Pra

"Sexy and fu
human and
evoke the right blend of tears as well as laughter."
—*RT Book Reviews* Top Pick, 4.5 Stars

"Auspicious...a warm cuddly tale full of dogs, cats, kids, and genuinely likable adults. This heartstring-tugger is certain to win fans."
—*Publishers Weekly* Starred Review

"The head might lead you in one direction, but what's in the heart will always win in the end... I really enjoyed this warm, wonderful story."
—*Romance Junkies*

"Pet lovers will adore all the animals introduced in Burns's sweet romance."
—*Booklist Reviews*

"A ragtag cast of supporting characters, human and otherwise, shines... Which is sweeter: reading to find out if heated disagreements will turn to hot romance, or a shelter full of animals all waiting for their forever homes? It's a toss-up, but both are pretty darn sweet."
—*Foreword Reviews*, 5 Stars

Also by Debbie Burns

A New Leash on Love

First in the fresh, poignant Rescue Me series
from award-winning author Debbie Burns

SIT, STAY, LOVE

🐾 A RESCUE ME NOVEL 🐾

DEBBIE BURNS

sourcebooks
casablanca

Published by Sourcebooks Casablanca, an imprint of Sourcebooks, Inc.
P.O. Box 4410, Naperville, Illinois 60567-4410
(630) 961-3900
Fax: (630) 961-2168
sourcebooks.com

Printed and bound in Canada.
MBP 10 9 8 7 6 5 4 3 2 1

To Dad,
Thanks for serving, and for all the
great little things ever since.

"Dogs do speak, but only to those who know how to listen."

—Orhan Pamuk

Chapter 1

KELSEY SUTTON HAD BEEN ON MORE HOME VISITS THAN SHE could recall. Most had proved to be run-of-the-mill experiences. Others were memorable for one reason or another. Never before had one brought to mind a jungle rendition of *The Twelve Days of Christmas*.

But here it was, mid-September, and this afternoon's peculiar home visit had the Christmassy tune flowing through her mind. Four fluttering finches. *Or maybe there'd been five in that cage. It was hard to tell with all the floating tufts of down.* Three squawking macaws. *How long will my ears keep ringing like this?* Two unique homeowners. *Weird. Let's face it. They were weird.* And a corgi in a hurry to leave. *Poor, sweet little Orzo.*

The whole fiasco made Kelsey more committed than ever to finding the precocious little corgi the perfect home. As lead adoption coordinator for the High Grove Animal Shelter, that was her current mission.

As she turned from the house's brick walkway onto the sidewalk, Kelsey was thankful she'd parked a few blocks away on the car-lined city street. She needed a minute or two to walk off her did-that-really-just-happen feeling. Orzo, who was typically a stop-and-sniff sort of fellow, was all too willing to keep up with her brisk pace. The only looking around he did was the occasional glance up at her, as if to make sure she hadn't fallen behind. His unusually serious demeanor made her laugh off her disbelief.

She didn't have to be a dog whisperer to know the residential Rainforest Café she'd just left wasn't meant to be Orzo's forever home. No amount of cajoling would have called him out from behind her legs. Hands down, it was Kelsey's most unique home visit ever. A dense jungle scene was painted on the far wall of the living room, and two enormous faux trees flanked the sides of it. Elsewhere, the house was adorned with more bird and jungle pictures, decorations, and furniture than Kelsey's active imagination could've conjured up. Especially for a house smack-dab in the middle of the United States. But the over-the-top decorating hadn't been what bothered the puppy-faced, five-year-old tan-and-white corgi.

What troubled the normally easygoing dog was the incessant, ear-piercing squawking and thunderous flapping of three upset macaws who weren't at all in agreement with their owners' desire to bring a dog into their family. By the time Kelsey had called it a wash and hoisted the terrified corgi into her arms, the air was so chock-full of downy feathers that she felt like she was trapped in a snow globe.

Thank goodness they'd decided to do this home visit. Kelsey's shelter prided itself on finding forever homes for the animals they took in. Potential adopters had to pass an interview, plus reference and background checks. When they did, home visits weren't typically required. These homeowners, two sisters, had passed all three. In that short time with them, it had become clear the sisters were animal lovers. However, during their interview, Chance, the shelter's resident blind cairn terrier, had sniffed something amiss. He could read people better than any animal or person Kelsey had ever known. It was unofficial shelter policy to take Chance's reactions to potential adopters seriously, so this afternoon's appointment had been made. In this case, he'd probably been smelling the exotic birds.

"I promise you, Orzo," Kelsey said as they reached her bright-yellow Corolla and she clicked the remote to unlock the doors. "We're going to find you the *perfect* home."

As soon as she had the back door open wide enough, Orzo made an impressive jump considering his short legs, forgetting that earlier he'd needed a boost.

"I'm going to make sure of it," she added, leaning in to scratch his back. She saw a pale-blue tuft of down sticking up from underneath his collar and pulled it free. "And even though you had a turn last week, you're coming home with me tonight." Orzo's tail began to wag like a piano metronome set for high speed.

Kelsey's decision to take a different shelter dog home every night had started by accident a few years ago. After moving out of her parents' house and renting an apartment, she was excited to adopt a shelter dog of her own. But the decision as to *which* dog had been nearly impossible. The forty or so dogs in the shelter's care were each lovable and adoption-worthy. While trying to narrow her choice down to a few, she started the overnight fostering and realized she was probably doing the greatest good with the quiet night's sleep and individual attention she offered all the shelter's dogs in turn.

And after this afternoon's crazy experience, Orzo deserved to be bumped to the front of the line.

Kelsey shut the back door and sank into the driver's seat. Orzo circled a few times, then plopped down with a sigh. Before turning on the ignition, Kelsey checked her phone. Megan had texted to see if Kelsey would still be stopping by the Sabrina Raven estate to feed the cat who, along with an entire estate, had been bequeathed to the shelter upon Sabrina Raven's death eight months ago.

Kelsey replied that she was headed there next. She was a bit surprised when Megan texted she'd meet her there. *Odd*, Kelsey thought. The Raven estate was a twenty-minute drive from the shelter, but close enough to Kelsey's apartment that she'd taken on the task of feeding the cantankerous cat each morning and evening. The fact that Megan wanted to meet there on her day off had to mean there was some sort of news.

Wondering if the news might involve the estate itself, Kelsey flipped on the ignition and buckled her seat belt. Whatever it was, it certainly couldn't be as eventful as her and Orzo's afternoon had been. After all, what topped a life-size feather-filled snow globe?

———

Hands down, it was the weather that Kurt Crawford was most looking forward to on coming home. There'd been enough times over the last eight years when he'd found it impossible to recall the sensation of a cool breeze against his skin. Scorching heat had been an all-too-constant companion during his long military service.

After completing his military training as a working dog handler in Texas at the Lackland Air Force Base, he started his enlistment in the army doing customs support on the U.S.-Mexican border. A couple years later, he was granted a transfer to the marines and found himself committing to multiple tours in Afghanistan and being paired up with new dog after new dog. Winters had offered a splash of reprieve from the unbearable desert heat. He'd even been in Kandahar during the one snow they'd had in thirty years. It was an experience he'd never forget. The snow had been thick and clumpy, yet dry, as if the endless desert sands had had a role in making it.

Most recently, he'd been stationed in Honduras, training Honduran troops' dogs to detect IEDs. There, the weather went from hot and sticky to hot and incessantly rainy.

With his sixty-pound military-grade duffel hoisted over his shoulder, Kurt dodged through the crowded St. Louis airport and headed outside to passenger pickup. Fortunately, for a midwestern day in the middle of September—which could've seen any temperature extreme—today didn't disappoint. As the flight attendant had announced, this afternoon St. Louis was pleasantly cool and partly cloudy. A light breeze blanketed Kurt's skin, welcoming him home.

He was tempted to close his eyes and savor it—and would have if it wasn't for the other passengers milling about. He suspected that closing his eyes on purpose in a crowd wasn't something he'd be comfortable doing for a long time. His edginess in the packed baggage claim area ten minutes ago had been proof enough. While waiting for his duffel, he kept catching himself scanning the crowds for signs of hidden weapons. It would take more than a signature on paper and a handshake for him to be able to let down his guard.

In the throngs of people waiting for rides and shuttles, Kurt spotted a working guide dog. The black Lab, who was old enough for her muzzle to be sprinkled with gray, sat patiently at attention beside an older man with stooped shoulders and Coke-bottle glasses. As if sensing Kurt's attention, the dog turned her head and met his gaze. Her brown eyes were soft and intelligent. An unexpected calm loosened Kurt's stiff-from-traveling muscles. The Lab may not have been trained for combat, but dogs were instinctively good at sensing danger, and this one was decisively calm.

He gave her a wink, and the dog pumped her tail before turning to look longingly at two small kids nearby whose ice-cream cones were getting drippier by the minute.

Things Kurt had once taken for granted stood out starkly. Ice-cream cones. All-terrain strollers. Bulky SUVs whose sole purpose was to transport children from school to the park to play dates. Patient service dogs. Well-marked handicapped zones. Kurt was undeniably stateside. He was home. His eight-year military career was over.

Less than 150 miles away, in his hometown of Fort Leonard Wood, he had a grandfather and mother he needed to face, and he would. Tomorrow. Maybe even tonight, depending on how hard jet lag kicked in.

For this afternoon though, he was going to hang with his buddy Thomas and savor the other thing he was most looking forward to on coming home: his newly renovated '69 Mustang Boss.

A few years ago, while on leave and hanging out at a bar with friends, Kurt had overheard a guy trying to off-load the car. Even though it needed work, Kurt was a sucker for Mustangs, especially late-sixties models. The drunker the guy got, the more willing he was to haggle. When they shook hands on a price, Kurt thought he'd gotten the better end of the deal.

Seeing the car in daylight the next morning, he wasn't so sure. The original paint coat had been more rust than red, the tires were threadbare, the leather interior was ripped and in disrepair, and the car went little more than a quarter mile before overheating. But that was where Thomas came in. Kurt's Mustang was Thomas's biggest and best restoration yet. Thomas had sent him enough photos and video for Kurt to be certain of it. With a gleaming coat of classic red paint, the rebuilt engine, custom wheels, and an all-new interior, the renovated Mustang looked even better than Kurt could've imagined.

Unfortunately, none of the cars idling in the passenger pickup zone was the one he was looking for. Not that Kurt was surprised. Thomas had never cared much for being on time. Thankfully, he didn't keep Kurt waiting long. Before his ADHD could get the best of him, Kurt heard the Mustang's purr a few seconds before he spotted it coming up the ramp. It looked even better than it had in the videos. A smile broke out across Kurt's face as Thomas let out three quick honks and pulled into one of the open spaces up the row.

Kurt was winding through the crowd as the little kid closest to him let his cone-holding wrist flop sideways. As quickly as the kid's scoop of ice cream fell onto the concrete, the old Lab was ready. She lunged to the edge of her leash and inhaled the messy treat with a flick of her tongue. After that, she was once again sitting at attention at her master's side without him seeming any the wiser. The kid, who'd at first looked about to cry, started to giggle. Kurt couldn't help but laugh as well. God bless the USA.

———∿∿∿———

Kelsey's tires hugged the curb as she parked in front of the Sabrina Raven estate. Megan was already here, at work picking weeds out of the overgrown landscaping. Hands down, the massive old mansion was the most peculiar item ever donated to the shelter. Probably ever donated to any shelter anywhere, Kelsey was willing to bet.

She stepped from the car and opened the back door. Orzo hopped out and looked around, sniffing the air as if to affirm they weren't returning to the strange and scary place he'd just come from.

"Guess who's with me," Kelsey called across the wide spans of lawn.

Tossing a handful of weeds behind a bush, Megan headed her way, smiling sympathetically. Even though she'd seen her yesterday, Kelsey blinked at her supervisor's swollen belly. She was still getting used to the idea of pregnant Megan, partially because Megan hadn't announced her pregnancy until she was starting to show.

Megan met her and Orzo halfway across the yard, motioning in Orzo's direction. "I'm guessing the home visit didn't go well?"

"Not very. Have you ever heard of a fruitarian? Because I hadn't. Not until this afternoon. To each their own, but they seriously wondered if their diet of fruit, seeds, and nuts might work for Orzo."

Megan laughed. "Oh my. I guess when you enter enough homes, you eventually see it all. I was skeptical about mixing dogs and macaws, but I knew you'd make the right call."

"Thanks. I recommended our dog-walking program. If I heard right over all the squawking, I think having a dog to take on long walks was what one of the sisters was most excited about."

"Good thinking," Megan said, extracting a two-inch-long red downy feather from Kelsey's thick, blond hair.

Kelsey suspected the reason her bra was itching her skin so badly also had something to do with a macaw feather. "I may be finding those for a while."

A cloud pushed in front of the sinking sun, making it seem closer to dusk than it was. Kelsey glanced at the 114-year-old house. She had stepped up to the task of feeding Sabrina's cat because she lived closest, not because she was particularly fond of the drafty old place. It would be nice to have Megan's company for once while feeding Mr. Longtail.

Kelsey scanned the perimeter and found the gray-and-black Maine coon sprawled out in the far corner of the front porch, grooming his long, glorious fur. She urged a sniffing Orzo along as they headed toward the house. "So what's up? Why'd you want to meet me here?"

Megan bit her lip and looked away guiltily, which piqued Kelsey's curiosity. Whatever had brought Megan here this afternoon wasn't something inconsequential.

"I had an idea. Kind of."

"You *kind of* had an idea?"

"I was thinking that since you come here every day to feed Mr. Longtail and staffing's pretty good at the shelter for the first time in forever, maybe we could put your time here to better use."

Kelsey was at a loss. She'd certainly never expected Megan to comment in this direction. "You want me to put the five minutes I swing by here on the way home from work to better use?"

Megan smoothed back hair that was already nicely confined in a wrap. "Remember what you said a few weeks ago about what you really wanted for your birthday?"

"A thigh gap?"

A laugh lightened her serious look. "Not that, the other part. About shaking things up and all."

"I know you're not saying you want me to spend more time at this creepy, dilapidated house so I can shake things up. While I'm taking care of an ornery cat that half our employees hope will one day disappear so we can honor Sabrina Raven's request and not sell her estate until after Mr. Longtail is in cat heaven."

"It's just… What if while we're waiting for whatever eventuality comes our way regarding this place, we make use of it?"

Kelsey shrugged. "How so?"

"By keeping a few dozen animals here that we can't keep at the shelter because of insurance regulations."

"What sort of animals?"

Megan plunged ahead, talking fast, which showed Kelsey how important this was to her. "I've looked over Sabrina's will. I even ran it by our lawyer this morning. Her only real stipulation on leaving the house to us was that we care for Mr. Longtail until his eventual passing. We wouldn't be in violation as long as he stays on the property and we continue to care for him. If you remember, Sabrina's will states we have the right to sell everything left here at our discretion and to use the house as we wish as long as that use doesn't displace the cat."

"I know that. So are you saying you want to bring more cats here?"

Megan chewed on her lip. "I don't suppose you watched the news last night or this morning?"

"No, I babysat my nieces last night, and it was a string of princess movies. This morning I didn't have time. Why?"

"There was a large-animal confiscation centered around St. Louis. It's a really big one. It has expanded to three states so far."

"Like a ring of cat hoarders?" Kelsey asked playfully.

"I wish. That would be so much easier. It was a dog-fighting ring. A big one. They've confiscated over 150 dogs already. They're raiding a few more houses that may be involved."

Kelsey's heart sank into her toes. "That's horrible. It's beyond horrible. It's sickening."

"I know, Kels. These dogs… You know we can't take any of them at the shelter since they're fighting dogs and we're a public facility."

Kelsey turned away from Megan to take in the house. "And the Sabrina Raven estate isn't."

The massive brick mansion could realistically house three times as many animals as the shelter. If those creaky hardwood floors didn't give way. And even though the house was smack-dab in the middle of South City, it was at the tail end of a quiet street, and the yard was a half acre or more. The backyard was huge, mostly reclaimed by nature, and surrounded by a tall privacy fence. She could see why Megan had thought of the house.

"No," Megan said, "it isn't." She paused, letting Kelsey take everything in. Finally, she added, "I made some calls earlier. If we act now, they'll make sure we get dogs that pass high on sociability and health tests. Ones that can be rehabbed for certain. The guy who's taken the lead in the rescue said he'd help find a trainer to do the retraining. You'd oversee their basic care. And I'm sure volunteers will be stepping up in droves to help. But you're the only one I trust to take this on. I'd do it if I wasn't nearing my third trimester." She cocked an eyebrow hopefully. "There's going to be a trial, and there's still so much red tape to sort, but I think in a few months' time we could start bringing them into the shelter for adoption."

Kelsey's stomach did a flip like when she was in school and about to do an oral report. Letting out a controlled breath, she caught the gaze of Mr. Longtail. His yellow-green eyes narrowed into slits, and he gave a twitch of his impressive tail before letting out a hiss, as if expressing his opinion on the idea. Orzo replied with an eager bark.

An untold number of dogs needed lots of loving care. The shelter had been given the perfect place that they could use to step in to help. And Megan trusted her to lead it. The whole thing felt a bit surreal.

But Megan was right. Her birthday wish on turning twenty-seven last week had been that she really wanted to shake things up. She just hadn't decided how. Never in her wildest dreams would she have imagined like this. "I'm in. You know I'm in. I don't know a thing about rehabbing fighting dogs, but you know I'm in."

Chapter 2

KURT PASSED HIS FIRST TWENTY-FOUR HOURS IN FORT Leonard Wood without placing the call he most needed to make. Finally, knowing he'd put off the inevitable reunion long enough, he borrowed Thomas's cell phone and arranged to meet his grandfather.

It wasn't so much that he dreaded reconnecting with the stalwart man who'd raised him. The problem was that seeing him would make it impossible to deny that his grandmother—Nana—was gone. Forever. His grandfather had been an upstanding, stern, and dedicated parent figure. Nana, on the other hand, had been comfort, love, and understanding.

Half an hour later, Kurt met his grandfather outside Tilly's, the quiet pub that escaped the craziness frequenting some of the more popular bars and taverns around Fort Leonard Wood. His grandfather was stepping out of his ten-year-old emerald-green F-150 when Kurt pulled up.

William Crawford nodded his way, squinting in the bright afternoon sun. He hardly looked a year older than he had when Kurt enlisted, certainly not eight years older. They exchanged handshakes rather than hugs and headed inside, taking seats at the bar.

Kurt found himself blinking at the familiarity of the place as they settled into awkward conversation highlighted by more silence than words. He shifted on his stool and swigged from his longneck beer. It felt like a lifetime since he'd been at Tilly's. Nothing here had changed, not even the glowing Miller Lite sign whose *M* flickered sporadically or the chipped pool table at the back of the bar. Kurt felt eons older than the twenty-year-old he'd been when he enlisted. But here time had stood still.

Beside him, his grandfather lifted his glass of bourbon to give it a swirl. Kurt couldn't remember a night the man went without one. When he was little, he'd watched him pop open a Coke along with the Maker's Mark, watched the careful way he mixed and stirred. For the last fifteen or so years, William Crawford had drunk it straight.

Kurt had never seen his grandfather drunk. One glass, sipped slowly, deliberately. Without variation.

He knew from the set of his jaw that his grandfather was still pissed. Kurt didn't blame him. His grandmother had given Kurt everything, and he hadn't made it to her funeral. Kurt tossed around the idea of telling his grandfather why, but he'd probably have more luck composing a sentence in broken French than he would telling his grandfather something with such heavy underlying emotion. The truth was, Kurt didn't have a good reason, other than that he hadn't been ready to accept her death. You slip. You fall. You hit your head. That wasn't reason enough for a life to end. Especially not hers.

And besides, his grandfather wasn't the type to let anyone talk him out of his anger until he was good and ready to let it go. Kurt would have to wait him out.

"You eating okay? Without her?" he asked instead.

"Well enough." William sipped his bourbon, then

added, "Been eating out mostly and having eggs when I don't. Not in a hurry to get my cholesterol checked."

If his grandfather had been eating poorly, it didn't show. For someone who'd recently turned seventy, William could still claim the fitness of a much younger man. He was just shy of six feet and lean. He wore his salt-and-pepper hair as short as when he'd been on active duty, and perhaps out of pure stubbornness, he'd made it all his years without as much as a pair of reading glasses.

"I miss her tortillas," Kurt said, thinking how different a pair they'd been. His grandfather met his nana when he was on leave and partying down in Mexico. She was from a proud, wealthy family who traced their ancestors back to early eighteenth-century Spain and had turned silver mining in Guanajuato into a fortune that had lasted for generations. Her decision to elope with an American army brat with no connections had led to her being ostracized by her family, though in all the years Kurt knew her, he'd never heard her complain about it. "When she made them fresh. The way they melted in your mouth. I'd have dreams about them back in Afghanistan."

This brought a smile to William's face. "Bet that was a sorry disappointment when you woke up to base slop."

"It was."

"Military food didn't stunt your journey into manhood, at least. You've muscled up a fair bit from the scrawny kid who left."

Kurt noted the compliment, something his grandfather rarely handed out.

After a few minutes of quiet, William pointed to

the flat-screen TV in the corner. "You been following this story? It's gotten more airtime than that attack in Baghdad. Old Rob's getting his fifteen minutes, that's for sure."

Kurt glanced at the screen. He blinked in surprise at the familiar face being interviewed. He'd first met Rob Bornello when he was six or seven. Back then, Rob worked on the base. He was the best K-9 trainer around, and Kurt made it his business to learn as much from him as he could. Rob left years ago to train dogs in the private sector, though Kurt continued to shadow him every so often until he enlisted.

Kurt wished the TV wasn't muted. "No, what happened?"

"A fighting ring was exposed in St. Louis. A big one. At least a dozen different dog men were involved. Rob came out of the woods to organize the rescue."

"Shame about the dogs," Kurt said, suspecting the sad story would set his restless mind afire. "That Rob. I wondered what had happened to him the last several years."

"He shows up at the post once or twice a year, and from what I know, he never gave any of it up. Heard he was calling around yesterday looking for dog handlers who might be able to help him out. Asked about you specifically. I got a call from Ham."

Kurt felt a rush of pride. It'd been eight years since he'd seen the man who'd been his mentor. "I take it as a compliment that he thought of me, but that's a mess I'm not interested in."

William raised a meticulously trimmed eyebrow. "That's a relief. Most of us have to grow up sometime. Not everyone can make an honest living playing with dogs."

Kurt's teeth ground together. It wasn't an argument worth having. He'd decided of his own volition that he was done working with dogs. His grandfather's long-held prejudices over which careers accounted for an *honest living* wouldn't change and shouldn't bother him.

But he could feel the retort, cynical and accusing, building in the pit of his stomach. Right before it reached his throat, soft, thin fingers clamped over his eyes, and a body, a distinctly feminine one, pressed against his back and hips.

"Kurtis Crawford, if I hadn't missed you so much, I'd be reading you the riot act for waiting so long to come home."

The muscles from the base of his skull to the back of his calves went rigid. Instinct at being caught off guard—honed over eight years of service—and not having heard her over the Johnny Cash pouring out the speakers, urged him to react, to throw her off him. But a secondary reaction pulsed a split second behind and kept his hands locked around his beer. He was stateside and in a friendly bar. And besides, he'd have recognized her if she'd caught him off guard the same way in the middle of a desert camp. The softness of her fingers pressing unwanted against his eyelids. The smell of her freshly applied Cashmere perfume. The touch of a southern drawl she'd most likely perfected to drive men crazy.

"It's just Kurt," he said, twisting to slip from her grasp. "Says so on my birth certificate." He shot a glance his grandfather's way. As always around her, William's look was a touch disapproving, but he didn't seem surprised that she'd shown up either.

So his grandfather had told her of their plans to meet here. What was wrong with facing only one of them at a time?

"And you really shouldn't sneak up behind someone who's fresh off a tour," Kurt added. "Though we all know you know that."

He swiveled to face her but kept seated on his stool. Maybe it was in the water. Maybe it was genetic. Maybe it was dumping every spare dollar she earned on beauty products. But she wasn't aging. She wore her long, raven-black hair full and free. The blue eyes she'd gotten from her father sparkled in a way that was distinctly hers. It was a cool September night, but she was still wearing cutoff jean shorts and a flowing shirt shoestringed together in the center, plunging low, highlighting her full chest.

"Look at you," she raved. "God, you're handsome." He was enveloped in a bear hug before he could stop her. "Like a damn bottle of Grey Goose to sit on a shelf and look at but not drink."

Kurt felt the heat rising up his neck, burning his jawline. He allowed his hands to close loosely over her shoulder blades. It hit him how petite she was. "Hey," he said, tiring of the confining hug well before she was ready to let go, "seriously."

She finally took a step back. "How about you scoot over, Kurtis, so I can have a seat smack-dab between the two most important men in my universe."

William cleared his throat or outright scoffed. Kurt couldn't tell over the music. His grandfather's face, as usual, was poker perfect.

Kurt slid over without complaint, having no desire to

be locked in between the two of them. Then he waved at the bartender, knowing he'd need another beer to get through the next hour. Hell, who was he kidding? He'd need another two or three. A fresh wave of fatigue swept over him, reminding him why it'd been easier to extend his tour than to finally come home.

But he'd been away long enough. The truth was, he'd shut them out long enough. Nana had once phrased it perfectly. Though he could no longer remember her exact words, he remembered the gist. Living, ostracized, dead, or embraced, your family was still your family.

"Mom," he said, "what is it you're drinking nowadays?"

Kurt hoped the two-and-a-half-hour drive back to St. Louis the next morning would be the distraction he needed. He awoke an hour before dawn from chaotic dreams that were the detritus of his years of service. He'd planned to spend the last part of the day catching up with some old buddies still stationed at the post, but he was too antsy to wait around until they were off duty.

And after surviving the uneasy family reunion last night, the idea of hanging around Fort Leonard Wood an entire day with no solid plans wasn't enticing. His mother had mentioned she had the day off, but try as he might, Kurt could only tolerate her in small doses.

His thoughts circled as he headed east on Interstate 44. Reconnecting with Rob Bornello was long overdue. Kurt had never gotten around to seeing Rob when he was home on leave, and he genuinely missed his mentor. He'd like to believe that driving nearly 150 miles back to St. Louis less than twenty-four hours after landing had nothing to do with the images of the dogs that had flashed across the TV screen last night.

But Kurt was getting better about not lying to himself. He wouldn't rest easy until he got inside that warehouse and saw the dogs for himself. He just needed reassurance they were being rehoused into centers with caring, competent staff. Whatever he saw today, Kurt was determined not to get involved. He'd make a donation, but he was staying out of this mess. He'd lost too many dogs—and too many buddies—over the last several years. It was a commitment he'd made after losing Zara in Afghanistan a few months back.

He needed a break. Needed to immerse himself in something that didn't matter. Something physically demanding that would have him crawling into bed after a demanding day, something to exhaust his body and quiet his mind. And he intended to do it where it wasn't hot.

He knew Rob was going to try to put him to work, but in the long run, Rob would understand. Rob had introduced him to the K-9 world. Kurt had started shadowing him at the post as soon as his grandparents trusted him to bike away for the afternoon. Rob had kept in contact after he left the post, taking Kurt to exhibitions with him a few times a year.

By the time he pulled into a gas station a mile from the warehouse address his grandfather had shoved at him as he was leaving the bar last night, Kurt was surprised to find it wasn't even eight o'clock yet. He'd grab a cup of coffee and whatever prepackaged breakfast sandwich looked the best under the heat lamps and be on his way.

If Kelsey had any doubt diving into a dogfighting rescue would be controversial, it vanished as she and Fidel, her coworker, pulled in front of the warehouses in north St. Louis County where the confiscated animals were being held. It was only eight in the morning, and the picketers were already here, polka-dotting opposite sides of the street. Peacefully it seemed, so far anyway.

Kelsey scanned the handwritten posters as she stepped from her car. The clearly animal-rights side wanted harsh punishments for the dog men and demanded an end to vicious dogfighting. A few people held posters with enlarged pictures of themselves snuggling with well-known fighting breeds, pit bulls mostly. Some had even brought their dogs along. Kelsey counted at least four leashed pit bulls, two Rottweilers, and a few breeds she couldn't identify milling among the group of supporters.

Her cheeks flamed hot as she took in the posters on the opposite side of the street. It wasn't only the glare of the morning sun that caused their posters to burn her retinas. A quick skim made it clear these protesters didn't want the animals being rehabbed. *Once a killer, always a killer. Protect our neighborhoods, stop killing sprees before they happen. Humanely euthanize now and save human lives.* One poster asserted that animals existed to serve humans, and fighting dogs didn't serve anyone.

She chewed hard on her tongue to keep from stalking over with a mouthful of statistics none of them would likely care to hear. Fighting with fired-up protesters wouldn't change their minds and would only give her a headache.

Fidel, who'd been finishing up a phone call with his wife, stepped out from the passenger seat and surveyed the scene. He made a guttural sound, and Kelsey wondered if she might have to guide him away from the protesters. Fidel grew up in the slums of Mexico City and credited a unique childhood relationship with a stray basenji as the reason he kept away from the city's violent gangs.

"We should head inside," she suggested. "I told Mr. Bornello we'd be here at eight. I'll text Megan that we're going in. She can join us when she gets here."

"*Sí*, let's do."

Her heart sank as she eyed the two police officers guarding the warehouse entrance. The few times she'd been with Fidel around the police, he'd fallen quiet and turned pale, the veins in his temples bulging. The only thing Fidel had ever shared about his journey to America was that it had been complicated. When he was hired four years ago, he presented all the necessary paperwork. Neither Megan nor Wesley, the now-retired shelter founder, were ones to question it.

When she'd asked Fidel to come along this morning, she hadn't thought of the extra stress it might cause him. She'd only thought of how she and Megan could use his advice in picking out the animals. Of the shelter's five full-time employees, Fidel knew the most about dogs. Sometimes she'd swear he spoke dog. He'd be perfect for leading the rehab project, if it wasn't for the fact that his wife was pregnant with their fourth child and on bed rest. As a result, his schedule had become unpredictable the last month and would continue that way for a while.

Kelsey held her breath as they passed the protesters. She had an odd sense of a crowd gathering for a parade, only no one seemed to be having any fun. Fortunately, she and Fidel made it down the sidewalk without more than a few halfhearted calls directed at them.

The two policemen squared off in front of the double doors as they neared. "No visitors," the shorter one said. "Registered guests and rescue workers only." His tone was blunt but not rude. The middle button of his light-blue uniform shirt had come undone, exposing an unsightly bit of flesh. Kelsey figured it best not to point that out.

"We're expected," she said as Fidel gritted his teeth. "I am anyway, and I asked Fidel to come with me. Our supervisor is meeting us here. We work at the High Grove Animal Shelter. We've volunteered to take some of the dogs once they're cleared to leave. My name is Kelsey Sutton."

The taller one lifted a clipboard from a chair. He scanned it, then glanced her way. "I'll need some ID."

As Kelsey fished through her purse, a loud, red classic Mustang pulled into the lot and parked. She wondered if it was another protester, and if so, why the driver hadn't parked off to the side with the others. The driver, a guy, popped out and headed purposefully down the sidewalk toward her. He was around her age and incredibly fit, precision-toned almost.

It had to be instinctive, the way her insides melted, because anyone *that* fit almost certainly couldn't be her type. His level of fitness spoke of high-maintenance diets and protein powder and lots of time in front of the mirror. She'd seen too much growing up with two older, self-absorbed weight-lifting brothers to believe otherwise.

Sliding her license from her wallet, she handed it to the taller cop with the clipboard.

He took his time studying it, looked pointedly at her, and frowned. "I'd put you at five nine or ten, not five eight."

Kelsey felt the heat flame up her neck as the driver of the Mustang stopped right behind them. *Dear God, don't let him mention my weight.* "Five nine," she managed, "when I'm not in these running shoes."

"You'll want to update that next time you're renewing your license."

She nodded but stayed as quiet as Fidel. They were offering to rehab confiscated dogs. Why did she feel like she was a crime suspect all of a sudden?

The tall one pulled out a radio to make contact with someone inside the warehouse. "I have a Kelsey Sutton and acquaintance from the High Grove Animal Shelter in Webster here to see Rob. She's on the list for an eight o'clock arrival." After a bit more of an exchange, the officer nodded at her. "Just a minute. He's on his way."

The officers shifted their attention to the man standing behind her. "Are you expected, sir?" the short one asked.

Sir?

Unable to resist, Kelsey stole a glance over her shoulder. To her dismay, he met her gaze full on. He was in jeans and a dark-gray T-shirt, but something about his demeanor radiated military or police. He had olive skin, short brown hair, and chestnut-brown eyes. And he was so fit.

He flicked his gaze to the officers, most likely

forgetting her existence on the spot. He slipped an ID from his wallet. "Kurt Crawford. Military dog handler, marines most recently. Army before that. I'm here to see Rob as well."

"Of course," the tall one said, not even giving the clipboard a glance. "He'll be right out."

Chapter 3

KURT'S SKIN WAS CRAWLING, AND THE TIGHTNESS IN HIS JAW had migrated to his temples. His shoulders and spine tensed as he scanned the parameters of the long, open warehouse like he was on patrol. The rear of the building was blocked off by accordion-style dividers. It bothered him that he couldn't see past them.

It was the smell setting him on edge, he finally realized. Not the obvious smell—the smell of hot, unbathed dog multiplied by 150. That smacked you in the face when you stepped through the doors. Unnerving him was the underlying scent of fear radiating from the expansive rows of crates that were dwarfed by the thirty-foot ceiling and five-thousand-square-foot floor.

Dogs didn't have sweat glands, so it wasn't as if the smell was coming out of their pores. But he'd been in the service long enough to know fear when he smelled it—his own, another human's, a dog's. Metallic and salty—like blood, only subtler.

The gushy blond accompanying him on the tour wasn't setting him at ease either, as she squatted down and talked to every crated dog. The bumper sticker on the back of her Corolla—the bright-yellow car he'd parked by had to be hers; he'd seen her keys—was a telltale enough sign she wasn't right for this job. I BRAKE FOR TURTLES. He didn't know what Rob was thinking, sending a bunch of trained fighters off to be in this girl's care.

The bumper sticker wasn't the only thing he noticed. She was tall and strikingly pretty in an understated, natural way, and she had an hourglass figure.

Not that her looks mattered.

What mattered was that Rob didn't make the ludicrous decision of sending a bunch of dogs off to end up hammering her. Dogs treated the way most of these had likely been treated—stuck in crates or tied to chains and freed only to fight—needed much more than soft words and treats passed through the bars of their crates. The blond's Hispanic coworker seemed to know a thing or two about how to handle fighting dogs, but from what Kurt understood, he wouldn't be working at the site where the dogs would be kept.

"What do you think of her, Fidel?" Her voice was easy and calm like the slow pour of honey. "She seems sweet enough," she said of the mastiff mix displaying submission along with a good deal of stress while being stared down through the door.

Fidel squatted to inspect the info sheet in the plastic sleeve attached to the side of the crate. There must have been something on it that the man didn't like because his forehead knotted into a V and he mumbled something Kurt couldn't hear.

Kurt gritted his teeth as she pulled free a yellow sticky and pressed it on top of the crate. *Yellow. Seriously?* Her and her stickies. He'd stifled a laugh earlier when he figured out her system. Pink for definitely, yellow for maybe, blue for pass. She'd only used one blue sticky so far, and the way that Rott had attacked the cage door, Kurt wouldn't have been surprised if he was rabid.

The next dog they came to was a giant. Rather than

being crammed into one of the crates, he was in an over-sized kennel. He stood when they approached, making it easier to inspect him. The long hair around his neck and along his upper back pricked straight up, declaring the animal's unease.

His fluffy brown-and-black coat bore markings similar to a German shepherd, but he was much bigger and fuzzier than any shepherd Kurt had ever seen. He'd place him at a hundred and fifty pounds easy. With the dog's massive size and powerful build, Kurt figured he must be part Neapolitan mastiff or Great Dane, or both. And unlike most of the gigantic dogs Kurt had come across at one time or another, this one seemed anything but easygoing.

With his tail stuck straight out, the massive animal looked at each one in the group alternately, fixing them with a striking stare that in Kurt's mind was akin to a dare.

"He's *so* beautiful. Definitely a yes, don't you think?" the blond asked her coworker. "Look how calm he is."

Kurt was opening his mouth in protest when Rob unexpectedly pulled him in for a second hug.

"Boy, you feel like a tree trunk." Rob let go and ruffled his hair. "With you extending your service like that, heading off to hell and back again, I was starting to think you had a death wish."

Kurt nearly sent him sailing over a crate for the unanticipated hug. Had Rob forgotten his service years completely? Then he remembered that Rob had never left the States. His entire military career had been as a dog trainer and instructor. He didn't know how impossible it felt to let go of the hypersensitivity it took to stay alive in a war zone.

"No death wish, just a larger than necessary sense of duty." Kurt forced a smile as the blond pressed a pink sticky on the front of the giant dog's kennel. So, she'd be throwing a man-sized dog with a heavily alpha demeanor into the mix, wherever she was taking them.

"Well, I'm glad you're back. And still in one piece. So many of them boys…" Rob shook his head and seemed to realize they had the girl's full attention. "I'm really glad you're back. To stay this time?"

"Stateside for certain. I'll be looking for work. I was thinking somewhere cool. Maybe Alaska."

Rob laughed heartily as if the Alaska comment had been a joke. He waved toward the crates. "Son, I've got work."

"Thanks. But like I said, I'm finished working with dogs."

Rob chuckled some more. "The question you should be answering is whether they're finished with you. However bad it went in Afghanistan and Honduras, I suspect they're not."

That was Rob for you. Taking things where you didn't want them to go. Kurt forced his gaze not to stray to the blond, not to give in to the part of him that wanted to see her reaction.

Not liking the turn the conversation was taking, he nodded to the partitions blocking off the back of the warehouse. "What's behind door number three?"

Rob's lips pursed almost imperceptibly. "Long shots and TLCs. None these guys need to see. For the long shots, it'll be a bit before we have a sense of whether or not they can be rehabbed into traditional homes. The others will stay until they need less intensive care."

Maybe the dogs in those cages would shake some sense into the girl. "She should know what she's getting into. Know how bad it can be." He gave himself permission to look at her. Her eyebrows furrowed as she listened. She closed one arm over her stomach, wrapping her hand around her other elbow, drawing his attention to her chest, though he knew not intentionally. She reminded him of one of those ancient hand-carved fertility statues. No makeup that he could see, light-brown eyes with flecks of gold, and hips in perfect proportion to her chest. And he had the distinct feeling she had no idea of the heads she turned every day.

She was dressed for a day on the job in faded jeans and a V-neck tee that was the color of orange sherbet. It read *ADOPT*, except that there was an impression of a dog paw in the middle instead of an *O*.

"I wouldn't mind seeing everything," she said, watching two young guys Rob had introduced at the start of the tour rolling a crate behind the blocked-from-view partition after bringing it in through a side door. "You're getting more dogs this morning? Do they all start back there, and once you evaluate them, you bring the ones you're ready to send out up here?"

One side of Rob's mouth pulled up into a half smile, half grimace. "That was a string of questions. Let's see. No new animals are coming in until this evening. The pit my guys are rolling back was in surgery yesterday. A couple local vets have volunteered their services. And right now, it's triage. They're helping the ones that can benefit most from the immediacy of surgery. Some of the guys back there were injured a while ago, and any surgery they end up getting will be more reconstructive in nature." He tapped his fingers against his temple and gave a light shake of his head. "Come on, if you want. I'll let you see."

Kurt fell to the back as they headed toward the partitions, a wave of guilt passing over him. After seeing Rob's hesitation, he knew it wasn't going to be good. He could stomach it, and he suspected Fidel could too, but he was fairly certain Kelsey was going to end up crying, throwing up, or both.

When Kelsey was little, Chaz and Brian, her brothers, were always confiscating the TV to watch horror movies. Because horror movies kept her awake at night, she'd get grounded if she was caught in the family room while they were on. But when her mom was out shopping or busy with yard work, there were still opportunities to catch a few minutes. Kelsey'd watch the gore until her stomach started to roll and bounce, and she knew it was time to leave the room.

This morning her stomach did neither. She made it past the first three crates—the malamute with a missing front leg, the mastiff pocked with more old scars than brindles, and a Great Dane mix missing most of an ear. She was trying so hard not to cry that she wasn't even thinking about her stomach.

By then, Rob's two workers had coaxed dog number four, a pit bull, out of his crate and were offering him a bit of water now that the sedation from yesterday's surgery was worn off. She saw the dog first from behind. He was leashed and wearing a bright-blue collar. He had a fairly lithe build for a pit bull, was very muscular, and the guy holding his leash was talking in low, easy words.

Their small group walked around the dog in a wide, respectful arc while Rob reminded them how these dogs gave everything that was asked of them, especially the pit bulls. How they never stopped fighting until they absolutely couldn't.

And then the dog turned to face them. For a couple of seconds, Kelsey could only blink, waiting for her trick vision to clear. It didn't. The vanilla latte she savored on the way over became a hazard as her stomach pitched wickedly.

It was impossible. No animal could have been hurt like that and still be walking around. Still be interested in drinking water. She had to blink to realize it wasn't a fuzzy rose tattoo on his left shoulder, but a thick circle of stitches. There were other, smaller patches on his neck. But the hardest to see was his face. The right side was fine, but the left side was a bustling city road map of stitches. From where she stood, it looked as if the eye was stitched shut. His left jowl was a jagged mess, almost as if he was giving their group a mocking smile. As the dog studied them, a wet, pink tongue flicked out, brushing over his nose, over the stitches perforating his jowl.

Kelsey's blood raced into her stomach, leaving her dangerously light-headed. With an odd sense of disconnection, she felt her body sway in a circle, as if she were warming up in yoga class. A strong hand closed underneath her arm, keeping her upright.

It was thoughtful of Fidel to help her. To understand. *Only he's on the other side of Rob*.

Thoughts circled slowly, as though they were trapped

in fuzzy cotton. Racing fast ahead of them was her unsettled stomach. All she had time to do was double over as her latte reintroduced itself. Her vision was too pinpricked to be sure, but the liquid was probably splashing atop her shoes. And, she feared, the boots of the hot soldier with the accusing stare.

The one keeping her upright.

Later, when she was home buried under the covers, she'd probably be humiliated. Right now, she was too distressed to give it much thought. She stayed doubled over until she was certain the nausea had passed.

The guy—*curt Kurt*, she'd thought earlier from the clipped way he carried out his end of the conversation—neither cussed nor backed away. He stood beside her, holding her arm. The fuzzy cotton in her head cleared, and her knees strengthened. She stood up, wiping her mouth, and waving him off with a "thanks."

She shot Fidel a pleading glance. Even under his brown skin, it was obvious he was blushing. Her first thought was that he was embarrassed by her. Then, knowing Fidel, she understood it was more likely because he hadn't been the one who'd noticed she was about to faint and stepped in to help her.

"I'm sorry," she managed, hardly daring a glance Kurt's way. "I'm fine now."

Fidel stepped forward. "If you have a mop, I'll clean it up."

"No, it's fine," Rob said. "I should've known better. These things take getting used to. We've got hoses for this. Let's go up front. There's a break room with a couch by the office. And we have Gatorade if you think it'll help."

Kelsey nodded. "Yes, please." The pit bull was staring straight at her with his good eye, and she couldn't look away. He was a beautiful silver blue with a white patch on his chest running up his chin, only it was stained yellow-red in patches. Kelsey hoped from disinfectants used in surgery. He released what sounded like a sigh and turned back to the dish of water, tentatively lapping up some more.

The others started to move, but Kelsey stayed and fumbled through her purse. Kurt stopped and waited, like he'd been assigned Kelsey duty. After a few feet, Fidel and Rob stopped too. Finally, her weak fingers clasped hold of the pink stickies, and she pulled one off the top.

She headed over to the pit's empty crate and pressed it on top. "When he's ready," she said. "I'll take him as soon as he's ready."

Chapter 4

"IF YOU DON'T MIND ME SAYING, YOU'RE JUMPIER THAN A jackrabbit, son," Rob said, swiping a half piece of toast over the mess of yolk on his plate. Seeing Kurt nearly leap from his seat at the sound of a dish breaking in the kitchen hadn't escaped Rob's notice. "It's a shame they don't do more for you boys on coming home. It's like when you've been down in the deep of the ocean too long. Come up without acclimating, and you burst from inside."

Kurt swallowed his last bite of crunchy bacon. *Son.* It was likely little more than slang, but nevertheless it scraped his ears every time Rob said it. How often had he fallen asleep as a kid wishing Rob were his father? Wished for it in a different way than just wanting *a* father, any father. But as Nana said, you make lemonade from the lemons you have. His grandfather was the best he'd get in that department. Half of his genes would remain a mystery. That was that.

"You think I have the soldiering bends?" Kurt laughed, half surprised something with such a heavy undertone had tickled his funny bone. "And you're trying to talk me into working with a bunch of dogs on the verge of exploding exactly as you said."

The server passed by, refilling their coffee and dropping off the check. Rob dragged a napkin over the salt-and-pepper stubble covering his dimpled chin. "I think," he said after the server left, "that getting on a lumber or road crew out West isn't going to settle what's churning under your surface. And the sooner you deal with it, the better you'll be. Take some time. Think it over. I don't have to tell you how nice it would be to have you here in St. Louis for a while."

When Kurt stayed quiet, Rob added, "If donations keep pouring in like this, I'll double the pay I've offered you."

Kurt swirled the last of the coffee in his cup. He kept seeing the blond walking over on shaky legs to press that pink sticky onto the pit's crate. Kept letting his thoughts sway to how seeing her do it stirred awake something burning hot in his core. "The thing is, I don't know—" His mouth stayed open, but no more words came. *Don't know what?* The truth was he had no idea. "I don't know."

If it was anyone else, he'd give an adamant no. But it was Rob. "I'll think about it," Kurt added, even though he knew the answer. He wasn't going to get involved.

However, things wouldn't sit easy with him until he said his piece. "That girl. I don't care how many years' experience she's had with positive training, most of those dogs are going to need a more assertive hand than she'll be able to give them. She didn't even have the sense not to drag a giant alpha who probably outweighs her into that ragtag mix she's going to take off your hands. You have to know that without me telling you."

"I do. And that's why I won't deliver them to her until I've got a trained handler ready to take the lead on rehabbing. I know he's not your favorite, but Tommy Sintras is giving it some serious thought. He's working over in Kansas City. He called me when he saw the story. If I'd been able to offer him more, he'd have dropped everything. From what he said, he's up to his elbows in pampered, inbred pooches."

A rumble of discontent rolled through Kurt's chest. Tommy Sintras had been in training down in Texas with him. Tommy hadn't passed the handler test on the first run. He'd been too quick to let frustration get the best of him. Military service dogs needed calm, assertive leadership, not an overly dominant, excitable handler. "Tommy, huh? Let's hope he's cooled off the last few years."

"Guys I trust are backing him. Not that I'm saying he'd be as chivalrous or stay as calm as you were about having a mess splashed all over his boots." Rob chuckled as he pulled out his wallet. "Good thing for that hose, huh?"

Tommy was a player too. There was no reason that should be bothering Kurt, but it was. Besides, from the little interaction they'd had, he suspected Kelsey would be better at putting Tommy in his place than those dogs. But Tommy would keep coming back for another shot. That body and those eyes were worth the effort. Kurt tried shoving the image of her into the same deep pit where he shoved everything he didn't want to think about, though it didn't work. He hadn't been that close to a woman in a while. Unless he counted the mother invasion of last night.

The surface of his hand still tingled from the smoothness of the blond's arm as he'd kept her from toppling over at the sight of the pathetic pit bull. The citrusy scent of her shampoo circled his nostrils. The soothing tone she'd used with the dogs reverberated in his head.

"You know what I haven't gotten an update on?" Kurt asked, needing to change the subject. "Soccer."

One of Rob's eyebrows shot into his forehead. Rob was fifty-two and still playing on a year-round team. He pretty much lived for two things. Dogs and soccer.

Soccer proved to be the change of topic Kurt needed. It monopolized the conversation until they paid and headed outside. They parted ways with him promising to give Rob a call and not to stay a stranger. He was halfway back to Fort Leonard Wood when he realized he hadn't been able to put the morning's events out of his mind for a second. Why couldn't his mind grasp that right now, his best chance of feeling good was to take a stab at something else entirely?

There were butterflies in Kelsey's stomach the next morning. Half from excitement, half from nerves. Change was hardly something she embraced, but it wasn't something she hid from either.

She sat at her desk at the shelter, looking it over with a rare scrutiny as she waited for Patrick to finish getting ready to head over with her to the Sabrina Raven estate. She'd spent most of her waking hours here the last seven years. Half the letters on her keyboard were so worn they were indiscernible. The miniature dog and cat glass figurines lining her monitor riser had collected enough dust to dull their colors. There was a pile of nonessential paperwork off to the right she never seemed to get to. The faded glass fishing float she'd found as a kid on vacation on the Oregon coast rested by her pen jar.

Kelsey picked up the glass orb, wondering how many

years it had been since she paid any real attention to it. These blue-green antique floats were abundant in the coastline shops but rare to find washed up on the beach. Her dad had hugged her tight after she found it all crusted with sand while walking the beach. He insisted it proved she was remarkably lucky.

She wondered if he still thought so, considering she'd only been taking classes part time since dropping out of Truman State University halfway through her sophomore year. Or considering she hadn't been on a date in forever, and her career had stagnated four years ago after she was promoted to lead adoption coordinator. In a full-time staff of five.

Ugh, you're psyching yourself out again, Kels. Glancing at the dusty framed photo of her family on the far side of her monitor didn't help ease her nerves. It had been taken six years ago at her brother Chaz's wedding. Chaz, Brian, and her dad were in suits that complemented their well-muscled physiques and dark-brown hair. Kelsey had been a bridesmaid and was in a fantastic lavender dress. Wearing it with ample makeup and an updo, she looked more like a younger, taller version of her mother than she typically did. Her mom, also a natural blond, had a gift for accessorizing that Kelsey probably couldn't acquire even if she had a degree in fashion.

Even though they had their differences, she loved her family and they loved her. And over the last couple years, they seemed to have accepted that her job at the shelter wasn't a phase, and that she and corporate America would never be a thing. Of her family of five, she was the only one who'd been bitten by the animal bug. As far as Kelsey was concerned, strong benefit plans and retirement accounts paled in comparison to warm, brown eyes and four-legged affection.

But working at a shelter was a lot different from leading a fighting-dog rehab effort at a secluded old mansion. Her dad and brothers were going to think she was nuts, and her mom was going to worry. And maybe she'd be right to do so.

This was probably why Kelsey had put off telling them last night when she'd gone to her parents' for dinner. Chaz was out of town with his wife, and Kelsey's parents were keeping their four- and five-year-old granddaughters for the week. Kelsey was crazy about her nieces, so it had been all too easy to keep the attention focused on them and not dive into the news yet. But maybe she should've gotten it over with.

Kelsey gave her shoulders a brisk shake. This thing with the fighting dogs. She could do it. She could run the rehab operation. *In* the Sabrina Raven estate. She'd even sleep there if she had to. More than enough furniture was still there, waiting for someone to use it.

Okay, so maybe she wouldn't take it that far.

But she was bound and determined to rock this rehab. She could feel the little breath of excitement that had been building in her stomach. Before yesterday, she hadn't realized how much she needed to do something gutsy.

And she wasn't going to go at this alone. Her parents at least could be comforted by that. Rob had called late last night to tell her everything was in order. He had secured a trainer to work with her, some ex-military dog handler named Tommy Sintras. She'd Googled him and found a half-dozen pictures as well as a few online newspaper articles in which he'd been interviewed. He was around her age and okay-enough looking, but there was something about his eyes that seemed beady and set up her guard.

She should be thankful. It could be worse. She could be working alone in that big house with the other ex-military dog trainer, Kurt. Curt Kurt. The weighty feeling in her chest last night on learning she wouldn't be working with him wasn't disappointment. She didn't know what it was, but it definitely wasn't disappointment.

He'd been chivalrous, yes. And he was good-looking enough that her pulse quickened when she looked at him. And maybe her mouth salivated a bit. Which was humiliating because judging by the sharp way he'd looked at her, there might as well have been a fluorescent light above his head declaring she wasn't his type.

And then there'd been the whole getting-sick-on-his-boots thing.

All in all, she should definitely be thankful to be working with someone else.

She was about to go look for Patrick when he stepped in from the back kennels wearing a clompy pair of rubber boots that reached his knees. Coupled with the thick rubber gloves half crammed into his jeans pocket, the boots make him look ready to disinfect a triage center rather than help tidy up the Raven mansion.

"Ready?" she asked.

"Yes, but I double-checked the van. We've only packed four baby gates, six leashes, and twelve collars. You said thirty-seven dogs are being delivered tomorrow. The only thing we seem to have enough of are the boxes of towels, blankets, water bowls, and stuffed toys."

Kelsey pursed her lips. Thirty-seven suddenly sounded like an enormous number. Yesterday at the warehouse, she'd felt like she wasn't committing to enough. "I know, but even with volunteers helping, it'll be awhile before the dogs will be together in any number. They'll eat in secluded rooms at different times. We can disinfect dishes between meals. And not all thirty-seven are coming tomorrow. Several of them still need to be spayed or neutered and may still be in recovery. Especially the ones having surgery today."

Patrick nodded and asked if two bottles of bleach would be enough to disinfect the estate.

"With two bottles of bleach, we could disinfect the whole street," Kelsey said, forgetting he would probably start calculating the possibility. "But keep them. That empty, old house has to be crawling with mice and who knows what else."

She was grabbing her purse when she noticed a Channel 3 news van pulling into the lot. Since they hadn't made any sort of announcement, it seemed unlikely the visit was related to the rescue operation. She glanced at the calendar on her desk. Channel 3 featured one of their dogs or cats every month, but the shelter was another week out from needing to send this month's photo and video. The thought reminded her that she'd need to pick someone to take over that project while she was at the Raven estate.

"What do you think this is about?" Kelsey asked, collecting herself before heading to the door. "We're keeping quiet about the dogs so we can stay out of that media storm."

Patrick followed her gaze. "The protesters," he said after a moment of thought. "You said you saw them in front of the building yesterday. It would be easy to trace your plates. Easy to connect you to the shelter."

Kelsey's butterflies changed to bats. "Megan has a doctor appointment this morning, doesn't she? Of all mornings."

"You can always decline comment."

"If I decline comment, it'll come across looking like we're guilty of something. Besides, it's Channel 3. They love us."

Patrick pursed his lips. "Maybe. But the news is a business. They'll air what generates the most viewership."

Kelsey pulled out her phone and shot off a text to Megan. The cameraman had the back of the van open and was pulling out a camera. Kelsey stared at her phone screen, willing Megan to reply. But she was probably on a table looking at an image of her baby right now.

And even though Kelsey didn't want to go it alone, Patrick's blunt honesty had the potential to make things messy. She finger combed through her mess of thick, wavy hair, then smoothed the front of her shirt. "Hey, why don't you stay inside, and I'll see what they want."

Patrick shrugged and said he'd look through the supply closet for anything else they might need at the mansion.

"Thanks," Kelsey said, rolling her shoulders. This was one of the rare occasions when she wished she carried some makeup in her purse. "How do I look?"

Patrick narrowed his eyes in inspection. "Pale," he

said, "and your cheeks are a bit blotchy. And you have a few beads of sweat on your forehead."

Of course. Of freaking course. If you aren't looking for the truth, her dad would say. She dragged her forearm across her forehead and swallowed hard. "Thanks, Patrick. Wish me luck. I shouldn't be long."

The quiet of the internet café outside Fort Leonard Wood was a welcome reprieve from the bustling USO cyber café Kurt tried earlier. Only a handful of diligently working soldiers dotted this café, a stark contrast from the noise and commotion of earlier. Here, perusing laborers-wanted postings online was almost relaxing. He emailed responses to about seven listings—three in Idaho, two in Wyoming, and two in Montana—before taking a break to order a large black coffee and a chocolate long john from the flirtatious girl working the counter. He spent a few minutes answering her questions and watching her flip her hair as he inhaled the doughnut.

He was rusty, but he suspected if he asked for her number, she'd give it to him. And he'd lost count of how many times he'd been distracted by her plunging neckline since walking in. He hadn't been on a date in nearly three years, and starting with something potentially easy and noncommittal was appealing. He was tossing around how best to ask when she twirled her hair around one finger in a way that reminded him of something his mother might do.

His mom had nearly twenty years on this girl, but he suspected she still spent enough of her time doing the same thing—hanging out on the outskirts of the post, hooking up with soldiers who had no thoughts of commitment. The connection sucked the question from his tongue, so he headed back to his computer at the first break in the conversation.

When Kurt sat down, rather than starting a new search in Washington State as planned, he entered *illegal dogfighting ring, St. Louis* almost unconsciously. He blinked in surprise at the image linking to a new Channel 3 story that had aired earlier in the morning. It was a still shot of the blond. Kelsey something or other.

His index finger hovered over the mouse, twitching. She was standing outside what must be the shelter where she worked, a nondescript redbrick building brightened by pots of colorful flowers and a bright-purple-and-green sign above a set of wide glass doors. Her delicate brows were drawn into a knot, and she was biting her lip. The caption next to the story image read *Family-Centered Shelter Takes on Animals Trained to Kill*.

The voice in his head—the one he credited with keeping him alive after more close calls than cats had lives—sternly announced he needed to get back to the job search.

His fingers didn't listen. He clicked on the story, maximizing it to full screen. His heart sank as he realized it had run first as a live story. *What was she thinking, agreeing to a live story?* That was something Rob would only do with great caution, and only after confirming the questions before filming began.

The piece started with a perfectly composed reporter updating viewers on the horrific dogfighting rescue story while images of the confiscation flashed across the screen. Then the voice-over images ended and the reporter reappeared. She was speaking in a this-story-is-more-important-than-anything-you've-heard voice that grated on Kurt's nerves. Kelsey stood beside her, looking fairly composed.

The first questions were benign, with the reporter asking how long the shelter had been in operation—eighteen years—and stating that it had long been a favorite organization in the Webster Groves community.

Then, after relaying that the shelter had made the controversial decision to take on a large number of the confiscated dogs, the reporter asked Kelsey point-blank her thoughts about embarking on what could be a life-threatening mission.

Kelsey seemed to freeze as the question sank in. The reporter had to nod her on. Finally, Kelsey gave a light shake of her head. "I don't think anything about this rehab is life-threatening."

That was it. She offered nothing else.

The reporter seemed to realize that she'd need to be the conversation starter. "But are you aware there are twenty to thirty deaths from dog attacks every year, most of which are committed by notorious fighting breeds like the ones you're taking on?"

Kelsey pressed her lips together and looked at the camera before angling her body awkwardly toward the reporter. "I'm aware and it's certainly tragic, but there are often extenuating circumstances the media doesn't disclose." She sucked in her cheek while shooting a glance at the camera. "And it's important to state that the shelter is acting responsibly. The dogs we're taking will be kept in a secluded location. Plus, their training is being overseen by a professional. He's on his way from

Kansas City." She stopped and raked a hand through her hair.

So, they were bringing in Tommy Sintras after all. Kurt's shoulders and neck tensed.

The reporter gave Kelsey a look of what seemed like mistrust. "Critics are calling for immediate humane euthanizing and are filing a lawsuit to that effect. Does your shelter have a formal response?"

"No, nothing formal." Her internal reaction to the reporter's question was obvious to Kurt. Her shoulders dropped, and she stepped half a foot closer. She no longer looked like she was trying to ignore the camera either. "But I'm happy to give you my opinion about that news. These dogs… In most ways they aren't different from dogs we adopt out every day. We're a shelter. Most of the dogs we take in have picked up undesirable behaviors. They swipe food off counters, tear up bedding and couches, eat shoes, you name it.

"Our goal is to redirect those behaviors and to help new owners do the same thing. And most of the time, it's easier than you'd think. So that's what we're hoping to do now, just on a different scale. The dogs we're bringing in have been trained to fight other dogs, but that's a *learned* behavior. They may have a way to go, but in the end, it's a matter of training and learning to trust."

The reporter cocked her head as a half smile escaped. Kurt had the distinct feeling she was playing chess and calling check. "So the opinion of the High Grove Animal Shelter is that teaching one dog not to fight another dog to the death is no different from teaching another one to sit or stay? I can't help but wonder how many viewers are shaking their heads at that."

Even from the screen Kurt could see how Kelsey's cheeks reddened. "I didn't mean to imply it was the same thing. It's a slower, more complicated process. Dogs naturally trust humans, but these dogs have been abused. They've been placed in environments where they have to fight to survive. So that's the first goal: rebuilding trust. Typically, those bonds can be rebuilt easier than you'd think, considering the lives these dogs have had."

"Typically." The way the reporter weighted the word, it sounded profoundly impossible. "What is your response to critics' claim that if you're wrong, the price could be very steep indeed?"

Kelsey fell silent a second or two as her forehead knotted together. Kurt was willing to bet she'd all but forgotten the story was airing live. "My response is that while I'm committed to complete caution, I'm also committed to second chances. Just last week, Channel 3 aired a story about a ten-year-old boy who'd been caught stealing, and it turned out he'd been taught it by his mom. He'd been stealing for her ever since he was in kindergarten. I don't recall anyone wanting to prosecute him because of his mother's poor judgment.

"These dogs..." Kelsey continued, closing her hands tightly at her sides. "They didn't have any say in their lives either. They were bred or purchased or in some cases stolen off people's property. Yesterday, I met a sweet Doberman whose microchip traced back to a caring home in Kansas. She was reported missing nearly a year ago, and her owners are overjoyed she'll be coming home. They're committed to helping recondition her. Fortunately, they aren't turning their backs on her."

She was angry and starting to ramble, Kurt thought. He wanted to shout *oorah* when she got back to the reporter's accusation. "What I'd ask people to remember is that every one of the dogs who has been brought in has something in common with that Doberman. They didn't ask to fight, but that's the life they were handed. Just like that boy who didn't ask to steal. We're going to do our best to give these guys a second chance. A bit of support to do it is all we're asking. Because that's what everybody deserves, isn't it? A second chance."

Checkmate, Kelsey.

It was the reporter's turn to fidget. She asked a few more questions before wrapping up, one about the location, which Kelsey wouldn't disclose, and another about the number of dogs the shelter was taking. Thirty-seven. Kelsey divulged the number as if it were no different from the variety of flavors of ice cream. Like she had no idea what she was getting herself into.

When the interview was over, Kurt replayed it twice, trying not to fixate on Kelsey's sculpted face and translucent expressions but doing it anyway. When he was finished, he headed to the counter and the cute barista. The little voice that had gotten him through everything so far screamed at him to ask for her number. To keep on the safer course.

Instead, he asked to borrow her phone.

He was half surprised when he remembered the number after not dialing it for so long. "Rob," he said when his mentor answered on the third ring, "it's me. Tommy Sintras... You got somewhere else you can send him?"

When Rob said yes but asked why, Kurt was nearly

as surprised to hear his reply spoken aloud as Rob sounded. "Because I'm coming back up. I'll take it. I'll take the job."

Chapter 5

THE THING ABOUT A DESOLATE 114-YEAR-OLD MANSION WAS that there was more work and cleaning to do than could possibly be done. Kelsey was the first to admit she wasn't a neat freak. Her clothes often went from the dryer to slung over a chair until she was ready to fold or hang them. She went on cleaning binges only when it was obvious the effort would show. She was often guilty of using the clean dishes in the dishwasher before unloading them. Still, she was accustomed to a level of, well, *newness* she wouldn't get here.

The plumbing worked—reluctantly—but the water needed to run a full minute before the reddish tint went away. The bases of the sink faucets were corroded with rust, and the handles required two hands to turn. The faucet in the best condition was in the guest bathroom, up a set of beautiful, winding hardwood stairs, of which about a third had boards that were precariously loose and needed to be hammered tight.

The toilets flushed and didn't leak, but the bowls were stained from the rust in the water. The thought of using them was about as appealing as using a porta-potty. Then there were the showers and tubs in the upstairs bathrooms. Even after Patrick's bleach attack, the lingering mold spots had convinced Kelsey to use the outside hose if one of the dogs needed a bath.

That covered the plumbing. The electricity worked,

but the way the lights dimmed when voices were raised or doors were shut unnerved her. The paint—which was most likely lead-based—was peeling off many of the walls and windows. Sheets of wallpaper were coming off the walls too. And thank goodness it was mid-September, because the air-conditioning system that had been installed in the late eighties didn't seem to be cooling any longer. She and Patrick had managed to pry open more than half of the original windows, and Kelsey was fairly certain at least one or two of them were now stuck open permanently.

In the kitchen cabinets and pantry and along the basement shelves, they'd found more rodent droppings than she could count. While she was normally a live-and-let-live kind of girl, she and Patrick had stopped at the Home Depot and loaded up on traps. She shuddered at the thought of having to deal with what was caught, but she wouldn't consider poisons that might hurt the dogs or other animals, and sharing the mansion with rodents while rehabbing the dogs simply wasn't sanitary.

So, the other night before leaving, when her muscles were screaming from the exhaustion of the long, demanding day of scouring the house, she and Patrick had carefully placed traps inside cabinets and along shelves where Mr. Longtail couldn't wander upon them while skulking around the house.

And skulking he was. You'd think a cat who hadn't had much human company in the last eight months would be grateful for the commotion. He wasn't. He followed them around indoors and out—using his cat door—while hissing and twitching his long tail. She kept bracing for him to attack her ankles, but so far he hadn't.

And he didn't seem to care about his lack of hunting ability. With that much pent-up frustration, the house should be mouse-free. As Kelsey checked the traps to see what might've been caught overnight, he followed along, twitching his tail.

Even braced for it, she let out a loud gasp when she encountered the first victim in the pantry at the back of a shelf. It was thankfully very dead. She shot Mr. Longtail a glance after grabbing a bag to dispose of it, trap and all. "I should let you examine this up close. It's a mouse. If you've forgotten, you're a cat. You're supposed to be keeping the house free of them. And I hope to have this place mouse-free and looking better when my parents come check it out later this week."

Even as exhausted as she'd been last night, Kelsey had forced herself to go to her parents' house and tell them the news about an hour before an expanded version of the story ran a second time on the evening news. Her parents had seen other stories about the dogfighting ring, but they could hardly seem to wrap their heads around the fact that Kelsey would be involved in the rehab until they watched her stuttering about it in the interview. Afterward, they were both excited for her and a touch worried. Kelsey knew once they saw the dogs firsthand, they'd feel better.

She was walking out the back kitchen door to drop the mouse in the Dumpster at the side of the house that had been delivered for the rehab when she heard a horn from up front. She dropped the bag in unceremoniously and headed around to the front.

As she'd hoped, the first to arrive was Megan. She was stepping out of her new prepped-for-baby Enclave, which she'd agreed to after reluctantly parting with her trusted but seen-better-days RAV4.

Watching her longtime friend and supervisor navigate the merging of her life with Craig, her older and much-better-off-financially fiancé, was an experience for Kelsey. Not only had Craig made an enormous impact on the shelter with a critically timed big donation, but he was a really good guy and great with Megan.

"I missed you yesterday," Kelsey declared as she and Megan met and hugged. Megan's doctor's appointment had run long, and then she'd gotten stuck at the shelter—probably dealing with the aftermath of Kelsey's fiasco of an interview—and hadn't been able to join her and Patrick here.

"I'm sorry I didn't help clean. I saw Patrick as I was leaving the shelter this morning. He said yesterday was productive, but more productivity awaited."

Kelsey laughed. "That's a good way of putting it. I'm holding my breath that Mr. Tommy Sintras doesn't take a look around and hightail it out of here. Especially considering he's actually going to be living here the next few months."

"You know, with a bit of money and elbow grease, this place could look really nice again." Megan eyed the old mansion appreciatively. "However many years it is from now when Mr. Longtail passes away and we sell the place, I really hope it's to someone who'll restore it, not knock it down and put up something new."

"Me too, but whoever attempts it is half-crazy. It's such a giant mess."

The estate was on a double lot at the end of a quiet street. Kelsey's attention was drawn to the street by a set of commercial vans approaching. Her stomach rolled like she'd swallowed a goldfish. This was really happening.

Megan glanced at her watch. "Looks like they're early." She gave Kelsey a hopeful smile. "You ready for this?"

Kelsey took a practiced, slow breath and joked, "I thought I was, but now I'm worried I may fail, and after yesterday's fiasco of an interview, the world will know."

Megan draped an arm across Kelsey's back. "You're going to rock this, Kels. You know how you're always saying I should trust my instincts? Well, something tells me this is going to be really good for you."

Kelsey's mouth went dry as the first van pulled into the circular drive and parked behind the Enclave. She'd worked at the shelter for seven years and would bet she was immune to most levels of barking. The noise erupting from the first van was different. Even through the enclosed vehicle, it was a sound she'd associate with a Category EF5 tornado, not a dog. And from the sound of it, it was coming from a single dog. Few dogs she'd met were capable of producing the level of sound that was blasting into the afternoon. *Kelsey Sutton, what on earth did you get yourself into?*

Swallowing a titanic wave of fear, she headed over to greet Rob and his passengers. Then she spotted a sports car pulling in behind the second van and did a double take. A classic red Mustang was pulling into the circular drive of the Sabrina Raven estate. *The* red Mustang. "What's he doing here?" The words came out in a whisper, but somehow Megan heard over the din of barking. She must have been reading Kelsey's lips.

"Who?"

Kelsey worked to shrug it off, to draw in enough air to clear her head. "No one." Her heart was thumping wildly. He was supposed to have driven back to Fort Leonard Wood the other day.

Engines shut off, and the barking quieted a decibel or two. Kelsey dug her thumbnail into her palm as everyone piled out.

Rob, lanky but confident Rob, made introductions. Kelsey managed to hold on to none of the helpers' names but hoped Megan did. In addition to Rob and Kurt, three people had gotten out of the vans. Two were guys and neither looked like the guy she'd Googled who was supposed to be helping her, the one whose name suddenly escaped her. Maybe he was coming later.

Rob seemed to be saying something important, but Kelsey's ears were buzzing, and the intense barking of that single dog was distracting. She tried not to gawk at Kurt as he studied the old mansion after giving her a long look. She'd almost swear he was assessing it the same way he'd assessed her at the warehouse. She got the sense that the way he read people, the way he related to them, was entirely different from that of anyone she knew.

Megan brushed Kelsey's elbow, trying to get her attention. Kelsey struggled to play back her friend's last few words. If she was correct, Megan wanted them to head inside for a quick tour before unloading the crates. Kelsey nodded in agreement. "Yeah, of course."

"No one, huh?" Megan whispered as Rob motioned for two of his helpers to open the back van doors before they headed inside. "The way you two were looking at each other, I'd say that's anyone but no one."

———

Maybe it was the light breeze sweeping across the tall, ancient oaks that spanned the yard, causing the leaves to chime in the wind. Maybe it was a trick of the mind on seeing the historic home. Kurt could swear he heard his nana's voice brushing over his ears.

It made sense she'd come to mind now. She'd left an older mansion than this for the chance to be with his grandfather. It wasn't the money she'd missed but the history. Whenever they'd come across old places like this, she'd reach for Kurt, knowing her touch helped draw his ever-roaming attention.

"Can't you feel it, Kurt?" she'd ask. "This home's history is clinging to its walls, to the branches of the old trees shading it, to its windows and doors. Think of the family who lived here when the house was new. And when it was only as old as I am now. What secrets would those windows tell if they could speak?"

He'd never had much of an imagination, but her questions always got his mind churning. He'd picture things like top hats and bustles and gramophones, though as a kid he'd had no clue about the names that went with those images.

Kurt studied the house as Rob finished introductions, and felt the rightness of his decision swirling over his ribs. He'd come here to help the girl. To keep her out of trouble. And while here, he'd keep the dogs at a distance. He needed to. The girl too, for that matter. But he knew even before stepping inside that he'd embrace his stay in this house fully. Nana would want him to, and he owed her more than that.

He'd stayed so many places while on duty the last eight years, seen so many homes with such dramatically different histories. He'd learned how to read the energy of a house. This mansion had a lingering pulse that brought to mind the laughter of small children, the fervent whispers of young lovers, and the quiet wisdom of the elderly.

Kurt was the last in the group to head up the weed-covered stone path to the front porch. He'd picked up on the curious look the pregnant supervisor gave him during Rob's introductions. She whispered something to Kelsey, who turned red and seemed to have trouble following the conversation, making him wonder if Rob had failed to give her a heads-up that Kurt was coming instead of Tommy. Even though he'd been focusing on the house, Kelsey hadn't looked his way since. He'd have felt it if she had.

He stepped through the double doors into the foyer and took in the expansive entry, curving staircase, and muted light pouring through the tall windows. He planted his boots on the dusty but rich hardwood floor spanning the first level and felt the hair prickle on the back of his neck and the goose bumps rise on his arms. In a good way. The scent filling his nostrils reminded him of bleach mixed with an old bookstore he'd once walked into before remembering that getting through an entire novel was next to impossible with his level of ADHD.

He wasn't sure how long the house had sat empty. It had the air of a place that was once a bustling, lively home and had been snoozing, waiting for the dogs and volunteers that would soon be filling it.

As inspiring as the old mansion was, it was also a great space for the dogs. Rather than large, open rooms, there were several smaller rooms so the staff could separate the crates. The still half-furnished rooms had once served as parlors, a music room, a library, a drawing room, and a dining room. Now they'd be temporary holding spaces for a bunch of canines with their fair share of emotional and physical wounds.

Kurt counted four fireplaces on the main floor, two small and two that were imposing. The ceilings were impressively high—twelve feet, he guessed—and there were transoms over the tall windows.

The eyesore of a kitchen stood apart from the rest of the remarkable old home. It looked to have been rehabbed last in the late sixties. Even if the retro look was in, the cabinets, countertops, and appliances were too dated to ever be considered in style. Not that he was one to care about style.

He was taking in the chipped, sky-blue cabinets and matching rust-covered appliances when a massive gray tabby cat pushed in through a pet door in the door leading to the backyard. The cat was huge and had silky, somewhat unkempt fur and the longest tail Kurt had ever seen. The feline eyed the group and hissed, then hopped up onto the counter, twitching its impressive tail.

"This is Mr. Longtail," Kelsey said, still making eye contact with everyone but Kurt. "He's the reason this estate was willed to us. His owner didn't have any family to take the house, and she didn't want him relocated, so she left the house to us on the condition that we care for him here until he passes away."

"I wondered why an animal shelter owned a high-maintenance old place like this and had it just sitting empty," Kurt said.

"We've only owned it about eight months," Kelsey answered, holding his gaze for a second or two. "Once or twice we've considered bringing a few overflow animals here, but dividing the staff never made sense. Until now, anyway. Eventually, when Mr. Longtail is gone, the house will be sold, and we're hoping to use the money to expand on the north side of our building. We'll name it in Sabrina Raven's honor."

"So it's just been him and this old house for the last eight months?"

"Yeah, but he doesn't like people much, so I'm not sure that he minds. If you leave him alone, he won't bite."

"How's he like dogs?" Rob asked, chuckling.

"Probably not any more than he likes people, but as long as they're on leashes and can't hurt him, he'll be fine."

"I have a feeling he'll be putting them all in their place fast enough, with an attitude like he seems to have," Rob added. "And he still has claws, right?"

"Yes, but he likes to use them on the last of the wallpaper that's still hanging and not on the mice taking over the house."

Kurt headed to the aged, yellow Formica countertop and held up a finger a few inches in front of the cat, allowing the undaunted animal a chance for a sniff.

Mr. Longtail smelled Kurt's finger for several seconds, then rubbed his cheek hard against it, twitching his tail like a whip.

"Maybe he just needs someone to understand him,"

Kurt said. He wasn't a cat person, but this cat was different. He could stand up to a room full of strangers and remind them that this was his house and would still be once this rehab was over. At the very least, the animal was worthy of Kurt's respect. And he had an odd feeling that, like the house, the cat had an intentional place in his life. For the time being, at least.

"What is it you think he wants us to understand?" Megan, the pregnant supervisor, asked. Her tone was without sarcasm. "Because we've certainly not gotten the message. Kelsey's tried every way she can think of to befriend him, but it hasn't worked. Sabrina Raven sure loved him though."

"I can't say," Kurt replied. "Cats don't communicate like dogs. They're solitary hunters by nature. I suspect we'll figure each other out soon enough, considering we'll be roommates the next few months."

"Well, if you figure it out, let us know. It'll make caring for him easier, won't it, Kels?"

If Kelsey heard her, she didn't show it. She was suddenly looking right at Kurt for the first time since he'd gotten out of the car. Her head was cocked sideways. "You're…you're staying? It's *you* who's doing the retraining?"

So Rob hadn't told her. Kurt actually felt her surprise, picking up on the insecurity and heat that rushed over her the same way he picked up on fear. He hadn't counted on how her feelings might affect him when he'd made the decision to come here.

He could handle his own feelings; he'd become a master at that over the last eight years. But something told him hers wouldn't be as easy to dismiss.

This knowledge unnerved him more than anything else had since leaving the jungles of Honduras.

"Yeah," he said, cocooning himself in the sarcasm he could always call on. "Figured I couldn't handle the guilt if the next report I saw on this story was about how half these dogs had gone missing and you were nowhere to be found. That wouldn't get any of these guys new homes, would it?"

His comment had the effect he'd hoped for. Settled that wildly beating heart of hers and sent a flush of embarrassment to her cheeks. What he hadn't counted on was how big of an ass he'd feel like for embarrassing her like that.

He swallowed back a sigh of regret as the rest of the group suddenly looked everywhere but at the two of them. One thing was for sure: it was going to be an unprecedented few months.

Chapter 6

THANK GOODNESS FOR THE ENTOURAGE OF CRATES PILING into the mansion. The dogs took precedence over Kelsey's newfound apprehension. Eventually, things would settle down and the fact that she'd be working intimately with Kurt would be catapulted into the forefront of her thoughts again, but for a few hours, she could focus on the dogs.

As crates began filling the old house, Kelsey started noticing little details about the place she'd not paid attention to before. Like the fact that the ceilings were nearly as tall as most of the rooms on the main floor were wide. The rooms led into one another through wide doorways and had always felt more spacious—*uh, more like looming*—than they actually were. The presence of the dogs warmed the rooms and melted away the coldness she'd felt here with only Mr. Longtail.

The handcrafted molding that lined the ceilings and doors suddenly stood out in comparison to the plastic crates in which the dogs had been transported. At one time, the house really had been a work of art.

Now that the dogs were in, thirty-seven brand-new wire cages were being assembled in various rooms. The cages were a generous donation from a local pet store in response to Kelsey's interview, and something she was very touched by. They would be roomier than the plastic crates the dogs had been living in the last few days, and the manager of the store had even thrown in comfy bed liners for each dog. These cozy liners were something Kelsey suspected many of the dogs wouldn't have had in their previous homes. To their owners, they'd been fighting dogs, not pets.

Now it was time to change that.

The crates and bed liners weren't the only support the shelter had received for the rehab since the story aired. Megan told Kelsey that the shelter's online PayPal account had received a record number of donations over a single night. People from all over were calling to see how they could help. There'd also been a handful of complaints and questions from concerned viewers, but from what Megan had shared, none of them had been too heated.

After the dogs were inside, it became apparent that only five or six dogs would fit in each room, allowing a bit of distance between cages. Deciding which dogs should be placed in rooms together was like putting together a complicated puzzle. This task was left to Rob and Kurt, while Kelsey and the others assembled the cages. The two men took the dogs out of their crates one at a time and walked them on leashes out to the backyard and then, when they were deemed sufficiently calm, past the other crated dogs. Kelsey was amazed at the way the dogs were immediately reactive to some but not others. Even while busy assembling the cages, she could tell that a handful of the dogs were strongly dominant, though most seemed amazingly relaxed for all they'd been through—in life and in the last few days of being pulled from their homes and everything familiar.

There was a showdown of sorts in the first hour,

minutes after Patrick showed up, that left Kelsey breathless. Kurt was walking the giant tan-and-black shepherd mix on a tight, controlled leash. He was the dog who'd been causing the incredible commotion as the vans had pulled in. He'd stopped barking, but judging by the ruffled hair on the back of his neck and his raised tail, he was anything but relaxed.

At first, everything stayed calm and quiet. Then, out of nowhere, the anxious dog bolted toward one of the crates, yanking Kurt to his knees and snarling at the door. It happened nearly too fast to process, but Kurt was on his feet again in seconds. Somehow, he got the dog to sit at attention. Judging by the giant dog's tense muscles and gaze that darted back and forth between the crated animal and Kurt, it was begrudgingly.

As soon as the chaotic barking that had erupted throughout the house quieted, Kurt looked her way, his face lined with tension.

"I won't let him catch me off guard again, but I know a dog who's going to be a lot of work when I see one. If you're set on him staying, no one, absolutely no one, handles him until I say so."

Kelsey nodded. "I'll make sure of it. Promise." Beside her, Patrick let out a troubled *humph*. He drummed his fingers against the pocket on the outer thigh of his cargo pants like he did when he was thinking through something.

Kurt gave a light shake of his head but said nothing further about the dog leaving. Megan used the break in the conversation to excuse herself and leave for the shelter, where a different mountain of work was waiting. While Rob and his guys were polite enough, Kelsey was glad Patrick would be sticking around to keep her company this afternoon. The companionship of her shelter coworkers was immensely comforting in the face of all this upheaval.

Patrick didn't lose a minute before he dove into cage assembly. Kelsey knew she shouldn't be surprised when one of his pants pockets held a thin but sturdy pair of wire cutters that snipped through the zip ties securing the unopened cages better than the rusty metal scissors she'd found in a kitchen drawer.

"Nice kennels," he said, jiggling the snaps in the corner that were meant to hold water bowls snuggly in place. "Some of the dogs may need to adjust to the openness of the wire. The ones who've mostly lived in enclosed crates."

"I thought about that."

"We can cover them with light blankets if needed."

"Yeah. We'll see what they say." She nodded toward the two guys in the next room, who were deep in conversation about a Rottweiler that Kurt had on a leash.

"You're in charge of the dogs' basic care."

"I guess I am," Kelsey said, not feeling quite as confident as Patrick sounded. Hearing several of the dogs snap and growl had solidified the knowledge that they'd been trained *not* to get along with one another. In a ring, at least. Many probably had lived docilely with other dogs in their house.

Kelsey suddenly realized that these dogs had no idea they hadn't been brought here to fight. This made her want to comfort them all. As she was considering how to do that, Kurt looked directly at her from the adjacent room.

"I think this Rott is pregnant," he said. "She's probably not more than three or four weeks along, but I'm betting she is. The vet didn't catch it, most likely because she's underweight by fifteen pounds."

Kelsey stood up from the crate she and Patrick were working on and headed into the next room. With her approval, Rob had brought over a few females who were still due to be spayed. With so many dogs having been confiscated, and some of them in worse shape than others, there was a backup on spaying and neutering. Kelsey had offered that the shelter would pay for the spaying of the few females they were getting who still needed it.

She eyed the dog carefully. She was fairly good at spotting a pregnant dog, but she couldn't see what Kurt had noticed in the Rottweiler. "How so? She doesn't look pregnant to me."

"There isn't a single male she's tolerated, and her nipples are a bit pink and swollen."

Pink, swollen nipples. *Of course.*

"Want Rob to take her back with him?" he continued, scratching the dog on the back of her neck while she stood obediently alongside him.

"To the warehouse? To go somewhere else?" Kelsey's shoulders squared defensively.

Kurt let out a soft sigh as if he knew her answer. "That's what I'd suggest."

"No way. Who knows where she'd end up. Here we can give her whatever TLC she needs."

"If you ask me, this op doesn't need the extra chaos. We have to focus on retraining these dogs. Puppies and pregnant females are a distraction. Added to that, she's underweight and looks a bit malnourished. Who knows how it could play out."

"I'll take care of her. I have a lot of experience getting weight back on dogs."

"She seems docile enough with people, but if you're serious, you should know there isn't a male dog here she likes, and there are twenty-eight of them stuck in crates all around. And most of the female fighters we've taken in don't like other females."

Kelsey tugged on her earlobe. "Then let's keep her in a room by herself."

"We've filled all the ones down here, and until the stairs are fixed, the dogs won't have access to the top floor."

"There's the screened-in half of the back porch. It's September, and the weather's good. We can keep her out there until we can get her upstairs."

Kurt pursed his lips and looked at Rob, most likely hoping he'd back him. Rob simply shrugged. "If she's willing to take on the extra work."

With a slight shake of his head, Kurt offered the leash in Kelsey's direction. "Why don't you take her for a walk around the yard and see how you two get along? And ask your friend to go with you, just in case."

Kelsey took the leash and had to refrain from jolting backward when their fingers brushed. Her skin prickled as if she'd gotten a shock. Kurt immediately locked his hands around his hips as he stepped back, drawing her attention to his lean torso. It was a really, really nice torso.

"I don't think I need to remind you to stay on this property. With all the dogs. Until they've passed several handling tests."

She nodded and let the pretty girl sniff her closed hand. Having worked so long around dogs who were mostly mysteries, she'd committed the basics to memory. Always read the dog's cues when interacting with them for the first time. Stand straight or drop to a squat, never lean over them—it was threatening—and avoid direct eye contact until the dog relaxed. "You don't. I know. The yard's plenty big anyway."

One of his eyebrows rose slightly. "Then I'll let you get acquainted."

―⁓―

"Pepper, definitely Pepper. Don't you think?" Kelsey looked at Patrick for confirmation. Since most of the dogs' names weren't known, finding the right name for each of them was one of Kelsey's top priorities.

Patrick gave the stocky Rottweiler another once-over before answering. "I think you're right. Pepper suits her."

"Then Pepper it is."

They'd been outside for twenty minutes when Kelsey sank to the ground in a warm patch of sun at the far edge of the front yard, a spot nestled under the yard's most enormous trees. Kelsey figured they had to be as old as the house.

The Rott had been super laid-back with Kelsey, and Patrick was seeing how she did with him. Most animals seemed to pick up on the fact that he was a bit different. Patrick had Asperger's. He was brilliant but a bit quirky. Most animals were comfortable around him from the start, though a few were skittish. Pepper seemed fine.

Kelsey crossed her legs and rubbed her calves,

enjoying the feel of the grass beneath her. She was wiped out from the intensive cleaning yesterday and from assembling the crates this morning. When the laid-back Rottweiler noticed her on the ground, she pulled Patrick in Kelsey's direction. The Rott collapsed in the grass alongside Kelsey with a plop. Since Pepper had trusted her enough to sit next to her, Kelsey decided to go with it, even if sitting on the ground beside a powerful dog who might still be wound up from an unstable past wasn't the most responsible of ideas.

They sat together for several minutes. Pepper was content to lie still and have her ears rubbed. Her nubbin of a tail wagged contentedly.

Maybe she didn't have much trust to reestablish with people after all.

Even as underweight as the dog was, Kelsey guessed she was at least eighty pounds. She was thin for a heavy-set Rott, but she hadn't been starved. The vet had put her at about five years old, and by a simple glance at her belly and the two rows of exposed teats, it was clear she'd had at least one litter already. And, unlike many of the dogs, she didn't have any visible scars.

"Maybe she was only bred and not fought. She seems so trusting of people," Kelsey said.

"Most breeds that end up in the fighting rings were originally bred to have strong trust in their owners." Patrick's tone was matter-of-fact, but Kelsey knew it wasn't because he didn't care. He just had difficulty connecting with his emotions. He rarely got upset, but when he did, he immersed himself in a laborious project and didn't stop until he was physically spent. He was cute with his soft brown eyes and always disheveled hair. He drove her nuts at times with his penchant for routine, but he was one of her favorite people.

"True." Kelsey let out a sigh and forced thoughts of Pepper's past out of her mind. Animals were often better than people at living in the present.

Mr. Longtail emerged from a thick hedge at the edge of the yard. He headed toward the group with his tail erect and unusually fluffy. Kelsey shortened the leash that Patrick had passed her way when Pepper sat down. Pepper watched the cat approach with only mild curiosity, as though she'd been around cats before and knew they weren't prey, which definitely wasn't something you could say about many dogs.

To Kelsey's surprise, the cantankerous cat walked right up to the Rottweiler and started to sniff, first the dog's face, then her paws and down her side. Pepper did nothing more than wag her tail, after glancing Kelsey's way as if in confirmation that this was okay.

"Well, she could easily be adopted into a house with cats," Kelsey praised, patting her. She relaxed and resumed rubbing Pepper's ears, which the dog seemed to really enjoy.

Finished with his sniff test, Mr. Longtail rolled onto his back and wiggled back and forth, marking his scent. Clearly, he didn't mind that the dog next to him was practically ten times his size.

"I see why Sabrina Raven liked him," Patrick said. "He's not your average cat."

Kelsey shook her head as Mr. Longtail stood up and strolled toward the back of the house without seeming to give them another thought. "No, he definitely isn't. And I'm no longer worried about him getting too stressed out by all the dogs. He's just so full of himself. He probably thinks they're here for his amusement."

"Possibly." Patrick watched the cat appreciatively before turning back to his Swiss Army knife. He was using the pair of microscissors to trim his nails. "Does the contract Megan signed tell which of you has more say? You or the handler?"

Kelsey's brows furrowed. "No, but he does, I would guess. He's the professional."

"He's letting it be your decision to keep Pepper."

"I suspect he's being courteous."

Patrick pressed the scissors back into the thick knife and slipped it into a pocket in his pants. "You blush when you look at him."

Kelsey stopped rubbing Pepper's ear midway through a stroke. Patrick had always been one to call things as he saw them. And they knew each other too well for her to try to hide her thoughts. "Back at the warehouse when I saw the shape one of the dogs was in, I pretty much threw up on his boots. And it's obvious he thinks I'm not cut out for this. He said as much this morning before you came."

Patrick frowned. "I thought it was because you two liked each other." Patrick was twenty-six and seemed to have zero interest in a relationship of his own. It came as a surprise that he'd have even the remotest interest in her finding one.

Kelsey glanced at the house, a blush stinging her cheeks. She couldn't see anyone through the open windows, but she was reassured that she and Patrick were too far away to be heard. "I'd have to be blind not to notice he's good-looking," she admitted, "but that's as far as it goes."

Having had her ears abandoned, Pepper let her head sink to the ground and licked her lips contentedly.

Patrick nodded but pursed his lips like he did when he disagreed but thought better than to say it aloud.

"Patrick, I appreciate your enthusiasm, but he and I are going to be working together for a few months. Anything like you're suggesting could get, I don't know, *weird*."

"It was good for Megan to fall in love," Patrick said as matter-of-factly as if he was stating that the sixty-five-degree day was refreshing.

A hearty laugh bubbled out of Kelsey, and it caught Pepper's full attention. The dog lifted her head and stared straight at her. With more agility than Kelsey would have given her credit for, Pepper was on all four feet in a flash. The hairs on the back of her neck ruffled as she stared Kelsey down.

Kelsey realized how naive she'd been to allow herself to remain so comfortable on the ground next to such a powerful dog with a possibly traumatic history. "It's all right, girl," she chanted, keeping her voice calmer than she felt. "It's all right."

Pepper took a step closer, and Kelsey dropped her gaze to her lap as she chanted the simple phrase. In the same calm voice, she added, "Don't move unless you have to, Patrick."

There was a flash, and Kelsey felt a warm, wet tongue swipe the length of her cheek. The relief that swept over her brought tears to her eyes. Patrick let out a sigh like a balloon deflating as Pepper inundated Kelsey with fresh licks.

Taking Patrick's outstretched hand, Kelsey stood up

and gave the dog a pat on the shoulder. She wiped her cheek dry with a shaky hand as Pepper shook her massive head, her collar jangling. "You'd almost think she'd never heard anyone laugh before."

From the direction of the house, a door swung open. Kurt and Rob appeared on the stoop of the front door, frowning in Kelsey and Patrick's direction. They'd seen what happened from the windows. *Because of course*.

Kelsey's growing confidence about being a good fit for this rehab disintegrated. Now for sure Kurt had to think she was an idiot. And if Patrick had been harboring hopes of Kelsey making a love connection while here, they were probably vanishing into thin air too.

Everyone kept silent as Kelsey and Patrick walked Pepper toward Kurt and Rob. When they got close to the house, Kurt said calmly, "Can we please agree to stay standing around the dogs until we know them better?" Now that she was closer, Kelsey could see two deep lines making a V across his forehead.

She wanted to sink into one of the dry cracks in the ground but instead locked her shoulders as they headed up to the porch. "We can if you can accept that I do know some things about dogs. I've worked in a shelter for seven years, and I haven't misjudged a dog's character yet."

Color flashed above Kurt's collar. As he opened his mouth, Rob placed a hand firmly on his shoulder.

"Of course you do," Rob said, smiling congenially, "or none of us would be here today embarking on this rehab. Kurt, why don't we walk them around inside and show them where we've placed the dogs? Kelsey, we've set up our biggest kennel on the screened-in half of the porch for the Rottweiler. And before I leave, we'll go over the feeding schedule these dogs have been introduced to the last few days."

Kurt's features softened a bit, and the lines disappeared from his forehead. Kelsey felt the muscles around her spine relax in response. Although something told her this wouldn't be their only disagreement, she gave Rob a nod.

What on earth would happen when no one was around to play peacemaker?

———

She wasn't getting it. That's what irked Kurt most. Undeniably, it was best to be calm and comfortable around any dog. But this wasn't the shelter. The thirty-seven dogs brought here were going to be put to the test. He might not be able to accurately determine their individual stress levels. However careful he was, one of them could snap before this was over.

And Kelsey needed to understand this. But Kurt suspected she intended to dive in like Snow White, singing and turning them into her soul mates. Maybe that would be fine, and maybe it wouldn't.

And that had him on edge. So did the people who kept driving slowly down the street and gawking at the house as if they suspected what was going on inside. That was the thing about the world now. So much information was at anyone's fingertips. It was public record that the estate had been donated to Kelsey's shelter. It wouldn't take much detective work for anyone who'd listened to Kelsey's interview to figure out this was where the rehab would be taking place.

Kurt suspected that protesters would be camped on the street out front by tomorrow. And there'd be nothing he could do about it. The mansion stood at the end of a quiet city street, but unfortunately not a private one. As long as no one came onto the property, people could protest all they wanted. And that would likely set Kelsey and anyone else coming in to volunteer on edge, which the dogs would notice. Hell, just having come off duty as he had, the potential of an angry mob out front made the muscles in his arms and legs practically lock up. Which wouldn't serve him well when it came to working with the dogs.

Directly across the street was a big house with lots of scaffolding on the outside and a half-dozen sawhorses visible through the windows. He guessed it was empty and being rehabbed. That meant their only actual neighbor was immediately to the east and blocked by a long row of hedges. The second story was partially visible through the expansive trees, and Kurt had caught a glimpse of an older woman in one of the windows watching Kelsey and Patrick as they walked the Rottweiler.

Thankfully, the mansion's backyard was big and very private. After he was caught up inside, Kurt would head out there to inspect the privacy fence for weak spots. He'd need to run to the store to get hefty locks for the gates as soon as he had time. He also needed to start building a few separated exercise runs as soon as possible. Hopefully, he'd have time to make a mental supply list and get those items tonight.

What he could really use was Rob's help for a few more days, but Rob had a warehouse of other dogs that needed his attention. There was Kelsey's coworker,

Patrick. Kurt wasn't quite sure what to make of him. Patrick's conversation and demeanor were a bit unusual, and Kurt wasn't convinced all the dogs would take to him, but he seemed handy enough. If he kept hanging around, Kurt hoped to put him to good use.

It was the first day, and he could feel his ADHD kicking into overdrive. Everywhere he turned, something needing his attention called to him. The stairs. The fence. The far-east corner of the roof that seemed to be leaking. The electricity. Thirty-seven attention-deserving dogs.

Kelsey was a hard worker and would match him effort for effort. He knew this before the afternoon was halfway over. It was nearly three o'clock, and she hadn't slowed down for as much as a bite of food all day. And while she wasn't the frail type that looked like a strong wind could blow her over, he could see the fatigue setting into her features.

"Pizza," he said after passing her in the kitchen and deciding to act on a whim. She was at the sink, washing the new stainless-steel water bowls. Rob and Patrick had left twenty minutes prior, and it was Kurt's first attempt to break the silence that had been hanging in the air ever since. "And not the crappy chain kind. I'm talking traceable-to-a-genuine-Italian recipe."

Kelsey's lips pressed together as if she was working to keep back a smile. Switching to a new bowl, she turned to face him, resting one hip against the sink as she worked her thumb under the edge of the sticker. The sun was streaming in the window, causing her long, golden highlights to shine. "Was that supposed to be a statement or a question?"

"Unless you're superhuman, you have to be hungry.

I'm hoping that since this is your stomping ground, you'll know someplace worth trying. I haven't had a really good slice of pizza in years."

"Hmm, that seems pretty close to torture. What kind of crust do you like? Are St. Louis–style cracker crusts popular in Fort Leonard Wood?"

Kurt made a face that made her giggle. "Popular enough, but for now I'd like to skip any pizza that's associated with the word 'cracker.' The best pizza I ever had was in this little mom-and-pop shop down in Branson. The owners were first-generation Italian. They said the secret's in the crust. It should be hand-tossed and made fresh in-house. And not too thick or too thin. Know any place like that? My treat."

"With you having been deprived of good pizza for so long, it's a lot of pressure, but I think I can come up with something. What are your favorite toppings?"

"I'm not picky as long as they're processed in a factory and not grown in a garden."

She laughed again. "I would've figured that."

"Let me guess. You're a vegetarian?"

"No, I'm not. I've given it consideration, but I haven't been able to go more than a few weeks without Philly cheesesteak sandwiches calling my name. Black-and-blue cheeseburgers are pretty high up on my list too."

"Both worthy candidates, if you ask me."

He could practically see the tension falling off her and knew it wasn't a good time to mention that he wasn't ready to leave her here alone in case she'd want to play Snow White with one of the dogs while he was away. Instead, he chose a safer route.

"Come with me. I could use a tour of the area," he said,

locking the dead bolt on the back kitchen door in case one of the passengers in the cars that had been casing the place decided to try something stupid. This reminded him that the Rott was kenneled alone on the back porch. It was screened-in but could be broken into easily. He unbolted the door. "On second thought, let's put the Rott's kennel in the kitchen before we leave. I'll move it if you'll walk her out back for a bathroom break."

Kelsey bit her lip. He'd done his best not to leave her an out. Maybe that was a mistake. She seemed pretty willful.

"That wasn't a question, and you didn't say please," she said, her voice light, "but I'll go with it, considering you're still acclimating back into a world where people actually do say please and thank you on a regular basis."

Kurt splayed his hands. "You've got me there. Kelsey, would you please accompany me on a quick excursion for takeout pizza and beer?"

"I am a bit starving, so yes I will—what was it Rob called you?—Staff Sergeant Crawford?"

"Kurt will be just fine. I'm hoping to settle into civilian life as effortlessly as possible."

It was Kelsey's turn to make a face. "Should I remind you that the cops at the warehouse the other day seemed to pick up on your military vibe even before you shared it with them?"

"There's a Semper Fi sticker on the back of my Mustang. I'm guessing it was that more than any sort of vibe. Though we can go with vibe, if you'd like."

"Oh," she said. "Makes sense now."

She followed him to the back porch, and their hands brushed again as Kurt passed her the Rott's leash. The hair on his arms stood on end, and a wave of yearning rocked through his core. It'd been a while since he'd been with a woman and even longer since he'd been with someone who stirred him the way she did.

The wind picked up, and Kurt caught her soft scent— flowers and a touch of citrus. He didn't know whether it was perfume or a hair product. He wanted to lean in and smell it again. Wanted to brush his thumb along the ridge of her jaw. Wanted to wrap his arm around the small of her back and pull her against him.

The fact that Kelsey didn't seem the type to let anyone do any of those things until she was ready made him want her even more.

He cleared his throat hard and hoisted the bulky kennel as she headed for the backyard, talking softly to the dog. He wished the kennel was heavier. Wished it was more of a distraction. He'd be needing a lot of distractions over the next few months. Without them, he was going to end up letting her in.

And doing that would make a complicated rehab even more complicated.

Chapter 7

KELSEY TOOK A CALCULATED SWALLOW OF BEER. ANY MORE than half a bottle and she'd start to get tipsy, something she wasn't about to risk while working. She couldn't remember the last time she'd had a beer in the middle of the day. When Kurt ran into the grocery store while she held the pizzas on her lap, she hadn't been thinking about how unappealing the tap water here seemed or that the jug of water she'd brought with her this morning was empty. When it had come to a bottle of beer or a glass of sketchy tap water, she'd chosen the beer.

Kurt had no worries about drinking water from the faucet, but she bet his system had tolerated worse. He'd downed a glass before they headed out and didn't comment on the rusty taste. Now he was enjoying a beer, but she was thankful he wasn't going for a second when the dogs still needed so much attention.

They were seated at a bulky iron table on the half of the wide back porch that wasn't screened in. After Kurt had scoured the privacy fence for holes, he'd turned one of the pit bulls, a recently spayed female, loose to roam the yard while they ate. She sniffed around for a while, then clambered up the four wooden steps to the porch and eyed him curiously as he ate slice after slice.

He had purchased three large pizzas after making sure one of them had Kelsey's favorite choice of toppings. When Kelsey commented that it was enough pizza for an entourage, he said the leftovers would be something to put in the empty fridge.

Kelsey settled back in her chair, taking a moment to savor the day. The weather couldn't be better. No humidity, sunny, blue skies, and temps in the sixties. "So how long were you in the marines?"

"Five years. And about three with the army before that including basic training." Kurt had just finished his fourth slice of pizza and was reaching for her longtime favorite, ham and pineapple.

"That's a lot of service." She was halfway through her third slice and regretting it. If it weren't for the dogs needing human attention, she would have had a hard time getting motivated. The last couple days had been a whirlwind, and she was feeling it.

At least she could go home tonight to her quiet apartment and sleep like a log. After she stopped by her parents', anyway. They had invited the whole family over for a cookout around the fire pit in their backyard, and Kelsey hadn't seen her nieces in several days.

Kurt would stay here, and even if the house didn't seem as creepy now that the main floor was alive with the sounds and smells of the dogs, Kelsey doubted it would be a peaceful night. The house was creaky and drafty, and the dogs were sure to be unsettled their first night in a new place.

"It felt like enough," he said, answering her unasked question about his length of service.

When he didn't add anything else in clarification, Kelsey wondered if he might not want to talk about it. Before she could bite her tongue, her curiosity got the best of her, and another question slipped out. She'd never met a military dog handler before. "Were you hoping to work with dogs when you enlisted, or did you fall into it?"

"Dogs, no question. Rob was my mentor. He worked at the post before he retired. After he did, he focused on training guard dogs in the private sector."

Since Kurt didn't seem opposed to talking about it, Kelsey continued. "My whole life, I wanted to work with dogs, but I never thought of the military."

"Yeah, well, you didn't grow up on a post, did you?"

"You mean you lived at Fort Leonard Wood before you joined the army?" She'd also never known anyone who grew up in circumstances so different from her traditional suburban background.

"My grandfather is an instructor there. He's a retired consultant now, but he taught weapons instruction for most of his adult life. I was born in a post hospital down in Texas. My grandfather transferred to Fort Leonard Wood when I was a kid. We hardly ever left except on vacation to visit other posts."

"Wow. No wonder you decided to be a military dog handler. At first I thought I'd be a vet, but I ended up coming home from college halfway through my sophomore year. It was how I connected with the shelter though, so I don't regret it. I still take classes part time. I'm a senior credit-wise."

"What will you do when you have a degree?"

She shrugged sheepishly. "Probably still work at the shelter. It just fits. I wouldn't have to take many additional classes to be a vet tech though, and I love the medical aspect of animal care. Dr. Washington, our vet, lets me administer shots when he has the time."

"You'd be a good vet or vet tech, whatever you decide on."

Still at Kurt's feet, the dog let out a sigh and rested her head on her front legs as if having determined she wasn't going to be offered a slice of pizza. Earlier, Kurt had requested that for now, treats only be given at the end of the dogs' training sessions. There'd be a time for pampering, he'd said, but it wasn't yet.

That made sense to Kelsey, so she didn't object. She wasn't surprised that Kurt had a natural alpha-male demeanor that the dogs seemed to pick up on immediately. That was especially obvious with this dog. The single, short introductory session Kurt had had with her seemed to have cemented in her mind that he was the boss. She hardly even glanced Kelsey's way. They weren't even a full day into training, but Kurt's talent was undeniable.

The dog was slender for a pit bull and seemed to be one of the calmest and most easygoing animals here. She was a light cream with a circle of white on her nose. Kelsey thought she was adorable. Suddenly, she noticed that the dog's front legs were crossed daintily underneath her resting head.

"Hey, we don't know her name, do we?"

Kurt shrugged. "I don't think so."

"We should call her Lady. Look how she's got her front legs crossed."

Kurt sat back in his chair and cocked an eyebrow at the pit, who immediately popped her head back up. "Yeah, that fits. That reminds me. How about bringing one of your fail-safe shelter dogs over in a few days? A neutered male who's right in the middle of the pack, not too alpha and not too omega. Obviously one you're betting has never been abused or in a fight."

"Sure. What for?"

"There are a few who should be ready for the first steps of socialization soon. Going on short, leashed walks with another dog, activities like that."

Kelsey immediately thought of Orzo. He was exactly the dog Kurt was describing. "Sure. I know who I can bring. A little corgi who gets along with everyone. And he's really laid-back."

"That works. And by the way," Kurt said, lifting the last of his slice of ham and pineapple into the air, "this is surprisingly good. I didn't think I'd like it, but I do. Almost better than the meat lover's deluxe."

"That one is too much meat for me. The straight pepperoni is good though. Maybe next time you'll be ready to add a few veggies."

He made a face. "You ever notice how dogs will eat almost anything, but they turn their heads from vegetables?"

"True, but they're carnivores. I believe humans evolved eating more plants than animals."

"Yeah, well, I've been told my soul is really canine, so that explains a lot."

She laughed. "You've just given me a second mission while we're here: getting you to like veggies. At least some of them."

"Honey," Kurt said, finishing off his beer, "I'm betting we'll have more success rehabbing these dogs than you will doing that." He set down the bottle and picked at the label. "Though miracles happen."

Honey. Kelsey could feel a deep blush rising above

her collar. She couldn't remember the last time anyone under the age of seventy had called her that.

His show of camaraderie this afternoon wasn't something she'd expected. All of this—right down to sitting here on the back porch eating pizza with a so-hot-he's-hard-to-look-at ex-marine—still felt surreal.

But whether she was ready for it or not, they'd be working in close quarters and getting to know each other very well over the next few months. He liked dogs—and was great with them—so she was inclined to give him the benefit of the doubt as far as being a good person. Whether he was or wasn't, she'd discover soon enough.

You figured things out about people, working alongside them. And as good-looking as he was, that wouldn't make up for a bad personality if he were hiding one. She'd be a liar to deny she was crushing on him, and she was hopeful he'd turn out to be as nice on the inside as he was outside. Really, really hopeful.

Finishing off his last slice, Kurt stood up and stretched, drawing her attention to the amazing torso under his formfitting T-shirt. "As they say, daylight's wasting." Then he gave the pit—Lady—a rub behind her ears.

"Thanks for the pizza," Kelsey said, combining the leftovers into two boxes. "I think you've got dinner, a late-night snack, and breakfast covered, though I'll let you do the apologizing to your arteries."

He gave her a wink as he reached for the rest of the six pack of bottled beer to take inside. "It's nothing a little liquid smoke won't cure. It's so damn artificial, it'll unclog anything."

Kelsey laughed. "It seems I have my work cut out for me."

"You've no idea. I've been told more than once that I'm stubborn in every way a guy can be stubborn. I get it from my grandfather. So, I'll go ahead and apologize for every bit of future contention right now."

His tone was playful and easy and not at all hard to match. "I'd ask how you know there's going to be contention, but in all honesty I'm betting the same thing." She lifted the boxes and followed him into the kitchen, wondering what Sabrina Raven would think of the bustle suddenly filling her quiet old house.

⚉

It had been years since Kurt had felt genuine peace slip over him after the sun sank below the horizon and stars studded the sky. In Afghanistan and in the jungles of Honduras, he'd rarely been able to relax, even on nights when he was tucked in a bunk and crowded with the sounds and smells of other marines and a handful of dogs not far away. He hadn't expected to be able to do so here either.

But the calm cradled his skin despite the surprise that accompanied it.

Standing under the stars, Kurt set his beer on the table and headed into the screened-in half of the porch. The pregnant Rott let out a whine as he approached. Kelsey had taken her outside an hour or so earlier, after making sure she ate a plentiful dinner.

Kurt hooked a leash onto the dog's collar and led her around the yard long enough to ensure she was calm and obedient, then asked her to sit on command. When she did, he gave her an affectionate pat and a treat from his pocket, then made a show of letting her off leash.

He needed all these dogs to understand that freedom was earned and not taken. Elsewhere, most dogs could fail to understand this and there'd be little risk associated with it. Here that wasn't certain. Most of these dogs matched or exceeded his strength, and their journeys so far in life hadn't given them much reason to trust people. Even though it was in a dog's nature to trust humans, seeing how willing and obedient the dogs were still amazed him.

Free from the confines of a leash, the Rott—Pepper, as Kelsey was calling her—gave her massive head a shake and trotted off into the yard before squatting to pee. Kurt headed back onto the porch for his beer. As a rule, he drank water, coffee, and beer—a variety of it—and, every once in a while, a cold glass of milk. He didn't care for soda, and since he was eighteen, he'd never drunk anything with an alcohol content greater than beer. And as with his grandfather, none of his acquaintances since high school had ever seen him inebriated. Drunken sprees and ADHD weren't a good combination. Thankfully, he'd figured that out without causing any harm.

It had been dark when Kelsey left, and she'd looked tired. She'd commented before heading out how it was ironic that before this started, she swung by here every night on her way home from the shelter to feed Mr. Longtail. Now, she'd be leaving here and heading back to the shelter to pick up a dog to take home with her for the night. She didn't have a dog of her own, she'd explained. Instead, she brought one of the shelter dogs home every night, and if she broke the habit now, she'd feel too guilty to sleep a wink.

She was all heart. This both touched and troubled him. Working with her would be a pleasure, even if it was one he wouldn't allow himself to truly embrace. Everything would be fine so long as he kept her at a distance.

Other than when Kurt had looked out the front window and seen the Rott staring her down, only inches from that remarkable face of hers, Kelsey had proven to be smart and rational and to have a way with dogs. He thought back to that split second this afternoon when he'd bolted for the door, bracing himself for whatever was about to happen outside and knowing he was too many feet away to prevent it.

It had been all he could do not to hold Kelsey by the shoulders and lecture her until he was certain she understood what could've happened out there. He was committed to getting her through this with no harm coming her way or to the dogs. But he needed her not to take unnecessary risks. He'd managed to hold back, but she'd seemed to understand his thoughts anyway. And she'd shown she wasn't one to back down easily from an argument. That was one more thing he liked about her.

Taking a swig of beer, Kurt eyed the silhouette of an owl standing watch on an exposed branch of an enormous oak tree at the back of the yard. If Kurt hadn't been outside when it let out a series of soft, low hoots, he wouldn't have known the owl was there. It seemed to be watching the dog sniff around the dark yard as if it had come across an interloper in its nightly hunting spot.

Inside, the rest of the dogs were quiet and calm, having settled down for the night. Out here, a cool, gentle breeze swept over Kurt's skin. He was thankful to be back in the temperate zone where he'd grown up. Thankful to be out of the heat. The dry oven that was the desert, and the wet, stifling tropics. He wondered how long it would be before he forgot the sensation of the heat rising off the desert sand late at the night as if he were holding his hand over a radiator. Or standing guard in the jungle at night, listening to the howler monkeys crossing the tree canopy while he scoped openings in the thick, tropical forest for insurgents. One night he'd spotted a small, wild cat hunting at the edge of the base. About the size of a slender coyote, it had unusually large eyes and a sleek coat with spots and stripes. It was the most magnificent wild thing he'd ever come across. Later, he'd learned it was an ocelot.

He was still thinking about it when a very different feline stalked into view. Mr. Longtail. Who knew where the unusual cat had been this evening, but he was headed confidently toward the Rott, in full view of the owl. The enormous Maine coon was too big to ever end up dinner to an owl, but Kurt wasn't so sure about the off-leash Rott. Setting down his beer, he whistled confidently.

Pepper—the name was sticking even though naming these dogs would create unnecessary emotional attachment—pricked up her ears and looked his way.

"Come here, girl," Kurt called, half holding his breath as the cat trotted directly into the dog's path. Like this afternoon, Pepper didn't disappoint. She dropped into a play bow and woofed. Mr. Longtail stopped midstep as the hair along his back and tail stood out stick straight. As if he'd had no idea a dog was capable of such a baritone woof. Pepper didn't seem to notice. She sniffed the cat all over, nudging his hind end off the ground with her strong head. Then, seemingly satisfied, she jogged around him and met Kurt halfway up the path.

He emptied his pocket of treats for her. Mr. Longtail followed, walking underneath her, straight to Kurt's legs to rub against his jeans. The cat meowed, and Kurt was surprised to hear a deep, thrumming purr radiating from his chest. Kelsey had said she'd never heard the feline purr.

Kurt leaned down to scratch the cat's chin. In return, Mr. Longtail rubbed contentedly against Kurt's fingers. "Maybe you just didn't like all the solitude."

After getting Pepper back in her kennel, Kurt headed into the kitchen, Mr. Longtail following. He fed the cat and helped himself to a slice of cold pizza. He considered hunting down a notebook and pen and making a to-do list of all the items bouncing around his head, but even if he could find a pen and a notebook, he doubted he'd get halfway through writing the list before becoming distracted. Experience had proven he could tackle projects of almost any size, but he couldn't make a list to save himself.

So instead, he dove into repairs of the Sabrina Raven estate the way he did everything else—focusing on whatever came to the front of his thoughts. It was a little after nine, and he figured he'd work until about one in the morning, doing what he could with the tools he'd found in the old carriage house at the back of the yard. Then he'd catch a few hours' sleep and rise with the sun and the dogs.

He sorted through a bulky metal toolbox for all the flooring nails he could find. The toolbox was an antique and one of the favorite things he'd come across so far.

If he was still around when the shelter held an estate sale, he'd purchase a few things for himself. The toolbox would be one of them.

"Come on, cat," Kurt said to the watchful Mr. Longtail. He slipped the nails into his pocket and fisted the hammer, heading out of the kitchen. "You and I could likely use each other's company. Let's see if I can get those stairs to be a bit less of a hazard so I can make it up to one of those old feather beds you've been sleeping on."

With a twitch of his tail, the cat followed him out of the kitchen, and Kurt suspected he was on the way to making an unlikely friend.

Chapter 8

THE JOB THAT LAY BEFORE THEM WAS JUST SO MASSIVE. AT the very least, they were going to need help from a few trusted volunteers. Kelsey suspected she'd have a hard time convincing Kurt to let some tasks fall to other people, but she couldn't see how else the rehab was going to work. He'd requested that for a few days, he be the only one taking the dogs in and out of the kennels and furnishing their meals, top areas where aggression could arise.

However, that left him with an enormous job.

He was fine passing dogs off to her once he'd walked around with them and made sure they were calm and attentive. Kelsey then did a "middle" shift with each dog, taking them for walks around the backyard while he readied their breakfast. After she passed the dogs off again, he had them sit at attention, then fed each one a little by hand before placing the bowl in front of them. From start to finish with all the dogs, the whole process ended up taking the better part of four hours.

During it, Kurt was quite different from the laid-back guy he'd been during their meal yesterday. He didn't say a word that wasn't related to the training, and she suspected there were times he forgot she was there. One thing for sure, she'd never met anyone with his ability to communicate with and train dogs. As he worked, she could almost see him shedding layers of his world until it was only him and the dog before him.

He was commanding and alert without being harsh or overpowering. During her years working at the shelter, she'd witnessed harsh and overpowering from a few people who'd come in claiming to have a way with dogs but who just intimidated them until the dogs were uncomfortable and submissive. In no way was this Kurt. His voice was never raised, and his movements were slow, fluid, and a bit exaggerated. Easy for the dogs to observe.

By the time the morning was over, Kelsey was willing to bet all thirty-seven dogs in their care had accepted him as an alpha and master. All except one, that was. Judging by the dog's behavior both in the kennel and out, Kelsey was harboring doubts the cranky giant of a dog could be won over by anyone. He snarled when other dogs passed within six feet of his kennel, had all but refused to reenter it after a late-evening bathroom break last night, and pulled away from any sort of human touch or affection.

It was something, watching Kurt work. And a good experience for her too. That clingy feeling she'd carried around the last two days—reminiscent of a few embarrassing high school crushes she'd had—fell away like crumbs off a cookie. In its place, true admiration formed.

And after a dozen passes of the leash, she even stopped feeling the hiccup in her stomach every time their hands brushed. But that also might've had something to do with the fact that each leash pass was exponentially easier than the first when he'd placed both hands tightly atop hers to show her the best way to hold the extra leash for maximum control. During those few seconds, she'd grown seriously light-headed. His hands were perfect. They were well muscled, and the skin of his palms was tough without being overly calloused—and just maybe a part of her would've been okay with having him hold on forever.

That had happened while she was taking over care of the Akita so Kurt could get the dog's breakfast ready. The observant dog had turned around to look at Kelsey as if it had picked up on her raging hormones. Thankfully, Kelsey had pulled it together and not let her mind trail deeper into the land of hand-touching fantasies.

After that, perhaps due to being shamed by a dog, she held the leash exactly right and didn't need any more reminders. She forced her focus to be on all the amazing things she was likely to learn from Kurt over the next few months.

After the next-to-last dog was back in her kennel, Kurt looked directly at Kelsey for the first time in over an hour. "Let's save the cranky giant till your friend Patrick arrives. You saw that it was all I could do to get him back into his kennel last night. And I've got the sense that dog has a stubborn streak bigger than mine. We might need a third set of hands around him for a while. I suspect he'll be testing us the next couple of days."

"Something tells me you're right. Patrick should be here in another hour or two."

"So, uh, well done this morning. You're easy to work with. That doesn't happen often. I know it's a big job, but before long we'll have enough of a system in place to bring in those volunteers you mentioned. I know when we do, it'll give the dogs more time out of their kennels, but let's give it a few more days. I'd like to get a good grasp on the rest of their personalities."

She nodded. "That makes sense."

"So how are you at building fences?"

Kelsey felt her eyebrows arch. "I can't say I've ever tried."

"I think our first order of business when the dogs aren't demanding our attention is to get a few runs set up out back. If any of those volunteers are itching to help, we could use a hand there."

Kelsey pulled out her phone. "We have an email hotline set up for such a thing. I suspect a few people will show up if I put out a call for help. What time should I tell them to come?"

Kurt glanced at his watch. "It's a little after eleven. How about one o'clock? I need to run by a hardware store first, and since neither of our cars will hold all that we need, I was going to rent an hourly truck at the nearest Home Depot. If you'd give me a lift there, I'd appreciate it."

Kelsey's mind flashed to the less than perfectly clean interior of her Corolla. She liked to think there was a link between it and her busy life. Her dedication to bringing a shelter dog home each night meant there were always stray hairs floating around. To protect the backseat from resulting wear, she'd covered it with a sturdy quilt. Its bright, colorful pattern didn't exactly add serenity to her car. On top of that, with her packed schedule, she was often grabbing meals on the run. Try as she might, crumbs got into hard-to-clean places.

At least she carried trash and recycling out after each trip. There was that.

Yesterday, she'd seen that while Kurt's restored Mustang might be old, it was meticulously clean inside and out. Which was probably what you'd expect from someone who'd just gotten out of the marines.

"Sure. I can meet you out front whenever you're ready."

"I'm ready."

So much for a fast cleaning spree. He bolted the house doors after she grabbed her purse. If he didn't need her at the Home Depot, she was going to swing by the grocery store for some grab-and-go snacks. For a while at least, sitting down for a meal would be a rarely afforded luxury. And they'd need to have something to offer the volunteers.

Her car was unlocked, so Kurt let himself in. He gave the Chihuahua bobblehead on her dashboard a soft flick and set it to bobbing. Kelsey started the ignition, a touch apprehensive about driving under his watch. "So how was your night? I can't believe you slept on one of those beds."

"Would you believe me if I told you it was the best night's sleep I've had in a while?"

"Now that you say it, you do have an air about you that says you wouldn't let a drafty, eerie old house disturb your rest."

"That cat tried to take over the pillow once. That was the only thing to wake me up."

Kelsey's jaw nearly hit the floor. "Mr. Longtail slept with you?"

"I suspect he was being more territorial than affectionate. So, what is it about the house that you think is eerie?"

"Let me see. How long do you have?" This made him laugh, a gentle, rolling sound that made Kelsey's heart flutter. She gripped her hands on the steering wheel again and forced her focus on the road and away from the well-muscled thighs shaping his jeans. He hadn't shaved this morning and had a touch of five-o'clock shadow complementing his olive skin. "It's creepy, for one thing."

"You said that, but I'm looking for specifics."

Specifics. She went with the first few that came to mind as she drove out of the residential area and merged onto Arsenal Street. The house was at the end of an unusually quiet neighborhood, and it was easy to forget how close it was to bustling South City. "It's so abandoned and—I don't know—*isolated*. Though I'll admit that with all the life packed in it right now, it seems warmer and more welcoming than it did before. And there are the creaks that sound like moans. The house sounds like it's protesting just about every step you take. And creepiest of all, in the back of the basement where it becomes an unfinished cellar, the temperature drops a solid ten degrees in a matter of a foot or two. One night when I was down there looking for Mr. Longtail, that whole area seemed foggy. I made sure it was still daylight whenever I went into the house for a few weeks afterward."

He gave her Chihuahua bobblehead another soft flick, this time sideways as she headed west toward Kingshighway Boulevard, which was a few blocks from the store.

"Unnerving but definitely cool." He looked her way and gave her a crooked smile. His eyes were warm and rich like chocolate syrup.

Kelsey had never thought of herself as an easy

blusher, but her cheeks superheated. She focused on driving and not trying to notice him in her peripheral vision. Driving right past the entrance to the hardware store a few minutes later didn't help either. She turned around in a gas station and backtracked. "So how good is that sense of direction of yours? With no cell, you've got no access to Google Maps. Can you get back to the house okay?"

"I can, but I appreciate the concern."

Kelsey stopped in front of the main doors and slipped her car into Park. She bit her lip, not sure what to make of the way Kurt's gaze traveled over her before he got out. Or the way he paused the longest over her lips before looking into her eyes. This made her mouth turn dry. She swallowed, and the sound seemed loud and awkward in the quiet car.

"I'm running by the store for snacks. Can I pick anything special up for you?" she asked.

"You chose well on the pizza. I'm sure whatever you get will be fine." Kurt pulled out his wallet, but she waved him off. "The pizza was on you. It's my turn."

"Fair enough. I'll see you back at the house in an hour or so."

"Sounds good." She rolled down her window as she drove away, hoping to cool her burning skin. This whole rehab thing would be so much easier if she didn't find Kurt so attractive. Thankfully, he'd been so distracted by her bobblehead that he'd hardly seemed to notice her missed entrance to the store.

The most convenient grocery store was a mile from the house, so she headed that way. The mental focus needed to zoom through the aisles would get her mind off the way she'd salivated just a bit at the sight of his sculpted hand toying with her bobblehead. Working with him was one thing. The dogs demanded most of Kurt's and her attention. But she needed to get ahold of herself when it came to things like this. She wouldn't deny she was crushing on him. But that was all it was going to be, an I'm-not-telling-a-single-soul crush.

He was too different from her for anything real to happen between them. He was an ex-marine, and before he'd agreed to the job, she'd overheard him make it clear to Rob that he had no intention of staying in Missouri. But this was her home. She loved it. Loved being close to her family and watching her sweet nieces grow up. Loved the shelter and the pulse of this just-big-enough city.

And besides, she wasn't ready to put herself out there by falling for another guy only to be rejected. Once had been traumatic enough. It happened during her sophomore year of college and had turned into one of the worst experiences of her life. Steve had been her chem partner, and they were both pre-vet. They met freshman year and had become great friends. They hung out all the time and were dedicated study partners. One night right before December finals, she threw caution to the wind and went for it.

Kelsey had thought taking it to the next level with Steve was the natural next step. She was even having secret thoughts about marrying him and running a vet practice together. They were great together. They had so much in common—from favorite movies to a love of animals to a weakness for Philly cheesesteak sandwiches, steak fries, and mochas with extra whipped cream.

They were sitting on the same side of a booth in a popular coffee shop, cramming for their biology final, when it happened. He'd snuck in a bottle of Baileys for their coffees, and she was just tipsy enough to let go of her inhibition. He'd turned to whisper something in her ear about the kids at the booth in front of them, and she'd been so close to his lips. She'd kissed him and even leaned in more when he started to pull away before the kiss got deeper.

While the kiss was her lead, taking it the rest of the way was his. She'd dated a guy in high school for over a month, and they'd done a lot. A *lot* lot. But not everything. So, it surprised her how easily she accepted Steve's offer to go to his car and slide into the backseat. He was putting on a condom when she told him she loved him. He stopped long enough to look at her and say her name, but the three words she thought for sure would follow never came. Instead, he kissed her full on the mouth, and in the swoop of minutes, her virginity was a thing of the past.

Maybe it had been true love on her part; maybe it was a crush. Either way, her feelings hadn't been reciprocated. After the bio final the next day, he broke her heart. He didn't only break it; he crushed it. He'd been fidgety and nervous and had a big, sheepish smile she'd only seen once or twice when he really felt stuck in a corner. "I'm sorry, Kels," he said. "I just didn't feel it."

With those few words, she lost her best friend and secret dreams at the same time. Somehow, she made it through the rest of her finals, bombing a few and doing fairly well on the rest, even as she and Steve avoided each other like the plague. She went home for Christmas with nothing more than a giant basket of dirty clothes, assuming that however bleak things were, she'd be back the second week of January.

It was over break that the crippling monster that was depression hit. It was the darkest, the ugliest, the worst time of her life. She hardly ever let herself think of those days. Somehow, in a world of gray nothingness, she found the shelter, around the same time she started medicine. And after the longest winter of her life, the sun came out again.

Kelsey had just turned twenty when Wes offered her a full-time job. In the months that followed, she turned away from everything that was gray and sad. She made the connection between the seven colors of the rainbow and the days of the week, and bought a different-colored adoption-focused T-shirt to wear each day, coordinating the day of the week with its corresponding rainbow color. She focused on the shelter and her family and, eventually, evening classes at a nearby university.

She had her life together again. Even though things were feeling a bit repetitious and empty before this rehab started, she wouldn't risk experiencing hurt like that again.

Remembering the few glimpses she'd had of Kurt's perfectly sculpted core underneath his T-shirts as he worked—and the resulting churning feeling in her midsection, the one that reminded her of the ocean before a storm—she knew it wouldn't be hard to fall for him. Not only was he a pleasure to look at, but he was so natural and calm with the dogs.

Maybe she'd been wanting to kick life up a notch, but crushing on Kurt wasn't the answer. She was here to help dogs that deserved the best second chance they could get. That was enough. For seven years, her work at the shelter had been enough. It would be enough at the Sabrina Raven estate too.

For stocking up, Kelsey focused on the peripheries of the crowded store, choosing a variety of easy-to-eat fruits, precut veggies, hummus, and several packages of natural granola bars. She couldn't pass up a box of freshly baked cookies from the bakery but promised herself she'd leave them to Kurt and the volunteers. Mostly. As she was inventorying her cart, she remembered string cheese and bottled water and circled back, hoping they'd now be set.

In addition to them having the groceries, Megan had texted earlier that she was bringing a hot meal over tonight. Most likely Megan's meal would be enough to feed a small army, so they wouldn't need to worry about dinner for a few days, even if several volunteers showed up.

Megan loved to cook, and whatever she was making was sure to be fabulous, though Kelsey had stopped asking for her recipes after several failed attempts to replicate her incredible cooking.

Kelsey was steering her cart next into line at the register when she remembered paper plates. Normally she was a wash-and-reuse kind of girl, but she hadn't inventoried the stash of dishes that came with the house. She left the cart to hold her spot in line and jogged to the paper goods aisle, grabbing the first package of recycled paper plates she could find.

She made good time in the store and wasn't surprised to make it back to the Raven estate before Kurt. The grocery store was much easier to navigate than Home Depot. And he was renting a truck.

She was, however, surprised to find two cars parked on the side of the street in front of the house and five people milling around them. The hair on the back of her neck prickled knowingly as she took them in. Protesters.

Kurt had mentioned they might show up, but Kelsey had doubted him. Who'd want to protest on this quiet, forgotten street? *Apparently, they would.* She recognized one woman from the warehouse. Kelsey had read the sign now hanging loosely at the woman's side the morning she chose the dogs: ONCE A KILLER, ALWAYS A KILLER.

A rarely felt anger bubbled up. The warehouse had been unfamiliar and foreign. But this was shelter property. *How dare they!* She pulled past them and into the circular driveway. Rather than grabbing the groceries, she squared her shoulders and crossed the front yard.

"Is there something I can help you with?"

There were four women and one guy. *Self-righteous* wasn't a word Kelsey liked to label anyone with, but it certainly fit the bill this time. She could feel the indignation rolling off them. Several lips curled as she approached. The woman from the warehouse stepped forward, as if indicating she was the ringleader.

"We saw your interview. I doubt there's anything you'll be willing to help us with, so we'll be helping ourselves. We're getting a court injunction to shut this down before someone gets hurt."

Shock and anger rocketed through Kelsey. The

possibility that someone might try such a thing had been discussed among the group at the shelter, but it had seemed like a worst-case scenario. No one would wish them *that* much ill will. But clearly someone did. Five someones. And they were standing right in front of her.

With thirty-seven dogs, the shelter might be over regulation as to how many animals could reside there permanently, but the rehab was temporary. And thanks to a volunteer with great connections on the city council, they'd been given a waiver.

"I suspect you won't have much luck with that," Kelsey responded. "We have permits. And we're keeping the dogs confined to the property while they're being retrained."

Somehow, the woman's face was both pasty and pink at the same time. "Oh, it'll happen. We have God on our side."

Kelsey's anger flared like a lit match. "Oh really? Because I'm pretty sure God loves all creatures."

"That house is full of killers," the man interjected. "God holds no love for killers." He had a creepy look about him that made Kelsey feel squeamish. He was wearing a tight sweatshirt with an iron-on picture of two dogs trapped in a savage embrace, teeth bared in ferocious snarls. The caption underneath read *Not God's creations*.

Kelsey's blood pressure was spiking. No good would come from talking to these people. And inside the house, there was important work to be done. She needed to focus her energy and attention on something that could make a difference. But the boiling-over-with-anger part of her couldn't hold back. "I'm curious. Do you eat beef? Or wear leather? Or do you protest the existence of cows too?"

All five protesters looked at her like she was crazy.

"I'm just saying, when you're done making a mess here, maybe you should protest outside a cattle farm. I'm sure you know the stats. Cows kill about as many people each year as dogs. Only there are a zillion more dog-and-people interactions than there are cow-and-people interactions, so statistically speaking, cows are far more dangerous to people than dogs. Even dogs like these that have been placed in fighting rings."

The leader shook her head, her lip curling as if Kelsey were diseased. "You don't know what you're talking about."

"Oh, I don't?" Kelsey leaned forward, setting her hands on her hips. "Google it. And if you would kindly step off the grass, I won't have to call the police. It's a free country, and this is a public street. You're welcome to stand there and protest to all the people *not* coming down this deserted street all day long. But step on our property, and I'll have you arrested. It's that simple."

She turned and headed at a controlled walk toward the car. They tossed insults the whole way, calling her and the dogs a variety of nasty names. She kept her anger in check and took her time getting her bags out of the trunk, even pausing to check her phone.

Sticks and stones, Kelsey thought, heading inside and taking a deep, calming breath once the door was closed. If anything, their taunts had made her more determined to make a fantastic success out of this venture.

Chapter 9

KURT COULD DETERMINE SOMEONE'S WORK ETHIC WITHIN ten minutes. So far, he was impressed with the group from the High Grove Animal Shelter, staff and volunteers alike. Kelsey gave the enclosure-building her all, even though she had to be exhausted from these first two packed days. In addition to her, six others showed up and stuck with the project till it was complete. This included Patrick, who was smart, strong as an ox, and a bit peculiar with his routines and general rigidity. Kurt was only half surprised when he learned Patrick had Asperger's.

Donna and Mickey, two women in their fifties, worked hard but consistently made jokes that kept the mood light and fun. There was Jim, a retired electrician who Kurt was hoping would have a look around inside. The wiring seemed safe enough, but two different fuses had shorted since he'd arrived. There was also a retired couple, Barbara and Ron. After an hour of working alongside them, Kurt learned it was Barbara's second marriage and Ron's fourth. They'd only been married to each other a year and had met while volunteering at the shelter.

Kurt was pleased with the work the group had done, and it was only five thirty. Eventually, he'd cement the corner posts into the ground and bury eighteen inches of the galvanized mesh fencing underground to keep the dogs from digging out. For now, the runs would be a supervised way to give the dogs some much-needed time out of their kennels.

Afterward, the volunteers and Patrick stayed around, watching the first two dogs experience the ten-by-four-foot runs. Two of the runs were purposefully built side by side. These two runs would be a safe way to see if the dogs were truly able to get along with one another when they were ready for a greater level of socialization with other dogs. For now, only one of the side-by-side runs would be used. The third run stood alone at the back of the yard. The mess of a dog, the giant who was causing more commotion and concern than most others combined, was given the largest side of the joint run.

Kurt was hoping a good stretch of his long legs and some fresh air might take the dog's edge off a little, but every time someone walked within ten feet of his run, the hair on his neck and upper back ruffled, and his tail stuck straight out. The massive dog sniffed and scent marked until it was hard to believe there was a hint of moisture left in him.

In the other run at the back of the yard, the lively Argentine mastiff was more interested in dropping into a play bow and dashing around the enclosure than he was in doing much scent marking. Like most Argentine mastiffs, he looked like a cross between a Great Dane and a boxer. He was eighty-five pounds of pure muscle and had the energy of a smaller, lighter dog. The vet had put him at about a year and a half. His sleek coat had minimal scars and none from cuts or bites that had been severe, indicating he hadn't spent much time in the fighting rings.

Although Kurt wasn't ready to share it aloud, he

suspected the rambunctious dog would be easy to integrate into a new home, possibly even one with another dog.

The dog's playfulness made him think of Zara, the last dog he'd had in Afghanistan. It had been difficult to keep her on task those first few months. She was willing to do the work, but underneath the surface was a playful and carefree three-year-old German shepherd. She wasn't a fan of the heat, but she was smart and loyal and willing to work. The best dog he'd ever had. In training, she'd been the first in her group to successfully sniff out IEDs. When she was finally acclimated to the scorching desert heat, she excelled in the field, staying on task as long as she was asked.

It was hard to think of Zara without thinking of how she'd passed. She was hit by the debris of an IED and lived just long enough afterward to slip away on a medevac transport back to base. To keep from experiencing the suffocating loss that was attempting to rush in alongside his thoughts, he conjured an image of a steel lockbox, visualized shoving his feelings inside and tossing away the key.

Sometimes it worked. Sometimes it didn't. He'd told one person—his best buddy and fellow marine, Zach— about the imagery he conjured to lock away the feelings of pain and loss. "Kurt, my friend, forget the box," Zach had said. "Forget the lock. Nothing does well being locked away. Picture yourself standing alongside something peaceful, like the ocean. Picture yourself not having to hold it in. Picture yourself letting it go."

The advice seemed to make sense, but Kurt had never been to the ocean, and he had no idea how to simply let go, but he'd seen lots of boxes and lots of keys, and he knew how to hold things in. So Zara and the pain of losing her—along with a whole lot of other shit that really stank—got locked away in the heaviest steel box he could imagine.

She wasn't the only dog he'd lost during his service, but losing her had hurt the worst. It wasn't the way she got hit with so much shrapnel or that she struggled. It was how she'd looked at him before she died. Like she still trusted him to make things better.

After her, he didn't take on another dog of his own. In fact, losing her had been part of the reason he'd transferred to Central America. He was done with the desert, and he was done with the horror of IEDs.

But he found that training Honduran troops in the jungles of Central America wasn't any better than the desert. Their world was just as full of insurgents, only they were camouflaged guerillas of the forest, fighting against a government they believed was tyrannous. Fighting to protect the cocaine they smuggled into America and to provide for their families. It was a jungle, not a desert, but IEDs were still the enemies' best friend.

After several months of this, Kurt was ready to come home. Now, a little over two weeks past earning his discharge, he was knee-deep in something else bigger than himself. Like saving the lives of his fellow marines, rehabbing these dogs was an honorable path and one Kurt could be proud of. It didn't matter that his grandfather had dragged a hand slowly, deliberately over the top of his thinning hair when Kurt had told him; Kurt knew he'd made the right decision.

He'd felt it seeing the old mansion for the first time yesterday morning, and felt it again last night after he'd collapsed onto the musty featherbed and lay in the dark, listening to the quiet hush that fell over the house. He'd brought his own pillow and a light blanket to toss over the top of the bed till he could find time to do a load of sheets, assuming the old washer and dryer worked.

As he'd drifted off, he'd heard the dogs downstairs breathing and shifting in their kennels. There'd been a soft breeze through the open windows, and for the second time, he could have sworn he heard his nana's singsong voice carried on the wind.

Looking around at the dogs making themselves at home in the runs and the enthralled volunteers, Kurt suspected he was meant to be here. It wasn't just the remarkable blond, or the house whose many projects called his name, or the thirty-seven dogs who deserved better lives than the ones they'd come from. It was all of them put together.

This sent his thoughts spiraling into a tangled mess of questions while most of the group laughed at the Argentine mastiff's continued antics and Patrick studied the giant from far enough away to not to disturb him. If Kurt was meant to be here, then something intentional was supposed to come of this. And he wanted to know what it was.

But who was he kidding? He'd stopped believing in fate when one of his buddies was severely injured after passing Kurt and his IED-detecting shepherd because Kurt had paused to give the animal a drink. Things happened, or they didn't happen. Those who survived moved on.

Locking himself off from his thoughts, he finished wrapping up the extra mesh fencing, then rejoined the group. The volunteers had drained their bottles of water but were hanging around until the mastiff was finished putting on a show, which didn't seem like it would be anytime soon.

Perhaps tired of them all, the giant German shepherd mix urinated on the gate, then, having stood guard for half an hour, plopped to the ground with a muffled sigh. Kurt wondered how many homes the big dog had passed through. And in how many of them he'd been traumatized. The cautious dog had no reason to believe this new set of circumstances would be any different.

But that was okay, Kurt thought, feeling a surge of hope. It would be their job to show him otherwise.

Chapter 10

IDA GREENE COULD COME UP WITH A DOZEN REASONS TO BE upset over the goings-on next door, but at her doctor's advice, she'd been practicing "complete tolerance" for twenty-three days. If she broke her streak now, all the good she'd done in naturally lowering her blood pressure might be for nothing.

Instead, she determined to bake a pie for the young couple inhabiting her late sister's house the last three days. Baking always settled her nerves. Thanks to the four mature apple trees in her backyard, she didn't need to fire up the old Camaro and make a trip to the grocery store either. Both the Pink Lady and McIntosh varieties were crisp, delicious, and ripe for picking. Under the watchful eye of Mr. Longtail—he came to visit every day—she used the handle of her broom to knock down apples until she had a basketful.

The girl, a tall, pretty blond, had been coming and going for the last eight months, feeding Mr. Longtail per her late sister's directions, when it would've been so much easier for Ida to do it. Of course, this was as Sabrina had instructed in her will, and Ida knew to leave well enough alone when it came to Sabrina's wishes.

Ida had meant to introduce herself to the girl long ago, but nothing seemed to happen fast at her age. The first several months she'd been reeling from the loss of her sister, and then there'd been the whole high-blood-pressure scare. In the scheme of things, today seemed like as good a time as any. A young man was staying in the house now too, it seemed. She'd caught a few glimpses of him working late into the evening the last two nights. If her trifocals weren't deceiving her, he was as fine as young men were back before the world grew so complicated and soft at the same time.

She'd seen the report on Channel 3 and had put two and two together. She'd known they were bringing those mistreated dogs here before the vans had pulled up. But she hadn't been prepared to see so many crates being unloaded. Her sister's quiet house was being packed full of dogs. And not just any dogs. The dogs Channel 3 flashed across the television screen were intimidating, to say the least.

But the pie making sent Ida's worries away. The girl who'd been feeding Mr. Longtail was competent enough. In all these months, she'd never forgotten to take care of him. And hopefully, that shelter Sabrina had been so fond of knew what it was committing to.

Ida lost track of the afternoon as she readied the crust. There was nothing quite like dusting the countertop in flour and rolling out a fresh, buttery crust or hearing the thin, fine scrape of the sugar and cinnamon as she mixed them with the apples. And of course there was the smell. Few things on earth smelled better than an apple pie baking in the oven.

When it was done, she let the pie cool as the sun sank low on the horizon. She watched the protesters pack up from their second day of protesting. Thank heavens they were leaving. The idea of people picketing outside Sabrina's house was disturbing. Ida hoped they had realized how quiet the street was and determined to take their picketing elsewhere. Or, better yet, abandoned it entirely. That was more consistent with the benefit-everyone way of thinking her holistic practitioner had been trying to teach her.

When the ceramic pie dish was cool enough to carry, she covered the pie with her best dishcloth and slipped a small flashlight into her pocket. If the young couple was the welcoming type, she might well be walking home after dark. Mr. Longtail met her halfway between their two houses. He meowed and beelined in front of her, nearly causing her to trip and send the pie sailing, which would have been a shame. It had turned out lovely.

The young man answered the door, looking both more guarded and more handsome than he had from far away. "Can I help you?" he asked, eyeing the heavy pie that was growing heavier by the second.

"I'm Ida Greene, your neighbor. And you can be a dear and relieve me of this pie."

He took it off her hands and cocked an eyebrow. "If I do, I may not give it back. It smells incredible."

"That's good to hear. I baked it for you. It only seemed right that you get more of a welcome than those protesters have offered you."

He smiled and shifted the pie to the flat of one hand as he extended the other in her direction. "Kurt Crawford. Nice to meet you, Ms. Greene."

He was enough of a gentleman to impress her. And he had remarkably strong hands. After the introduction, Ida craned her neck to look into the parlors flanking the entryway. Rather than studying the crates, she took in the condition of the walls and light fixtures. "It's funny, but my memory of the house as it was twenty years ago is more vivid than that of how it looks now. And look what that crotchety cat has done to the beautiful old wallpaper!"

Kurt followed her gaze to the strips of wallpaper that the cat had clawed away. "You know this house?"

"Yes, very well. Sabrina was my year-younger sister." She pointed toward her house. "I moved next door after my husband died twenty-one years ago. Sabrina lived here much longer, nearly sixty years in fact."

Kurt's eyebrows arched upward. "Would you like to come in?"

Ida's thin fingers closed around the doorframe for support. She could almost see her sister, decades ago, barefoot and in a cornflower-blue summer dress, carrying a basket of laundry down the stairs, singing as she went. "I very much would, Mr. Crawford. I very much would."

~~~

If it wasn't for Ida taking a seat at the kitchen table after touring the house, Kurt doubted he would have remembered his dream from last night, his second night in the house. As it was, only snippets came to mind. It had taken place here in the kitchen. He remembered the soft, yellow light pouring into the kitchen from the window behind the sink, making the god-awful aged counters shine a brighter yellow. Kelsey had been at the stove stirring something in a pot, and his grandmother, Nana, was standing alongside her, smiling with approval.

Nana had looked younger, like she did when he was a kid, and she was wearing her favorite slippers and an apron over a cotton dress. He also remembered the powerful sensation he'd experienced watching them, one that had made his insides swell up like a balloon. It had been so long since he'd felt something that strong in real life, so the best he could equate it to were peace and contentment. Like everything was exactly as it should be.

Ida showing up with her pie and her wrinkles and her old-person manners must have stirred the dream into conscious thought. Kurt rarely remembered any dreams. The ones that stuck tended to wake him in a cold sweat and were nothing to reminisce over. He hoped time out of the service would change this.

"This kitchen," Ida said, shaking her head and smiling. "It stood out as much when they had it installed as it does now. The first time I saw it was in the early sixties. They'd only been in the house a few years. Back then, I lived in my childhood home of Connecticut with my husband and two sons. With Sabrina having settled so far away, she and I were only able to see each other every few years.

"When she and her husband bought the house in the late fifties, it needed considerable plumbing and electrical repair, and the kitchen needed a complete revamping. It was already half a century old then. Since the work was completed, little about the house has changed. Sabrina replaced the stove and refrigerator again in the late seventies with the models here now. She had to pay an arm and leg to keep the vintage look because hardly anyone was making it then."

Kelsey, who'd brewed a fresh pot of coffee to go with the pie, carried a steaming mug to Ida. Not wanting

Kelsey to feel as if she needed to serve him, Kurt got up to pour his own cup.

"We have milk but no sugar," Kelsey told Ida. "No creamer either. Sorry. We're still getting things up and running."

"A splash of milk will be fine. And I understand. At this house's age and after a full year with no inhabitants, there's likely to be a bigger-than-average to-do list. And to be fair, the house hasn't had the care it deserves the last several years. After Sabrina's husband passed, she spent more time next door with me than she did here. Fewer memories, you understand."

"I can only imagine," Kelsey said. "If your sister was from Connecticut like you, how did she end up in St. Louis? If you don't mind me asking."

"I don't. Jeremy Raven, her husband, led her here. He was raised in this very house, in fact. His parents died when he was young, and the house was sold. Through the grace of an aunt, Jeremy went to medical school at Cambridge. He and Sabrina met in Weston-super-Mare, a seaside town in southwest England, while he was on break from the university. And theirs was quite the meeting. At Weston, at low tide, the water recedes about a mile offshore. It's something to see. Everywhere you look, boats are trapped in the sand.

"My sister had traveled there by train and was walking alone at low tide looking for seashells when she got stuck out in the mudflats. Jeremy was on the beach with friends, celebrating the end of another term. He ran out and attempted to save her, and ended up stuck himself. They were thrown a rope, thankfully, and pulled from the mud as the tide was rushing in."

"Wow. That's both very fortunate and wonderfully romantic at the same time," Kelsey said. She met Kurt's gaze, and her cheeks flushed pink.

"She sounds brave to have traveled on her own like that, especially for a woman back in the 1950s," he said, surprised by an urge to run his hand down Kelsey's back.

Ida let out a soft *humph*. "Brave she was. In her younger years, she was a bit of a black sheep, at least in my parents' eyes. Her way of doing things tended to be a touch unconventional. They never could see eye to eye. Our father was a minister, so maybe it's no surprise. After one particularly big argument, Sabrina left home in a fury and made for Europe. She was just seventeen. It caused such a scandal in my hometown! She lived like a gypsy for nearly two years, sending me postcard after postcard from one city to the next before she and Jeremy met. She claimed if it hadn't been for his complete devotion to her, she'd never have settled down.

"Jeremy was six years her senior and ready for a grown-up's life by the time he earned his medical degree. To my entire family's surprise, Sabrina allowed Jeremy to make her his wife and bring her to St. Louis. They lived in a small apartment in Soulard, but Jeremy bought back his childhood home the first chance he got. And, obviously, they lived out the rest of their lives here."

"Wow," Kelsey said, closing her hands over her mug. "That's really cool. I had no idea."

Ida smiled as she finished cutting the pie into slices. She transferred the slices to chipped and faded blue-flowered serving plates that had belonged to her sister. "I always thought this colorful kitchen was Sabrina's way of stating that she wasn't going to tame down entirely."

Kurt eyed the bright-yellow countertops and light-blue cabinets with a new appreciation. He wondered what Ida thought of her sister leaving this home and its contents to the shelter. Personal things like paperwork and pictures had been cleared out, but so much remained. He also wondered what Ida thought of all the crates of dogs filling up the house. She'd been polite but quiet during the tour. But knowing the dogs were here, she'd brought him and Kelsey the pie and was extending this welcome. Since all this felt too personal to ask, he went with something simpler. "Was your sister a gardener?" Although that area of the backyard was grown over, he'd spotted the makings of what once might've been an impressive garden.

Ida smiled as she pressed her fork into her slice of pie. "Yes, Sabrina loved to garden. Late summer to fall, she was always canning something. After Jeremy died six years ago, she couldn't find the energy, but she kept an impeccable garden for decades."

"After I get the yard cleaned up, I'll give you a tour of what remains. There seem to be a few pumpkins hidden in the tall grass."

Ida smiled. "I would very much enjoy that."

"Oh my gosh, this pie is incredible." Kelsey had taken her first bite. "I have a weak spot for apple pie, and this is absolutely perfect."

Kurt followed suit. Kelsey was right. It was hands down the best slice of pie he'd ever had.

"Why, thank you. We used to compete, Sabrina and I. Good-naturedly, of course. I made the best apple pie, and she, the best peach cobbler. These apples are from my yard. You may not have noticed, but you have several peach trees on the side of the house and a pear tree at the far end of the lot. The peaches will all have dropped, but there might still be pears. They make a good pear butter."

"It's so awesome to hear these stories," Kelsey said, meeting Kurt's gaze before she refocused on Ida.

It was a pleasure seeing how animated Kelsey had become. Maybe Ida's stories would give her a better opinion of the house. Help her see it in the same light he'd seen when he first set eyes upon it. This thought brought Kurt back to last night's dream, and he remembered a new snippet. He'd been standing at the stove next to Kelsey, his hand on the small of her back, smelling whatever she'd been cooking. Remembering the perfect, easy connection he'd felt between them, he was thankful he was now seated. His knees weakened from the desire of wanting to feel something that strong in real life. Clearing his throat, he forced his attention back to Ida.

"Your sister," Kelsey continued, oblivious to his thoughts. "She was so kind to leave her house to the shelter, but none of us knew anything about her other than that she'd adopted her cat from us. Was she a big animal lover?"

"Yes and no," Ida said, shifting in her chair. "She and Jeremy always had a dog or a cat to keep them company over the years, but if anyone had told me my sister would leave her beloved home to an animal shelter, I'd never have believed them. But their only child lives in England, teaching at Cambridge, believe it or not. He was married about twenty-five years ago in a little stone church in Weston-super-Mare in honor of his parents.

Unlike my worldly sister, the only time I ever left the country was for that wedding."

Ida paused to eat a bite of pie and have a sip of coffee. "It was both strange and fitting, the way she decided on leaving this house to your shelter. My nephew is established in England, and my sons are happy in Connecticut. So, with no heirs for her home and an inoperable cancer diagnosis—yes, it was cancer that took her," she said in reply to Kelsey's look of sympathy, "though I don't have the strength to talk about that today—Sabrina was motivated to find the right buyer for the house. She had a dozen real estate agents and appraisers come by, and she contacted two different historical societies. You see, the house was built by a brew master of the South City brewery."

Kelsey raised her eyebrows in surprise. "I wasn't aware of that."

"That fact was never touted, though I don't know why. My sister had a few lowball offers from contractors who intended to gut more than they would have kept. The idea of this happening to her beloved home set her blood to boiling. Then one afternoon I came over, and she had your shelter's newsletter in her lap. She was pretty weak by then, but she looked at me with the brightest eyes and told me that she intended to leave the house—furniture and all—to the shelter so long as you all would agree to care for Mr. Longtail." Ida paused and gave a small huff. "I mean no insult when I tell you the idea seemed preposterous to me at first, but when my sister set her mind to something, it was set."

Kelsey smiled and shook her head, her honey-blond

hair tumbling over her shoulders. "I can't tell you how awesome it is to hear this. I had no idea."

"Thank you, dear. I saw you on the news the other day," Ida said. "And I knew right away you intended to bring the dogs here. At first, I was a bit worried, but I suspect this is exactly what Sabrina would've wanted. The busier and bigger and more vivacious life was, the more she enjoyed it." She motioned toward the front rooms. "And from what you showed me as I came in, you certainly seem to have everything under control." She paused to point a thin finger at Kelsey. "And just like you did yesterday afternoon, dear, she'd have given those protesters a piece of her mind. I was sitting on my porch when you came upon them. My sister would've liked you."

Kurt felt surprise wash over him. So Kelsey stood up to the protesters. Of course she had. She simply wasn't the type to rehash it. He wished he could have seen the confrontation himself.

"Thanks," Kelsey said, swiping a lock of hair behind her ear. "It's such an honor to meet you, and it would've been an honor to meet your sister."

"You two would've gotten along well, I'm certain." Ida folded her napkin and stood up, bracing her frail hand on the edge of the table. "When you're more settled, if you have the time, I'd be happy to show you some of my sister's photographs and tell you some of the stories that took place here over the years. There are many delightful ones. But how could there not be? A lot of living was done inside these walls. And, young man," she said, turning to Kurt, "feel free to climb my apple trees any time you'd like. The best ones are always up high."

He and Kelsey showed her out together, but Ida refused his offer to walk her home. She pulled a flashlight from her pocket and promised she was fine. Kurt closed the door and caught Kelsey taking in the foyer and curved staircase with a look of renewed interest and admiration.

"Nice," he said, "to have such an interesting neighbor."

Kelsey shook her head and hooked a thumb in the belt loop of her jeans. "She's incredible. And clearly her sister was too. I had absolutely no idea. I've been feeding Sabrina's cat for eight months, and I had no idea about any of it."

Kurt shrugged. "Sometimes things happen like that. So, did that remarkable pie give you the energy for another couple hours' work with the dogs?"

Kelsey rolled her shoulders in a stretch. "I'm going to sleep like a log tonight, but yes, I'm good to go."

"Great. There are a couple dogs I'm feeling confident enough about to let you do the whole thing."

Kelsey gave the cuff of his T-shirt a soft tug as they headed into the first parlor. "Look at that. Dogs impressive enough to gain the trust of steel-hearted Kurt Crawford."

He winked as he reached for a leash. "That doesn't only go for the dogs, you know. You've made it clear you allow some of that knowledgeable mind of yours to rule along with your *I brake for turtles* heart."

Even in the semidark room, he could tell his words made her blush.

"Thanks," she said, "but just so you know, the whole world should brake for turtles."

Chapter 11

AFTER SUCH PACKED DAYS, WHEN KELSEY ARRIVED AT THE Sabrina Raven estate the next morning, it felt like the rehab had been in full swing for the better part of a month. As she'd anticipated, she'd been tired enough to sleep like the dead last night. Committed to not skipping a night of bringing home one of the shelter dogs, but knowing she was too exhausted to give a high-energy dog the attention it would need, she'd chosen Max, a laid-back, eight-year-old bulldog who was content to snuggle the night away.

And despite leaving the estate so late, driving back and forth for Max, grabbing a bite to eat, and forcing herself to do a load of laundry, she'd still managed to get eight hours of sleep. As a result, she was rejuvenated and ready to face another physically and mentally demanding day.

Though she'd only known him a few days, she wasn't surprised to find Kurt not only awake but knee-deep in a house project while waiting for her to arrive. She glanced at her watch, reaffirming that it was in fact only minutes after seven. How long had he been at it? It seemed he needed remarkably less sleep or downtime than the average person. He just went, went, went, reminding her of a ping-pong-ball taskmaster, when he wasn't hyperfocused on the dogs. When he was with them, he was slow and purposeful, and time fell away.

And even though she should've guessed he'd be tinkering with one project or another, she was still a tad thrown off at finding him on his knees with the upper half of his body buried in the cabinets underneath the kitchen sink. This left the rest of him, from mid-chest down, on display. Her pulse quickened instinctively. The man truly didn't have an ounce of fat on him.

Growing up, her brothers had been so engrossed in bodybuilding that she'd almost been turned off muscles entirely. But nothing about Kurt turned her off. Not only did he have the perfect physique, but he was equal parts Cesar Millan and the Property Brothers.

And unlike with her reflection-addicted brothers, she'd not once caught Kurt gazing at himself in a mirror. He didn't eat like a weightlifter either. With her brothers, it had been egg whites, chicken breasts, and protein shakes. Kurt, on the other hand, ate anything. Actually, he ate a *whole lot* of anythings. He seemed to have a metabolism of fire that magicked food straight into muscle.

Dropping her purse on the table, Kelsey forced out a loud, confident good morning. Rather than his typical blue jeans, Kurt was wearing a pair of khaki cargo pants and a dark-gray T-shirt that had slipped upward enough to show off the smooth olive of his lower back. *Wow*.

How long had it been since she'd fantasized about someone she worked with? The answer slowed her pulse a beat or two. As if she could forget. College. Sophomore year. Lab partner and best friend, Steve. *Sorry, Kels, I just didn't feel it.*

"Morning," Kurt said, looking at her from over his shoulder while still inside the cabinet. "Mind joining me?"

Join him? Under the sink? "Um, I think we've reached the point in the morning that I admit I don't know anything about plumbing."

He backed out from the cabinet and rested against the balls of his feet. His smile was easy and fabulous, and his teeth gleamed white. And there was a grease smudge running across his bicep. Kelsey hadn't known grease smudges could be sexy.

"You don't have to know anything about plumbing. But your hands are smaller."

As much as she might like to, this wasn't something she should opt out of. For this rehab to work smoothly, they needed the house—plumbing included—to be functional. She tugged off her hoodie, not wanting it to get dirty. When it was halfway over her head, she said a quick prayer that the wash of cool air on her belly wasn't because her T-shirt had come up with it. She was two inches taller and fifteen pounds heavier than she'd like to be, and he was most certainly out of her league. That was fine. But the last thing she wanted was for him to think she was putting herself out there like she'd done with Steve.

There were some lessons she didn't need to learn twice.

"Where to, boss?" There was no use wasting time. She needed to deflect her nervous energy.

"Why don't you take the left cabinet? You'll be able to reach the pipe easier. I'll take the right."

Pulling free the elastic tie she kept on her wrist, she shoved her thick hair into a knot, then sank to her knees. "Am I going to be loosening or tightening?"

"Tightening," he said, shifting to give her space. "See

the new elbow joint? It's PVC. Nothing in this house was PVC."

"I'm not going to ask if that's a good thing or a bad thing." She felt the wetness of the cabinet base as she crawled half in. "Was it leaking?" Suddenly he was cramming into the other half and sucking the air right out of her lungs. He smelled so good, and he was *so* close. Their hips and legs were only inches apart.

"It started dripping last night." He passed her a pair of pliers and pointed with a pen-sized flashlight. "See where I'm pointing? Those are compression nuts. I can't fit my hand into the crevice with the pliers to tighten them enough to seal it."

Compression nuts. *Hold it together, Kels.* Thank goodness for the elbow joint separating them, though it did nothing to block out his smell. It took her a few inhalations to discern what it might be. Bar soap, like the basic kind her mom had bought when she was a kid; Axe deodorant, like her brothers wore; and a touch of sweat all blended into the perfect male potpourri.

Her skin was humming with energy. She felt like she was waking up from hibernation, and she was starving for… *For what?* she wondered. *Him? His body? Sex? All of the above?*

She dropped the pliers on the second half turn.

"Sorry if it's uncomfortable," he said, passing them back.

"It's righty-tighty, isn't it? It *feels* like I'm tightening it."

"It is. A couple more turns, with a long twist on the last one, and you can move to the other nut."

A burst of laughter escaped, and Kelsey pressed her

forehead against the new elbow joint. "I'm sorry. We're in too cramped a space to talk about nuts without me taking it wrong."

"We're in too cramped a space to not talk at all, so pick a topic."

"How are the dogs?" she asked, choosing something familiar and safe.

"Nut-free, though a few of the females still have their ovaries."

Kelsey giggled. "I think you're delirious because you never sleep."

"I got a full six hours last night. I never get more than that. If I'm delirious, it's that intoxicating perfume you keep putting on."

Kelsey jerked reflexively and banged the back of her head on the bottom of the sink. "*Ow*. And I'm not dosing myself in perfume to rehab dogs, thank you. It's body wash, citrus mint, and it wakes me up better than coffee."

"Citrus mint, huh? Any chance you'll switch it for a bar of Ivory soap so I can work around you easier?"

She dropped the pliers again. *Did he really just say that?* Thank God for all those years of learning how to be snarky with her brothers when they were dishing out their endless jokes and pranks. "I think I got it on the last turn there. And I have this. I don't need you in here for the last one. And no to the Ivory soap. I like my body wash. It makes me happy. You can spend the next couple minutes looking for nose plugs if you'd like."

It was Kurt's turn to laugh as he backed out of the cabinet and sank against the balls of his feet again. "No thanks. I'll deal."

"Or I could pick you up a bottle. If you start using it, it'll be like we belong to the same citrus-mint tribe."

"No thanks. Too girlie. If I used that stuff, the dogs might no longer recognize me as the alpha male." He stood up and headed over to the toolbox, facing away from her. This made her a little less self-conscious about her rear end sticking up exactly like his had been. She forced her focus back to the job at hand. It was no use wishing for a tiny, petite body. Besides, her height came in handy often enough, and thanks to being so active, those extra pounds were mostly stuck to her curves.

After several turns, and sprouting a hand cramp, Kelsey managed to tighten the next nut till it no longer budged. She scooted out and left Kurt to test the faucet as she headed to the screened-in porch for Pepper. Kurt had given Kelsey the green light to handle the loyal Rottweiler whenever she wanted. This morning, Pepper could hang out in one of the runs while they started on the other dogs.

When she got to Pepper's crate, Kelsey found it empty. A look out into the backyard proved the Rott had already been let out into the single run at the far edge. In one side of the double run, there was a quiet and calm hundred-and-twenty-pound bullmastiff. He was a striking brindled color and so easygoing that Kelsey had decided to name him Buddy.

With two dogs in the runs, it was time for the morning feeding routine. Kurt followed her into the main parlor where they'd been starting the lengthy process. Kelsey could hear the kitchen faucet running and figured he was testing it to be sure the leak was stopped.

"I thought this might help move things along," he

said, pointing to labels he'd stuck to the floor in front of the wire crates. The closest dog, a Doberman who Kelsey had named Lucky, had a green circle drawn on the top left line of his label. Beside the circle were the Greek letter beta and the number one. Below that line, *possible companions* was written, along with a blank underline. Kelsey guessed that meant Kurt would be trying to determine who to eventually pair Lucky with in the double run. "Phase two of the op," he'd called it yesterday.

"I know you had your own color code with those stickies you used at the warehouse," he said, crossing his arms and making his biceps stand out even more in his tight, gray T-shirt. "But I thought green, yellow, and red were more universal. And this is for the volunteers who'll be coming in too. The Doberman was one of the few who got a green, because he's so obedient. I'm not sure he'll be able to be placed in a home with another dog, considering all the ring time he's had, but I think he'd roll over for a toddler who asked him to."

Kelsey had named the Doberman *Lucky* because, at nine years old, not only was he the oldest dog here, but she wouldn't be surprised if he'd been in more fights than most of the other dogs combined. He had the faded scars to prove it. "And you gave him a label of beta because he's not as macho-acting as some of the others?" she clarified.

"Pretty much. Their pack order will either be alpha, beta, or omega. I won't confuse things by breaking it down any further. Betas, you probably know, are the least likely to give us trouble. Alphas might well test us, and omegas may act unpredictably if they feel a lot of stress."

"That makes sense. And why the number one?"

"We'll have more betas than him obviously, so I gave them numbers. I started with him since we've been starting our rounds with him first."

"Shouldn't that be where his name comes in? It's Lucky, if you forgot. If you tell me where the marker is, I can add it."

"Kelsey," Kurt said, stopping her by closing his hand over her elbow. "I didn't forget that you want to call him Lucky, but this place is going to be full of volunteers who will be helping us out. And I get why you give all the shelter animals a name right away, but names instill a certain camaraderie and connection with an animal. When it comes to these guys, I'm not sure we should be promoting that right now. Everyone who'll be working with them needs to keep alert and—"

"Wait a minute," Kelsey interrupted, her emotions flaring. "Are you saying you don't want these guys to have names? After all they've been through, you don't think they deserve *names*?"

Kurt's shoulders sank. "I'm not saying they don't deserve names. They do, and we'll get there. What I'm saying is that everyone who'll be working closely with them needs to keep in mind these animals were trained to fight, and as a result, they're unpredictable. The dogs need training and consistency over affection right now."

Kelsey shook her head. She was starting to see red. So Pepper and Buddy and Lucky were just supposed to be *numbers*?

"No way. I've listened to you on everything, but not this. You have a way with dogs, and I can see that, but no way. They're going to get names and they're going to be transferred to the shelter, and sooner rather than later they're going to be adopted into *loving* homes. All of them." She was upset enough to tap him pointedly on the chest. "And if *you'd* let your heart do a little co-ruling with your I-have-everything-under-perfect-control mind, you'd get that."

Both of his hands immediately closed over hers, lifting off the finger she'd pressed against his well-muscled pec. One by one, he spread her fingers apart, then pressed his thumbs against her palm as he splayed her hand flat. The skin-on-skin contact was disarming, pulling Kelsey away from her anger.

"I was a soldier in enemy territory for longer that I care to recount," he said calmly and slowly. "I've lost far more buddies and dogs than fingers I'm touching. And I can confidently tell you that letting your mind rule you will do little other than psych you out. Let your heart rule, and you'll never pick up the pieces as you fall apart." In a smooth movement, he pressed her hand low and tight against his abdomen, right below his belly button. "The way to survive is listening right here. The little whispers that form here are right a million times more than they are wrong. And my gut is telling me that your helpful shelter volunteers—and you, for that matter—need to respect the fact that many of these dogs have fought others to the death. That isn't something you can hug away, Kelsey."

It took her three solid seconds to react, to process that her hand was in fact pressed against his phenomenal, rock-hard stomach. His brown eyes held her gaze. A part of her wondered if he was taunting her, pressing her hand against him like that. But the only emotion visible in those warm, brown eyes was concern.

She yanked her hand away and practically shook it in hopes of dissipating some of the unexpected heat surging through her. "That was inappropriate." *Um, you touched him first.* "And besides," she added, forcing her thoughts back to the dogs, "I'm not backing down on this. You can give them numbers if you'd like, but I'm giving them names. The volunteers and I will respect your rules *while* the dogs start learning their names." She stopped and swallowed. Her mouth was uncomfortably dry. It hadn't disappeared yet, the feeling of his washboard stomach against the flat of her hand. How long would she be able to recall it so precisely?

"The faucet's still running," she said into his steely silence. "I think you'll be able to tell by now if the leak has been stopped."

He headed for the kitchen without saying anything else, those deep lines of worry etching a V across his forehead once more. Still reeling, Kelsey squatted to the eye level of the Doberman and let him lick the back of her hand from the other side of the kennel door.

"How you doing this morning, Green-Beta-One?" she said quietly enough that Kurt wouldn't overhear. "Yeah, it doesn't do much for me either. With that sweet face, those old, faded scars, and those wizened-beyond-your-years gray hairs, you're definitely a Lucky to me."

———

It was on the tip of Kurt's tongue, in hopes of lightening the mood, to say the fluffy-tailed three-year-old Akita he and Kelsey were working with reminded him of his mother. Maybe that was because the temperamental pup had an undeniable swagger, or maybe it was because the dog made it clear she only enjoyed being around males, not females. In any case, Kurt held the comment back. Bringing up his mother, and all her eccentricities, wasn't what he wanted to do.

Two minutes later, when he heard a vehicle pulling into the circular driveway and looked out the nearest window to spy his grandfather's emerald-green decade-old F-150 pickup, he was particularly thankful he hadn't. There were two people in the cab: the first, his sinewy grandfather; the other, his curvy, vivacious mother.

"Ever notice how when things get off to the wrong start, it's difficult to get back on track?" That came out before he knew he was going to say it.

Kelsey looked directly at him for the first time since they started working with the dogs twenty-five minutes ago. Her eyebrows knotted into little peaks. She'd noticed the truck too. "Protesters?"

"Worse," he said, dragging a hand through his hair. "We could kick *them* back to the street and off the property. It's my family."

"Oh." Still holding the Akita's leash in one hand, Kelsey smoothed the front of her indigo-blue T-shirt. This one read *You can't buy love, but you can rescue it*. She then pulled out the elastic band that had been holding her hair in a messy knot and finger combed through it. Kurt usually wasn't one to notice hair, but hers was thick and wavy and an intoxicating honey blond. The few times he'd seen it down and loose, he'd been overwhelmed by the urge to lose his hands in it while he busied his mouth with that smooth skin of hers.

As he watched her primp, a smile tugged at the corners of his mouth. *She wants to make a good impression.*

She got the Akita back in her crate confidently and unhooked the leash. It was Kelsey's first time doing the whole process with the dog without asking anything from Kurt except a bit of guidance.

"Nice job with her."

"Thanks." She joined him at the window as his mother stepped down out of the truck. Kelsey's jaw dropped. "Your sister's so beautiful."

Sister. Kurt wasn't surprised by this. Whenever he and his mother were together, people who looked close enough to notice their resemblance assumed they were brother and sister. Others assumed they were a couple. Sara Crawford had sixteen years on him, but few would guess it was more than five or six.

Nothing short of typical, his mother was dressed in a flowing white shirt with a deep V in front and cutoff jean shorts with a belt complementing the western boots that drew attention to her sculpted legs.

Kurt cleared his throat, but the necessary clarification eluded him. *Oh well.* Kelsey would figure it out soon enough.

As soon as he opened the front door, his mother let out a coo. "Kurtis Crawford, you didn't tell us you were working in a damn mansion. Look at this place." She sprung up the steps and caught him in a bear hug.

He returned it, if a bit half-heartedly, wondering if his mother would ever remember that, like his grandfather, he enjoyed his personal space. Pulling away, he met his grandfather's gaze. William offered a slight nod, and Kurt thought the word he mumbled was *son.*

"Oh my," Sara said, spying Kelsey, who was hanging back a few feet. Reminding him once more of the Akita, his mother clicked her tongue. "You didn't tell us you have company."

"Actually, I did, if you remember," Kurt said, motioning in Kelsey's direction. "Kelsey, this is my grandfather, Colonel William Crawford, and my mother, Sara, also a Crawford. Guys, this is Kelsey Sutton. She works for the shelter that will be taking in these dogs once they're rehabbed."

"It's great to meet you." Kelsey's smile seemed sincere.

"You too, you sweet thing. And aren't you a brave one." Sara wasted no time drawing Kelsey into a hug.

"Oh, I don't know about that," Kelsey said as they separated. "The dogs are all a lot more docile than you might think."

Sara flashed the grin that had won her best smile in high school and had been commented on ever since. "I meant working in such close quarters with my son. If he doesn't try your patience at least a fraction of what he did mine when he was growing up, you can call yourself lucky. His doctor said his ADHD was off the charts."

Seriously? She's going there in less than sixty seconds? Kurt shoved his hands in his back pockets, doing his best to shrug it off. Unlike the rest of their small family, his mother had always been one to tell everything just like she saw it. Nana had said a dozen times that she was a creature of God who'd been born without a filter.

Kelsey's expression conveyed more camaraderie toward him than Kurt would have expected after the disagreement they'd had. "Well, if he does, I'll try to keep in mind he's the hardest working person I've met. And in all my years working with dogs, I've never seen anyone with his skills."

Kurt looked sharply toward his grandfather, who was reaching out to shake Kelsey's hand. One of his grandfather's eyebrows peaked slightly in response to her praise. "Nice to meet you" was all that he said.

"I didn't know you guys were coming."

His grandfather pulled a phone from his pocket. "That's kind of hard to know when you're incommunicado." He tossed the phone at Kurt, who caught it easily. Kurt was all but out of the technology loop, but the iPhone looked like a recent model.

"I've been meaning to get to a phone to call. It's been a busy few days."

"Your mom and I figured if you owned a cell, that might be easier to do."

"You mean you're giving this to me?"

"A bit selfishly, Kurtis." Sara offered him a wink. "You're going to need to use it to check in every so often. When you were overseas, there was always a number to call. Though Miss Kelsey here looks like she'll be able to help us keep decent tabs on you."

"Thanks," he said, "but you didn't need to do that. I'd have gotten around to getting one eventually."

"It was your grandmother's. It's under contract awhile yet. She upgraded just a month or so before…" William fell silent and focused on the curving staircase instead of on them. "She didn't have it long," he finished.

Out of the corner of his eye, Kurt saw Kelsey chew her bottom lip, probably putting two and two together.

He wondered if later, when they were alone, she'd ask questions. There was so much he'd love to tell her about Nana. Kelsey was the type of person who'd listen expertly, who'd genuinely want to hear about her. And maybe, somehow, make the whole mess a little bit better.

Adding how much his grandmother had meant to him to the fact that he'd all but missed the last eight years of her life hadn't made her death easy to swallow. The desire to confess it all to Kelsey took him by surprise.

"I appreciate it."

"We took it by the store yesterday," Sara said. "It's a new number, but I thought you might enjoy her pictures, so I had them put back on. There aren't many."

"Thanks. I appreciate it." He sounded like a broken record, but at the moment, Kurt found himself as limited to clipped speech as his grandfather usually was.

He slipped the phone into his back pocket without examining it further. He wasn't sure he could stay in control if he looked through Nana's pictures. He'd save that for another time. "So, would you guys like a tour?"

William glanced at his watch. "A short one. Your mother has an appointment. I'd like to swing by later today, if you're up for it."

"What an amazing house," Sara said, jamming her thumbs in the front pockets of her shorts and rocking back on the heels of her boots. "And you get to sleep here and everything until this job is finished? Both of you?"

Kelsey shook her head at Kurt's yes, which was spoken over Sara's last question. "Just Kurt. I have an apartment about five miles from here. Kurt didn't know the house's history when he took the job, but it has an interesting one."

Just yesterday morning, Kelsey's friendly and perfectly normal parents had come by to tour the house and meet the dogs. He couldn't help but wonder what she thought upon seeing his unconventional mother and tight-lipped grandfather. She gave them a quick recap of how the house came to belong to the shelter, and included the bit about Ida Greene that they'd learned yesterday. "There's some of her apple pie left in the kitchen," Kelsey added. "It was fabulous."

"Homemade apple pie," Sara said, giving William a playful scratch on the chin. Kurt didn't think there was another person on earth who could get away with that and not be put in their place. "If you've got hot coffee, the Colonel won't be turning it down, will you, Pops?"

William stepped back half a foot and gave his watch another glance. "The truth is, I'll enjoy it more this afternoon." He gave Sara a deliberate glance. "We're supposed to arrive early."

"Where is it you're headed?" Kurt asked for the second time.

"Your mother has an appointment." William set his shoulders determinedly and somehow managed to stand a half inch straighter. Wherever the two of them were headed, Kurt understood his grandfather wasn't ready to discuss it. This set Kurt's thoughts churning; it must be something important to make them drive so far from home. But if there was anyone in Missouri more stubborn than William Crawford, Kurt had yet to meet them. The truth was, he wouldn't learn their business until his grandfather was good and ready to share it.

Chapter 12

KELSEY BLINKED IN SURPRISE LATER THAT AFTERNOON WHEN she pulled into the circular drive of the Raven estate a mere fifteen minutes after leaving for a quick errand. Unlike last time, her surprise wasn't caused by the protesters. After a few long, quiet days without getting any true attention, the group seemed to be taking a day off.

Her surprise was at finding Kurt twenty feet off the ground on an extension ladder leaned against the north side of the house. He had a tool belt slung loosely around those remarkable hips of his and was working on the frame of one of the second-story windows.

Grabbing the two bottles of IBC Root Beer and the bag of freshly baked pretzels she'd bought, Kelsey left her purse and keys in the car and made a mental note to grab them before going into the house.

So glad he waited for a spotter. She hadn't even known they had an extension ladder. He'd probably found it while poking around in the garage at the back of the yard. The detached building was framed by cobwebs, and Kelsey had never done more than glance in the dirty windows. After learning from Ida yesterday that it had been built to be a carriage house and converted for cars in the forties, the old building had more appeal, though Kelsey was fine waiting until Kurt had scared away more critters before checking it out further. Not only was it likely chock-full of spiders, but a few months ago, on the first warm summer day, she'd noticed the largest black rat snake she'd ever seen sunning itself in front of the old carriage doors.

As she got closer to the side of the house where Kurt was working, she noticed Mr. Longtail milling around underneath the ladder and rubbing his cheek against its base. "Please, God, say that's stable."

Kurt smiled, his teeth gleaming white in contrast to the dark brick behind him. "With the stabilizer, it's safer than if someone was down there holding it."

"Let's hope." Kelsey shooed the cat out from underneath. "So, tell me, what little fire are we putting out now?"

"A storm's coming, and the cracks around the side of this window are nearly big enough for a bird to fly through. It's causing a mess in the front bedroom. The wall around the window is rotting, and the wooden floor underneath has water damage. Not only could we use a new window and frame here, but the brick needs tuck-pointing. For today, a bit of duct tape will do."

Shifting the bag of pretzels and root beers precariously to one hand, Kelsey pulled her phone from her pocket and clicked open the weather app. He was right. There was a seventy percent chance of thunderstorms late this afternoon. "I was about to ask how you knew, isolated here as you've been, but then I remembered you're now the proud owner of a smartphone."

He shifted on the ladder, causing it to bounce and jiggle. Kelsey grabbed ahold of one of the lower rungs, nearly dropping her phone in the process. Apparently unconcerned about the jiggling, Kurt stopped taping and brushed a hand over his back pocket, drawing her attention to his fabulous derriere. "If you want the truth, I forgot I had it. Can't you feel the air pressure dropping? I'm no weatherman, but I can tell when a thunderstorm is coming."

Kelsey made a face. "When the winds pick up and the sky darkens, I can."

He chuckled and ripped off another piece of duct tape. From here, the window frame blocked the silver tape from view, so hopefully it wouldn't be visible from the street either. Not that duct tape would stand out much in comparison to the couple of missing bricks or the peeling paint on the shutters and porch or the run-down carriage house out back.

Kelsey was surprised by the rush of emotion that swept over her as she thought about all the work the house needed to really shine again. At one point, she wouldn't have cared if the old mansion was torn down and a new one was built in its place whenever it went up for sale, or if, like the dogs, it was rehabbed. Not anymore. Now she'd be willing to put up a battle to make sure whoever eventually bought it was intent on restoring it. The old place had way too much history to be knocked down. Whoever the eventual new owners were, they just *had* to pump the life back into it that Sabrina Raven had given it for so many years. And hopefully they'd get her garden going again too.

"That should do it," Kurt said, dropping the tape and X-ACTO knife into the worn leather tool belt.

Kelsey held the ladder for his first several steps down, then backed away as his feet reached chest level. He quite possibly had the best rear end she'd ever seen, and she could feel her cheeks flaming hot to prove it.

"I made a pretzel run," she said, holding up the bag and hoping it drew attention away from her blush. "And I hope you like root beer. It's so warm today that I thought it would hit the spot."

"Sounds perfect. Thanks." He took one of the extended bottles and twisted off the cap. He slipped the cap into his pocket rather than tossing it on the ground. None of it was intentional, but he was passing so many tests. She couldn't have a crush on a guy who littered. Or who wasn't kind and gentle with the dogs. And even though he was cautious about naming them, he was a genuine dog whisperer.

"Want to sit a few minutes?" she asked. "Some part of you *has* to be tired."

One side of his perfect lips turned up in a half smile. "Now that you say it, the rocking chairs on the front porch have been calling my name."

"Awesome. I've always wanted to sit in them, but I've never taken the time." Kelsey walked with him around the house and up the wide brick stairs. "Have you heard of Gus' Pretzels? Depending on how you get off the highway, you probably passed it as you came here. I'd guess you could say they're a bit of a St. Louis landmark."

"Like the pizza joints that use a cracker for the crust?" Kurt teased, pulling one of the long pretzel sticks from the bag and then collapsing onto one of the old wooden rockers.

Kelsey took a seat in the adjacent one, wondering how many times Sabrina and Ida had sat here together.

"They're good."

"And addictive," she added. "Which was fine when I was swinging by here to feed Mr. Longtail. It was on my way home, and the place was closed. But now it's right up the street and so *available*."

"You say it like that's a bad thing."

"It is if you're watching carbs."

"I don't know why you'd be doing that." His gaze dropped to her body for only a second or two, followed by one or two seconds when she wanted to disappear. They had to be just empty words. He was too physically perfect not to want someone who could double as a Victoria's Secret model. Right?

Thankfully, Mr. Longtail jumped up onto the side of the porch and meowed his loud, pervasive meow, drawing Kurt's attention. The cat stalked over to him and rubbed against one calf.

"If I didn't know better, I'd swear you switched him with a double. Eight months of trying, and he wanted none of my attention. You're here a few days, and he's following you around like a lost puppy."

Kurt brushed a few pieces of pretzel salt off his thigh, then swooped the cat onto his lap. "I opened an old can of sardines for him last night. He was definitely a fan."

"Did he sleep with you again?"

"Either that, or someone was trying to suffocate me with a fur pillow around two or three in the morning."

Kelsey giggled. "Some things you have to see to believe." The Maine coon was a giant cat and took up all of Kurt's lap, but that didn't stop him from getting comfortable. He plopped down and started kneading Kurt's knees. Kelsey could hear the cat's sharp claws getting stuck in Kurt's cargo pants. She pulled out her phone. "Do you care if I take a picture? Megan will never believe me."

"Knock yourself out." A second later, he winced as Mr. Longtail's sharp claws dug into his skin. Kurt extracted the claws carefully from his pants, then began to pump one foot softly, causing his leg to jiggle and Mr. Longtail's head to bobble like her Chihuahua bobblehead. The movement stopped the cat from kneading but didn't seem to disturb him otherwise. He curled into a ball, exposing part of his stomach, and began to purr. Kelsey snapped a picture as Kurt's free hand disappeared into the cat's mass of thick, gray belly fur.

She inspected her work, promising herself that even though Kurt looked incredibly sexy with his broad shoulders, strong jawline, and shadow of stubble, she wouldn't pull out her phone later just to stare at the picture.

"Sorry about earlier," he said after swallowing a bite of pretzel. "My mother's a bit much, if you didn't notice."

"For a second there, I thought you were talking about not naming the dogs."

"I'm a pretty good judge of when a battle has been lost."

"So you're consenting? You're okay with me naming them?"

"I'm consenting. Let's leave it at that. And I named one while you were gone. I'll leave the rest up to you."

"Who?"

"I'll let you figure that out later. I wrote it on his crate."

Kelsey cocked an eyebrow. "I know what I'm doing as soon as I finish this pretzel."

He smiled and ate a bite of pretzel.

"Your mom was nice. Does she live in Fort Leonard Wood too? I know you said your grandfather teaches there."

"She's not too far outside the post. She lives in a trailer park a few miles away actually." Kurt swigged his root beer, then added, "She left my grandparents' house when she turned eighteen. I was a little over a year old. To hear her talk, you wouldn't know it, but my grandparents were the ones to raise me. Back then, she pretty much came and went as she pleased. At least that's how I remember it."

Kelsey wasn't sure how to respond. He didn't say it like he wanted sympathy, but she'd put the pieces together about the cell phone having been his grandmother's. If his grandmother had been more involved in raising him than his own mom, her passing had to be especially hard. "I'm really sorry about your grandmother."

"Me too," he said, looking at the house across the road. Two carpenters were there today, and somewhere inside the house, a table saw kept going off. "Nobody was expecting it. She was in her late sixties but healthy as can be. She was in the grocery store when it happened. She fell and hit her head, but it was a stroke that caused it."

If they were closer, Kelsey would've put her hand on his shoulder. Instead, she busied herself by breaking off a piece of her pretzel stick.

"She was an amazing woman," Kurt continued, keeping his focus on the house across the street. "Small in size, lots smaller than my mom even, but she was big in spirit. She was born in Mexico and came from money—loads of it, to hear her tell it. Her father was very proud and traditional and wanted to keep all the money and property in his family line. When she was eighteen, she found out he wanted to marry her off to her third cousin.

While the relationship was distant enough not to have any genetic risk associated with it, they'd been raised in the same extended family and she wanted absolutely nothing to do with him.

"She and her father were having big rows about it, so he sent her on vacation with her mother and aunt to a beach in Baja, California, in hopes she'd cool down. That was when she met my grandfather. He was a few years older and stationed down in Texas back then. He was on leave and vacationing with his buddies. They eloped after meeting each other three times. She never went home."

As this last part settled in, Kurt stroked Mr. Longtail, who clearly loved having his belly rubbed. Kelsey could practically feel the cat's deep, thrumming purr reverberating in her chest.

"Not even for vacation?" she asked. The idea of never seeing her own mom, dad, or brothers again was almost unfathomable.

Kurt raised an eyebrow. "She reached out to them after my mother was born, but her father made it clear she'd been excommunicated. To hear her tell it, my very stubborn and set-in-his-ways grandfather was a pussycat compared to her dad. However, a year or so before I enlisted, she got a letter from her hometown in Mexico. I don't think she ever opened it. At least if she did, it was something she never shared. She said sometimes too much water can pass under a bridge."

"Wow. I can't imagine having my family turning against me because of who I wanted to marry, but I don't have that kind of heritage either. At least she handled it okay. She sounds like an amazing person."

"She was the best." Kurt rolled the side of his empty bottle along the edge of his chair. "She really was. She had endless patience with me, and my mother wasn't kidding about the ADHD. My grandmother was a saint to put up with all she did. I started a garage fire when I was ten that forced us to stay in a hotel for a month and could've been much worse. Then, when I was twelve, I got caught trying to drive my grandfather's old truck off post property. If it had just been up to my grandfather, I'd have gotten spanked more times than I could count."

Kelsey grimaced. "I hope that's a figure of speech."

Kurt gave her one of the half smiles she was starting to love. "Let's go with that. Then I became a teenager, and the trouble really started. If it hadn't been for my grandmother and for the chances I had to work with Rob and his dogs, I'd probably have ended up in juvie."

"You don't seem anything like that now." She held out the bag, offering him another pretzel. The tips of their fingers touched as he took one, giving Kelsey an electric jolt. Yep, she was definitely crushing hard. Learning more about him wasn't helping extinguish those flames either.

Over to the west, it was starting to cloud up and turn gray. The rest of the sky was still blue and sunny. She wondered how many hours they had before the storm hit and what kind of anxiety it might stir up in the dogs. She was opening her mouth to ask if they should start the evening feeding rounds early when she spotted his grandfather's truck coming down the street. This time, there was only one person in the cab.

"Looks like it's only your grandfather this time," Kelsey said, nodding toward the street.

The slightest hint of a frown appeared on Kurt's face. He set his bottle on the porch floor and lifted a perturbed Mr. Longtail off his lap. The cat meowed and twitched his tail at having been disturbed, then strode to the center of the top step and started licking his long fur.

"As long as you're good with it, while you guys talk, I can switch out the dogs in the runs—after I discover who's newly named." Offering him a smile, Kelsey made a show of crossing a finger over her heart. "And I promise to handle only the green betas whose names I know you're going to love using very soon."

He chuckled and brushed off his pants. "Sounds good. Yell if you need me."

After waving to Kurt's grandfather as he pulled into the circular drive, Kelsey headed inside. She couldn't be sure, but this morning she'd gotten a strong sense that Kurt's grandfather was holding something back.

Chapter 13

KELSEY WAS OUT BACK WATCHING LUCKY AND PEPPER ENJOY some time in separate runs when Patrick stepped out of the house onto the back porch.

"Hey, when did you get here?" she called as she headed over.

Patrick glanced at his watch. "Three minutes ago. Kurt said that if you're able to help, I can go ahead and get the big shepherd mix out of his kennel. Kurt will join us when he's finished. He's on the front porch talking to an older man with a similar face shape. I think they're related."

Kelsey swallowed a giggle. "That's his grandfather, but sure, I can help. These two guys are fine out here for a bit. What are you going to do with the shepherd mix today?"

She'd been only slightly surprised to find that Kurt had named the big shepherd Devil. The dog knew all the basics like *sit* and *stay*, and he seemed to respect people, even if he held no obvious regard for them. On the other hand, he'd already eaten through one kennel and had destroyed every chew toy he'd been given, even the most indestructible ones. And whether he was in his crate or out, he passed most of the day anxious and unsettled. He had zero tolerance for other dogs. All of that paled in comparison to how difficult it was to keep him on track during training sessions. When he

was out of his crate, he always seemed to be searching for something that was just out of sight. Treats and
affection were wasted on him. His only interests during
his training sessions were in scent marking, snarling in
the direction of other dogs, and searching the road for
signs of who knew what.

"He doesn't want to be here," Patrick said as they
headed inside. "Maybe none of them do, but none of
them seem to feel as displaced as he does."

"The poor guy has probably had it really rough."

"Maybe." But the way Patrick said the word,
it seemed to imply *maybe not* more than *maybe*.
"Appropriate name," he added when he spied Kurt's
addition to the tape on Devil's kennel designating him
as red alpha seven.

Although the giant had given no indication that he
would ever snap at a human, he was the only dog here
being treated as a high-risk possibility. This meant rather
than simply hooking a clip leash to his collar after his
kennel door was opened, Kurt or Patrick needed to get
the generally uncooperative dog to step into a slip—or
noose—leash first. Once it was on and the dog proved
to be calm, a regular clip leash was hooked to his collar
and the self-tightening slip leash was removed.

From there, it was pretty much business as usual.
Except that Devil had no interest in receiving their
praise or in any of the reward toys the dogs were offered
when they were well behaved, and only a mild interest
in even the best of treats.

"What's on the agenda for him today?" Kelsey asked
a second time.

"Music."

Kelsey pressed her tongue to the roof of her mouth. She'd hoped for a better explanation but suspected she wouldn't get it.

Rather than allowing Devil to drag him toward the front door, Patrick coaxed him out the back and down the rear porch steps to the grass farthest from the newly installed runs. Across the yard, Lucky barked several times, causing the long, fuzzy hair on Devil's back and neck to spike high as he sniffed the air. He urinated a long, unending stream on the closest tree while staring the dogs down. Afterward, the massive dog seemed to dismiss both Lucky and Pepper as he turned his attention to the side of the house that had a rickety gate in the privacy fence.

Patrick asked him to sit, though he had to step between Devil and the gate to get his attention. On his third repeated command, Devil tucked in his massive haunches and sank into a sitting position, eyeing Patrick for a split second before stretching his head at an awkward angle to refocus on the gate.

"He has a very determined focus."

Kelsey was considering whether she should comment on Patrick and Devil's shared similarity when Patrick took out his phone, pulled up a playlist, and handed the phone to her. Kelsey frowned as Neil Diamond's "Sweet Caroline" burst from the speakers.

Sometimes back at the shelter, they played music for the dogs, but making music a part of one of these training sessions seemed too peculiar even for Patrick.

"I believe twenty seconds should be enough to get a reaction, assuming we're going to get one, so I made a playlist with twenty-second recordings of a variety of songs. We'll see if he reacts to any, or if he treats them all like white noise."

After the "Sweet Caroline" snippet ended, a song Kelsey didn't know but that would qualify as hard rock played, then a popular country song, then a piece of classical music, followed by a song by Kygo.

In Kelsey's opinion, Devil seemed to ignore each of them equally. His interest was in the gate, though he was distracted for a few seconds by a small flock of birds taking off from a nearby tree. He paid little attention to Patrick or Kelsey, sinking back into a seated position only on repeated requests from Patrick, who rewarded him with a few nibbles of a savory treat.

It was on the tip of Kelsey's tongue to ask what Patrick was hoping to get out of the song playing when a bluegrass song came on, and Devil looked pointedly at Patrick's phone, his ears pricked forward.

"Bluegrass," Patrick said aloud, shifting Devil's leash to one hand and reaching for his phone. When it was over, he typed in "most popular bluegrass songs."

When he began "Come All You Fair and Tender Ladies," Devil cocked his head at the first plucks of the banjo. After a few seconds, he whined, then his gaze flicked from the phone to the gate and back again.

"It could be that his only interest in it is that it's unusual," Patrick said, letting the song play for a full minute before passing the phone back to her and letting it play out.

"Or?" Kelsey asked. Patrick clearly had a point to this. He just wasn't making it clear to her.

"It seems to me there's a reason he has no interest in connecting with us. Or any interest in teaming up with any of the other dogs. He doesn't show it often, but he's well trained. He's unhappy and unsettled. And he lets that be known. Affection and praise are lost on him, but that doesn't mean he's never received it."

Kelsey watched as Patrick sank to a squat, balancing on the balls of his feet. Although she wasn't afraid of the cantankerous, massive animal, she felt enough caution around him that her back muscles tensed. With Patrick in a squat, it was obvious that Devil nearly matched him pound for pound.

Patrick extended his right hand. "Shake." When Devil made no movement to acknowledge him, Patrick slipped a single, moist treat from his pocket and held it in his left hand. Devil took a whiff but ignored Patrick otherwise. "Shake, boy," he repeated.

Almost absentmindedly, with his sharp brown eyes still fixed on the gate, Devil lifted his giant paw and dropped it into Patrick's hand.

Patrick shook the paw, then lifted the treat within swiping distance of Devil's quick tongue. "Good boy. Good, good boy." Then, standing and directing his next words to Kelsey, Patrick said, "I don't have the answer, but nothing about him fits. The music. The tricks. His discontent. He's waiting for someone, and I want to find out who."

"Someone who likes bluegrass?"

"Possibly."

Devil's microchip had never been registered and the vet who inserted it didn't have his owner's new contact information. Finding out who had owned this guy felt like an impossibility, but Kelsey did her best to never say never. In her seven years at the shelter, she'd seen the impossible happen more than once.

—♦—

Thanks to the wind picking up and carrying the smell of rain, as soon as Kurt's grandfather left, he and Kelsey dove into the evening feeding routine. If she'd been put out that he'd named the cranky giant Devil, she hadn't commented. The tenacious dog was promising to give Kurt a run for his money when it came to retraining him. Thankfully, it looked like Patrick was going to be a huge help in figuring out the complicated animal.

Unlike the relaxed conversation he'd enjoyed with Kelsey this afternoon, tonight they worked in silence. Yesterday, she'd commented playfully that Kurt's vocabulary all but eluded him while he was intently focused on the dogs. "I swear I can almost see the right side of your brain taking over," she'd joked.

He hoped she attributed his quiet to that this afternoon. He tried to hone his usual focus, but it evaded him. He kept replaying his grandfather's words, rehashing what he hadn't been prepared to hear. Thankfully, he and Kelsey had worked out a seamless routine over the last several days, and she always seemed on top of her game.

They had finished feeding and giving each dog a short walk around the side of the house when the first crack of thunder rumbled across the sky. Zeus, the newly named Argentine mastiff, and Pepper were still in the runs, having a turn to stretch their legs. Zeus was barking and chasing every leaf that blew inside his fence. The Argentine mastiff's all-white coat looked especially bright under the darkening skies. Pepper was standing at the gate of her run. She wanted to roam the yard, and probably to hang near Kurt and Kelsey, but Kurt wasn't in the space today to introduce two dogs, even through a fence. And when he did, he wouldn't start with a pregnant Rottweiler. He was positive by now that she was. Just a few days of good meals, and her belly was visibly rounding out.

As far as Zeus went, Kurt would put money down that the dog had never been fought. His tail wagged too damn much when other dogs passed his kennel. Tomorrow, Kelsey was going to bring Orzo, a laid-back corgi, and if Zeus did well, Kurt would step up his socializing, including taking him on walks off the property. A few of the other dogs seemed ready for the same thing. If the court order was no longer in place, Kurt was starting to feel hopeful that within a month, at least five or six in the group would be headed for the shelter. He suspected the rest would take a while longer. A part of him worried that a few, like Devil, might never be ready to live as a pet in someone's home. There were options for dogs like this, but Kurt wasn't ready to spend time thinking of them. For now, he was committed to optimism.

To accomplish this, he'd turned one of the bedrooms into a private training room, and whenever things were slow, he'd head in there with one of the dogs. Instilling basic training in these animals was essential, and it went so much deeper than sit or stay. But he was becoming confident they'd get there.

A brilliant flash of lightning danced across the sky. Kurt could feel the electricity in the air, circling over his bare arms and neck. "I think it's time we get them in."

"Agreed." Kelsey set a fresh bowl of water in Pepper's kennel and followed Kurt down the back porch into the yard. Seeing them headed his way, Zeus made a move that looked an awful lot like a bucking bronco, then plunged toward the door of his run. The gangly dog skidded into seated attention, stopping just shy of slamming into the door.

Kelsey laughed. "I can almost imagine him finding his place in a circus." She headed for Pepper's run but waited for Kurt to head inside first with Zeus.

She was latching Pepper's kennel door when Kurt stepped out of the house and joined her in the enclosed half of the porch.

"I've been a fan of thunderstorms since I was a kid, and I can confidently say that I don't ever again want to live too long in a place that doesn't get its fair share."

"Where were you stationed?" Kelsey asked, joining him in front of the floor-to-ceiling screen.

The wind was picking up, and he could hear the rain pelting in the west. In the distance, he spotted the deluge headed their way. "Look, you can see the rain rolling in." He fell quiet, watching it rush toward them at an angle. "Afghanistan mostly," he said finally, responding to her question. "Texas with the army at first. I finished out in Central America. There, most of the time it's like the rains are ruled by a light switch. It's either raining heavily, or it isn't but feels like it just did."

"It would be cool to see more of the world, but I agree about thunderstorms. I'm a sucker for changing seasons." A fresh blast of wind circled across the porch, lifting Kelsey's hair off her shoulders. She shuddered. "I hope Mr. Longtail found his way inside."

"I just saw him. He's sprawled across the kitchen counter." Unfazed by the storm, Pepper was curling into a ball to sleep. Her kennel was far enough from the screen to stay dry.

The circling winds stirred up Kelsey's citrus-mint scent. Kurt resisted the urge to pull her close and breathe her in until he was sufficiently calm inside. Instead, he tucked his hands into his back pockets, palms facing out.

"*So*," she said while he was still trying to block out her intoxicating smell, "I may not have known you long, but I'd bet a million dollars that you're not the gabby type. However, I want you to know that I'm here if it would help to talk about whatever it is that's bothering you."

Kurt pulled his attention from the storm to look at her. It had been a long time since he'd met someone who could read him so easily. It had also been a long time since he'd brushed his lips against lips like hers, full and sexy and moist. And those eyes. They were the rich, soft brown of amber and just as inviting, and the lashes framing them were thick and long and sultry.

He swallowed hard. The energy of the storm matched the energy building inside him. Rain and bits of hail began to hammer the roof. The pretend box deep inside him where he locked things away seemed to have the lid stuck open. He realized it was kiss her or tell her everything, or quite possibly both. Coming here, he'd been so damned committed to keeping her at a distance. Could that possibly have been less than a week ago?

Dragging a hand through his hair and putting some necessary distance between them, he strode the length of the porch. When he returned, he made sure to stop a full arm's length away.

"Turns out my mother went in for her first ever

mammogram a month ago. They found a lump. Apparently not a nasty one, at least," he added at Kelsey's gasp. "She and my grandfather have spent the last few weeks working out a plan. They'd decided on doing the treatments here in St. Louis even before I took this job. The only really good hospital down at the post is military and, not having been in service herself, my mother doesn't have access to it."

A flash of lightning lit the darkened porch, and a clap of thunder filled his ears. Kelsey folded her arms across her chest. Kurt got the feeling she wanted to touch him as much as a part of him wanted her to.

"I never would have guessed," she said when the thunder quieted. The rain was coming in slanted, forcing them both to step back from the screen. "She looked so happy this morning. That's good though, right? You said it's not one of the bad types. Maybe she's not that worried."

"My mother's never been one to worry about anything. Or at least she's never been one to show it. It's my grandfather who's taking it hard, even if he denies it. I guess you wouldn't expect any different, considering he lost his wife a couple months ago."

Kelsey nodded sympathetically and folded her arms tighter over her chest after a strong blast of cold wind swept across the porch. "I don't know if it helps, but several of our shelter volunteers are breast cancer survivors. I walk with them every summer in a breast-cancer-awareness walk downtown. I'm not trying to downplay it, but from what they say, massive strides have been made in breast cancer recovery the last ten or fifteen years. Where's she getting treatment?"

"Siteman Cancer Center. Based on the conversation with the surgeon this morning, they've decided not to go through with a full mastectomy. Ten years ago, it probably would have been recommended. From what my grandfather said, a whole team of people made the recommendation, but today she only saw the surgeon. He recommended she have a lumpectomy followed by radiation. Based on the biopsy, it looks like she won't need chemo. Thank God she won't have to deal with that."

Overhead, the rain that had been pounding on the roof of the porch abruptly slowed to gentle tapping, and the wind dropped as brusquely as it had begun.

"It's not exactly the Hyatt, but now that you've fixed the stairs, the bedrooms are easily accessible," Kelsey said. "If they don't want to deal with that drive while she's recuperating, I can ask Megan if it'd be okay if they stay here."

"Thanks for the offer. They're talking about renting a place close to the hospital, which would suit her better. As cool as she thought the house was, she freaks if she spots a spider indoors." He shrugged, shaking his head. "I'm not kidding. It's her thing. But don't be surprised if my grandfather makes himself useful around here."

"Then he's good with dogs too?"

Kurt let out a small laugh. "No, for a reason I've never figured out, he's kind of anti-pet. I meant with the house. He always says if he hadn't stayed in the army, he'd have become a carpenter. He joined Habitat for Humanity when I was in high school because he'd run out of things to repair in our house. He'd have a heyday here."

"Well, he certainly couldn't hurt anything if you

want to give him that tool belt of yours and free range of the house."

"No, he couldn't, could he?"

"It'd probably be good for him too, considering..." Kelsey said, her voice trailing off as she looked out to the west where the cloud cover was thinning and the setting sun was poking through. "Seems like it's clearing. And we're ahead of schedule. Maybe we could take an hour or two off. The dogs will be good for a while. Earlier, you said your trips with your family to St. Louis were mostly limited to the Arch, the zoo, and the City Museum. Those are amazing, of course, but there's so much more to show you. We're a city of fantastic little neighborhoods like this one here in South City. I could give you a tour of the area, and we could grab something to eat afterward."

It was probably because of what he'd just shared, but she was offering to spend a considerable amount of time with him. Without the dogs. He needed to say no and send her home. Give her a night off. He could get lost in the dogs and the one-on-one training each one needed. If he accepted her offer, he'd be letting her in even more when he'd promised himself he wouldn't. He was searching for a polite way to say no when an insanely close blast of lightning struck, reminding him that some of the biggest strikes were often at the tail end of a storm. Before the flash of brilliant white dissipated, the kitchen and hall lights visible through the windows went out simultaneously.

He huffed. "I guess there's no working with the dogs in the dark, is there?" he said when the accompanying boom quieted.

"No, but with any luck, Hodak's won't have lost power. Since I've absolutely blown my diet this week, I might as well introduce you to the place. It's the best fried chicken in the city, and it's within walking distance."

Kurt smiled, feeling the tension he'd been holding in since talking to his grandfather start to lift. "Somehow, you're reading my mind. Fried chicken and thunderstorms were two of my biggest must-haves on coming home."

She waved him off, smiling playfully. "You're from the Midwest. Chances are slim that fried chicken wouldn't be high on your list."

"Probably so. Hey, I know it's your tour and all, but are you good with taking the Mustang?"

Kelsey clicked her tongue. "This is going to be a walking tour, Staff Sergeant Crawford."

"What happens if it storms again?"

She shrugged. "Then you'll have to find us suitable cover. All those years of service, I'm betting you're a real-life MacGyver. That *was* duct tape you were using earlier, after all."

He laughed and savored the warmth filling him. "Watch it, or I'll strap on that tool belt before we go."

Chapter 14

"So, HOW EXACTLY DO YOU DEFINE 'WALKING DISTANCE'?" Kurt asked after they'd been walking for about thirty minutes.

Kelsey was pointing out interesting shops and popular taverns he might enjoy while staying at the Raven estate. The *while* part was a bit of a downer for her. He and the dogs and the house had become such a sudden but immense part of her life that it would be strange to swing by the quiet, empty house to feed a cat who'd probably be crankier than ever when Kurt was gone. And *strange* wasn't the right word for it. It would be downright sad.

"Without the detours we're taking, it's about a mile and a half," she answered. "I'm guessing with them, it'll be about double that. You aren't getting tired, are you? When you go to Hodak's, it's important you're sufficiently hungry."

"Trust me. I'll be sufficiently hungry."

She brushed her fingers over his triceps before thinking about it. "One more detour, but trust me, it's worth it. This one is the best of all. I'm hoping it won't be too dark to see it."

He followed her down a side street without comment.

It had taken him less than three minutes, but he'd jogged upstairs before leaving and come down in a black V-neck long-sleeved shirt, perfectly molded blue jeans, and a pair of understated cowboy boots. Considering the short time he was upstairs, he couldn't have done more than finger comb his thick, brown hair. It was just messy enough without being unkempt, and Kelsey could easily imagine slipping her hands into it.

She was super thankful she'd still had a basic faux-cashmere sweater in her trunk from a planned family dinner she opted out of the other night when things took longer than expected at the Raven estate. Not only was it considerably cooler now that the short storm had blown through, but she'd been told more than once the snug-fitting lilac sweater looked great on her. She'd also ditched her tennis shoes for the pair of comfortable, tall leather boots she'd had in the trunk.

"Here," she said a few minutes later.

Kurt seemed skeptical as he took in the narrow but deep empty lot they'd stopped in front of. It was sandwiched between an antebellum home in the process of being renovated and a single-room brick house with the windows boarded up. Dusk was setting in heavily, making the edges of the lot hard to distinguish. The streetlights were kicking on, but none were close enough to really light up the area.

"Let me guess," he said. "You're hoping to turn it into a dog park for dogs who don't play well with others?"

Kelsey giggled. "I don't think I could get a permit for that if I tried. I thought you'd like to know that we're standing in front of what's believed to be an Underground Railroad site."

Kurt raised an eyebrow. "Really? Cool."

"Like about everything around here, this story ties to the caves that spiderweb through this part of the city.

The house that used to be here had a tunnel hidden under the back porch that connected to caves leading to the Mississippi River. The river's less than half a mile that way as the crow flies. If you believe the old stories, escaped slaves would hide in a now-demolished graveyard down the street until one of the German abolitionists who owned the home came and got them under the cover of darkness. After feeding them a good meal, they'd send the escaped slaves on their way through the caves to the river. From there, they headed north. Unfortunately, the house was torn down by the city before it was officially registered, but there've been a few archeological digs here since. Several archeologists believe the artifacts they found here prove it was part of the Underground Railroad."

Kurt rocked back on the heels of his boots as he surveyed the area. "That's freaking awesome."

"I think so too. Unfortunately, the construction of Interstate 55 tore up miles of caves, as have a lot of the demolishing and new construction around here, which makes the claim all but impossible to prove."

"That's a shame, but sometimes the mystery of a place is what keeps it famous. Think of all the old ghost tales that are told."

"True. That's the other thing about this area you've probably heard about. These last five or six square blocks make up what is considered one of the most haunted spots in America."

"I remember watching the *America's Most Haunted* episode that was filmed here awhile back, but I didn't realize the Raven estate was so close to here. And I thought you didn't believe in hauntings."

"I don't believe in *hauntings*. That doesn't mean spirits don't linger, does it?"

He grinned. "No, I guess it doesn't."

She waggled her eyebrows at him. "I hope this little tour tidbit doesn't make sleeping in that big house all alone a problem for you."

He chuckled the soft, rolling laugh that made her chest turn to pudding. Or at least thick molasses. "I suspect I won't miss any more winks than I already do. But this is great, Kelsey. All that you've shown me tonight. Consider me a bona fide fan of South City."

"You can't say that *before* you've tried the chicken. It was supposed to be the tipping point."

"Speaking of chicken…" he said, placing the flat of his hand over his wonderfully carved abs and reminding Kelsey how it had felt to touch them. "If we don't get there soon, I think my stomach is going to start eating itself."

"We don't want that, do we?" At her lead, they took off in the direction of the restaurant, their arms accidentally brushing against each other. Kelsey knew she should be hungry too, but the whirlwind of sensations in her stomach had nothing to do with hunger.

───※───

Kurt sat back in the booth and stretched. He'd have to give serious consideration before eating a single additional bite.

"That was pretty much an entire chicken you just ate," Kelsey said. "I thought you were messing with me when you ordered two entrées. I figured you were going to take one home."

Home. It'd been a figure of speech, he was sure, easier to say in conversation than *the Sabrina Raven estate*, but the word lingered, reverberating through his mind. Aloud, as he examined his plate, he rebutted, "I only doubled the chicken, not the sides. A breast, thigh, wing, and drummy didn't sound like enough." He pointed to his two untouched pieces. "And the second wing and drummy are still ripe for devouring, if you're hungry."

Kelsey shook her head, laughing, sending her thick, blond hair tumbling over her shoulders. "No, I feel like I won't be able to eat for a week as it is."

"Nice place," Kurt said. "You chose well." He looked around, once again taking in the impressive collection of chicken and rooster decorations covering every wall. *Vegans, beware*. He finished his beer and pulled his credit card from his wallet. When she popped off the back of her phone case to pull out a credit card, he added, "No, I've got this. You bought the pretzels earlier."

She looked about to protest, then shrugged it off. "Thanks. I'll get coffees on the walk home. My weight-lifting brothers would be curious to know how you stay so fit and eat like you do."

"If you want the truth, I don't pay much attention to it. I'll admit I worked out a lot in the service. It was a good way to release tension. Lately, I haven't had time to do anything aside from a couple dozen push-ups and a few rounds of pull-ups in the attic using the support beams. I feel better when I'm not lazing around."

"Of course," Kelsey said, giggling. "The man who never stops moving 'lazing around.' Now I have this image of the ceiling rafters giving way and you being trapped under a pile of rubble. When I have time, I'll swing by my parents' and see what weights I can find deserted in their basement. My brothers moved out over a decade ago, and my parents have long since claimed the right to donate whatever they didn't take to Goodwill. My mom just hasn't gotten around to it. You're welcome to come along and have a look. I'm sure my dad would love another chance to talk to you. He served in the National Guard to help pay for college. If my mom hadn't gotten pregnant with my brother Brian and they got married, I think he'd have ended up joining the marines when he finished."

"That's a nice offer. Thanks. Your parents are cool, by the way. And very supportive of you."

"I think they finally gave up hope I'd find a better job with benefits and whatnot. It took a few years, but they seem to get it now."

"I think it'd be impossible not to. It's easy to see how much you love your job. Which reminds me… I talked to Rob earlier, new cell phone and all," he added, winking at her. "Were you serious about that pit you saw when you toured the warehouse? The one with those facial injuries?"

Kelsey sat straighter, her face revealing her sudden rapt attention. "Please tell me he's doing okay."

"He's fine. He's healing well and has no sign of infection. Most of his wounds were superficial, though he's probably not going to be a pretty boy. Rob's happy to bring him over when he finds a spare minute. That is, if you haven't changed your mind. You're going to have your hands more than full in a few weeks when those Rott pups are born. Keep Devil in the mix, and things will start to look like a zoo, not a rehab."

"Are you kidding? Of course I want him." She closed her hand over Kurt's wrist automatically. "I keep dreaming about him. We're going to find him the best home in St. Louis. The absolute best, I tell you."

Experiencing her touch, hearing her words, Kurt remembered a snippet of a new dream. Unlike his typical dreams that took place in random homes or buildings that were quite different from anywhere he'd ever been, his dreams with Kelsey were in the house, the Sabrina Raven estate. The only differences were that there were far fewer dogs and the house and yard looked beautiful once again. Sabrina's old garden was overflowing and surrounded by flowers and buzzing bees. Ida was next door, but in the dream, she was blended into his memories of Nana.

These dreams were light and happy and created a fullness in his chest he wasn't sure he'd ever experienced in life. He'd never had dreams as powerful as these. This brought to mind Kelsey's comment about lingering spirits. He toyed with the thought half a minute, wondering if it could have anything to do with why he'd been so comfortable there from the start. If there were any spirits hanging around in the Sabrina Raven estate, he had no fear of them. He could almost swear the house had its own energy, and it was one he enjoyed.

"You okay?" Kelsey asked, pulling her hand away.

Kurt was struggling to find the right thing to say when the server walked up and took his card, promising to be back in a cluck.

"I think I'll take you up on that coffee" was all he said when they were alone again. After that, the conversation lost its easy, natural flow. He had a feeling Kelsey was wondering if she'd said something wrong.

As promised, the server was back in no time. Kurt tipped and signed, and they headed outside into the dark night. A few stars shone between patchy, rolling clouds.

"Holy crap, the temperature keeps dropping," Kelsey said, closing her arms over her chest. "Poor Pepper's going to be cold."

"When we get back, we can move her to one of the upstairs bedrooms."

"That would be good." She shuddered and drew closer to the brick wall they were passing as they started heading back.

"I'd offer you my jacket, but I don't have one. Would you like my shirt instead?"

"Thanks, but I don't think the world is ready for your pecs."

Kurt broke into a laugh. He wondered if she was doing it on purpose, keeping the mood so light and airy to stop his thoughts from straying back to his mother's predicament. The fact that Sara was only sixteen years older than he was and had breast cancer kept washing over him in waves. Even though he'd been unable to shake much of his long-held resentment in regards to her, he still loved her. He couldn't lose her in the wake of losing Nana so unexpectedly. Neither could William. It just couldn't happen. Hell, maybe this would be the scare that Sara needed to get her life together and stop chasing one loser after another.

This wasn't just Kurt's opinion of the guys she went for either. She was the first to say that if a guy had his crap together, there wasn't a thing about him she'd find attractive. That might have worked when she was a teenager, but sooner or later, she needed to face the fact that she was in her midforties and start living like she knew it.

That's what Nana would say, only in a softer tone.

Deep in thought, Kurt draped his arm around shivering Kelsey. She stiffened at the precise second he realized he'd done it. "Better than my exposed pecs," he said, which made her laugh and relax.

They fell into step, and it felt so damn right to have his arm around her, to experience her curvy hips brushing inches below his, to feel the cool air sneaking in from the hourglass of her figure where their sides weren't touching, to smell her citrus-mint body wash that made him want to stop and inhale. The wind picked up, sending her thick, silky hair blowing across his neck.

"It's this next street," she said, pointing. "If you're still in the mood for a good cup of coffee."

"I won't complain if it isn't good as long as it's strong."

"How about we make sure it's both?" In the west, there was the distinctive rumble of thunder. "Shoot, I guess the storm was predicted to come in waves, but the sky looked so clear to the west before we left. Here's hoping we make it home before the next round."

Home. Again, he thought of his dream. The air had been light and breezy, and the house had smelled like apple pie. Kelsey had wrapped her arms around him, and he'd closed one hand over the back of her hair. How could he have known it felt like this? Her hair kept blowing across his shoulder and brushing the skin of his neck.

They made it to the corner coffee shop with only a few more cracks of distant thunder and the wind picking up slightly. Loosening his hold on her was harder than he would have anticipated.

"What do you like?" she asked, eyeing the chalk menu over the bar.

You. "Just a large black coffee will be fine."

"Oh, come on, they have so many good drinks. While I'd bet my last dollar you aren't the pumpkin-spice type, that doesn't mean you wouldn't like the rosemary–brown sugar or a mocha or even a simple latte."

"Tell you what, I'll run to the bathroom while you order for me."

"Okay, but were you serious about the extra caffeine? Because I can have them do a double shot."

He raised an eyebrow. "Hit me, lady."

He headed for the bathroom and stopped in front of the sink. He was struck by the stranger facing him in the mirror, the one with the hint of a smile playing on his lips and the calm in his brown eyes. He might be a long way from not feeling the need to assess every crowd or jump to attention at every plate that crashed, but his tension fell away when he was with her. She'd felt so right against him that his muscles still felt like rubber bands. The implications sent his mind spinning. Should he risk it? Should he let her in?

No, idiot. Keep to the course you can handle.

For the first time in Kurt's life, he wondered if that little voice he'd attributed to keeping him safe and alive always knew the best decision.

—⁓—

By the time Kurt stepped back into the shop, Kelsey was picking up their coffees from the barista. A flash of lightning lit the western sky.

"Seems like we're going to get hit with another

round. Want to make a break for it? It's about a half a mile from here, isn't it?" he asked.

"Probably closer to three-quarters." She was still working to ignore the impression that his arm had left against her body. "Let's step outside and check it out. There are awning-covered shops for the next quarter mile. We could get closer at least."

"I hate to break it to you, but I don't think awnings offer much protection from lightning."

They stepped out into the dark, quiet street. On the way to the restaurant, the area had been bustling with people. Now, everyone seemed to have taken heed and headed home.

"So, may I ask what I'm about to have the pleasure of drinking?"

"Sure. I couldn't decide, so I asked the barista, and she thought it was best to go with a basic mocha with whipped cream. And honestly, I've never met anyone who doesn't enjoy a mocha. However, if you want, we can switch. I chose the rosemary–brown sugar tonight."

"And here I thought for sure you'd pick pumpkin spice for yourself. And this is good."

They walked in silence at a clipped pace. Kelsey missed his arm around her, but with the coffees and the speed they were walking, it wasn't warranted. They'd reached the end of the shop-lined street and were about to turn onto a residential one when a flash of lightning lit up the entire sky and thunder boomed all around. Before it quieted, large splashes of rain began to fall.

Kurt grabbed her hand and started to backtrack. "It's too close. That covered bus stop a hundred feet back is the safest thing around."

Kelsey nodded, needing no convincing after that flash. The individual splashes became a downpour twenty feet before they reached the bus stop. "Holy crap, this rain is so cold!"

She felt lost when they made it inside and he let go of her hand. The rain was coming in at an angle, so they huddled as close to the back wall as possible in the narrow space next to the bench.

Using his thumb, Kurt brushed a drop of water off her cheek. As much from his touch as from the run, Kelsey's heart pounded louder than the rain.

"Are you cold?"

She shook her head. "No, not anymore."

He was staring at her, not the rain. *Thunderstorms are on the top of his list. He should be watching the storm*, she thought.

How long had it been since he'd been with someone? she wondered. He might have been on active duty, but that didn't mean he hadn't had opportunities. But he didn't seem like the type to get laid just to get laid.

Her mind was racing. She needed to focus, but he was staring at her as though he couldn't see anything else. *Say something, Kelsey.* "Want to try mine? It's not quite as sweet." *Seriously? That was the best you could do?*

"Yes." He sat his cup on the bench and reached for hers. Their fingers brushed, and a jolt of electricity raced up her arm.

She blinked in confusion as he set her cup next to his. When he turned toward her, his gaze was on her lips. He slipped one hand into her hair, gently cupping the back of her head above her neck. With his other hand, he traced her lips. She wanted to keep her eyes open, to know when the kiss was coming, but they closed involuntarily as his fingers moved lower, tracing her neck and sternum. Her lips must have parted because she felt his thumb return to her mouth, brushing over her lips and connecting with her teeth.

Then he shifted and his lips pressed against hers softly, as if seeking permission. She opened her mouth in reply, and the kiss intensified. It was like nothing she'd ever felt, the sweetness of his mouth against hers. His lips were firm, and he tasted so damn good. His hand left her neck and slipped underneath her sweater, caressing the skin at the small of her back.

Kelsey's knees were turning to jelly. She draped her arms over his shoulders, lost her fingers in his hair. *Please don't ever let him stop.* The kiss deepened, and his tongue met hers. Their bodies pulled together like magnets.

She was getting lost even further when he pulled away abruptly, stepping back just far enough to break the magnetic connection. "You're wrong," he said, his voice thick and husky. "It's the sweetest thing I've ever tasted."

Then he started kissing her again, and Kelsey was fairly certain nothing would ever be the same.

Chapter 15

SPOTTING MEGAN'S ENCLAVE IN THE SHELTER PARKING LOT at seven o'clock the next morning brought the same sweet relief as when Kelsey had painstakingly finished the 5K run she'd signed up for on a whim last year. Better yet, the lot was otherwise empty. No one else was here. She couldn't think of a time when she'd needed her friend's advice more than at this moment.

Unlike on the last several days, Kelsey turned off the ignition rather than letting her bright-yellow Corolla idle while she zoomed inside to put away whichever dog she'd brought home. She stepped out and stretched her exhausted and overworked body, then popped open the back door to let Millie, a senior golden retriever and last night's companion, clamber out.

After giving Millie a quick potty break, Kelsey headed inside to find Megan sitting crisscross on the floor in the front room in a patch of sun. Chance, the shelter's resident blind Cairn terrier, was snuggled on her lap. He looked as content as could be, curled around Megan's swollen belly, his head and hind legs draping off onto the floor.

"I was wondering if you'd been by already," Megan said. "Seems like you've been keeping longer and longer hours the last couple days."

Chance lifted his head off Megan's lap, sniffed the air a second or two, gave a quick wag of his tail, then dropped back into cuddle mode. Chance might be blind, but he knew the staff by scent and sound. Normally, he was quick to greet Kelsey at the door, but Megan's undivided attention had proved too much of a distraction.

"I won't argue that, which probably explains why it feels more like a month than a week since I've worked a full day here."

Megan's smile was sympathetic. "Are you in a big hurry, or do you have a few minutes?"

"I've got some time," Kelsey said, thinking of all the things she hadn't shared during her and Megan's short phone calls the last few days. And then there was last night. Just skimming the surface of all that had happened a mere few hours ago would take more time than she could afford to be away from the Sabrina Raven estate. "Let me get Millie put away, and I'll be right back." Kelsey picked up on the wonderful aroma of freshly brewed coffee halfway to the kennel doors. "Thank God you started the coffee. I didn't take the time at home. I'll grab a cup and be back in a sec, and I'm guessing you don't want one?"

"No thanks. I've had my morning herbal tea," Megan said. "Quitting caffeine wasn't as hard as I feared it might be, though if I wasn't brewing up a baby, I doubt that would be true."

"Better you than me," Kelsey joked as she headed into the back with Millie. She got the sweet-tempered golden set up in her run, remembering to put in her favorite chew toy, a worn stuffed animal monkey, then made a quick stop in the break room for a steaming mug of coffee.

It had been well after two in the morning the last

time her sleepless self had looked at the clock before finally dozing off. No wonder she'd slept through her five-thirty alarm this morning.

She returned to the main room, sipping her coffee. "I meant to ask… With the expansion that's planned, will there be room for a sofa or two? Because if that's the case, I may never leave."

Megan hadn't moved from her spot on the floor against the wall. She smiled. "A sofa would be much nicer than those plastic chairs up front and much softer than this floor. But you're right… We'd never go home. So, how's 'the op' going?" she asked, making air quotes and referring to Kelsey's comment yesterday afternoon about Kurt's pragmatic solder-like views on the rehab.

"Oh, where to begin," Kelsey said. She sank to the floor and scooted back to lean against the nearest adoption desk. "We haven't had a floor date in eons." Katrina, their resident three-legged cat, spotted Kelsey's open lap and hopped down off the counter in front of the cat kennels where she'd been napping. After a quick stretch, Katrina claimed Kelsey's lap and started to purr even before Kelsey began scratching next to her cheek. *Plenty of cats like me fine*, Kelsey thought, thinking of Mr. Longtail. "Remember that night we sat out here till midnight playing and cuddling with that abandoned litter of Saint Bernard puppies?"

"I was thinking of that the other day. They've got to be close to three years old now. We still get Christmas cards from some of their owners."

"I remember reading some last year. Hey, did I tell you that Pepper's definitely pregnant? She's due in three or four weeks, Kurt's guessing. Right around the time of your reception."

"*Aww*. I don't think there's anything cuter than Rottweiler puppies with their portly little bodies and big heads."

"I know. I can't wait."

"Hey, you bringing up the reception reminds me… Did you find a dress? I'm still happy to go shopping with you, if you'd like."

"If you've got the time, that'd be great. My mom wants to go with me, but I don't have to tell you how we'll never agree. She won't like anything that isn't extravagant or full of sequins, and I won't like anything that is. Thanks for inviting my parents, by the way. I've been meaning to tell you they got the invitation. That was nice."

"Of course. I love your parents. And while your mom is awesome, I agree you probably shouldn't go dress shopping together, unless it's for a dress for her. A love of frills that runs that deep almost certainly has to skip a generation."

Kelsey giggled. "I still can't believe you're getting married in two weeks."

"Why ever not?" Megan smirked, patting her growing belly. "Because I only met my fiancé eight months ago? Or because I'm headed to the altar a solid six-months pregnant?"

Megan and Craig would be flying to a private island off the Georgia coast for their nuptials. Craig's two kids—both of whom had spent enough time at the shelter that Kelsey felt confident saying they were truly spectacular kids—would be going with them. Megan's mom, stepdad, and two younger half siblings would be there as well. Afterward, Megan and Craig were staying behind for a few days' private honeymoon. Then, a day or two after the newlyweds returned home, there was going to be a large reception about an hour away in the Missouri wine country. They'd rented out a winery for the event and a few dozen rooms in a nearby inn for guests who wanted to stay overnight.

Before the rehab at the Sabrina Raven estate was even a thought in the wind, Kelsey had decided she'd like to stay overnight, thinking it would be a fun break. Now, she was wondering how she'd find the time to get away at all. She also thought of how she'd RSVP'd that she wouldn't be bringing a guest. But now, after last night, she couldn't help but wonder if maybe she should be bringing a date. But she hadn't even known Kurt a week. Trying to imagine how their relationship might progress over the next several weeks was like trying to envision the true vastness of the oceans from the mere glimpses she'd had while standing on the beach.

"Funny, but none of the above," she said in answer to Megan's playful question. "It's because eight months and one day ago, your life was one way and now it's totally another, and it still suits you perfectly. Like a fairy tale almost. And look at all the good things that have happened since you two met. And it's not just you and Craig and his family. The shelter's undergone a complete turnaround because of you two."

Megan gave a humble shrug as she scratched Chance's belly. One of his back legs thumped the air rhythmically, matching the beat of her scratches. "I'm very blessed. I'll give you that. If you want to know the truth, I was sitting here taking it all in. The baby did this whopping somersault when Chance barked as I walked in, like he or she knows how much I love this place. That's what I was doing when you pulled up, sitting here with Chance being thankful."

"And that's why you deserve every good thing that's happening to you."

"It's going to happen to you too, you know."

Kelsey wasn't positive her face flushed until Megan called her out on it.

"Kels, I can't believe I missed it, but something's up, isn't it? Because all of a sudden you look like Chance when he's eaten something he wasn't supposed to but isn't sure that we know yet."

Kelsey giggled. "It's that obvious, huh?"

"Totally. Was it Kurt? What am saying? It *has* to be Kurt. I saw those looks you were giving each other the day when the dogs arrived. And I've been on the other end of our phone conversations lately."

Kelsey curled forward into a ball, pressing her forehead against the top of Katrina's head. The curious cat twisted in her lap and started to lick Kelsey's temple.

"I *really* like him, Megan," she said, sitting upright again. "He's so good with the dogs. And he's sweet. He's got the worst ADHD I've ever seen. Unless he's focused on the dogs, which he's incredible with, he pops around the house doing chores like a Ping-Pong ball. And he's a really good person. He was raised by his grandparents. His mom was only sixteen when he was born, and he never even met his dad. And he's seriously a dog whisperer, if I didn't mention that already."

Megan nodded slowly. "I can see why you'd be

attracted to those qualities. The only thing you forgot was that he's so hot, he's smoking."

Kelsey dragged her hands through her hair. "I'd like to say you get used to it, but I haven't yet. I swear, it's like my pulse is racing all day, and half the time I'm salivating. I'm not even kidding."

"So, have you told him how you feel, or are you keeping all this to yourself?"

"What would I tell him?"

"A few of those things you just told me might be a good way to break the ice."

"I think it's already broken. I took him on a walking tour of South City last night. We got stuck out in a thunderstorm, and we ended up making out in a bus stop shelter."

Megan pressed the flat of her hand against the floor. "Stop! You're kidding! Why didn't you break down the door starting with *that*?"

Kelsey shook her head, exasperated. "I was working up to it. Megan, what am I supposed to *do*? We work together. It's going to be weird."

"Weird? It's going to be sexy as hell for you; that's what it's going to be."

"I don't know that though. Something could go wrong. A lot could go wrong. And then I'd still be stuck in the middle of a rehab with him."

Megan lifted Chance off her lap and got up to join Kelsey. She sank beside her on the floor against the adoption desk, more awkwardly than normal because of her belly. "Kels, listen to me. You're the best person I've ever seen when it comes to working with people. You have an easy confidence and kindness that pours off you. There's no reason in the world that confidence shouldn't extend into your relationships."

"That's different though."

"Does it have to be?"

Kelsey chewed her lip, which was chapped from all of last night's kissing. "What if everything goes wrong?"

"Are you hearing yourself, Kels? You're the queen of positivity. Do yourself a favor, and let that positivity extend into your love life. You deserve it. What if everything goes *right*?"

Closing her eyes, Kelsey let her friend's words sink in. Megan was right. Kelsey had worked hard to always see things in a positive light. She'd simply have to find a way to put aside her fear and doubt. "It'd be easier if he wasn't so cute," she said, voicing her fears. "If he was just average."

"It might be easier, but would it be as fun? And give a pregnant lady a break, will you? The suspense is wearing on me. Details, please. Lots of them. Including how you guys left things."

"You don't even want to know," Kelsey said, rolling her eyes. "It was like a dream at first. Better than a dream. It was like a fantasy. It was just us and the night and a storm and a bus stop shelter. It went on, like, forever. My lips are actually raw. But kissing him was the best thing I've ever experienced. Absolutely, hands down, the *best*. He's an amazing kisser, and he was knee-bucklingly seductive without being too handsy for a first kiss. Or at least a first series of kisses. But then this loud honking brought us back to reality. Awkwardly back to reality."

"How so?"

"It was the MetroBus driver. It had practically stopped raining and the bus had pulled up, and all of a sudden we were being honked at. The driver wanted to know if we were 'getting on or getting off,' and it was so embarrassing. There weren't that many people riding, but the ones who saw us applauded."

Megan covered her mouth to stifle a laugh. "That's not so bad, Kels. Look at the bright side. You've got one hell of a first-kiss story."

"Maybe so, but wait till you hear what happened next. That was enough to stop the kissing, but we held hands the rest of the way back, and we laughed about how the driver had looked at us like we belonged in jail. But as we got closer to the house, all these thoughts kept racing through my head like 'Do I sleep with him?' and 'If I do, will the same thing happen that happened with Steve?' and stuff like that. It was so stressful. I didn't know what to do."

Megan nodded slowly. "And? What'd you decide?"

"Nothing. Everything fell apart from there. When we got back, the house had been vandalized. I know it was one of the protesters. It had to be. A brick had been thrown through the lower-right front window. There was a message tied to it, and the wording was too close to what they'd said that day we talked for it not to be them."

"Those wicked people. What'd it say?"

"'Creatures of the devil won't find their heaven on earth. Euthanize now before it's too late.'"

Megan gasped. "That's horrible. That's worse than horrible. There's an implied threat."

"I know. We called the police. Thankfully, Kurt had written down all the protesters' license plates and the makes and models of their cars. Since it was only one window, I'm not sure how actively the police will pursue it. Yesterday, when the protesters didn't show up, we thought maybe they were giving up. Now I think they're just ready to play dirty. After putting a brick through the window, I doubt they'll show up to protest today."

Megan pressed her lips together. "Yeah, about that. You sounded like you were dealing with enough yesterday when you called. I didn't want to add more stress. They didn't show up there because they came here."

"Oh shit."

Megan nodded. "I know, Kels. It sucks, but they stayed next to the road. The police drove by several times. And the people who know us are really showing their support. It's going to be okay."

Kelsey let out a sigh like a deflating balloon. "I hope so. At least now I'm too worried about what kind of stink the protesters are going to cause here to worry about it being awkward around Kurt. Speaking of which, I'd better get going. He really needs me there to help with the feeding routine." She gently scooted Katrina off her lap and stood up, then extended a hand for Megan. "We're starting to work volunteers into the schedule so we'll be able to give all the dogs a bit more time, which they desperately need. There are so many dogs you're going to love when you get to know them, Megan."

"I already do, from all the stories you've told."

"Did I tell you I'm bringing Orzo today? A few of the dogs seem ready for phase two of 'the op,'" Kelsey said, making air quotes.

Megan gave Kelsey a tight hug. "I love you, girl. And I know I've told you, but you're rocking this. And as far as Kurt goes, my advice is to give it one day at a time. Eventually you'll know if he's worth the awesome love you have to offer."

Kelsey rolled her eyes playfully. "I'm not sure if it's hormones from that baby in your belly or what, but I swear you're starting to sound like Oprah. But thanks. And as for the protesters, have you tried unleashing Patrick on them? Once he starts relaying stats, they won't even know what hit them."

Megan laughed. "Patrick. Of course. Why didn't I think of that?"

<hr/>

By the time Kurt spotted Kelsey's bright-yellow Corolla pulling into the circular drive at eight o'clock, he was starting to feel a touch foggy-headed from lack of sleep. From his unbelievable experience with Kelsey to coming home to the threat and damage from the protesters, he'd been completely wired last night. He'd only managed to doze a couple hours before abandoning the idea of sleep entirely around four thirty, and that wouldn't be enough to keep him going all day.

His early morning had been worth it though. He'd extracted the broken window and was the first patron through Home Depot's doors at six that morning. He'd purchased five motion-sensor floodlights and a temporary single-hung window, as well as a few No Trespassing signs. He was wrapping up the installation of the floodlights when he spotted Kelsey's car. He'd put four of the lights around the house and one on the garage.

Ida had walked over a little after seven with a fresh, wrapped-in-wax-paper bacon-and-egg sandwich that had tasted almost as good as Kelsey's kiss. Ida had hung around for twenty minutes or so and watched Kurt work before heading home. She'd seen the police car on a trip to the bathroom last night and had been concerned. The kind old woman was troubled not to have witnessed the act of vandalism herself. She'd heard an unusually loud and quick eruption of barking as she was drifting to sleep just before nine. Kurt suspected it had happened then. But both his and Kelsey's cars had been in the drive. How had the vandals known no one was here? Or had they not cared? Likely the power had still been out, and they'd assumed no one was inside.

Kurt gathered the empty cardboard packaging and dumped it into the outside recycling bin as Kelsey parked and turned off the ignition. He headed over to meet her, wondering if it would make things easier between them to kiss her as soon as she stepped from the car. It might, he thought, but it would also make it harder to focus on the dogs, and there were thirty-seven of them waiting inside, needing his and Kelsey's undivided attention.

"Hey," she said, glancing down before making eye contact.

The reason that she was quick to look past him to the house was nerves, he realized.

"Those floodlights are new, aren't they? I've never been able to get the exterior lights to work. It's always been pitch-black out here after dark."

He gave a one-shouldered shrug. He still had the floodlights in the on position, and even in daylight, they were bright. "I just finished installing new ones. Cross your fingers they don't overload that iffy circuit panel. So long as they don't, I'm betting they're effective. I texted Jim, your volunteer electrician, about coming out to have a look. He's going to stop by later this afternoon. And Patrick texted. He's coming out earlier today to work with Devil. He should be here by the time we're done feeding. Or, as he put it, about ten minutes to ten."

Kelsey grinned. "He's a prompt one, our Patrick. And that's awesome about the lights. But did you sleep at all?" Her delicate eyebrows knotted into peaks as she studied him, apparently past her earlier wave of shyness. "You're getting dark circles under your eyes."

"I'll catch up tonight. Promise."

"I hope so."

She bit on the corner of her lip, calling his attention straight to her mouth. She didn't seem to have a clue that she stirred him to life like a pharaoh that had been disentombed after a millennium of stillness. Or, for that matter, that by now there was hardly a surface of the house, porch, or yard where he hadn't at least briefly imagined their bodies joining together.

Last night, she'd fit against him so perfectly. Her mouth was supple and yielding. Her skin, at the least the small bit he'd experienced, was like silk, and her curves churned what had previously been smoldering desire into an inferno.

"You slept on that worn-out couch in the front parlor, didn't you? I'm betting you didn't even take your shoes off."

He smiled. "There's something to be said for being ready."

Kelsey let out a soft sigh. "I found out the reason they weren't here yesterday was because they were protesting in front of the shelter."

"If they show up there today, then at least I won't have to waste any time looking for them," Kurt said, cocking an eyebrow.

"You and me both. Megan and I talked about sending Patrick out to them. No one can outtalk Patrick. He's got a photographic memory."

"He can talk all he wants. As for me, there's a lot I'd like to do, but talking's not high on my list."

Kelsey pursed her lips, clearly not liking his comment. He suspected she was debating whether to call him on it. Behind her, through the open car door, there was an almost inaudible whine. "Oh, I almost forgot. I brought Orzo."

"Thanks," Kurt said, switching to a lighter topic, "but I'm not really the pasta-for-breakfast type. And Ida was kind enough to bring over a sandwich about an hour ago."

"Ha. That was sweet of her." She glanced toward Ida's house. "I really need to move it higher on my to-do list to bake her something in return." She shut the driver's-side door and opened the back passenger door. "And I know you know I was talking about our little corgi. Kurt, meet Orzo. I don't allow myself to pick favorites, but if I did, it might be him."

Kurt sank to a squat and let the brown-and-white corgi sniff his hand. He noticed that the dog's tail was relaxed, not curled down around his haunches or forced upward on display. Orzo wagged it a few times before facing the house and sniffing the air.

Inside, not surprisingly, the house was starting to smell like dog, and Kurt had all the windows wide open. "What's his story? Seems like he should be adoptable."

"He is. Very. Like all our dogs really. He's a special case though. His old owner operated a struggling bakery. When it started going under, she stopped buying dog food and fed him bakery leftovers. The woman's mother finally brought him to us. Orzo came in so overweight he could barely walk. He had high blood pressure and was on the verge of being diabetic. But he was a rock star when it came to getting healthy. After six months of exercise and a healthy diet, he was cleared for adoption. That was a month ago. He's had a few people show interest, but most folks are wary because, even with the weight loss, his sugar levels are a little off. He was almost adopted once, but that's a story for another day."

Kurt gave the puppy-faced corgi a gentle rub on the back of the neck. "The world is full of stories, isn't it?"

"It is," Kelsey agreed, "but I'm a firm believer that most of them are happy, or at least they wind up that way."

Kurt stood and smiled, resisting the urge to pull her in for a deep kiss. How was it that in the few short hours of sleep he'd had, he'd dreamed about her again? They'd been inside the house, in a warm, sunny room upstairs. The room had a fresh, bright coat of paint, and they were lounging in a wide, comfortable bed. They'd been talking, and their fingers were entwined. The almost-constant ache he carried in his groin around her had fallen dormant. Instead, his chest was bursting with a sense of connection that didn't come from sex, or at least not from sex with just anyone.

In real life, he'd never felt that connection with anyone, though last night he'd felt a brush or two of it

with her. He'd had buddies and even dogs in his care
that he would have laid down his life for, but he'd never
been in love. Being the son of Sara and who knows who
else, he wondered if that gene might be missing in his
DNA. But he was also a descendant of his grandparents.
They'd spent their lives loving each other, despite differences in culture and family traditions and religious
beliefs. His grandmother was a devout Catholic. His
grandfather was an atheist. Yet, even in their subtle,
understated way, their love for each other had been
immense. Why should it surprise him that some innate
part of him seemed to want to make this old mansion his
home and Kelsey his wife?

He'd only met her a week ago, and the old house
belonged to the shelter. And inside, it was full of dogs
who needed breakfast and a break from their kennels,
and then some serious one-on-one training.

Thankfully, foggy-headed as he was, not only was
there still a half a pot of coffee warming in the kitchen,
but he could count on the occasional brushes of fingertips or elbows with Kelsey to keep him stimulated.
"Speaking of happy stories, we should get to work
ensuring that a few more end up that way."

———◆———

"We've got to get this on video," Kelsey said later that
afternoon, reaching into her pocket for her phone as
Zeus dipped into a play bow next to Orzo. "Patrick,
you don't by any chance have the shelter's DSLR in
one of those pants pockets, do you?" Then, seeing that
he was taking her literally by the way he cocked his
head in contemplation—probably wondering how she

could be insensible enough to think the bulky camera could fit into one of the pockets in his cargo pants—she added, "Kidding."

Both dogs were on leashes—Zeus with Kurt and Orzo with Patrick—and had spent the last fifteen minutes walking around the front and side yards together. Now, they were hanging out by the side of the house under the massive oak trees whose leaves were turning yellow and orange.

Kurt had remained cautious, even though from the start it seemed as if Zeus was nothing but happy to have Orzo's company. Kurt kept Zeus engaged by issuing commands and rewarding him with gentle pats, praise, and a couple treats here and there. When asked to do a command, Zeus seemed to forget the presence of the calm corgi merely feet away. He sat at attention, lay down, and heeled according to Kurt's instructions.

Finally, Kurt gave the Argentine mastiff free rein the length of the leash. And the only thing Zeus seemed interested to do with it was play. When his play bow wasn't enticing enough to draw Orzo in, he wagged his tail and barked, then spun in a tight circle and dropped into another play bow. Picking up on his energy, the corgi wagged his tail and barked in return.

Kelsey, the only one of the three observers not holding a leash, had just pressed Play on her phone when Zeus rolled onto his back and Orzo stepped in close to lick his cheek. Suddenly, Zeus was on his feet and moving in a blur. Kelsey flinched before realizing the two dogs were full-scale playing. A grin broke out across her face as she recorded them dropping into play bows respectively and circling around one another in a crazy, wild dance. Zeus was easily four times Orzo's size, but he didn't seem to know it. He rolled onto his back a second time, wriggling his big, white body. Orzo came up next to him, not quite tall enough to see over Zeus's barrel chest, barking and wagging his tail. The little corgi even turned around to expose his back, a sign of play and relaxed submission.

The romping went on for several minutes, with Zeus twice getting excited enough to jump up on Kurt to try to lick his face. The giant dog was big enough to reach it too. Even excited as he was, Zeus heard and listened to Kurt's command of "Down." Unfazed, the Argentine mastiff dropped back to all fours and then went back to playing with Orzo.

Finally exhausted, the two dogs stood side by side, mouths agape, looking as if they were wearing big grins as they panted. After a few seconds, Orzo plopped to the ground and collapsed onto his side, tongue lolling, resembling the pasta he'd been named after. Zeus leaned over to lick the side of Orzo's face before sinking to the ground to rest as well.

After zooming in, one at a time, for a close-up of each of their contented faces, Kelsey finished recording. She fisted the sleeve of Patrick's polo in disbelief. "Patrick, if this is half as good as I think it is, you *have* to get this on Facebook today."

A few years ago, Patrick had taken over management of the shelter's social media accounts. At first, it had seemed like a strange turn of events, considering Patrick's difficulty discerning emotions, but his posts were well edited and spot-on, and he always ran the more emotional posts by Megan or Kelsey first. Once

they added the adjectives and adverbs that made the
story shine, he saw to the ins and outs of posting at
the right time and ensuring the right followers saw and
reposted the content.

Over the last few years, their social media following had increased tenfold. Kelsey was willing to bet this
large Facebook following had helped Channel 3 choose
to focus on the High Grove Animal Shelter over other
area shelters six months ago for the weekly pet adoption
stories the station had decided to produce.

"I suspect it'll be as good as you're hoping," Patrick
replied. "That was something. I agree with you, Kurt.
It's unlikely Zeus spent any time in a fighting ring."

Kurt nodded. "He's going to have an easier path
than most of the other dogs we've taken in, that's for
certain. There are a few others inside who could end
up in the same comfortable place with other dogs, but
time will tell."

Kelsey understood that most of these dogs would only
be placed in single-dog homes. Significant ring time had
left many of the dogs inhabiting Sabrina Raven's home
with as many emotional scars as physical ones. From
here on out, they'd live quiet lives, and their new owners
would need to agree to keep them out of dog parks and
heavy crowds. But at least they'd be placed in loving
homes. They'd get to experience what every dog should.

Her real hope was that the dogs would turn out to be
more resilient and trusting than anyone expected. She
liked to imagine every one of them not only learning
to trust people again, but also learning to trust other
dogs too.

Kurt and Patrick had Zeus and Orzo on their feet,

and the group was heading around to the front of the house when Kelsey spotted a plain, white van pulling into the driveway.

"Looks like Rob's on time," Kurt said. "Patrick, let's get these guys put away so as not to cause any more stress for our new arrival than necessary."

Kelsey's heart thumped in her chest. In all her years working with dogs, she'd never been as moved by one as she'd been by the resilient pit bull. "Patrick, here," she said, passing him her phone before he headed inside. She didn't want to get distracted and forget to give it to him later. "Take my phone with you when you head back to the shelter, please, so you don't lose any quality in transfer. I'll pick it up tonight when I drop Orzo off."

Patrick slipped her phone into one of his deep pockets and buttoned it closed before leading Orzo inside to the deluxe travel crate where the ready-for-a-nap corgi was spending his downtime today.

Kelsey headed for the driveway where Rob was stepping from the van.

"How you holding up, young lady?" He walked toward her, hand extended, and ended up pulling her in for a hug. "I sure do appreciate all the work you've taken on here. You're making a difference, that's for sure."

"It's been an honor to be part of this. And I'm learning a lot too."

"I expect you will. Hell, I expect my old mentee could teach me a thing or two anymore. He's a regular old dog whisperer, his buddies tell me."

"I won't argue with you there. It's something to watch him work." Kelsey followed Rob toward the back of the van. He opened the double doors and stepped back. She was surprised to find close to fifteen crates, each with a dog inside. "Where are the other ones going?"

"Couple hours away. A little rehab place outside Jeff City."

"That's great. I'm so glad you're placing so many dogs."

"We've been lucky."

"Kurt said the pit bull is doing pretty good," Kelsey said as Rob zeroed in on the nearest crate.

"Frankie? He's something, I tell you. A survivor. And a character at that. He really likes his tennis balls, so I've got a couple up front to give you. And before I forget, his stitches come out this week. His vet's information is up front too."

"Okay. Sure. And it's Frankie? Was that his name?"

"It is now, unless you can think of a better one. The boys named him. We never found out jack about him. The asshole that was fighting him so hard probably never bothered to name him. He had four dead dogs dumped out behind the shed where Frankie was kept. There were two others in crates still alive. One made it and went to a woman I know over in Illinois. The other pit was humanely euthanized."

Kelsey felt her eyes tear up. How could someone be so heartless? No, *soulless*. "Can I see him?" she asked, blinking back tears.

"Sure thing. For all he's been through, he's been a love sponge around people, which makes me think he wasn't living in the place where he was confiscated for long."

"Let's hope not."

Rather than asking her to help lower the crate as

Kelsey expected, Rob pinched the door lock open and took his time clipping a leash onto Frankie's collar. Kelsey's emotions were stirred up from Rob's words, so the tears stayed close to the surface as she watched the beautiful silver-blue pit bull emerge from the crate. The remarkable dog stopped calmly at the edge of the van floor, looking around the yard and blinking his eyes in the bright sun.

In the scheme of things, it hadn't been that long since Kelsey had laid eyes upon him. The swelling on the left side of his face had gone down considerably, though with his stitches, his expression still looked stuck in a wink and a half smile.

Kelsey let out something that was between a laugh and sob. "He's beautiful."

"Blue-nose pits are quite beautiful, if you ask me." Rob patted Frankie confidently atop his shoulder blades. Then, to Kelsey's surprise, he wrapped his arms around the dog and lifted him carefully down to the ground. "Don't want him tearing any stitches trying to jump."

Kelsey fished through her pockets and was happy to find a few leftover treats. She sank into a squat and let Frankie approach her. Keeping the treats back for a moment—knowing Kurt wouldn't approve of her offering a treat at the front end of a greeting—she let Frankie sniff her empty right hand. His eyes were the same silver blue as his coat and as clear, bright, and intelligent as those of any dog she'd ever met.

After a few quick sniffs, he turned his attention to her other hand, the one hiding the treats. His ears perked forward, but he waited patiently. She brought her left hand forward and let him swipe the treats off her palm.

He crunched them in a few chomps, then began to lick her palm contentedly.

"I know a love connection when I see one," Rob said, passing her the leash. "Other than keeping him clean and dry while he heals, you won't have any problems with him. So long as you keep him out of direct contact with other dogs until he's had considerable retraining. Maybe forever."

Kelsey nodded. "I understand." She pressed one hand against Frankie's chest and scratched him gently with the tips of her fingers. "From here on out, Frankie, you get a total redo. It's only the best for you, promise. Cozy beds, great foods, and people who love you. And how about homemade popsicles on Sundays? Beef, chicken, peanut butter, or pineapple—your choice. And I can tell you right now, that sweet face of yours is making it onto next year's calendar. Everywhere you turn, you're going to get nothing but love."

Finally, Kelsey stood up. "Kurt and I set up one of the upstairs bedrooms for him," she told Rob. "So long as he doesn't mind stairs, he won't have to be crated in the same room as other dogs. Once he settles in and is used to being here, we're going to try offering him free roam of the room too. We started the same thing with Pepper, the Rottweiler, today. I'm sure you remember her. She'll be next door to him. She's had free roam of her room since midmorning but still went into her kennel to nap. Otherwise, she's either been watching out the window or sitting behind the stair gate that's blocking off the room. She seems to enjoy being around people."

"You might be surprised how many of them do.

Often in cases like this, it's as if they don't connect the job they're given with the person who cares for them."

Kelsey was opening her mouth to reply when she realized they were no longer alone. Kurt and Patrick were back. She'd been so focused on Frankie that she hadn't heard them approach. Kurt was watching her intently, and Patrick was fastening the buttons of his side pants pocket.

"Afternoon," Kurt said, nodding at Rob. "That pit's looking better already. Looks like the vet really had skills."

Yesterday afternoon, Kurt had told Kelsey that Rob had shown him the "before" pictures that would be used in court. They were something she knew she was better off never seeing.

"Afternoon, son," Rob said cheerfully. He pulled his phone from his pocket and glanced at the screen. "I'm doing okay on time if you'd like to show me how some of these guys are progressing."

"Yeah, of course." Kurt glanced at Kelsey, motioning toward Frankie. "You okay walking him around the yard a bit? Patrick, you'll stay with her?"

Patrick glanced at his watch. "Yes. I have twenty-four minutes before I need to leave."

Kelsey pressed her lips together as Rob's eyes widened slightly in surprise. Clearly, he was trying to decide if Patrick was joking, even though his expression was serious.

"Perfect," Kurt said as if that was just the answer he was looking for.

Chapter 16

THERE WAS NO WAY AROUND IT. EACH DAY OF THE REHAB wound up seeming more like a week than a single day.

Kelsey fell into step behind Patrick as she walked him out for the night, a part of her wishing she could crawl into the passenger side of his old Tacoma and have him drive her home to her apartment—no, to her parents' house and her old room and bed that were still the same as when she moved out six years ago. To shed life's responsibilities and sleep in as late as her exhausted body craved.

Patrick scooped Orzo into his arms as they reached the truck. He'd come back out after leaving the shelter when it closed for the evening and spent an hour walking Devil around the front yard, allowing him to scent mark as he pleased.

The big giant was continually finding new ways to challenge them. This morning, Kurt had asked Patrick to take the lead in the dog's retraining. If Devil was ever going to be adoptable, Kurt had admitted, he was going to need a lot more one-on-one attention that Kurt was going to be able to give him. Although Patrick was hit or miss when it came to understanding the social cues of people, he was a genius at reading animals. Even not knowing him long, Kurt seemed to have picked up on this.

"Thanks again for your help. I know you're putting in

your regular hours at the shelter too. Kurt's not much of a talker, but I know he's impressed with how well you do with Devil." Kelsey gave Orzo, who looked quite content in Patrick's arms, a scratch on the forehead.

"I think that he wants to communicate."

"Kurt?"

"Devil."

"How so?"

"Whenever he lunges at the kennels or snarls at the dogs passing by him, he's quick to look me or Kurt in the eye. It's the same way when he looks down the road."

"Do you know what he's trying to tell you?"

"I will soon. He's a complicated animal. Not like Orzo, who just wants to sniff and eat and get petted."

Kelsey nodded. "I won't argue with you there. Let me know if I can help. I swear, there's always so much to do here. I think Kurt feels pulled in every direction."

Jim, the volunteer electrician, had been at the house for several hours too, working on the circuit panel. He had left for the evening after relaying that, while the Sabrina Raven estate needed a considerable amount of electrical rewiring, his patchwork would hopefully be a stent to keep the op running smoothly.

"You've made a lot of progress already," Patrick said.

Kelsey squeezed his elbow. "You're the best, Patrick."

He made a face like he didn't know how to respond, then muttered good night. He loaded Orzo into the backseat of the cab and took off after rolling down his window and offering a wave.

With hardly the energy to move, Kelsey watched him drive off, noticing exhaustion in atypical places like her joints and her belly. Finally, she headed back in. After quietly shutting the front door—the dogs had settled down, and most were dozing—she paused in place, wondering where Kurt had gone.

Butterflies fluttered in her chest, reviving her better than caffeine. It had been such a busy day that there'd been no time to wonder if the way they'd so easily gotten down to business this morning meant last night would become nothing more than a fantastic memory, or if it might happen again. She'd also not had time to gawk at Kurt's amazing lips or daydream about running her hand once more over his smooth skin and precision-toned core.

If she had a hope basket, she'd stick all her eggs in it, hoping she'd be lucky enough to experience him more than once. But starting something up again tonight wouldn't be the smartest decision. She wasn't the only one who was wearing out. Kurt was—finally—showing signs of fatigue. He'd yawned several times during the nightly feeding and once while intently focused on a training session with Lucky, the nine-year-old Doberman. For his fatigue to show during training, Kurt had to be tired. Hopefully, the floodlights he'd installed would enable him to relax and fall into a deep sleep tonight.

Kelsey headed toward the back of the house where she'd last seen him. She found him at the kitchen table. The ceiling light was off, and the last of the fading daylight was coming in through the south window. Mr. Longtail was sitting on the table in front of Kurt, lapping up milk from a half-empty glass. Kurt was bent over, staring down at his lap, ignoring the cat.

After twisting sideways for a closer look, Kelsey

realized he was asleep. His eyes were closed, and his breath was even and slow. Her chest swelled with new emotion. It was the first time she'd seen him look vulnerable. She wanted to pull him against her and run her fingers through his hair. She wanted to tuck him into bed and crawl in beside him and hold him while they drifted off to sleep—even if it meant sleeping in one of those questionable old beds.

And she never wanted to leave.

As she had with Steve, Kelsey wondered about the difference between a crush or fling—whatever this might turn out to be—and the real thing. She'd known Steve a year and a half, and her pulse had never quickened around him like she was a driver on an Indianapolis Motor Speedway.

Her feelings for Steve had been akin to fitting a questionable piece into a complicated puzzle. The piece seemed to fit, the edges locking together almost seamlessly, but sometimes you didn't know for sure until you assembled more of the puzzle. She'd thought she loved Steve. Before "I just didn't feel it," imagining a life with him had seemed so natural. They liked the same movies. They were always laughing at something. They loved animals, had been brought up similarly, and had similar career goals.

It wasn't the same with Kurt. Aside from his love of dogs, he was really nothing like her. Kurt was serious and intense and quiet and an ex-soldier, raised on a military post, with no clue who his father was and a unique mother who could've stepped straight out of a movie. It would be impossible to connect the dots from Kurt's dramatic life to her ordinary, suburban, plain-as-toast upbringing, her over-the-top brothers, and her ordinary but loving parents.

But no matter what their differences were, her feelings for Kurt were clearly "yes, please" and "a bit more, please" and "maybe another spoonful" too.

With all these thoughts rolling around in her head, Kelsey had no idea what to do next. Maybe it would be best to jot a note, sneak out, and deal with everything tomorrow. Maybe a good night's sleep would help her see things in a clearer light.

Wondering where she might find a notepad, she tiptoed to the table and, as soundlessly as possible, extracted the glass from underneath Mr. Longtail's draping whiskers. A supply of milk that size and adult cats didn't mix.

Then, as sudden as last night's lightning flashes, Kurt was bolting to his feet and slamming her backward against the wall. The back of her head and shoulders smacked against it as his forearm smashed into her collarbone. He pressed against her, larger size and superior strength immediately subduing her. For a split second, Kelsey could swear she grasped how it felt to be a deer facing a set of barreling headlights.

"Shit!" Letting her go almost as quickly as he'd grabbed her, Kurt stepped back, dragging his hands through his hair. "Kelsey, I'm sorry. I thought… I don't know what I thought. Did I hurt you?"

Her head was ringing, her adrenaline was racing, and everything seemed to be stuck in slow motion. Kurt's voice carried a touch of grogginess and fear that belied the aggression he'd just exhibited.

He reached across the doorway and flipped on the

light. The sky-blue cabinets, matching appliances, and yellow countertops gleamed fluorescent.

Kelsey shook her head, trying to clear it. "*Ow.*"

"Shit. I'm sorry," he repeated. "It was stupid to doze off like that." He opened the freezer and pulled out a frozen-solid package of peas. "Let's get you to the couch and get some ice on that head of yours."

Despite the ringing in her ears, Kelsey could hear the drips from the spilt milk hitting the floor. Mr. Longtail was now in the far counter, watching them with a look of immense dissatisfaction. Kurt's chair was turned over too. She hadn't heard it fall, but then, she'd been busy being shoved against a wall.

Reality was sinking in as she gingerly fingered the knot forming at the back of her head. She looked from the rock-hard package of peas to the troubled expression on Kurt's face.

There was another difference between them she'd not been thinking about. She hadn't spent the better part of the last eight years in one war zone or another.

He kept hearing it over and over, the *thunk* of Kelsey's head slamming into the wall. He'd hurt her. He hadn't meant to—hell, he'd move mountains to keep her safe—but he'd hurt her all the same.

He'd been sitting at the table, fighting off a wave of exhaustion so deep he'd barely been able to keep his eyes open. Clearly, he dozed off in spite of trying to fight off the urge, because the dream he'd been having while in the light sleep had been too easily confused with reality. If he could separate himself from the awful dreams—dreams of trying helplessly to assist a buddy or one of the dogs in his care who'd been unexpectedly hit by a blast from an IED—if he could stop having these dreams, maybe he'd start believing in miracles.

But that seemed like an impossibility.

It was in that uneasy doze that he'd reacted to Kelsey hovering over him before he could process what he was doing. And even in the darkened kitchen, he'd caught that look of fear and pain in her eyes as he'd jolted fully awake and realized what he'd done.

"Can you stop pacing and come sit by me, please?" Kelsey was curled into the corner of the couch, the bag of peas pressed against her head.

"You could have a concussion," Kurt repeated. "I think we should get you to an urgent care center to be sure."

"I don't have a concussion. I have a contusion. Here, feel." She reached for his hand as he obliged her request and sank beside her on the couch.

"It feels like a damn egg," he said. Her touch was more comforting than he expected. And the sensation of his hand in her hair was more than inviting; it was disarming. So was being so close to her remarkable lips again. "I'm sorry."

Sorry. What a weak, ridiculous word. *Sorry* never altered the past, no matter how far away or close by that past was.

Kelsey shrugged, a smile playing on her face. "You can stop saying you're sorry. Twenty times was enough. It hardly hurts anymore, and I should have known better than to sneak up on a sleeping ex-marine. But I *will* let you clean up the mess in the kitchen later. I think it goes back to my childhood and my rowdy brothers, but there's something about wiping up spilt milk that makes me want to hurl. And if I ever get a whiff of really sour milk, it's hurl city, just so you know."

Somehow, their fingers stayed entwined. Kurt began to stroke her palm with his thumb, and the smile she'd tacked on faltered. What had happened a few minutes ago had shaken her up more than she wanted to let on. That much was obvious.

All day, he'd been fighting the urge to take her in his arms and kiss her. Now he realized what an idiot he was. How could he think about drawing someone as wonderful as Kelsey into a relationship when he was part Jekyll and part Hyde? What did he think he was going to do… make crazy love to her, then send her packing before he fell asleep, just in case? How could he expect her to be okay with that? And what could happen if she was, and they tried it anyway?

"I guess now is good a time as any to bring up last night." Her tone was soft, unaccusing.

"Because you have a clearer idea of what you'd be getting yourself into?" He dropped her hand and started pacing again.

"Because I like you," she said, dropping the package of peas on the side table and tucking her hands under her thighs. "But like most things that are worthwhile, a relationship—if that's what this could be—seems complicated in the middle of what is probably that most important thing I've ever done. It is, you know, this thing we're doing with the dogs. And I don't know if what we have is a crush or something that could be real, but I don't want to mess anything up. On top of all that, not only are you really good looking, but you're amazing with the dogs, so it's quite possible I'm not thinking clearly to start with." She stopped and bit her lip. After a few seconds of silence, she shrugged her shoulders. "I'm ranting, aren't I? It's not like me to be this open, so maybe I'm still in a bit of shock, but I want you to know that all this, you included, is important me. When it's over, I don't want any regrets."

Kurt pressed his eyes closed a second and let out a slow breath. Couldn't she be coy and skirt the truth and make it easier to shut her out? Hell, he wouldn't be nearly as attracted to her if she could.

He sat beside her a second time and pulled her in for a soft kiss before either of them had time to think about it. But the thing about her lips was that a quick taste would never be enough. The kiss deepened and a flame of want ripped through him, sending a surge of fresh energy into his tired limbs. He pulled away long enough to offer a husky "No regrets." Rather than reconnecting with her lips, he found her neck and lost all thought.

He was damn close to climbing on top of her when several dogs jumped up in their crates and started to bark simultaneously. Abandoning the couch, Kurt headed for the nearest front window, being sure to keep to the side and out of view. Kelsey followed close behind him. Outside, an owl hooted loudly, and several of the dogs barked again. From where he stood, the yard looked dark and empty.

"Think it was the owl?" Kelsey asked after the dogs quieted down and nothing else happened.

"Possibly."

After another half minute of silence passed, he

headed for the front porch. The late-September night was cool, and an easy breeze flitted over his skin as he crossed over to the top stair. The neighborhood seemed calm and benign. From so far away that it was barely audible, he heard a car alarm going off. Maybe that had been what stirred up the dogs, not the owl. Over at Ida's, a few lamps lit the lower floor. Across the street in the rehab, one upstairs bedroom light was on. No cars were parked out front, and Kurt wondered if the construction crew had left the light on accidentally.

"I'm worried that you won't let yourself get any sleep tonight, and you *really* need it. Should I stay? We can take turns keeping watch, if that would help."

Tugging her by her closest belt loop, Kurt drew her in for another long kiss. "If you stay, neither of us will get any sleep." His blood pulsed so hot through his veins that it seemed to have an acidic tinge. "And after what happened in the kitchen, I think we both know you joining me in a bed could be a bad idea. For a while, at least." His words had an unexpected ring of permanency, and he didn't attempt to pull them back.

"Then what happens now?"

"You go home and get some sleep. Tomorrow morning, after we're finished feeding, we'll head over to the shelter together. I'd like to have a look at the stock so we can decide who to bring next. I need someone a little more imposing to really test Zeus."

Her eyebrows rose at the word *stock*, and he wasn't surprised at the exclamation that followed. "You're still pretty fresh out of a long string of soldiering, so I'll forgive that impersonal term you used to refer to some of the sweetest dogs in the world, and I'll agree. But I meant between us." She pressed her lips together. Her amber eyes were sincere and locked on his.

He traced his thumb over her lower lip, then down her neck, and finally down the length of her sternum. "I like you, and you like me. And we're going to take this one day at time. Yesterday, I learned that you have hands down the best lips of anyone I've ever met. Tonight, we learned that as much as I'd like to be, I can't be trusted in my sleep. Not now. Probably not for a while."

Kelsey traced the tip of one finger along the line of his jaw, making him hungry for her all over again. "I know you well enough to know you aren't going to believe me when I tell you that what happened in the kitchen is never going to happen again. Call it intuition if you want, but sometimes I just know these things. And one of these days that we're about to take one at a time, you're going to trust me on this."

"My grandmother was a strong believer in intuition. My grandfather always scoffed until he was proved wrong, so I'll refrain from comment."

"Good." She sucked in her cheek a second. "So, uh, I know we just talked about taking it a day at a time, but I was wondering if you'd like to go to Megan's reception with me. It's in three weeks. She's probably my closest friend, and I'd really like to bring you with me."

"I'd be honored," he said, running his hand down the length of her arm and feeling the goose bumps that rose as a result, "as long as the only dancing we do is in a slow circle. Otherwise, I'd probably do more damage to your feet than I did to the back of your head."

She smiled. "I'm good with that. And thanks. You

gave me the dress-shopping motivation I needed." She rose up and brushed her lips against his. "I should go. Promise me you'll try to get some sleep."

He gave her the promise she requested and went back in the house with her while she gathered her stuff. When they were back at her car, he savored another kiss and allowed himself to explore her phenomenal body until she started to moan and he was on the verge of exploding on the spot. Then he pulled away and closed his hands over her shoulders.

He might not have known her long, but he felt the permanency with which she'd entered his life with the deepest of certainties. He'd thought he was coming home to head west to lose himself in hard labor and wilderness. But here he was, falling in love with a girl and a house and a city and thirty-seven—no, thirty-eight—dogs all at once.

Rushing the next step would belie that permanency. He made a commitment then and there not to take her into his bed until he was certain he could not only fall asleep beside her, but also tell her this complicated truth without fear.

"Kels," he said, using the nickname he'd enjoyed hearing her friends use. "Good night. I'm looking forward to tomorrow."

A wide smile spread across her face. "Me too. In the meantime, sweet dreams."

He gave her a wink as she slipped into the driver's seat and tugged on her seat belt. "After what I did in the kitchen, you may not believe me, but I'm not lying when I tell you I've had some of the sweetest in my life after starting this with you."

"After having a few of my own, I'm inclined to believe you."

He watched her drive off, then headed toward the house, almost swearing he could hear one of Nana's favorite tunes carried on the rustling night breeze.

Chapter 17

IT WAS SUNNY, BRIGHT, AND PREDICTED TO BE A PERFECT late-September Sunday. Kelsey wasn't surprised to find the streets of Webster Groves bustling with activity as she and Kurt neared the shelter. He'd driven the Mustang, commenting that he'd had more opportunities to get behind the wheel in the service than he had in the last week.

He paused on the street outside the shelter parking lot, waiting to make a left turn into it. The shelter wasn't far from the town center, close to dozens of houses with perfectly manicured lawns, but also within walking distance of a number of shops, restaurants, and a park. It wasn't uncommon, especially on nice, weekend days, for the tree-lined street out front to be lined with cars.

But this morning, that area was an unparalleled bustle of commotion. People were everywhere. Wondering if a Webster Groves fall event had missed her radar, Kelsey took in the crowds while Kurt waited for a young couple to cross the street so he could pull into the nearly full parking lot.

Kelsey gripped the door handle as she looked around. They couldn't all be protesters, could they? She'd texted Megan earlier, asking if they'd shown up today, and Megan had replied that they had, but not to worry. Everything was under control.

Kelsey scanned the individual groups of people until

she spotted the core group who'd protested in front of the Sabrina Raven estate for a few days. They were here, and their group had multiplied. Kelsey estimated there were close to thirty now. With their camping chairs and rolling coolers, they were making themselves at home on the sidewalk under the tall trees. At least they seemed to be keeping off shelter property.

However, this didn't explain the bustle of commotion flowing out from the shelter. Two parking spaces immediately outside the main doors had been roped off, and people Kelsey had never seen before were covering a U-shaped row of folding tables with purple tablecloths. Another man was dumping a giant bag of charcoal into a portable grill.

"Looks like someone's having a party," Kurt said, pulling in and parking in an empty spot at the back of the lot.

"I saw Megan yesterday morning. She didn't say anything about this."

"From the looks of it, it's coming together as we speak." As they got out of the car, Kurt motioned toward two teen girls. They were huddled on the walkway near the main doors, making posters with poster board and marker. Ten feet away, a woman was dumping bags of ice into two large coolers. Two preteen boys were attempting to tie purple and green balloons to the concrete dog statue that stood alongside the big pots near the entryway. They didn't seem to be making much progress because they kept pausing to bonk each other on the head.

"It's like parade day," Kelsey said, shaking her head. "But that's in April."

Bypassing the strangers, Kelsey hurried inside,

determined to go directly to the source. Megan was behind the counter talking to Patrick and dabbing at her nose with a Kleenex.

"Please tell me that's a happy sniffle, not a sad one."

"I think it's best to show you." Megan looked pointedly at Patrick. "Patrick, you're at the helm."

Kelsey noticed the two had been looking at the iPad on the counter below them.

"Email, Facebook, or PayPal?" Patrick asked as Kurt and Kelsey joined them at the counter.

"Whichever you'd like," Megan said, heading around the counter to wrap Kelsey in a hug. "Girl, you aren't going to believe this."

She's smiling. Thank the Lord. It's good news. Those are happy tears. Kelsey bit into her lower lip to keep from spouting a million questions as Patrick turned the iPad their direction after pulling up Facebook.

"We've had over twenty-eight thousand likes since last night. You've really moved people, Kelsey," Megan said.

Kelsey grabbed Kurt's arm in excitement, pulling him in for a better look. That many likes in one night beat the old record exponentially. "You mean the clip with Zeus and Orzo? That's incredible! We're going to get adoption applications for those two boys ten times over."

"Probably," Patrick said, "but they've only had a few thousand likes, and they're riding the wave that this clip is generating."

Patrick hit Play and opened the video clip into full screen. Kelsey was surprised to be staring at herself. The video footage had been taken yesterday afternoon. She was squatting in front of Frankie, swiping tears off her cheeks as Frankie licked one palm. Then the clip switched to her swearing to Frankie that life for him was going to be really good from here on out. Patrick had been recording when she hadn't even realized he was there. He'd had the foresight to zoom in on Frankie's sweet face as Kelsey made those declarations. Frankie was staring straight at her and his mouth was open in a light pant, but with his stitches, he seemed to be grinning a lopsided grin.

Even in a state of mild shock—she'd never been a fan of seeing or hearing herself on video—Kelsey could tell the clip was immensely touching. Frankie was the star, and he'd be the one people would really notice.

The clip was simple and quick, only about forty-five seconds long. When it finished, Kelsey glanced at the number of likes. Megan was right. Just over twenty-eight thousand. Her heart fluttered. "How many online adoption forms have we gotten for him?"

"Almost seventy-five, the last we counted," Megan said, squeezing her arm.

Kurt closed his hand over her elbow. "Way to go, Kelsey. I knew it was going to be good, but I wouldn't have predicted it'd take off like that."

"It's our most powerful post yet. Patrick, click over to PayPal, will you?" Megan said. "We've not transferred anything yet, because it keeps growing so fast."

"What keeps growing? Donations?"

"Look here," Patrick said, as he switched screens and logged into the shelter's PayPal account. "We hit nineteen thousand dollars, and it's not even ten o'clock."

Kelsey's knees felt weak. "So all those people in the parking lot? It's because of this?"

Megan grinned. "Yes. The protesters arrived in

bigger numbers this morning too, but they've been quieted by this enormous show of support. We've had so many calls that I can't even keep the groups straight anymore. It's a Kiwanis club that's out front setting up for an afternoon barbecue, and a librarians' group is preparing a bake sale. Can you believe it? Oh, and Channel 3 called. They'd like to do a follow-up interview whenever you guys feel ready."

"I really can't swallow it all," Kelsey said. "It's awesome."

A bustle of commotion erupted in front of the building, catching everyone's attention. Beside her, Kurt visibly tensed as a high-pitched scream carried through the glass. The small group made for the front window, Kurt taking the lead.

Kelsey watched two teen girls jump up and down and clap their hands as they squealed. The preteen boy beside them was frozen in place, staring toward the parking lot, his mouth agape.

Kelsey followed their stares. A glistening red Dodge Ram was idling in front of the tables. The driver's-side door was open, and a man had stepped out. He was in jeans and a fitted white T-shirt, wearing a Red Birds cap. His grin was all charm, and he was shaking his head as he talked.

Kelsey had seen him before, countless times; she was just having trouble placing him. She stared hard, willing herself to remember. Something was off, and she couldn't place it. He was tall, fit, and classically all-American. Poster-worthy almost.

And nearly everyone in the parking lot was gawking in his direction.

That was when it hit. She looked to Patrick for confirmation. Patrick couldn't *not* know. His love of baseball nearly surpassed his love of the shelter. In the fall, like now, when it was nearing playoff season and the entire city population seemed clothed in red, she suspected sometimes it did.

Patrick's mouth had fallen open wide enough to catch flies.

"What am I missing?" Megan asked, clearly not having figured out that Mason Redding was standing in the parking lot of the High Grove Animal Shelter. "Why is everyone staring at that guy like he just stepped off the moon? Or at least out of a boy band."

"Tell her, Patrick," Kelsey managed to squeak. Knowing Patrick, he probably had a Mason Redding trading card in one of the pockets of his cargo pants.

"There's a game starting in three hours and fifteen minutes" was all that he managed.

"Oh shit," Kurt said. "Is that Mason Redding?"

Megan had enough time to suck in a breath as the Red Birds player who might possibly be in the running for MVP this year waved off the crowd and headed toward the door. And though they were no more than six feet away, not one of their group moved to welcome him in.

Mason Redding pulled the door open, and the bell jangled loudly in the suddenly silent room. "Hey there, folks. I'm, uh, looking to make a donation. The kids outside said to ask for Megan."

"I'm...I'm Megan," Megan said, stepping forward and shaking his hand. "And that would be wonderful."

He grinned a grin that Kelsey was willing to bet had its own insurance policy, like the legs of supermodels.

"I keep hearing bits and pieces about what your shelter's doing to help those dogs. It was absolutely the right thing to do." Suddenly, his gaze landed on Kelsey, and he pointed confidently her direction. "And you're the girl from the video I saw last night. I want you to know, your promise to that pit was pretty damn touching. I woke up thinking about it, and before I knew it, I was headed to a pet store. I wasn't sure what all you guys could use, so I threw in a little bit of everything."

Mason Redding had seen her on Facebook. And he'd been moved to make a donation. "Thanks," Kelsey managed, feeling her cheeks flame fire-hot. It seemed not everyone was only watching Frankie. "He's a great dog. Even sweeter in person."

"That's really thoughtful of you," Megan added. "We've been blessed with an outpouring of support from the community. Did you need help carrying everything in? And would you like a donation receipt?"

"Not for the toys and stuff, but if you don't mind, I'll take one for this." He pulled a check from his wallet and passed it Megan's way. "But if you give it to me now, I can tell you I'm going to lose it. If you can mail it to the address listed, I'd appreciate it."

"Of course." Megan took the check and stared at it a beat too long. "Oh wow. That's awesome. Thank you. Absolutely."

"My cell number is on top if you have any questions. I'd stick around to see some of the dogs you've got here, but I'm running late for the stadium as it is."

"Of course. This is awesome. Thank you so much."

Kelsey—who was standing next to Megan and had seen the figure on the check—offered her thanks as well.

Mason Redding was giving the High Grove Animal Shelter forty thousand dollars. Out of nowhere.

Kurt, who seemed the most unfazed by a famous St. Louis baseball player's sudden appearance, followed him toward the door.

"Can we post this?" Patrick asked. "Not the amount; that would violate privacy rules. Just that you donated."

Mason shrugged. "Certainly, as long as you say it's a personal one."

"Then I should take a picture," Patrick said, pulling his phone from a pants pocket.

In a blur of commotion, Kelsey found herself, Megan, and Kurt being filed against the south wall under the newly painted shelter logo for a picture with Mason Redding. When she ended up flanked by Kurt and Mason, with Megan on Mason's other side, she leaned close to Kurt and whispered, "When this over, I'm definitely going to let you pinch me."

Chapter 18

TIME AND AGAIN, THERE WERE TWO ASPECTS OF IDA'S LIFE that her acquaintances found peculiar. The first was her Camaro. She didn't blame them on that one. Not many women her age would still get behind the wheel of a Camaro Z28. She knew her reaction times weren't what they used to be, though in no terms did she consider herself a danger to anyone. She planned her errands at times of low traffic when navigating the busy city streets was easier. But getting behind the wheel and flipping on the engine gave her a rush that was unlike anything else she experienced in daily life, so she wasn't about to give it up. And she was okay that her 2002 Camaro wasn't as reliable as it once had been. She didn't intend to replace it. If it conked out before she did, she intended to look into that Uber thing people kept talking about.

She'd bought the car a few years after moving to St. Louis in memory of her late husband. He'd been driving a 1967 model when he picked her up for their first date. The purchase had been her way of saying that she wasn't settling into a quiet widowhood like everyone expected. Perhaps after living quietly through her youth while her sister lived loudly, it was also a form of self-expression Ida finally needed.

The second thing Ida's acquaintances were most apt to comment on was her love of a porterhouse steak. An eighty-one-year-old woman and porterhouses didn't go together, she'd been told. And even if she wouldn't admit it aloud, the mouthwatering steaks hadn't been easy on her stomach for over a decade. Knowing how they messed up her system for a few days after eating one, she only gave in to the craving once or twice a year. And to stave off some of their effects, she'd stick to oatmeal for breakfast and a brothy soup for dinner a few days before and after.

But today, a quiet Thursday afternoon framed by newly turning yellow, red, and gold leaves and a crisp, cool breeze that carried the promise of the changing season, she found herself with a craving for red meat that only a good porterhouse would cure. And since steaks were best with company, she drove by her sister's old place before heading to the grocery store to invite the busy young couple to dinner.

It gave her a chuckle to see the way Kurt cocked his head at the sight of her shiny black Camaro idling in the driveway when he answered the door. To his credit, he didn't comment aloud. And like the gentleman she suspected he was, after politely accepting, he asked what they might bring.

"Your time and company is all I'll ask for," Ida had said.

From there, she'd headed to the butcher shop that Sabrina's late husband, Jeremy, had claimed carried the best meat in St. Louis. After choosing three steaks that were each big enough to quell the appetite of a hungry grown man, she headed for the Soulard Farmers Market. There, she strolled through the open, high-roofed brick building for fresh salad fixings. Before she knew it, her basket was heavy with a head of iceberg, endive, watercress, and a few sprigs of dill, as well as a fresh cucumber, radishes, and cherry tomatoes. She also chose three baking potatoes that were handsome enough not to be undone by a porterhouse.

In those first months after her sister's death, she couldn't recall having tasted a single thing. Now, her mouth watered at the sights and smells of the bustling old market that was as much a tourist destination as it was a staple for those who lived near enough. She released a happy sigh as she headed back to the Camaro. How nice it would be to enjoy a good meal and charming company!

As she headed home, the purr of the Camaro's engine was so strong that she felt it vibrating through her thin fingers and down past her hands, all the way to her elbows. Sixteen years ago, when she'd bought the car, she hadn't needed to sit on a pillow seat to see over the hood.

Ida remembered being young and proud and hoping the frailty that came with a long-lived life would somehow not find her when old age did. How silly she'd been not to realize it was all part of a beautiful circle.

She'd been considering it for a while, but she knew the time had come to put the house on the market and head home to Connecticut where her children were waiting. Her sister was gone, and there was nothing but memories holding her here.

And she was almost ready to announce this decision to her family. Her sons had been in their twenties when their father died and she'd left to join her sister here in St. Louis. Her older boy had been living in South America, teaching English at a Brazilian elementary school. Her younger son had been in LA. She hadn't expected them to return home when they started families of their own years later. But they had. They'd been hoping she'd come back ever since, though it was something they'd never pushed for before Sabrina passed.

Ida had held off on announcing her intention to return to her childhood home and her family, knowing when she did, her kids would be anxious for her to start the process. But doing that would be leaving behind Sabrina. And before she was ready for that, she wanted to make sure the cogs her sister had set in motion would continue turning.

Though Ida had first been skeptical, she saw how right her sister's decision to leave her house to the shelter had been. During the long months it had sat abandoned with no life but Mr. Longtail and the mice he neglected to hunt, she'd had her worries.

But now she fell asleep lulled by the happy energy radiating out of it once again. Not only was her sister's beloved house essential in healing those dogs, but something very important in the lives of two humans seemed to be happening as well.

Ida was hoping that after dinner tonight, she'd be more certain of this.

───※───

If Kelsey kept a bucket list of the zillion things she wanted to do during her life, canning fresh fruits and veggies would've been on it. The urge to try canning stemmed from trips she could hardly remember to her great-grandparents' house. She'd only been five when they died, months apart, so her memories were sporadic. But one of them involved her great-grandmother's garden and the canning she did in late summer. The small farmhouse counter had been lined with glass jars, and a large pot had been simmering long enough to steam up the small kitchen window over the sink.

Kelsey couldn't remember what her great-grandmother had been canning at the time. From what her father had told her, she'd canned a bit of everything. Perhaps because her great-grandparents' quiet farmhouse life had been so different from her jam-packed suburban one, Kelsey had wanted to try canning ever since she could remember.

Now that she was knee-deep in a rescue op gone viral, Kelsey wasn't sure today had been the best time to experiment. But the refrigerator full of pears from Sabrina Raven's private orchard had been tempting her for the last week, and Ida's dinner invitation was the call to action she needed.

After finishing a few essential chores by late morning, she'd headed to the store for the supplies and returned with the hope of having the beautiful, fair-trade African basket she'd purchased filled with freshly canned jars of pears for Ida tonight.

After peeling four dozen pears and discarding seven or eight of them because they'd begun to rot on the inside, Kelsey had the rest sliced and simmering in the spiced sugar water.

She was scooping the discarded peelings from the sink into a paper shopping bag when Kurt came into the kitchen. He and his grandfather and Jim, the shelter's volunteer electrician, had spent the last few hours working on the roof of the carriage house, patching a large hole and strengthening a few support beams.

His grandfather had been a frequent presence in the house the last week, and the old mansion was getting a face-lift as a result. Kurt's grandfather and mother had rented a small, furnished apartment near Siteman Cancer Center for the course of her treatment. It was twenty minutes away, and when his grandfather wasn't with her, he was here, working on the house. While Kelsey couldn't exactly say she'd gotten to know him— he didn't stop working until he needed to leave—she understood where Kurt got his ceaseless work ethic.

Sara's surgery, a lumpectomy, had been outpatient. From what Kurt shared, she was recovering quickly. Her radiation was expected to start in the middle of next week.

After wiping his shoes on the rug—it had rained last night—Kurt joined her at the sink. His hand closed over the small of her back as he eyed the dozen jars drying on the counter and the steamy window next to the stove. "Hey, sweets. What're you doing?"

Kelsey felt a rush of pleasure at the small but intimate show of affection. This last week, there'd been little time for anything between them beyond a few quick and delicious make-out sessions. This was partially because their days were filled with nonstop work, and partially because the house had become a bustling hub for various volunteer projects—the canine ones led by Kurt, and the maintenance ones by William Crawford—and they'd had very little privacy.

While Kurt had said he intended to take it slow after what had happened, Kelsey's confidence sometimes wavered about this being the reason he walked her to her car every night after everyone was gone and the work was done, rather than up to his room. It had helped when last weekend, after he'd walked her to her car and they'd shared a heated kiss, he'd mumbled something about two more weeks. Two weeks that coincided perfectly with Megan's wedding reception. Maybe Kelsey wasn't the only one who was hopeful it might be the landmark night it had the potential to be. She'd told Kurt about the room she'd accepted at the bed-and-breakfast, and he'd insisted she keep it, promising he'd get Rob to fill in for him here.

"I'm finally canning those pears so I can bring a few jars to Ida tonight," she replied. "Only watch your step. I made quite the mess. I was ladling out some of the syrup because the pot was so full, and I spilled some. The floor's still sticky in front of the stove. I'll mop when I'm done." She opened the handles of the paper bag she'd filled with pear rinds and held it out to show him. "I don't really know anything about composting, but I thought I'd put these out behind that garden you're trying to revive."

His gaze flicked from the sagging-it-was-so-full bag to her happy grin before his toasty-warm brown eyes locked on hers.

Kelsey's phone timer chirped from the back pocket of her pants, alerting her that the pears should be finished boiling. There was something about Kurt's reaction, however, that momentarily froze her in place. The lightness in his stance had disappeared, and his smile had all but vanished.

"Did I say something wrong?"

He shook his head. "No, you never do." He slipped the bulky bag from her fingers and set it on the counter.

She knew he was going to kiss her before one of his hands closed behind her neck and he pulled her in to him. It was a zero-to-sixty kiss, not sweet, not slow, not timid. She was pressed against the sink as his body ground against her.

She didn't know what had caused Kurt's sudden intensity, but her body responded instinctively. Her blood heated as the ache of desire flamed hot and fresh. It was a hungrier kiss than any she'd experienced.

Piece by piece, the world fell away. The quietly bubbling pot. The sporadic hammer hits coming from the carriage house. The ceaseless grooming and shuffling sounds the dogs made as they rested in their kennels. It was just her and him and a humming in her ears.

He pulled away and pressed the palm of her hand against his mouth, then his lips and tongue trailed down her wrist until her damp shirtsleeve impeded him. "You taste like sugar."

"It's the sugar water," she managed to say. "The pears are done, by the way. I need to turn them off."

Kurt whirled the dial, and the soft gas flame disappeared. Then his lips were on hers and his hands were loosening the top button on her jeans and sliding them a few inches down her hips. She racked her brain, trying to remember which pair of underwear she'd pulled on this morning. She hoped it was something sexy but suspected she'd gone with comfort instead.

His touch superheated the space between her legs. She felt like a rocket readying for lift off. It became a war of hands, the victor the one to find the most soothing flesh first. His smooth skin and toned core were silk against her fingers, but she was still the first to relent. It was too much to explore and receive at the same time.

His hand moving against her was the single best thing she'd experienced. She tilted her head back and gripped the counter. Her mouth fell open, and she tried not to lose herself in the moans threatening to break out of her throat. Not only would sounds like the ones she wanted to make set the dogs to barking, but the windows were wide open and who knew how far those moans might carry.

He curled close, pressing his forehead against her neck as he matched his breath to hers and continued those perfect strokes. She floated between conscious thought and pleasure so intense it was without form. She'd never climaxed in the presence of a guy. Not with Steve, the only guy she'd gone all the way with. And not with the ones of lesser importance whose names currently escaped her.

Though it hadn't been for lack of trying.

If she'd had the presence of mind to debate the possibility of doing so in a kitchen in a house filled with kenneled dogs and a pesky cat who was suddenly and persistently rubbing against their calves, her boyfriend's grandfather and a shelter volunteer not quite a hundred feet away, and a heck of a lot of open windows, she'd have bet against the possibility.

Kurt sensed it was going to happen a second before she did. His free hand pulled her face against his chest, muffling the gasps that escaped with her NASA-worthy liftoff. He didn't stop his perfect exploration until the swell of pleasure peaked and finally receded.

Kelsey was left numb and shaky, but the blood

returned to her head faster than she would have predicted. At some point, she'd let go of the counter and was grasping him around the neck. Her heart was beating like she'd run a mile, although this had been anything but dreadful. Mr. Longtail had abandoned the floor and was on the kitchen table, grooming himself.

Something between a laugh and a gasp escaped. "I've never done that before." She was breathless and stunned and spent a split second debating whether she should clarify the statement before deciding not to.

It was an open-ended declaration, and she didn't necessarily want Kurt to know how little experience she'd had. It would be surrendering a vulnerable part of herself, and she wasn't ready to do that. Not until she was sure he wouldn't pull a Steve. She wasn't looking for a proposal, but she didn't intend to give her heart away again unless she knew she wouldn't be rejected.

Kurt pressed his lips against hers, drawing the kiss out as he buttoned her jeans. Things were beginning to intensify once again when Jim called Kurt's name, the sound traveling clearly through the open windows.

They pulled apart, and Kurt let out a sigh. He tucked a lock of her hair behind her ear and leaned close to whisper as a pair of feet could be heard bounding up the back porch steps. "It's probably a good thing that we're never alone, because I wouldn't get any work done. Especially now that I've gotten a real taste of you."

Chapter 19

KURT WATCHED THE TAILLIGHTS OF KELSEY'S COROLLA until they disappeared in the darkness. The two of them had managed to find a spot behind one of the trees where they could stand without setting off the floodlights while saying good night after their evening at Ida's. Knowing he'd trigger the lights and disturb the calm hush that had settled over the yard when he headed back toward the house, he stood in the quiet a while longer.

The great horned owl that hunted in the area was across the street in a tall pine. Its low hoots punctuated the crisp night, along with the sporadic chirps of a handful of crickets. It was forecast to be the coldest night yet as fall finally crept into the area. The dropping temps made Kurt contemplate closing the windows, even though he was always in favor of fresh air. However, with all the body heat around them and the brick insulation of the house, the dogs wouldn't get cold.

In the darkness, Kurt studied the big, quiet house. Like the rustling leaves and the late-summer insects, the Sabrina Raven estate seemed to pulse a beat of its own into the night. For 114 years, it had stood watch over this quiet end of the street. The house might be up there in age and in need of some TLC, but it could shine again.

How he'd become so certain that this would happen under his watch, he didn't know, but he felt that certainty deep in his bones.

He thought of the look of surprise that had come over Kelsey earlier tonight. It had been after a second glass of wine when he'd declared his intention to buy the house when it went up for sale. She'd looked at him as if he'd said he intended to purchase Cape Horn. He couldn't blame her. Just a little over two weeks ago, she'd heard him declare to Rob that nothing could keep him from heading west. She'd likely been assuming he still intended to head that way when the rehab was over.

But like Nana had told him, when you got caught with your foot in your mouth, the best thing to do was take it out.

This house was meant for him. Or he was meant for it. He wasn't entirely certain which was which. He wasn't sure how, but he'd get the money. His credit was good, and he had solid savings and even a decent amount in investments from the money he'd earned the last eight years. He was confident he'd be able to get a loan when the time came.

It was the same way he felt about Kelsey. One way or another, they were supposed to be together. Every sorrow, every loss, every moment of bliss… They'd all been little moments leading him to her. He'd known it before now, had felt the truth of it in both waking and sleeping hours.

Then he'd walked into the kitchen this afternoon and Kelsey'd given him that happy grin and she'd been so at home in the house. Making him think his dreams might very well be becoming hers.

And then there'd been the feel of her. Half the evening had passed before his blood finally stopped boiling hot. He'd never get enough of her. He wanted her more than he'd ever wanted anything, but he also wanted her to be the last woman he brought into his bed. How could he start that without trusting himself to fall asleep beside her?

The last few years, he'd been wondering if he had it in him to fall in love the way his grandparents had. He'd been content being single. He could manage himself and his ADHD very well. Bringing Kelsey into his life the way he wanted to might cause complications, but he was confident they were complications worth experiencing. She'd also bring joy he'd scarcely believed he was capable of having.

When he'd appreciated the quiet yard long enough, Kurt headed into the house. Ida's incredible meal sat heavy in his stomach, as did his two glasses of Syrah. He was drowsy and content and deeply tempted to head upstairs to bed rather than collapse on the couch where he'd be quicker to react if anyone considered vandalizing the property again.

He did a check of the rooms, offering bathroom breaks to a few of the younger, more fidgety dogs, like Zeus. Aside from Devil, the older dogs were napping or gnawing on antlers or tennis balls, and a few were grooming themselves. Devil was five or six, and considering the shorter life spans of two of the breeds that likely helped contribute to his DNA—mastiffs and Danes—he was entering his senior years, even if he didn't look the part. He'd been gnawing at the doors of his crate but stopped when Kurt entered the room. Now he was on his haunches, staring at Kurt with rapt attention, while tossing intermittent glances toward the front of the house.

"I'm getting the whole discontentment part, but what are you trying to tell me, guy? There's not one of you who wants to be here, and maybe you don't know it yet, but it's a hefty step up from where you were." Kurt knelt to inspect the kennel as Devil released something between a sigh and a growl.

"You're going to rip out your teeth gnawing at these bars." Just two weeks into the rehab, and it was Devil's second kennel. The first one had only lasted three days. He'd gotten out of it right at dawn, as Kurt was waking up. He'd heard the giant paws scratching against wood and had rushed downstairs to find Devil trying to get out the front door. When Kurt approached, the giant dog had run into one of the front rooms and begun pouncing and snarling at the dogs in the crates. The resulting commotion was louder than the roar of a jet engine.

Kurt opened the crate and clipped a leash to Devil's collar. Rather than taking him to the backyard, Kurt headed out front, doing his absolute best to make it apparent they were going out the front door because Kurt was allowing it and not because Devil wanted it so badly.

Judging by the minimal scarring on Devil's legs—legs were what would take the brunt of the damage on a dog his size—it was unlikely he'd been fighting for a long time. He'd been microchipped at birth, but the chip had never been registered. It traced back to a veterinarian who had stopped treating him just before he turned one when his owner moved out of the area. According to Rob, who'd talked to the vet, the owner's contact information was no longer valid, and it was against policy to release his name.

Devil overmarked on a popular tree trunk and, after accepting that Kurt wasn't going to give in to being pulled down the dark, quiet road, headed up to the porch. He took Kurt by surprise by stretching out on the ground next to the door and letting out a contented sigh.

"I can't let you sleep out here, guy. You might chew through your kennel again. We can't have you escaping mid-rehab and giving those protesters something real to complain about."

Kurt blinked in surprise when it hit him what he *could* do for the dog. Why hadn't he thought of it sooner? With so much German shepherd in him, Devil was a natural guard dog. Having a good view out one of the big front windows might help him feel at ease. They'd been keeping him in the side parlor with only one window, and a small one at that.

It took a bit of finagling, but in a matter of minutes, Kurt rearranged kennels so that Devil could spend his kenneled time looking outside. Once he had the massive dog settled, he'd swear Devil gave him a gentle look of gratitude. It was also the easiest time he'd had getting the dog back into the crate all week.

"Night, guy." Kurt headed upstairs with a smile on his face.

Pepper was in her room, napping in her kennel even though the door was open. Hearing him, she rolled over to attention, then clambered out. Kurt hopped over the stair gate and joined her halfway across the room. He sank into a squat after she greeted him calmly. He ran his hand along her back and down her side. When her only response was to wag her nubbin of a tail, he ran his hand along her belly. Her stomach was fat and swollen, and it didn't take much work to feel the bumps from some of the growing pups underneath.

Whatever extra chaos the arrival of the puppies might end up creating, Kurt was glad Kelsey had pushed to keep her. Pepper was a remarkable dog, and he suspected her pups would bring even more good publicity their way.

After a few minutes with her, he headed into Frankie's room. This week, Frankie had proven to be obedient and calm and eager to follow Kurt's commands. Unlike Pepper, Frankie hadn't gone back into an open kennel to sleep. Instead, once he'd shown a tolerance for Mr. Longtail and earned freedom within his room, Frankie had sprawled on the floor to nap, usually near the stair gate and door with a tennis ball or two within easy reach. He was the calmest and most content when he was near Kurt, Kelsey, or one of the volunteers.

"How you doing, old boy?"

Frankie wagged his tail enthusiastically and began to lick Kurt's hand. Frankie's stitches had come out yesterday. Now that the brief swelling from their removal had dissipated, he looked better than ever. The fact that Frankie would forever wear a partial wink and a lopsided grin would likely be something the slew of people wanting to adopt him would find endearing. The top half of his torso would be pocked with small scars as well.

"You want to know a secret?" Kurt asked, rubbing Frankie's chest. "I don't think Kelsey gets that Rob's guys called you Frankie because it's short for Frankenstein. So, I'm thinking we don't tell her. Frankie fits, however it came to be."

Frankie shoved past Kurt's hand to lick his chin.

Telling himself it was a part of Frankie's training, and not because he needed it as much as Frankie did, Kurt picked up the blankets that comprised Frankie's make-shift bed and carried them to his room. Frankie followed at his heels and Kurt refolded the blankets, placing them on the floor beside his bed.

"Frankie, lie down," Kurt said, kneeling to give the blankets a pat.

Frankie stepped on the blankets and circled over and over before curling into a ball. Kurt stripped off his clothes, flicked off the light, and collapsed into bed. He was tired enough to begin drifting off right away. Thoughts of Mr. Longtail pulled him awake. He got out of bed and shut the bedroom door. The last he'd seen, Mr. Longtail was skulking in the garden, but the cat had a habit of joining him halfway through the night.

Yesterday, he'd found Mr. Longtail in Frankie's room. The cantankerous cat had jumped the stair gate. He'd been drinking out of Frankie's water bowl while the gentle dog watched from his mats. Although Frankie hadn't shown an ounce of aggression or territoriality toward the unusual cat, he might act differently if he felt he were guarding a sleeping human. It was best not to test it. Besides, Kurt could use one night without fighting Mr. Longtail to see who got more of the pillow.

Spent as he was, he drifted off immediately, but not before hearing Frankie's contented sigh from the floor beside him.

Chapter 20

KURT KNEW HE WAS OVERDUE FOR A VISIT WITH SARA EVEN before his grandfather attempted to prod him into it. But with all the work that needed to be done, it was too easy to stick with a quick phone call most days. He'd visited her twice since the surgery, and she'd been to the house once as well.

So, he probably shouldn't have been surprised when William walked over to him the day after their dinner with Ida and reached for the shovel Kurt had been using in his trench digging. "Your mother could use some company for lunch." William nodded as he said it, as if the added confirmation was what Kurt needed. "With nothing more than me to keep her company, she'll be getting soured on Crawfords for sure. And you could use a breath of air that doesn't smell like dog or a pretty blond." His gaze flicked to the other side of the yard where Kelsey was finishing work on the compost pile she was creating. "I can dig a trench," William continued. "I'll finish up. Adam and Eve's paradise won't suffer."

Using the shovel, Kurt's grandfather highlighted the trajectory of the curve Kurt had been cutting into the ground to bury a new downspout extension to replace the old, disintegrated one. The downspout was flooding out the dog runs every time it rained. "You want it dumping out over there, right?"

Kurt nodded, wiping his hands on the hips of his soiled jeans. William had made the Adam and Eve comment once before. Kurt didn't find it particularly funny, and since as his grandfather had next to no sense of humor, Kurt suspected he didn't either. "I'll go if you'll sit down for lunch with Kelsey. Ten minutes, minimum."

Kurt knew it wasn't that his grandfather didn't like Kelsey. There wasn't anything about her not to like. He suspected their lack of communication to date was because William's conversation skills were highly inadequate, especially when it came to conversing with women.

"I hardly ever take lunch," William said, trading places with Kurt in front of the trench and beginning to dig.

"I'd like it if you got to know her. Since you're here and it's nothing but convenient, I'm hoping it won't put you out." Kurt hadn't asked anything close to this in twenty-eight years. He suspected the significance wasn't lost.

William sank the shovel just as deeply into the earth as Kurt had. "If it's important to you."

Kurt thanked him and headed inside. He showered and yanked on a fresh set of clothes. He was zipping on a clean hoodie when he noticed that Kelsey was in the kitchen. She was kneeling on the floor as she attempted to brush Mr. Longtail. The cat seemed to be putting up with it, though his lengthy tail twitched determinedly every few seconds.

"That's brave of you. Let's hope he's up to date on shots." Kurt hovered in the doorway, watching.

"I'm keeping an eye out for flashing teeth, that's for sure. But his long fur has gotten so nappy the last few months that it needs to be done. I guess it isn't surprising, considering the amount of time he spends outside."

"Why don't you put it off for later and I'll help you?" Kurt crossed the floor and pressed his lips against her temple.

"When you're free, there're more important items on the to-do list." She blushed as soon as she said it. Kurt suspected she was remembering those few minutes in the kitchen yesterday afternoon. "That's not what I meant," she said, shaking her head as she picked up on his smile.

"But it's true." He knelt, resting his elbows on his thighs, and leaned in to kiss her for real. "Unfortunately, I've got to run," he said, pulling away before his arousal took hold. "I promised my grandfather I'd bring my mom some lunch. To hear him tell it, she's William-Crawforded out."

"Is she? Maybe he talked her ear off."

Kurt chuckled. "Speaking of which, don't be surprised if he accepts when you offer him lunch today."

"What if he does? Without you here, it would be like scraping nails to come up with something more to say than 'nice weather, eh?'"

"You'll think of something." He placed a hand confidently on Mr. Longtail's belly and slid him close to rub underneath his chin. "You won me over fine."

Kelsey pressed her lips tightly together, failing to subdue her smile. "That's nice to hear."

"I won't be long. Text me if things get hairy."

He took off, knowing it was terrible that he was more excited about the half hour he'd spend in his Mustang picking up lunch and driving to visit his mother than he was to spend the hour with her. Nana was gone. His mother and grandfather were his family. He needed to embrace them.

Kurt called, took his mother's lunch order, and promised himself he was going to do his best to let his resentment go. Like Nana had said, for the most part, people did their best. Some people's best was just better than others'.

Sara answered the door wearing a pair of Victoria's Secret lounge pants and a baggy zip-up hoodie. The thick wrap of bandages she'd worn over the lumpectomy had been off for a few days, and she was moving her arms naturally, though she was still visibly favoring the right one.

She brushed the fingers of her left hand through his hair. "Look at that mop of yours. It still makes me blink to see you with something other than a buzz cut. It's growing out nice."

"Thanks." He held up the bag of Chipotle. "Steak burrito, white rice, hold the beans. Just like you asked."

She took the bag and pressed a light kiss against his cheek. "Come on in. I can't tell you how badly I've been craving one of these, but today's the first day I feel like I can stomach it. It's too cold to sit on the deck and stare out into the back parking lot, and the kitchen is as drab as the inside of a paper bag. So, let's sit on the couch and get crumbs on it to annoy William later. What do you say?"

Kurt chuckled softly. "Sounds all right with me."

"We've got soda and Gatorade in the fridge. Milk too."

"Water's fine. I'll get it. You sit down. What'll you have?"

"A Coke, I guess. I'm sick of Gatorade—and chicken soup and mashed potatoes, which means I'm getting that anesthesia out of my system."

He headed to the small kitchen and grabbed a soda and a glass of water, then joined her in the living room. The whole place was about seven hundred square feet, but it felt even smaller to him after having gotten used to the high ceilings at the Sabrina Raven estate. "How are you feeling? Ready to start radiation next week?"

She shrugged, her left shoulder rising higher than her right one. "Ready as I'll ever be. We Crawfords jump in and don't waste time thinking about it, don't we?"

"I guess so."

The TV was muted, but she'd been watching the Food Channel. A baking show was on, giving Kurt an immediate craving for cupcakes, something he hadn't had in years. He unwrapped his burrito, also steak, though he hadn't opted out of the beans.

She thanked him again for coming and moaned over how delicious her burrito was. After she'd eaten about a third of it, she sat the rest on the wrapper on the coffee table and scooted sideways, facing him and crossing her legs. "Did William have to twist your arm to get you away from that girlfriend and those dogs of yours?"

Kurt smiled through his mouthful of burrito. "He offered to finish digging a trench."

Sara laughed and made an imaginary check mark in the air. "Score one for motherhood. Sara Crawford out-rates trench digging."

"I'd have come anyway."

"Yeah, well, when he left, I told him you needed to come today. Between now and never, if it went any longer, I'm pretty sure I'd choose never. For part of this, at least."

Kurt swallowed hard. "What's going on?" He set his burrito on the coffee table and twisted to face her. "I thought everything was on track."

"I'm fine, if that's what you're thinking. At least, I'm right where a woman my age with stage zero breast cancer should be."

"Then what's going on?"

Sara pointed toward the kitchen. "There's a cardboard box on the table. I'll let you grab it."

Kurt wasted no time retrieving the box. It was lighter than he'd expected. It was folded closed but not taped. "What's in it?"

"Some closure for one thing, I hope. Who knows what'll come of the rest."

Kurt scooted his burrito toward his mother's, then sat the box on the coffee table. "Sara, in case you've forgotten, I'm not much for surprises and even less for suspense."

"Then open it."

Clenching his jaw, Kurt pulled free one of the corners. He blinked at the contents. They were both familiar and foreign. There was a framed picture of the four of them: Nana, William, Sara, and him. He'd seen it before, but it had been years earlier. Kurt was maybe five, which put Sara at just over twenty. It had been taken at Epcot. They were standing in front of Spaceship Earth. It was the one perfectly normal, all-American thing they'd done together, though Kurt scarcely remembered any of the vacation. Nana looked radiant, Sara was posing as if her crush had been taking the picture, Kurt looked two steps away from a grandiose meltdown, and William was looking grimly at the camera.

Next to the picture frame was the sock monkey that

Nana had stitched out of honest-to-God worn socks. It had been on Kurt's bed next to his pillow every day until fourth grade when a buddy came over and made fun of it. There were also a few toy cars, including a classic Mustang that looked a lot like the one he was driving now, except that it was black. His grandmother's favorite rosary was in there too.

"She'd want you to have it," Sara said as he brushed his fingertips over it.

Kurt wasn't sure he wanted the responsibility of keeping it safe, but he didn't want to refuse it either. At the bottom of the box were a couple folders stuffed with paper and a handful of children's books.

"Mostly that's your schoolwork. It was fun to look through it. There's a paper in there you wrote about dogs. You should read it later. Grab the top book though, will you?"

Kurt did. It was worn, and the cover was half torn off. The cover picture was a cartoon drawing of a beach and an old lady and a little boy. Memory rushed over him. Nana's singsong voice tickled his ears. How many times had she read it to him?

"I remember stopping by their house for one thing or another after I moved out and hearing her read it to you at bedtime. Do you remember it?"

Kurt nodded. He remembered the book more clearly than the trip to Disney World. It was about the adventure of a boy and his grandmother on the Oregon coast. It was a simple book, but Nana had loved it, so he'd loved it too.

"It always made me jealous, but she used to want to take you there. Just you and her. She was my mom and you were my kid, and it made me jealous. But I want you to know I'm sorry it never happened."

Kurt shook his head. "I'm sure she forgot about it."

"I don't know if it'll help or hurt, but it was actually one of the last things I remember her saying to me. It was maybe a week before she died. Like a premonition or something. She said it was one of her only regrets, that you two had never gone to the coast together."

Kurt shook his head. He didn't want to hear anything else Sara had to say. Nana was gone, and there was no use stirring up the past. *Did you hear that, you idiot? You're starting to sound like the Colonel.*

"Kurt, I have no real delusions about who raised you. I've got my game face off today, and when I put it back on, you may never hear this again, but my mom did an extraordinary job. You are this miraculous, amazing young man because of her. I know it. William knows it. You know it."

"What's this about, Sara?" He flipped absently through the book, his jaw so tight that his teeth hurt. Two envelopes fell out of the book onto his lap. One was letter-sized, the other large enough to hold a thin stack of unfolded paper. Both were sealed.

"It's about what I have to say next, actually."

"And what's that?"

"My mom's father died not long before she did, believe it or not. He was ninety-three. A cousin of hers came up from Guanajuato a month before her accident. My mom wasn't exaggerating, Kurt. Her family owns half a village."

"Did you meet her cousin?"

"Yes. He was nice. Different. Really different. Old

world and sophisticated. It explained a lot to me about why Mom was the way she was, always in a dress and collecting crystal and lace and whatnot."

"Did it make her happy or sad, seeing him?"

Sara took a measured breath. "Happy mostly, a little nostalgic too. She intended to tell you. She talked to me about it a lot."

"About what?"

Sara drummed her fingers on her knee. "About the money, Kurt. She was given a nice chunk of money."

"No shit? What's William got to say about that?"

"No surprises there. He doesn't want anything to do with the money. It's for us to split as long as we don't do anything wasteful, which I keep thinking coincides pretty perfectly with this," she said, motioning to her surgical site. "I'm forty-four, and this death scare got me thinking that the only real thing I ever did of any importance was give birth to you. Let's face it, finishing high school doesn't account for much. Neither does waitressing or shacking up with my fair share of the U.S. armed forces."

One side of Kurt's mouth pulled into a smile. "You mean a lot to a lot of people, Sara. That counts for something."

"But not to me."

He sat the book on the edge of the table next to the box and leaned against the couch. "So what are you going to do about it?"

"That's the burning question. If it wasn't for this scare, I probably would have wasted my half if William didn't stop me. I've been taking this time to myself to think things over. Promise you won't laugh?"

"Of course."

"I love clothes, and I like to run things. You know I run that diner, even though I don't get paid to do it. I was thinking of taking a few business classes and opening an upscale resale shop. They're all the rage now."

"I think that would be perfect for you. It makes me happy to hear you say it. William will be too, I'm sure."

"He said he'd help me get the space ready for customers, so I think that pretty much counts as his approval."

"I'd say so."

"Aren't you going to ask how much we're getting?"

Kurt dragged a hand through his hair. He had a strange feeling everything was about to change, and he stifled a desperate urge to shove everything back in the box and head out the door. "Honestly, I'm still trying to digest the fact that in the end, Nana wasn't cut out of her father's will."

"I think the whole affair ended up being pretty complicated. It was her sister's last wish that she be included. She passed away a year or so before their father."

"So how much did they give her?"

"Nine hundred and thirty-two thousand."

Kurt choked on the water he was taking a swig of. "Dollars? Not pesos? You're sure?"

"If it was a million pesos, I don't think we'd be planning much of anything. The money's in Mom and Dad's account. Mom never spent a dime, and Dad won't either. He wants to visit an estate lawyer to minimize taxes, but if you're doing the math, it's safe to say you'll have over four hundred thousand dollars to spend however you'd like. All the details are in the big envelope. And I'm telling you right now that you should start your own K-9 training rescue team or something of the sort. You're too good with dogs not to."

Kurt sat against the couch, his hands resting loosely against his thighs as Sara picked up her burrito and began to nibble again. She poked his knee with her bare toe.

"Or you could marry Kelsey and throw a big, ostentatious wedding and get her to start popping out babies right quick, because I think there's a good chance I'll be a much better grandma than I was a mom. But no pressure."

Her efforts to lighten the mood weren't going to work. He was numb from his fingers to his toes, and his mind was racing. It was too much to process. His mother's possible turnaround. His grandmother's family coming out of nowhere. A hell of a lot of money. That was when it hit him. "Then what's in the small envelope?"

Her smile faltered long enough for him to see this one made her nervous, not excited. She set the burrito down and sipped her Coke. Kurt waited, forcing a patience he didn't feel.

"I found him, Kurt."

She was looking at the table, not him, and her voice was soft. It took Kurt a minute to process her words. He played them over and over while she fidgeted with the tie string of her pants.

"I didn't think it could ever happen," she said into the silence. "I didn't think the world was small enough, but it turns out it is. I mean, we lived in Texas even."

Kurt swallowed hard and leaned forward, pressing his thumbs into his temples. He wanted to drown out her words, wanted her to stop talking. His stomach flopped like a fish on land. All these years he thought knowing was an impossibility. Thought he'd never know more than a handful of nonessential details. His father's name was Kurt. He had brown eyes and a kind smile. He was from North Carolina, and he wasn't in the military.

He was also the only guy she slept with the month Kurt was conceived.

"A friend of his—one of the guys he was hanging with the night we spent together—came into the diner. I wouldn't have recognized him from a hundred thousand other worn-out ex-soldiers coming to the post for a weekend brush of nostalgia. But he recognized me. He gave me a name and a number. He told me a little about what your father's doing now, if you'd like to know."

Kurt held up his hand and shook his head. "You know his name? His last name?"

"Yeah. His friend even had a picture on his phone. The resemblance was undeniable."

Kurt dragged his fingers through his hair. He crossed over to a window, not able to open it fast enough even though it was only in the midfifties outside. His skin was hot, burning even, and his fingers and toes were humming with electricity.

"Does William know?"

"Yes."

"What'd he say?"

"He's too much like you to say much of anything."

"Did Nana know?"

"No, this happened after."

Kurt walked into the kitchen and braced himself against the counter, drumming his fingers on the Formica. "I'd like to think about it."

"I understand. There's no rush. Look, if you decide

not to open it, no one's going to blame you. This is yours to do with as you wish." Sara stood up and placed the book, picture frame, and letters back in the box.

"Don't put that letter in there. Not if I'm supposed to take that stuff with me. Keep it here. I've got to think about it, and I don't want it with me while I do."

"That makes sense." She sank back to the couch like she was overcome with a wave of fatigue. "Kurt, should I not have told you?"

He drummed his fingers some more. "No, I'm glad you did."

"It doesn't have to change anything, if you don't want it to. But it might also offer you some clarity. Think about it."

"I will." He leaned forward and pressed his forehead against the cool Formica counter. Most of his life, he'd have given pretty much anything for this news. Now that the impossible wasn't impossible, it felt like he'd been handed Pandora's box.

He was a soldier. He'd been trained to stand his ground and fight. To face any adversary head-on. Bravery was in his blood. So why the hell did hearing this make him want to run and run and never stop running?

Chapter 21

"THESE HAVE TO BE THE CUTEST WEDDING FAVORS EVER." Kelsey held up a chubby, handblown glass honey pot, admiring it in the sunlight streaming onto Ida's covered front porch. Kelsey had just finished using raffia to tie on a wooden dipper and handmade paper tag that read *Sweet Beginnings*. On the tag's other side were Megan's and Craig's names and their wedding date, now just two days away. The four-ounce honey pot was small and squat-bottomed, and thanks to the honey inside, it shone with an amber glow in the afternoon light. "Would it be bad luck if I took mine home today? Maybe I should wait until after you text me beachside pictures of the big moment."

From her spot at the end of the eight-foot-long folding table that had been set up for this afternoon's craft project, Megan waved her hand dismissively. "Take one now. I'm not letting in any room for superstition or worry or anything else. And after you endure all this sticky mess with me, you deserve a giant pot, not a tiny one."

"These are perfect. I'm going to put mine where I see it all the time."

Megan had purchased three gallons of honey from a sustainable farm in the Missouri wine country not far from where they were hosting the reception next weekend, and now their job was to get the honey into the small pots. "They are cute, aren't they? Only I'm worried we won't have enough honey. I didn't really account for the spills in my calculations."

The front door pulled open, and Ida rejoined them on the porch. She held a glass measuring cup with a spouted rim and a plastic funnel. "These could help keep the outsides of the pots from getting so messy. What else can I get you?"

Kelsey had mentioned to Ida during their dinner that she'd volunteered to help assemble Megan's wedding favors. Ida had been so excited by the idea that she'd offered for the assembly to take place at her house and to provide lunch as well. Megan had been eager to meet her ever since she'd learned Sabrina's sister was living next door, and she was deeply touched by the offer.

Megan's wedding was approaching with lightning speed. Kelsey was impressed with how her friend was handling everything. Things were nearly as busy at the shelter as they were here, from all the recent publicity and with the construction in progress. On top of coordinating everything there, Megan was still settling into her new life, preparing for the baby that was on the way, and planning her wedding. Thankfully, the favors were the last big item on Megan's wedding to-do list. Kelsey suspected Megan had to feel like she was sliding into home base in the nick of time. She and Craig were flying out tonight to have a full day to relax on the island before the ceremony on Sunday. Megan wouldn't return from her short honeymoon until a week from today, which would be the day before the reception.

"These will help for sure," Megan said as she took the measuring cup and funnel from Ida. A honeybee, drawn in by the sweet smell, buzzed in a circle around her. "We should be good to go now."

"Yell if you need something. I've got a chicken pot pie in the oven, and I'm finishing the salad. And will tea do, or would you like lemonade?"

Kelsey and Megan exchanged looks of agreement. The sticky honey on their fingers and the pleasant scent in the air would be all the sweet they'd need. "Tea's fine," they said in unison.

"Kels," Megan said after Ida had headed back inside, "I want you to know that if I was having a traditional wedding, you'd be a bridesmaid for sure. Honestly, it'd just be you and Ashley, and Sophie and Tess for the little ones. I never wanted a big wedding, though I never considered whisking away to a private island either. It still feels a bit surreal."

"Everything about your life is surreal." Kelsey couldn't help but shoot a wistful glance next door. Kurt and his grandfather were inside, and an electric saw and a drill pierced the quiet afternoon at sporadic intervals.

Prior to this rehab, she'd have sworn her life was close to perfect, even if she wasn't sharing it with a committed partner. But then Kurt had shown up and stirred up a wild mess of emotions, and one thing had become clear. Despite any lingering insecurities or uncertainties, she wanted him in her life. And not only *in* her life. She wanted him to comprise a giant, integral, life-wouldn't-be-the-same-without-you part of her life.

Lately, he'd been really reserved. Worse than reserved. Withdrawn. Then this morning while they were working with the dogs, she'd closed her hand over the back of his arm, and it had seemed as if he'd stiffened at her touch.

She put it off to his level of focus when working with the dogs. Immediately after all the animals were taken care of, his grandfather arrived and the two of them dove into ceiling repairs on the second floor of the house.

She wished she'd had a few minutes with Kurt first, minutes where something else wasn't demanding his attention. Last night, he'd scarcely seemed interested in their good-night kiss. She'd put it down to exhaustion, but added to what had happened this morning, she wasn't sure.

"What's up, Kels?" Megan was suddenly all attention. Kelsey's thoughts must have been readable on her face.

She gave a one-shoulder shrug. "I wish I could say. Kurt's been a little weird lately, but I think he's just tired. All he does is work. And I'm not kidding when I say that. I've never met anyone with his drive. In between one tiring chore to the next, sometimes he even sneaks into the attic to do pull-ups with the rafters."

Megan laughed at the last part. "Well, considering the work you and everybody around puts into the shelter, that's saying something. Maybe he needs some guidance from you on how to relax. I'm glad you're bringing him to the reception. I can't say my short trips here have helped me get to know him. As long as you believe in him though, that's what matters. That and he truly gets what an amazing person he's hooking up with."

"I certainly won't tell you he's easy to get to know, but he's a really good guy, Megan. His softer side is cinnamon-roll soft. It's just covered by prickly pear cactus."

"There's a good visual." From her purse stowed

underneath the table, Megan's phone rang out with its fun, chirpy beat. "Good thing I cleaned my hands." She leaned sideways a bit less fluidly than pre-pregnant Megan. *It's Patrick*, she mouthed before saying hello.

Kelsey was getting the next pot ready when, after a bit of silence, Megan interjected with "That's horrible. How sad. Where did you hear this?"

Kelsey waited, watching Megan's expression for the level of tension lining her face—which expressed deep concern—until she hung up a few minutes later.

"You won't believe this, Kels." Megan dropped her phone on the table and let out a sigh. "Patrick heard on the radio that Mason Redding was in a car wreck last night. They announced he wouldn't be able to play in the playoffs if the Red Birds win tomorrow's last game. He's got a broken collarbone and a concussion."

Kelsey's jaw fell open in disbelief. After his wonderful donation, he wasn't only a high-profile baseball player that the shelter staff had had a brush of fame with. He was a great guy. Having met him and been moved by his sincerity and kindness, Kelsey felt this news much more personally than she would have otherwise. She suspected Megan and Patrick did too.

"That's so sad." She pulled out her phone and read the story that Channel 3 had posted. She gasped at the picture of an overturned, mangled SUV that had been tossed up on a grassy hillside by Highway 40. In the background were flares, several police cars, ambulances, and fire trucks. It had clearly been a serious crash. Kelsey skimmed the article and saw that Mason had been in the backseat. The article stated that while all passengers had been treated at a nearby hospital, two remained, and one was in critical condition. "That's so, so horrible. It doesn't say who the other people are. I hope they're okay."

She was sure the whole city would be abuzz. The Red Birds were currently neck and neck with the Voyagers, their biggest rival, and only one more game—tomorrow's—would decide who went to the playoffs. Without this season's best hitter, it would be a harder game to win. But Mason wasn't just a Red Birds player. He was a real person.

"We have his address," Megan said, probably thinking the same thing. "Do you think we should send flowers? Or a card at least?"

Kelsey nodded. "Yeah, definitely."

Megan closed her hands over her stomach absentmindedly and let out a long, slow breath. "Don't you wish there were no accidents?"

Megan's father had died in a highway crash when she was a kid. This was the kind of news she always took personally. Kelsey agreed as they resumed the honey pot assembly in a subdued mood. They'd known each other long enough that neither one tried to fill the silence with empty chatter as they absorbed the news.

As a single bee became four, all buzzing around them, Mr. Longtail hopped over the porch railing and onto the table. He planted himself in an open spot near the center. His tail twitched periodically, and his head moved in circles as he watched the bees.

Pepper, who Kelsey had brought along with Kurt's okay, lifted her head from a doze to eye the cat before collapsing back onto the cool, brick porch floor. The Rottweiler's belly was getting so round and full that

Kelsey was counting the days until the house would be full of portly little puppies.

"Hey, isn't that Rob's van?" Megan asked, drawing Kelsey's attention to the white commercial van heading past Ida's house and pulling into the driveway next door. "You aren't getting any more dogs, are you?"

"No. Maybe he's stopping by for a visit."

Kelsey wiped the back of her hand on a rag and watched from across the wide lawns as two people stepped from the van. Rob was indeed the driver. A woman about Kelsey's age stepped down from the passenger side. Kelsey felt a rush of appreciation at how pretty she was. A brunette with long, wavy locks, dressed in a sweater, leggings, and tall boots, she was eye-catching without a doubt.

Rob didn't have kids, but from here, the woman looked young enough to be his daughter. Kelsey was mulling over their connection to each other when she heard the front door of Sabrina's house pull open, catching on the frame as always. Kurt stepped onto the porch, brushing dust off his jeans and grinning. It was a deep grin, one she'd only seen half a dozen times.

He'd made it to the top step when the girl broke into a jog. From this distance, it felt like a movie, watching the girl run across the lawn, up the steps, and into Kurt's arms. Kelsey's ribs locked in tight around her heart. She told herself it was the girl doing the running and the deeper part of the hugging. And besides, it was just a hug. Family hugged. Friends hugged. Everyone hugged. *That's not just a hug, Kels. She's burying her face in his chest.*

They'd stepped apart, and the girl was clearly

brushing tears off her cheeks when Kelsey forced herself to look away.

She locked her attention on the pot in front of her and grabbed the funnel.

"Do you know who she is?" Megan asked quietly, carefully. Kelsey shook her head. She'd lifted one of the big jars and was about to start pouring when Megan added, "Looks like we're about to."

In her peripheral vision, Kelsey could see the trio headed their way. She was debating whether to act like she'd not seen what she'd seen when Pepper rolled up onto all fours. She let out a single but authoritative bark. Although Kelsey wasn't worried too much about Pepper being territorial, she'd tied her long leash onto one of the table legs for such an occasion.

Gathering courage she wasn't entirely sure she felt, Kelsey stood up and Megan followed. The girl, who was prettier and prettier the closer she got, walked in the middle of the group as they crossed the yards.

Whatever it is, it is, Kelsey determined, locking her shoulders and standing straight. Together, she and Megan headed down the brick steps to the stone path in front of them. Pepper let out a second ruff and wagged her tail, though she didn't try to leave her spot by the table.

"Kurt tells us there are wedding bells in the air," Rob called out by way of a greeting as they walked up.

Because it was the easiest thing to do, Kelsey kept her gaze locked on Rob.

"Kelsey, Megan, I'd like you to meet someone who gives Kurt a run for his money when it comes to her training ability," Rob continued. "Ladies, this is Tess. She's been living in Europe the last year or so and came home this week. These two kids traveled all over the Midwest with me when they were an awkward, gangly pair of adolescents, and while I'd like to think the credit for their talent is due to my tutorage, I know it's not. Tess, this is Kelsey—she's running the rehab with Kurt—and Megan, the shelter director I told you about."

Megan smiled warmly and glanced Kelsey's way in confirmation. "Nice to meet you, Tess. We'd shake your hand, but we're both a mess of honey."

Up close, it was clear Tess had in fact been crying. Her eyes were dry, but wetness still clung to her thick, long eyelashes, and the whites of her eyes were brushed with red blood vessels. As nicely dressed as Tess was, Kelsey would've expected her to be wearing makeup, but she didn't seem to be. With lashes that thick, she didn't need it.

Tess tucked a strand of dark-brown hair behind one ear. "That's okay. It's nice to meet you both. It's wonderful what the shelter's doing to help out so many dogs. I can't wait to meet them." She sounded sweet and a bit nasal from crying. Kelsey wondered what had happened to upset her. Hopefully, it wasn't anything too serious. And, a bit selfishly, she hoped it wasn't just a rush of heavy emotion at reconnecting with Kurt.

"Want to walk around with us while I show her the dogs, Kels?" Kurt asked.

Kelsey's ribs unlocked a bit at Kurt's words and the sound of her name on his tongue. She met his gaze, and relief flooded her. It was soft and pleading.

Whatever this girl meant to him, Kurt was clearly not putting Kelsey on the back burner. Maybe Tess's arrival added to the already complex muddle of their relationship, and maybe it didn't. The only way to find out was to keep in the running.

"Sure." She looked Megan's way. "Megan, want to come with us? I know we've got a lot to do, so I won't be long."

"Go for it. I'll hang here with Pepper since I'm already knee-deep in this mess."

"Sure. If lunch is ready, tell Ida I won't be long."

As they headed back toward Sabrina's house, Kurt's hand closed reassuringly over the small of Kelsey's back, making the whole experience a little bit easier.

Kurt wished that at least once over the last month he'd brought Tess up to Kelsey. But Tess had been in Europe and there'd never been a strong reason. She'd left her big Italian-American family behind in a huff and was working on a farm was all that Rob had shared with him. That and it was difficult to get in touch with her.

Kurt had been knocking out rotted plaster by a leaky window and trying not to think about the envelope he'd left at his mom's or the chaotic mess of nightmares he'd had last night, when out of nowhere Rob was texting him to come outside and check out the stray he'd picked up.

He had no delusions that Kelsey might've missed their greeting, and he hated to guess what she'd thought. What she hadn't heard was Tess's muffled sob of "My grandpa died, and I wasn't here to say goodbye."

Even knowing Tess so well, Kurt only had an inkling of the pain that must have caused her. Her family was tight knit, *smothering* as she'd often referred to them. He had no clue what had happened to make her run off. But he knew how it felt to be overseas and to lose one of the most important people in your world.

Hell, that was probably why Rob had brought her over like this without any notice. But Rob hadn't been thinking how pathetic Kurt's conversation skills were, especially when it came to something so personal. However much he might like to, Kurt had no idea how to console her. The one thing he could do was talk dogs. He was glad when Kelsey joined them and even gladder when the conversation settled into one that was easy and comfortable.

Kurt hadn't seen Tess in forever. She'd gone from a gangly teen to a woman in her midtwenties who most guys would find it hard not to look twice at. But Tess was Tess, and no matter how life or years had separated them, he cared about her as much as he had the last time he'd seen her eight or nine years ago. He'd traveled to St. Louis from the post with William. While his grandfather went about whatever business had brought him to the city, Kurt had met Tess for lunch at her aunt's sandwich shop on the Hill, a cozy Italian neighborhood he'd been meaning to take Kelsey to whenever there was a quiet hour. He'd been in his late teens and giving serious thought to enlisting. Tess was two years younger, still in high school and not at all interested in military life.

And back then, before they'd reconnected over lunch, he'd been wondering if, since they had so much in common, he'd ever think of her as more than the sister he'd never had. When he'd seen her and they started talking, the answer back then was just as obvious as it was now.

He'd walk through hell and back for her, but he'd never think of her as more than a would-be sister.

And out of all of this, what moved him the most was that somehow, without ever being told any of it, Kelsey had picked up on the important stuff. Her at-first-tense shoulders relaxed, and she fell back into her warm and inviting ways. With every dog they introduced Tess to, Kelsey told simple stories that made Tess laugh and brought the color back to her tearstained cheeks.

It was one of the things that moved Kurt most about Kelsey, the way words always came so easily to her. By the time Tess had been introduced to all the dogs and fallen desperately in love with Frankie, Kelsey was inviting her over to Ida's for lunch and to help finish assembling the wedding favors.

Tess looked to Rob before answering, probably remembering that even when it wasn't warranted, Rob was always in a hurry.

"I wish I could, but I promised to help at the warehouse this afternoon. I'd love a tour of that shelter of yours soon though. When you have the time."

"Are you staying in town for a while?" Kurt asked.

Tess gave a slight shrug of one shoulder. "I don't know. Maybe. I left my friends in a hurry, but right now I think my grandma needs me."

"If you stick around, you know Rob'll put you to work."

"If I stay, I'm going to want to be busy. I'll keep you posted. Rob gave me your number."

They headed down the stairs and out to the circular drive. Tess hugged Kurt hard, her thin body and wool sweater pressing into him, then hugged Kelsey without losing a beat. "It was nice to meet you, Kelsey. I knew from all that Rob said on the way over about you and your shelter that Kurt and these dogs were in good hands, and now I'm sure of it."

Kelsey's cheeks lit with a pretty blush. Like him, she was probably wondering what assumptions, if any, Rob had made about their relationship. Tess's words had an air of innocence about them. However, since Kurt had already asked Rob for overnight dogsitting during the reception next weekend, she likely knew he and Kelsey were doing more than just leading a rehab together.

Rob and Tess loaded into the van, and Rob gave Kurt a single knowing wink before flipping the ignition and heading out.

Kurt stood beside Kelsey as the van headed down the road. A mess of words rolled over his tongue, but none came out. He wanted to thank her for letting her guard down so easily when, aside from the few snippets that had come out during the tour, she knew so little of his and Tess's history.

But the words were stuck alongside all the words about the unexpected money and the forgiveness his grandmother must have felt toward her family, and the most befuddling words of all about a father and a connection that Kurt had given up all hope of.

He dragged a hand through his hair, and the words slipped further and further away.

A few hundred feet from them, Ida and Megan were on Ida's porch pouring honey that Kurt could smell even from here. Inside Sabrina's house, his grandfather was waiting for him to finish with a mess of plaster.

"Thanks." It was a small word and hardly worth saying without being attached to a string of others.

Kelsey tugged at the zipper of her hoodie while a bee circled around her hand. "Sure. She's nice."

"Yeah."

"I'd, um, better get back. We weren't even a quarter of the way through when I left." She turned away without waiting for a reply.

He was about to let her go when he caught her hand and pulled her into a kiss that was both deep and heavily curtailed at the same time. When he let her go, she brushed a wisp of hair back from his forehead.

"Kurt, whenever you're ready to talk about it, whatever it is, I'm here."

He nodded and felt his throat constrict. "I know. And right now, this is all I can do."

"That's okay. You're worth waiting for."

Chapter 22

THERE WERE PLACES WHERE YOU COULD GO A HUNDRED times and still feel like a foreigner or, at best, an interloper—the post office fit the bill for Kelsey—and there were places you could go only once and feel you absolutely, unequivocally belonged. This had happened the first time Kelsey visited the shelter.

She knew she belonged, and in a big way. Despite the small staff size, getting hired had fallen into place easier than many other things in her life. Seven years later, looking around the building as it underwent changes and renovations, Kelsey still felt the same sense of belonging and ease. She sank into the familiar, one-leg-was-just-a-touch-shorter-than-the-rest chair at her desk and placed her palms flat against the wooden top, savoring a moment of quiet.

Hearing the plop of one of her favorite human's bodies into a chair, Trina raced over and hopped up onto the desk with the grace and ease of a cat who wasn't missing one leg.

"I can always make time for you, girl." Kelsey leaned forward and let Trina sniff her nose and face before the attention-loving cat began to rub against her.

It was so nice to sit and do nothing. Even if it was only for a minute or two. At Sabrina's house, there was always another item to be checked off a seemingly endless list. Here, it was basically the same, but there was a coziness about the place that most everyone slipped into savoring from time to time.

And now was as good as any. All the volunteers had gone home early, and there were no customers. Fidel was in back clanging around by the kennels, and Patrick was out front using a hose with a nozzle powerful enough to wash away the bird poop that collected under the big oak that pushed the sidewalk up near the parking lot entrance. This was a chore he saved for when he needed to work through something. Since things were going so well here and his home life was usually predictably quiet, Kelsey suspected he was still reeling about Mason Redding's accident and the struggle the Red Birds were having in the playoffs this year. He was a Red Bird fan to the bone.

Since Megan had left for Georgia last Friday, Kelsey had been here a few hours during the midday rush each afternoon. The most eventful thing that had happened was when a laid-off construction worker came back for the senior Bernese mountain dog he'd surrendered three months prior. He'd found work and, with his first paycheck, had come back inquiring whether the old dog had been adopted. The man was quiet and reserved, and if Kelsey wasn't so head over heels for someone with a similar demeanor, she might have mistaken his feelings for indifference.

She'd seen his hands shaking and couldn't help wondering if he was someone who held everything in. He'd done nothing more than nod and swallow when she admitted that while a few people had shown interest, his dog was still here. Moose was a good, quiet dog, but at seven and a half, he was nearing the end of the average lifespan for the breed and was already down in his hips.

She'd pulled Moose from his run and brought him to the front room to reintroduce them. As soon as his master said his name from across the room, Moose let out a high-pitched bark and bounded over in a way that seemed to shed the years from him.

The man had dropped to his knees, breaking into tears and bear-hugging the ecstatic dog. There hadn't been a dry eye in the place, and this included a handful of visitors too. Kelsey waived the re-adoption fee and sent the man home with a two-month supply of Moose's new arthritis medicine.

The experience reminded Kelsey of how much she enjoyed witnessing the love connections that took place here every day. Some were small and subtle; others were so touching that she'd ride on the glow of them for days, remembering all the things she loved best about the world.

A small part of her wondered how it would feel to come back here full time, whenever that might be. If it'd be like she'd never left and the rehab had never happened. Some days, it seemed like the rehab would go on forever. That she and Kurt and the dogs and Mr. Longtail were right where they were supposed to be, and things were never going to change.

But what would happen when the court case was over and the last dogs were ready to be brought here? Just as she couldn't imagine leaving Mr. Longtail all alone in a big, quiet house again, she couldn't imagine not seeing Kurt for an extensive part of her day. She'd never hold the dogs back a single day from the new lives that would be waiting for them—and the more publicity they got, the more certain she was they'd all find loving homes—but moving on might very well crush her.

And what would Kurt do? Would he head west like he'd been talking about when they met, or would he want to go back to the post? Did he care about her enough to stay? Her heart thumped at the idea. Beyond any doubt, she wanted him to. She wanted him in her life. Every day. She just hadn't been able to gather the nerve to tell him.

If everything went as planned, tomorrow—Megan and Craig's reception—could prove to be a really defining day. Not only would there be dancing and music and all the wine and fine food they might imagine, but there'd be a fancy room in a high-end bed-and-breakfast with his and her bathrobes and a hot tub and a private deck and God knew what else.

Feeling a wave of excitement mixed with insecurity wash over her, Kelsey laid her head on the desk. She heard a soft clunk and the rolling of glass on wood, and something bumped the top of her head. Sitting upright, she picked up the handblown glass fishing float she'd found on the Oregon coast as a kid. It had rolled off her monitor riser. Every time she looked at it, she remembered the muted surprise of finding it on the beach half-covered by sand. She remembered her father's joy and his powerful hug and his exclamation of what a lucky girl she was.

She cupped the glass float in both hands. It was a little larger than a billiard ball. The cool, green glass was translucent and even prettier in the sunlight.

"You'd look good in the light that pours through Sabrina's kitchen window."

Talking to animals is one thing. Talking to glass orbs is another.

Still, she couldn't escape the feeling that this float needed to be rehomed to Sabrina's house. She'd had it on her desk forever. But she didn't need a float to bring her luck. What she needed was confidence.

And to arrive on time to the mani-pedi she'd scheduled for three o'clock, which was only ten minutes away. If she didn't take the time out today, she wasn't going to get it done. Tomorrow was going to zoom by in a whirlwind of activity. Not only did she plan to work the first half of the day at Sabrina's, but she'd also promised to help get everything set up at the winery, and she'd still need to find time to look her best.

Dropping the float in her purse, Kelsey gave Trina a quick scratch on the chin and headed for the door. With the dress she'd found, this mani-pedi, an updo, and some new makeup, she was hoping to knock a certain ex-marine's socks off.

Or maybe just his pants.

When she stepped outside, Patrick was rolling up the hose, talking to himself.

"Hey, I'm heading out," she called, walking his way.

Patrick dragged his wet fingers through his hair, leaving a visible trail of moisture. "Does Kurt need you to feed tonight? Are there volunteers coming in?"

"Um, there are a couple guys coming in. I could probably miss it, if needed. What's up?"

He grinned the same way he did when he watched puppies at play. "I had an idea. To make it work, I need you."

"Okay. How soon? I've got an appointment in a few

minutes to get my nails done. It shouldn't take more than an hour though."

He glanced skyward, working through something. "That should give us just enough time. Text me the address. I'll pick you up in one hour."

"Okay. Do you want to tell me what this is about?"

"No."

Her fault. Patrick took all questions at face value. *Oh well, there's the air of mystery to hold on to.* "Then I guess I'll see you in an hour."

<center>~~~</center>

Kelsey was still wearing foam thongs and had her nails under a fan when Patrick pulled into the parking lot of the strip mall. Her jaw dropped at the sight of the monster of a dog in the backseat of Patrick's old Tacoma truck. She'd ridden back there once. Clambering into it had been a chore. How Patrick had gotten the giant dog loaded, she couldn't fathom. And how he'd gotten Kurt to agree to taking him off property was an even bigger mystery.

She did a quick touch test of her toes and fingers. Deeming her nails sufficiently dry, she grabbed her purse and sandals and shuffled out to meet him.

Patrick had rolled his window down and was looking like a kid the night before Christmas.

"Patrick, why is Devil in your truck?"

"Because of my idea."

Patrick had gone to the Raven estate every afternoon for a week to work with the ginormous dog, but no great strides seemed to have been made in Devil's behavior. Moving his kennel to the window had kept him from gnawing it to shreds but hadn't kept him from lunging at the other dogs when he was led too close to their kennels. While several of the other dogs had now been introduced to Orzo on leash, the idea of seeing how he and Devil got along seemed liked a fairy-tale dream.

Devil tolerated people but had little interest in them. Patrick might eventually prove to be an exception. When he praised the indifferent dog for good behavior, Kelsey had actually seen Devil's ears perk and his tail thump a time or two.

"Is he going to be okay when I hop inside?"

"He should be, and he's harnessed in."

"How did you ever manage that?"

"He's irritable but consenting."

Keeping her movements calm and purposeful, Kelsey slid into the worn cloth passenger seat, feeling awed by the sheer volume of space Devil occupied behind her. He could tie a show pony in a shadow-making contest.

"So, can you please tell me where we're headed? The suspense has just quadrupled."

"Edwardsville."

She waited, hoping Patrick would offer more explanation on his own. The truck interior smelled like dog breath, and she focused on breathing through her mouth. Devil was panting, his head was cocked, and he was eyeing her with big, brown eyes.

"What's in Edwardsville?" she asked as Patrick merged onto the street.

"Devil's old vet. The one who microchipped him."

"I thought his microchip was a dead end."

"It was."

When it became clear he didn't intend to add anything

else—Patrick was a one-task-at-a-time guy, and now he was driving—Kelsey drew in a controlled breath. As soon as he stopped at a light, she blurted out, "So why are we going there now? What purpose do you think it'll serve?"

"Devil is different from the other dogs." Patrick drummed the steering wheel with his fingers. "Like I said before, he doesn't want to connect with us. I don't think he's watching the door and staring out the window because he wants to guard the house. I think he's looking for someone. Someone in particular."

Kelsey frowned. "His first owner? Devil's microchip wasn't even registered. Who knows if the person who first adopted him kept him. Dogs his size often pass through a lot of homes. And the vet stopped treating him before he was a year old."

"Yes, when his owner moved."

When the light turned green and Patrick didn't add to his train of thought, Kelsey determined she'd need to settle in for the forty-five-minute drive and learn his plan when they got there. With Devil's panting and pervasive dog breath, and Patrick keeping to the speed limit but choosing to drive in the left lane since highway studies had determined it to incur the least number of accidents, the drive was close to torture.

She sent thanks to the heavens when they pulled into the veterinarian's parking lot at ten minutes before five, with the office scheduled to close for the day at five.

Through the glass, Kelsey could see a woman leading a long-legged poodle toward the exit. Otherwise, the waiting room was empty.

"Will you go in ahead of me and tell them we have

a socially challenged dog coming in? I'll wait till you wave that the room is clear."

"Sure, but what if they ask how come?"

Patrick's forehead knotted in confusion. "A veterinarian's office should understand that dogs who've been in fighting rings need an extended period of—"

Kelsey held up her hand. She'd figure it out when they got inside. "Okay, got you." She passed the poodle and owner on the sidewalk and headed in. There were two people behind the desk, a guy and a girl. She gave them the heads-up Patrick had asked her to, but had no idea how to explain why they were here. Once Patrick was given the all clear, Devil hopped out of the back with more grace than Kelsey could've guessed.

The guy behind the desk huffed as he took in the sight of them through the large front window. With his massive head and giant body, Devil probably outweighed Patrick. The top of his head was just higher than Patrick's navel.

Kelsey held the door as Patrick led Devil in, the leash short and secured with both hands. The lobby was clean, sparsely furnished, and smelled of astringent. The hair atop Devil's haunches stood on end, but he seemed otherwise calm. He sniffed the air, and lines of drool started to form at the edges of his droopy jowls. He pricked his ears at a muffled bark coming from behind a set of swinging doors at the back of the building.

"How can we help you?" the guy behind the desk asked.

"This dog was microchipped here when he was ten months old. We'd like to get him home to his original owner."

The girl popped up from her chair and pressed her palms flat on the counter. "Oh my God, is this him? Is he the guy they called about who was captured in that fighting ring? We don't get dogs that size very often."

"Yes, this is the dog," Patrick replied. He dove into a Patrick-paced explanation of Devil's behavior and how he felt that what the dog needed more than anything was to reconnect with someone he'd bonded with prior to his traumatic fighting time.

"Poor thing. Denise took the call. I heard about it later. We'd love to help get him home, but Denise said we don't have a forwarding address or working phone number for his owner. She moved out of the area several years ago, and we only have her old address on file. The post office will no longer forward her mail either."

"But you have a name." Patrick followed this with an emphatic nod, as if that explained everything. He pulled a piece of paper from one of the pockets of his cargo pants. "This is the number of his chip."

The girl turned toward her coworker. He gave her a light shake of his head. "You can't give them her name," he said under his breath.

"His owner was a woman?" Patrick passed Devil's leash to Kelsey and pulled a small stack of index cards from a different pocket.

The guy looked at Patrick and nodded. "If I remember correctly."

Devil sank onto his haunches while Patrick sorted through the cards. "That narrows it down. I've been searching through all of the popular big dog blogs and messaging some owners that live in the Midwest. A few have responded, and I've ruled them out. I found seven

people within a half-hour drive of here, and from comments left by similar user names on other sites, I believe
I've linked two of those seven to bluegrass music by
their attempts to win tickets to local concerts. I suspect
Devil's owner is one of them."

The girl behind the counter shook her head. "I'm
sorry. I don't understand."

Patrick singled out two cards. "I'd like to give you
the names of the two women, and you can tell me if
one is a match. If it's one of them, I'll be able to lead
you through a Google search to help you find her contact information."

Kelsey felt a wave of admiration wash over her.
Patrick was an absolute genius at so many things. What
a miracle it would be if this worked! But what if they
found her, and she'd given him away? What if she
wasn't the one Devil seemed to be looking for?

Behind the counter, the two technicians huddled over
one monitor. The girl entered the microchip number and
clicked through several screens before flipping between
the two cards. When she looked at the second card, her
lower jaw fell open.

Kelsey grabbed Patrick's elbow. "It's a match, isn't
it?"

"Well, what do you know," the guy said.

"That's Tina's card." Patrick looked at Devil and said
her name again. Kelsey suspected the single thump of
his tail was more because he was becoming attuned to
Patrick's voice than anything else. "Tina F. was how she
signed in on the blog." He looked at Kelsey. "She didn't
disable the tracking stamp on her photos. I could find
her house. If she hasn't moved again."

Kelsey bit her lip. "I think it might be best to call or send a letter. It could be a bit much, you know."

"The dog was eleven months old the last time he was seen here. Before that, she had him immunized regularly. He's a month away from being six years old now." The girl passed Patrick back the cards. Immediately after the *F*, she'd added *erguson* and scribbled Tina's old street name underneath. "You're so close to getting there that it makes sense for this phone call to come from you."

Tina Ferguson.

They thanked her and headed for the door.

"Hey, will you let us know if it works out?"

Kelsey promised she would. With no other dogs in the area, Kelsey walked Devil around a mulch island for a bathroom break while Patrick searched on his phone.

As Devil was pulling in his haunches and taking a massive poop, Patrick let out a single *humph*. Kelsey looked over to find him engrossed in his phone. Pulling a bag from the nearby bag stand, she asked, "You found her number, didn't you? It's hard to believe it's that simple."

"It's become easy to find people if you know where to look." He offered Kelsey his phone and reached for the bag. "You should be the one to call. You'll come up with better words than I would. I'll bag it."

Kelsey let her thumb hover over the number. What happened if Tina had given Devil up and wasn't interested in reconnecting with him? She took a breath and pressed Dial. She was almost relieved when the call went to voicemail after the fourth ring.

She left a vague message, saying only that she was with the High Grove Animal Shelter and wanted to talk to Tina about a possible former pet. She ended the call and handed Patrick back his phone.

"I expected her to answer," Patrick said, his forehead wrinkling.

"We have her number now. We can keep calling if we need to." Kelsey squeezed his arm as they headed for the truck. "I've known you for five years, and hardly a week goes by that you don't amaze me with some crazy fact you know or something remarkable like this that you do."

Compliments weren't something Patrick processed easily. He gave her a confused look as he opened the passenger-side door. The seat was still flipped up. He was able to motion Devil in and hook up his harness with almost no cajoling. Then he snapped back the passenger seat and jogged around to the driver's side.

"Thank you for coming" was all that he said before he started the ignition and busied himself in the activity of driving.

Chapter 23

IF THERE WAS A MORE PICTURESQUE PLACE IN ALL THE Midwest for the celebration of Megan's wedding, Kelsey hadn't seen it. Nestled in the rolling hills of Augusta, the winery was surrounded by brilliantly hued trees, farmlands, and the quietly meandering Missouri River in the distance.

The historic brick buildings throughout the vineyard were quaint and inviting, the trees were lit by white marbled lights, and the reception hall was a sea of white, silver, dove gray, and blush. Megan had flown home yesterday, and she looked radiant and refreshed from her magical week away.

Kelsey had left Sabrina's house a little before noon, run by her apartment, and headed out to Augusta. After a few hours of helping Megan see to last-minute details at the winery, it had been pampering time.

Megan had done Kelsey's hair. It was mostly pinned into a gorgeous updo, but a few strands hung loose and would hopefully hold the curl.

After Megan left, Kelsey finished getting ready on her own. The inn's inviting king-size bed piled with pillows and a plush comforter made her salivary glands activate the way they did right before she ate something tart. It made her think about her and Kurt having the whole night here after the reception, and was probably the most exciting but intimidating thing she'd ever imagined.

A few of their make-out sessions had been more astounding than she'd ever thought possible, but none of them had been on a bed. Sabrina's kitchen, porches, and the darkened front yard by the cars had been impromptu rendezvous spots where she'd gotten to know him physically in the same way he'd gotten to know her. But a whole night with no dogs and no interruptions and a giant, cozy bed—and a Jacuzzi for two—was almost too much to process.

Focusing on her reflection in the full-length mirror didn't do much to ease Kelsey's nerves. Blue jeans and shelter T-shirts were her safety net. Sweaters and boots and sundresses were a fun escape here and there, but evening gowns and Kelsey Sutton didn't feel like they fit in the same sentence. Megan had helped her find a great dress, so she was thankful for that. The strapless, shimmery, champagne-colored dress hugged curves she had a hard time believing were hers, and the strapless push-up bra did exactly what it was supposed to. The dress was a great color with her skin and her warm-blond hair too. Added to that, her matching champagne-painted nails and three-inch heels gave her so-sexy-it-didn't-feel-real thoughts.

The reception was down the street, less than half a mile away, and a glance at the clock reminded Kelsey it was time to get moving. Kurt had texted nearly an hour ago that he was leaving the city and he'd meet her at the winery. He'd run out and bought a suit last week just for the occasion, and she couldn't help but wonder what it would be like to see him in one. He wore jeans and snug-fitting T-shirts so well that she wondered if he'd feel like he was playing dress-up too.

Her phone rang, startling her in the quiet room. "Hey, Mom."

"Hi, dear. We're here, fifteen minutes early, as usual. I'm not sure what I'll do if we ever end up being casually late somewhere. It's gorgeous though. Where are you?"

Kelsey drummed her fingers on the back of her phone. Her mom knew nothing about the room here. Kelsey didn't plan to go into it either. With any luck, most of her mom's and dad's attention would be on the newlyweds tonight. "Just down the street getting ready at the inn where Megan has a room." It was the partial truth, at least. "I'm on my way out the door though. I'll be there in a few."

"Don't rush on our account. The bar's open, and there are some delicious hors d'oeuvres."

After hanging up, Kelsey did a quick brush of her teeth, spritzed both herself and the bed with her nearly empty bottle of Happy perfume, and slipped into her heels. It was go time.

She stepped out of her room to a burst of applause from Megan down the hall. "Look at you, Kels. I actually had to do a double take to be sure it was you walking out of that room."

Kelsey stuck her tongue out playfully. "When I trip in these heels, you'll know it's me for sure."

The whole Williams crew was heading to the center stairway: Craig, Megan, and Sophie and Reese, his kids from his first marriage.

Megan had told Kelsey yesterday that after a bit of indecision, she'd chosen to take Craig's last name for her own and change her middle name to Anderson. The baby on the way helped with the decision, she'd said, and Kelsey understood.

Dressed in a high-waisted, full-length wisteria evening gown, Megan looked elegant and not even close to six months pregnant. She'd been married in a different dress, a cream one that Kelsey liked just as much. Photos taken during their ceremony would cycle on two large-screen TVs at tonight's event. Kelsey wasn't versed enough in men's clothing to know if Craig was wearing a suit or tux, but it was black and fitted, and with a white shirt and a wisteria tie, he not only complemented Megan, but looked absolutely stellar.

Craig nodded her way. "You look great."

"Yeah," Sophie said. "Beautiful."

"Well, so do you," Kelsey replied, admiring the gold flowered cocktail dress that complemented Sophie's changing thirteen-year-old figure, and saying nothing to directly acknowledge Craig. He was simply too good-looking for her to feel comfortable taking a compliment from him.

"I thought I was running late."

Megan wrinkled her nose. "I think we all are. Getting this group ready was nothing short of a miracle. But we'll make an entrance, *and* there isn't a single cell phone or video game on one of our bodies." She waggled her eyebrows in Reese's direction. "We're hoping to entice everyone to dance and have fun and make the most of a special night. And just saying, we may have had to bribe them with all-you-can-eat pancakes tomorrow."

"I'll go, but I'm not going to dance," Reese said, his hands shoved into his pockets. Kelsey had gotten to know the sweet but standoffish boy fairly well, and she'd certainly seen him look less interested in going somewhere, so that was something at least.

"That's a shame," Kelsey said, "because I was really hoping you'd help me break the ice out on that floor. I kinda feel like I won't see you in a suit again until you graduate."

Craig chuckled. "If Reese has any say in it, not even then."

"Do you want to ride with us?" Sophie asked as they descended the stairs together. "We're riding over together, but our housekeeper is going to bring us back here at eleven. Reese and I have our own room with two double beds, and we're allowed to stay up as late as we want."

"That's cool. And thanks, but I'd better drive. If I had to ride back alone with your dad and Megan, I'd feel like I needed to serenade them or something. If you'd like, you can ride over with me. I haven't seen you in a month, I don't think." Sophie was one of the shelter's junior volunteers and one of Kelsey's favorites.

She was thankful when Sophie took her up on the offer, giving her a bit of companionship and keeping her calm before her big night with Kurt.

Chapter 24

KURT HAD AN ITCH TO KEEP HEADING WEST ON INTERSTATE 70 and not stop till he reached the Oregon coast. Ever since he'd opened that damn box, the desire had swelled into a primal need. It was ridiculous to think a sandy beach and some rocks would somehow quiet his racing mind. But there was Nana in his dreams every night, a purple-and-gold shawl draped over her thin shoulders, strolling on some beach he'd never been to, beckoning him to join her. He suspected the old rosary he'd kept in his pants pocket for several days was the culprit, bringing her more acutely to mind.

It was ridiculous to think of going. Of driving all the way there. Or to believe that his rebuilt '69 Mustang could handle the two-thousand-mile trip. Just as importantly, there was a house full of dogs needing his attention. Besides, going there wouldn't solve anything. Nana was gone. And the money he'd come into unexpectedly shouldn't unnerve him. Nana wanted him to have it. If he wasn't afraid, he'd know exactly what to do with it. And if it wasn't for the last bit of news his mother had delivered, he'd probably now have a tune on his lips.

Kurt had been resigned to believing that half of who he was would forever be a mystery. He was a Crawford, a blend of nothing more than the three impossibly different people who'd raised him.

But they didn't have to account for his only known universe. Not any longer.

The hair on the back of his neck stood on end thinking about it. Of sitting down to coffee with some stranger and searching that stranger's features for physical similarities before delving deeper in search of more intrinsic ones. But the man whose name was inside that envelope probably couldn't give Kurt any of the answers he was looking for. Like why he felt more at home around dogs than he did people. Or why he'd never been able to sit still to save himself. And why, no matter how used to a place he got, he'd always felt like an interloper, at least before he came to Sabrina's.

He was on the verge of doing it, of heading west to see if it helped ease his racing thoughts. The suit he was wearing gleamed starkly in his peripheral vision, reminding him of his commitment tonight to the one person he was starting to care about above all others. She'd forgive him, but he'd have to find the words to explain, and he'd been a total failure at that of late.

His phone rang a mile before his turnoff for the two-lane highway that would take him to the winery where Kelsey was waiting.

He pulled it out and looked at the number. His mother.

He hadn't called her in a couple of days, and he'd ignored several calls from her. He canceled this one and dropped the phone onto the passenger seat. It rang again immediately. Gritting his teeth, he answered on the second ring. "Hey, I'm busy. Can it wait?"

"It could if you were answering my calls. But you're not, so not really."

"I answered now, didn't I?"

"Yes, and I don't want to waste my good luck. Guess what? I went on a date, Kurtis. Wait… Sorry… I'm trying, I really am. I called to ask how you're doing. I've been worried about you, and the Colonel's as tight-lipped as ever. The date thing just popped into my mind when I heard your voice because I think it's something you'll want to hear."

"Well, congratulations on the date, I guess."

"Are we talking about you first, or no?"

"There's nothing to talk about, so no." He'd taken the exit for Augusta and was headed southwest and away from Interstate 70 before he even realized it. *Thank you, Sara, for helping with my quandary*.

"Fine, I'll start then. Guess who I went on a date with?"

"All right. Bruce Wayne."

Sara refused to be baited. "He's a nurse. And about as nonmilitary as you can get. I met him at the hospital. He took my vitals when I was all padded up in bandages and didn't have makeup on and my hair was a mess and everything. Honestly, he's cute, but not in the way I usually seek out. And he's so damn sweet, sweet like you and Dad."

Kurt lost track of the conversation a second or two as he tried to picture William as sweet. It was like trying to picture Mickey Mouse in full military attire.

"And it was a day date. We met for coffee and he didn't even try to kiss me, but he did ask me on a second date."

"Yeah, where to?"

"The art museum of all places. Kurt, I think he's a keeper. We were talking and he put his hand over mine and the world kind of fell away. Do you even know what I mean?"

Kurt swallowed hard. His thoughts went to Kelsey standing in the kitchen canning those pears, the sunlight glowing in her hair. Yes, he did.

"That's nice, Sara. Really nice."

"I didn't tell him about the money, in case you're wondering. I won't. Not for a while. I want to be sure, you know?"

"That makes sense."

"So, what about you? For real."

His throat locked up like a hand had closed around it.

Even over the purr of his engine, her sigh was audible. "I shouldn't have told you, should I? I-I thought…"

"Mom, you didn't do anything wrong. It's just a lot to take in."

"I'll take that compliment, if you'll let me earn it."

"Earn what?"

"I can't remember you ever calling me Mom. At least not when you weren't being a bit facetious. And I know it's because I didn't deserve it, but it was easier to step aside when the most remarkable woman on earth was raising you."

Kurt released a long, slow breath. "Look, I don't know if William told you, but tonight's that reception Kelsey invited me to. I'm headed there now. I'll call you tomorrow. We'll talk. I promise."

"William did say he caught sight of you in a suit and that you cleaned up nice. I want pictures, and if I have to call Kelsey to get them, I will. And Kurt? She seems sweet enough, but as your mother, I have to say it."

"Say what?"

"That I hope she knows what a great guy she's getting. I hope she appreciates all the many things you are."

A dozen different images of Kelsey—grinning at him, laughing with him, running her fingers through his hair, pointing at him, letting him know he could do better, be better—flashed across his mind. "The thing is, Mom, she does. She absolutely does."

"Then I'll cross my fingers it's like a fairy tale for you from here on out. Lord knows, you've had enough of everything else."

Kurt said goodbye and dropped the phone back onto the passenger seat, wondering how the tide had turned so much that he was agreeing with his mother more and more.

———

Kelsey felt a buzz kicking in. A part of her wanted to feed it, to get lost in cuddly oblivion, but she suspected that if she did, all the many words she was holding back would stumble out in a torrent the first moment she had Kurt alone. There was so much she wanted to say—to ask, to clarify—that she knew if a single important thing came out, she'd never hold any of them back.

And tonight wasn't for clarification. It was for fun. The type of fun that didn't involve dogs or responsibility or clarifying relationship status. It did, however, appear to involve her parents. Kelsey wasn't sure what she'd been expecting, hoping for a romantic getaway night with Kurt *that her parents were invited to*. She couldn't figure out who was being clingier, her mom or her dad.

Kurt was taking it all in stride, answering her dad's questions about his military service and his upbringing on an army post, and both their parents' questions about his work with the dogs.

Kelsey was thankful when Patrick joined their small group twenty minutes into the conversation. Her parents loved Patrick. Last year, when his parents had gone on a cruise, he'd even accepted her parents' Thanksgiving invitation. However, after catching up with him, Kurt became the focus of their attention once more. Kelsey accepted it as payback for all the times over the last month when she'd been too busy to join them for anything more than a quick dinner. And having been so evasive about Kurt had made them more curious than ever. Add this to the fact she'd hardly had anything beyond a sporadic first date for the better part of a decade, and this was what she got. At least her brothers weren't here. They'd probably want to challenge him to an *American Ninja Warrior* competition on the frames of the grape trellises out back.

When it was clear she wouldn't be overheard, her mom leaned close and whispered in Kelsey's ear. "He seems like a sweet one, Kels."

Kelsey smiled and sipped her appletini, savoring the blend of sugary sweet mixed with tart apple.

Her mom reached up to fidget with the back of Kelsey's dress. "And since you say I never like your clothes, I'll admit I don't think I could have found a nicer dress for you myself."

"Thanks." Kelsey couldn't remember her mom complimenting her attire in forever. Certainly not since before she'd gone off to college.

"And I saw the way he looked at you when he came in. It's safe to say he approves as well. Those eyes. *Oh my* is all I can say."

"*Mom*, shh. Please." Thankfully, Patrick jumped in

with a list of questions about the menu, while Kelsey's dad switched out his empty glass of wine for a full one.

Kelsey glanced Kurt's way, and her neck grew warm. He looked so perfect in jeans and a T-shirt that she was surprised how natural he looked in a tailored suit. He reminded her of a suave movie star on a red-carpet night. Calm, confident, and just reserved enough to look like a pro. The dark-gray suit fit perfectly, only bunching a bit at the biceps as he held his drink. The thought of how all those extra clothes would make undressing even more fun tonight made her palms sweat.

Even though he looked content with a bottle of Guinness, she lifted the slice of Granny Smith apple off the edge of her glass and, after a nibble, offered him a bite. A hint of a smile tugged up one corner of his mouth. He gave a light shake of his head, though his gaze lingered on her mouth, not for the first time. "Later. But thanks."

Later. Her heart fluttered. *Yes, please.*

A new server passed by their small group, carrying a tray of crispy puff pastries filled with something that looked mouthwatering. "Artichokes and Alouette?" the woman asked.

Patrick shook his head, declaring that Alouette was too soft a cheese for his liking. Aside from Kelsey's dad, everyone else took one. Unlike her mom, whose biggest form of exercise was passing from store to store at the mall, her dad had recently gotten into biathlons—biking and swimming—after determining that running was too hard on his fifty-five-year-old joints. He was sticking to the passed trays that were primarily protein.

Kelsey's mouth watered at the savory blend of

cheese, pastry, and delicate artichoke. "I could eat an entire plate of these."

Patrick wrinkled his face in displeasure. He was the pickiest eater Kelsey knew. Megan had once chided him for having the palate of a six-year-old, and he didn't argue. Tonight, he looked cute but a bit uncomfortable in a dark suit that was just loose enough to make Kelsey suspect it belonged to his father. She couldn't remember the last time she'd seen Patrick out of his traditional pair of cargo pants and a single-pocket polo.

"Oh, hey, did Tina call back today?" Kelsey had called once more last night but with no luck.

His face darkened. "Yes."

Kelsey's heart sank. It didn't appear to be good news. "What did she say?"

"She didn't say very much."

Kelsey perked her eyebrows, waiting for more.

"She cried a lot. I think it upset her to know he'd been in a fighting ring. She's calling back tomorrow."

"That's a good sign, right? A great sign."

"I don't know what to think of it. She cried, but she gave him up a year ago last summer. The man who took him promised to stay in contact but didn't." Patrick frowned and sipped his root beer, clearly working through something. "If she didn't want him then, it doesn't seem probable she's going to want him now."

"You never know, Patrick. Let's wait and see."

Kurt nodded in agreement. "He won't be allowed to leave for a good while anyway. She's got time to get used to the idea of what it would take to fit him back into her life."

"I just thought seeing her might help him."

If the woman didn't intend to take him home, Kelsey hoped she'd stay away. Once Devil had time to adjust to living in a place that wasn't Tina's and wasn't a horrific experience, he might settle down on his own.

At the drop in the conversation, her dad eyed the tray of a server who was passing by with a second round of chicken satay with peanut dipping sauce. This time, her dad and Patrick were the first to accept because the chicken skewers neither lacked protein nor were on Patrick's list of unusual foods that should not be eaten.

The room was getting more and more crowded, and guests were starting to take their seats. Kurt motioned around the reception hall. "This is definitely the nicest room I've ever been in."

"Me too. Most of the decorating decisions were Megan's. I'm proud of her." The arched ceilings were hung with ribbons of delicate, soft-white lights, and a floor-to-ceiling stone fireplace flanked the far wall. Dressed in fresh, white linen, the tables each held beautiful displays of flowers and candles, and the chairs were covered to match. The flower arrangements were dove gray, silver, and blush, and the votive holders were a mercury glass that created a stunning, muted glow across the tables.

Kelsey was debating about finishing her appletini and wondering how her buzz could be setting in so heavily when she remembered that aside from a few bites of appetizers, she'd not eaten since breakfast. She knew it was a good thing when the rest of the crowd began meandering to their seats. Unless she wanted to slip from an easy buzz into a wild one, she needed food.

And better yet, Kelsey, Kurt, Patrick, and her parents had been placed at a table with two longtime shelter volunteers, Jan and Linda, and their teenage daughter. Jan and Linda had recently returned from a month-long excursion in Zambia, where they'd participated in a walking safari. Kelsey was hopeful their fabulous story-telling skills would take some of her parents' attention off Kurt so he could relax and enjoy the night.

Soon everyone at their table was seated and introductions had been made. When her parents weren't so overly interested in finding out more about a secretive possible boyfriend, they were great in a social setting. Her mom always knew how to keep the conversation flowing, something Kelsey was able to emulate when needed.

Feeling a wave of sympathy for how well Kurt had endured the attention so far, she placed a hand on his thigh beneath the layers of linen. He covered her hand with his, stroking it with his thumb. She'd experienced his touch enough to have committed the feel of his hand to memory. And not just the feel of it either. Even underneath the table she could envision the faded check-mark scar over the two center knuckles of his left hand, the swell of the muscle between his thumb and forefinger, and the smooth skin of his palm with a few calluses interspersed.

She'd never stop enjoying the feel of them against her skin. She leaned close and dropped her voice to a whisper. "Thanks for coming."

"Thanks for inviting me."

"I was kind of worried you might change your mind and not come."

He dropped his gaze a little too quickly, reminding

her of how quiet he'd been lately. She bit down on her lip to keep from spouting a dozen questions.

"How was everything when you left?" she asked when she was sufficiently composed. "Did both Rob and Tess come to the house?"

"It was quiet, and yeah, both of them. Rob's going to head back to the warehouse when they're finished for the night. Tess is sleeping over."

"Good," Kelsey said, even though she was suddenly a little jealous that another girl Kurt knew would end up sleeping over at Sabrina's house before she did. It took reminding herself why this was the case to be able to let the jealousy go.

Kurt shifted in his chair and leaned in close enough to whisper in her ear. "When I came in, if you hadn't been standing beside your parents, I'd have spent a bit more time telling you how amazing you look." He started to sit fully upright again, then changed his mind. "Not that you don't look perfect every day, cuz you do."

Kelsey's neck warmed ten degrees. His breath smelled like the rich stout he'd been drinking, and she wanted desperately to brush her lips over his. "Are you... Do you think you'll be able to stay? All night?" In her peripheral vision, she saw her mom begin to fidget with her napkin, and Kelsey wondered if, considering her buzz, she was really being as quiet as she thought. Kurt's answering soft chuckle suggested she wasn't. She hurriedly spat out a bit of clarification. "Or will you still have to go back early to check on the dogs?"

The romantic room waiting for them back at the inn was something her parents never needed to know about. Neither was Kurt's fear of how he could accidentally hurt her if he allowed himself to fall asleep beside her.

"I'm committed to staying for the entire thing." He entwined his fingers with hers, and Kelsey was fairly certain the only way she could feel any better would be if every animal at the shelter had just been adopted.

Dinner was enjoyed with highlights of Jan and Linda's safari. Their pictures and stories were captivating, and Kelsey became determined to include a few in the next edition of the shelter's newsletter. Volunteer spotlights were usually related to their service at the shelter, but that wasn't a steadfast rule.

Determined to make it through the night without slurring, Kelsey switched to a semisweet Vignoles when the server came by, while Kurt stuck with Guinness. The dinner choices were grilled filet of beef tenderloin or chicken stuffed with Boursin and wild rice with bordelaise sauce. Kurt chose the tenderloin and Kelsey opted for the chicken, which ended up being the single best piece of chicken she'd ever had.

After dinner was over, the dancing began. Megan and Craig kicked off the traditional first dance. The talented band, a trio, played a rendition of "Lucky" by Jason Mraz and Colbie Caillat. Kelsey didn't think there could be a more perfect song for them to dance to. They fit together better than a ceramic cake-topper couple. Their happiness seemed to wash over the room, and the dance ended in a hearty round of applause.

When the band began the next song and the lead singer, a woman, invited guests onto the floor, Kurt let out a soft *humph*. It took Kelsey a few beats before she recognized the song as Rascal Flatts's "Bless the Broken Road."

Kurt leaned toward her. "I'm not one for dancing, but I can't *not* dance this one with you, Kels. That is, if you'd like to."

He extended his hand, palm up and open, toward her. He could do *anything* with those hands, and all his attention was on her. It was enough to make her breathless. It took her a second, but she managed to collect herself. "I wouldn't say no for anything in the world."

He led her to the dance floor and pulled her close. She suspected her parents would be watching but didn't care. As his arms locked around her, somehow, even though the rest of the world was falling away, she made eye contact with Megan. Her friend wiggled her eyebrows at her from over Craig's shoulder. Kelsey smiled before burrowing her head against Kurt's smooth neck and breathing in his scent. He didn't smell like working Kurt tonight, his now-familiar blend of clean skin brushed with a touch of sweat and his delectable deodorant. Tonight, he was wearing a sultry cologne, underneath which she was still able to catch the familiar scent of his skin.

As the talented singer sang out the first lyrics, it occurred to Kelsey that they'd been so busy this last month that she hadn't really learned about Kurt's taste in music. Was it a general liking of country music that made him want to dance to this song, or something else?

She wrapped her arms tighter around him and savored the feel of him pressing against her. As she appreciated the singer's magnificent voice, the lyrics hit home. She'd heard the song dozens of times but had never imagined she could one day be what someone's broken road led to. The thought that she might be this for Kurt caused the hair on her neck and arms to stand on end.

She pressed her lips on the skin beneath his ear and above his jaw. "I love you." It came out so quickly she couldn't pull it back. Her words surprised her enough to lose a split second of the rhythm and have to find it again.

He stiffened enough for her to be certain it wasn't her imagination.

Please don't let this ruin things. Please, please, please. Her confidence was melting like Jell-O at a warm picnic.

He pressed his lips to her temple and left them there as they circled across the floor. The hand that was against the small of her back drew her closer. "I know," he said an eternity later, his voice low and husky. "Forgive me for not saying it back. It doesn't mean that I don't."

An uncomfortable heat blossomed in Kelsey's chest, neck, and face. What did that mean? What *on earth* did that mean?

Kurt stopped dancing entirely. "The moon's out and almost full. Want to step out on that amazing veranda for a few minutes?"

Not if it means you're going to break my heart. A numbness was washing over her. It was as if her head didn't belong to her body when she nodded.

Clasping her hand in his, Kurt led her across the dance floor, wove through the tables to the back of the room, and headed out the closest of the glass doors that led to the veranda. Like the room inside, the pergola roof of the veranda was woven with soft-white lights, and so were the trunks of several trees.

It was dark otherwise, and in the silvery moonlight, the rolling hills of the winery seemed to stretch on forever above the farmland below.

"It's beautiful here." She said it mostly to prove she was strong enough to find her voice. Her hands were shaky. She crossed to the edge of the veranda and placed them flat atop the wooden railing that separated the veranda from the stone patio that stretched out across the yard to the edge of the bluffs.

Kurt followed, stopping beside her and looking out into the night. "I've never been good with words. I know that. And lately they've been more locked up than ever."

"You don't have to say anything. I'm a bit buzzed, and it kind of slipped out. I don't even know if—"

Kurt held up a hand to stop her. "No, don't. Don't make it less than it was. Kelsey, I can't even begin to explain what's inside me. There's so much I haven't told you. So much you don't know."

His words gave her courage. "I don't have to know everything. And the important stuff—the part that makes you you—that's the stuff that's learned from actions, not words. I know you, Kurt, even if I don't know everything."

His answering sigh was like steam escaping from a kettle. His arms locked around her as he drew her tightly against him. She could feel his trembling torso against her stomach. His face was half-buried in her hair, and his words were muffled. "Kels, I came for you. To Sabrina's. I came for you."

Their lips met, and the kiss was both tender and intense. Tears of relief slid down her face. Not making a mess of the makeup she'd taken a half hour perfecting slid to the bottom of her priority list. Through the glass doors, there was a second round of applause after a muffled announcement was made.

Then, where Kurt's thigh pressed into her, she felt his phone begin to vibrate. When he didn't pull away, she followed his lead and allowed the kiss to linger. His lips left hers to press against her temple, then her ear, and down her neck. They were on their way back upward when his phone began to vibrate for a second round.

Kelsey pulled away enough to let her head clear. They had time for this later. An entire night with no interruptions. She didn't want to miss much of Megan's big moment.

"Do you want to see who it is? And I'm thinking we should head back inside. At least until the big stuff is finished."

"Yeah, sure." He pulled out his phone and shook his head. "It's a number I don't know." He pressed End and dropped his phone back into his pocket.

He'd locked his hand around hers, and they were crossing the veranda when he stopped and frowned. "Someone's persistent. I should take this."

"Yeah, okay. I'll meet you inside." A glance through the glass doors and across the crowded room was all it took to spot her mother craning her neck in their direction before hurriedly looking away. Kelsey clicked her tongue as she turned back to Kurt. "Something tells me we weren't as invisible out there as I thought we were. If you get lost in the crowd, just look for the middle-aged parents with a zillion questions."

Chapter 25

KURT PRESSED END AND DROPPED HIS PHONE BACK INTO HIS pocket. He could think of only one thing that could effectively come between Kelsey and this night of hers.

And it was happening.

He wove through the crowd until he found her tucking a pin into a young girl's hair at the edge of the dance floor. He stopped about ten feet away, taking a few seconds to commit to memory this side of her—the sexy heels and golden hair swept off her neck, the shimmery dress that called out to him to slip it off her enticing curves.

She noticed him before he was ready for her to. His hesitation must have been visible on his face, because her eyebrows knit together in concern as she stood, patting the girl before she bounded off to join a group of other little kids.

"Everything okay?" she asked as he joined her.

"Yeah, but I don't know how to tell you this. It was Tess. She thought we'd want to know."

Kelsey clamped a hand over her mouth. "Please don't tell me it was the protesters again."

"It wasn't. It looks like Pepper's gone into active labor. She was unsettled this afternoon, but I was really hoping we had another day or two. It's new territory for Tess, but Rob's willing to stay. They don't need us, but after seeing how crazy you were about Pepper, Tess wanted to make sure you knew."

Kelsey clutched the front fold of his suit. "Tonight! Are you kidding? Oh my gosh, you aren't kidding, are you?"

He couldn't help but laugh at her unbridled excitement. "No, I'm not."

"How soon does Tess think it will be? Is Rob able to guess? These things always happen at night, don't they?" She smoothed his suit back into place. "Oh, Kurt, we can't miss Pepper's puppies coming into the world."

"Honestly, there's no way to tell. Once the delivery starts, it'll go for several hours. They usually rest in between deliveries, and I'm pretty sure she's pregnant with quite a few. It's possible if we head back early morning tomorrow, we'll still catch a few being born."

Kelsey shook her head. "Something could go wrong. She could need us. She trusts us. Rob and Tess are strangers to her."

"It's up to you, Kelsey. Whatever you want to do. I know how important tonight is to you."

She let out a soft sigh, her shoulders dropping and her eyes closing a second or two. When she opened them, she leaned close to whisper in his ear. "Kurt, that room is so lovely. There's a Jacuzzi and a giant, comfy bed and candles, and you didn't even get to see it. When things settle down, I'm so taking you back there."

He closed one hand over her hip. "I'll hold you to that."

"Deal. Would you think we have another half hour or so? They're going to cut the cake and stuff soon. I'd hate to miss that. Shoot, I still have to go back to the inn and get my things."

"Why don't you stay here and hang out with your parents a bit longer, and I'll run to the room to get your stuff. That way I'll know what to look forward to later, and hopefully you won't miss anything too important here or with Pepper."

Kelsey brushed her lips over his. "That works, if you don't mind." She hurried to the table where she'd left her clutch and came back with an antique key rather than a plastic card. Kurt knew before seeing it that he'd approve of the room.

It was Kelsey's experience that return trips usually felt shorter than the way to a place. This wasn't the case tonight. First, the winding country roads seemed to snake on forever, then the highway did the same. She reassured herself that the whelping box had been ready for over a week, and a pile of blankets, scissors, and other supplies was already in the room.

It was almost ten o'clock when they rolled into the driveway. Rob was laid out on the couch in the front parlor, and Tess was descending the stairs. A few dogs, Zeus in particular, roused in their kennels and started to bark excitedly as Kelsey and Kurt walked through the front door. Kelsey felt an unexpected tug at her heartstrings. She'd grown to love walking into the house each morning, but this was the first time it felt like she was coming home instead of going to work.

Rob rose to his feet with a yawn. "Nothing yet, Mom and Dad. She seemed close a couple of times, but I think she's been waiting for you to get your butts back here."

"Yeah, she's been dozing the last twenty minutes, but I swear she heard your cars pull in," Tess said, joining them in the hallway. "She woke up and barked a couple times. We've been watching her on the nanny cam so as not to stress her out. She went into her whelping box on her own, and her temp is down into delivery range, so things could pick up quickly. And by the way, you look *amazing*, Kelsey. I'm sorry you're missing your friend's reception."

"Thanks, and it's okay. We were there for most of it. We saw the first dance and got the cake to go. There are several slices, if you're hungry. Which reminds me, I left it in my car."

Kurt waved her off and headed back out the door.

"Well, I've been going since about four thirty this morning," Rob said. "With the three of you here now, I'll follow him out. I've got another early morning tomorrow. And besides, working at a shelter, Kelsey, you've probably seen more births than I have."

"I've only seen a few, but I've watched a ton of them on YouTube this last month."

"I don't think you'll need it, but there's a number for a vet on the fridge. He's a friend. You can call him at any hour. Though these guys usually do fine on their own. And I suspect Pepper's an old hand at this."

"Thanks for hanging out with me tonight." Tess stepped forward and gave Rob a bear hug, which he returned, lifting her off her feet. She was average height but slender enough to pass for petite. Unlike when they'd met and Tess had looked like she'd stepped out of an upscale fall clothing catalog, tonight she was in yoga pants and fuzzy socks, and her hair was piled high on her head.

Rob gave Kelsey a wink as he reached for the doorknob. "Don't hesitate to call, no matter what time it is.

And when things settle down, make that boy of yours dance another few dances with you. I suspect you won't get him in a suit too often."

Kurt was jogging up the porch steps, and with the door ajar, Kelsey didn't have to wonder long if he'd overheard. "Oh, you never know, especially if she'll slip back into that dress." He stepped to the side to let Rob leave. In one hand, he was holding the boxed cake slices, and in the other, her bright Vera Bradley weekender bag.

Kelsey's cheeks felt hot enough to light a candle at the sight of it. But underneath the embarrassment, she was almost giddy. This was staying-power talk, and Kurt wasn't shying away from it.

After Rob headed out and the door was shut, Tess gnawed her lip as she eyed Kelsey's bag. "So, um, I've never actually seen a dog in labor, and I'm not going to pretend I don't want to now, but I don't want to be a third wheel either."

"Third wheel, my ass," Kurt said, ruffling her messy topknot after passing Kelsey her bag. "You're staying up with Kelsey if this runs late. Besides, someone's got to do the grunt work."

Tess wrinkled her nose at him. "Eight years of military service, and they didn't take the Kurt out of you."

Kelsey laughed. "I'd better get changed."

"Hey, did you guys get pictures? Because if not, you should. I can take some for you."

Kelsey met Kurt's gaze. "You know, we didn't think of that."

"She's right."

"Well, we have to change that." Tess locked her

hands on her hips as she scanned the lower floor. "Hey, how about in front of that beautiful staircase?"

Kelsey found herself being shuffled in front of the curved staircase that not long ago had made her hold her breath whenever she'd used it. Now, the steps were solid, and she bounded up and down them throughout her days here without a second thought. Kurt and his grandfather had been busy healing this house. Really busy.

She and Kurt each closed an arm around the other. While Tess flipped on a few extra lights, Kelsey leaned in to whisper, "I'm glad we didn't get a picture at the reception. Our first picture wouldn't have the same meaning if it wasn't taken here."

Kurt locked his gaze on hers. "It means a lot to hear you say that."

Tess centered herself about ten feet in front of them and held up Kurt's phone. "Okay, say 'puppies.'"

"Puppies," they said in unison. As if in answer, a determined bark drifted down from upstairs.

After posing for a few shots, Kurt said, "Sounds like we're getting close to go time."

Kelsey ducked into the hall bathroom to change into the clothes she'd worn earlier in the day. Sorting through her bag, she realized she'd been so busy the last several days that she'd forgotten to dress in rainbow-color order. Today, a Saturday, should have been a day to wear a purple shelter T-shirt, and she'd worn a blue one. And yesterday she'd worn a green one. *Maybe it's time to let go of the things you used to need to get you through*.

She'd no more than hung up the gorgeous dress in the coat closet when Kurt called from the top of the stairway. "Hey, Kels, come on up. It looks like she's starting to push."

Kelsey jogged up the stairs and hurried down the hallway. He wasn't kidding. Pepper was sprawled out in a corner of the whelping box, half panting, half moaning. "Oh, sweet little mama, you're going to be just fine." Pepper lifted her head and licked her lips at the sound of Kelsey's voice. She was on her side, her top back leg lifted off the ground at an awkward angle. "Can you think of anything else we should have on hand? I've read lots of blogs, and most say the same thing."

"I checked through your supplies. I think you thought of everything. How many times have you done this before?" Kurt asked.

"Only twice." The number sounded very small to her ears. "One of the live births that I saw was a seven-year-old Chihuahua. It was touch and go with her. One of our volunteers is a retired vet. She had to assist in the delivery of all three puppies, or I don't think the mom would've made it. The other birth was a Lab, and she was a pro like I'm hoping Pepper will be. How about you?"

"Zero. I helped deliver a baby to an Afghan woman though. 'Woman' is not the right word for it. She was fifteen tops. It was a nightmare."

Tess, who'd just come into the room, shuddered. "Were she and the baby okay?"

"Thankfully."

Not for the first time, Kelsey wondered how much Kurt was holding in from all those years of service. He'd lost dogs in his charge and friends who'd been working alongside him... She knew that much. Once in a while, he'd say something specific like this, but he'd never go into any real detail. He seemed to prefer to lock things away and keep too busy to dwell on them. She wasn't sold on the idea that this approach was healthy long-term. It would be better if he could find release. But that, she suspected, would be something he'd have to decide to do on his own.

From her corner of the floor, Pepper let out a determined groan. The dog's muscles tensed as she strained.

"She's contracting," Kelsey whispered. Sabrina Raven's house was about to be filled with new life.

Kurt motioned toward the whelping box. "I don't think she'd mind your company, Kels. Tess and I can hang back so as not to crowd her."

Kelsey wasn't about to argue. She stepped over the makeshift plywood playpen, its floor covered with old towels and blankets, and crouched next to Pepper. She stroked the dog's head and whispered a string of encouraging words. Pepper's nubbin of a tail wagged a few times before she had a few whole-body contractions. The metallic smell of blood mixed with pungent dog filled the air.

After a few minutes of crouching in place and petting Pepper, Kelsey started developing pangs in her knees. She was thinking about repositioning when Pepper curled around and started to lick underneath her tail.

"I see its face emerging," Tess whispered. "Oh wow, it's still in the sac. This is so cool."

Pepper began to lick vigorously as the first puppy slid the rest of the way out. Tears stung Kelsey's eyes.

Kurt stood at the edge of the whelping box, a towel and baby nasal aspirator in hand. "So far, so good. It's better to let her stimulate her pups to breathe than for us to do it."

With Pepper busy with her baby, Kelsey joined Kurt and Tess at the edge of the box. "I don't think there's anything cuter than Rottweiler puppies."

Kurt met her gaze and winked. "It looks like an encased link of sausage to me."

Tess laughed. "I hate to say it, but he's right."

After several minutes of vigorous licking, the puppy was cleaned of its sac, wiggling about, and whimpering.

"Well done, Pepper," Kurt said. "Look. It's already making its way over to nurse."

Even though it couldn't support its own weight, the short-legged puppy was clearly making a beeline wiggle toward Pepper's nearest teat. And still sleek and wet as the little thing was, the brown markings on its face and feet stood apart from the black body, and its squished face was the cutest ever. Kelsey snapped a few pictures to post on the shelter's Facebook page.

"I was wondering if the father was a Rott too. From the looks of it, he was," Kurt said.

"They can't see or hear, but they can sure smell and sense their mother's warmth, can't they?" The look on Tess's face made it clear she was as amazed by all this as Kelsey was.

After one dramatic attempt to shove forward, the little puppy rolled sideways, exposing its smooth belly. Pepper gave it a gentle nudge upright. "It's a boy," Kelsey said. She locked her hands together in front of her mouth. "It's all I can do not to scoop him up."

"Let him nurse a bit, then you can get him in the basket while she goes to work on number two. I've got the heating pad warming up."

Once the puppy was latched on, Kelsey shot a bit of

video. The soft suckling sound of such a tiny, helpless creature was almost too precious.

Pepper rested as her first puppy nursed. Less than ten minutes later, she was panting again. When it was obvious she was close to delivering another puppy, the first puppy was moved out of her way and wrapped in a soft hand towel. Kelsey, who took the first turn holding him, stayed at the edge of the whelping box so Pepper would feel at ease that her puppy was being cared for. After a few minutes, she passed the tiny guy to Tess, who cooed over him as he cuddled deeper into the towel and started dozing in her hands.

Puppies two and three came out one right after the other. The second pup looked exactly like the first. The third pup was much smaller and showed patches of white on its body even while still in the sac.

"She can't clean them both at once." Kurt handed Kelsey the nasal aspirator. "Want to suction the nose and mouth of the other one?"

Even though she was a little hesitant to aspirate such a tiny thing, Kelsey knew it needed to be done. Puppies had only a matter of minutes to start breathing after being delivered, and they often needed help from their mom or a human to clear away the sac.

Closer inspection showed the clear, membranous sac was already partially off and not covering the puppy's face, so aspirating was easier than she'd expected. After a bit of suctioning, the brown-and-black puppy was breathing on her own. "This one's a girl," Kelsey said. "And she's perfect."

The next several hours passed in a blur. Pepper rested between most of the deliveries, which gave the puppies a chance to nurse. Soon, there were four girls and two boys. Five of them looked like full-bred Rotts, and one, a little male, seemed to be part bluetick coonhound. He had a white underbody speckled with brown and the longest ears Kelsey had ever seen on a dog that was half Rott.

"Looks like Pepper had a midnight rendezvous," Kurt had said on seeing the little guy.

It wasn't uncommon in cats and dogs for a large litter to be comprised of offspring from two or three different fathers, especially if the mothers were allowed to roam. Since Pepper had been part of a fighting ring, it was unlikely she was intentionally bred to a hound.

Kurt brewed a large pot of coffee around four in the morning while waiting for puppy number seven to come into the world. He carried up a tray of three steaming mugs of coffee, forks, and the cake they'd brought from the reception.

"Thought the sugar and caffeine might get us through till dawn." Kurt sat the tray on the old dresser and carried over the cake and forks. He took a seat on the rickety full-size featherbed that Pepper had napped on until she grew too large to get up and down from it easily.

Kelsey continued standing, knowing if she sat on the cozy bed, she wouldn't be able to get up. Tess collapsed into a straight-backed wooden chair that had been carried in from Kurt's room. She yawned, rubbing her eyes and tucking her legs into a pretzel shape. She was only a year or two younger than Kelsey, but she had an innocence about her that made her seem younger than her midtwenties.

The cake was perfect. Kelsey's mouth watered at

the hint of almond and the rich, creamy icing. It and the coffee were the pick-me-up she needed. By the time puppy number seven, another girl, had entered the world, Kelsey was ready to keep going until sunup.

Kurt, however, had stretched back on the bed after finishing off a slice of cake and fallen asleep within seconds. He was dozing with his feet still touching the floor. His breathing was soft and even. His shirt had lifted, exposing his smooth, toned midriff, one that she intended to lose hours kissing someday very soon.

Her blood pulsed faster at the thought. If Tess wasn't here, Kelsey would have been tempted to wake him up for something that had nothing to do with the birth of Rottweiler puppies. Her thoughts brought to mind the last time she'd tried to touch him while he slept. Was he better now? Could he relax enough to fall asleep beside her when total exhaustion wasn't pulling him under?

Tess, who was squatting beside the laundry basket where they were keeping the delivered pups safe and warm, seemed to read Kelsey's mind. Perhaps she'd caught the direction of Kelsey's gaze. "Just like these little guys are going to be, he was a handful even before he went into the service. Dogs were the only thing that could slow him down when he was a teenager. Otherwise he was in hyperdrive. I think I knew him for two years before he willingly took the time to talk to me about anything other than a dog. And honestly, that first conversation was only because I was crying."

Kelsey had been gathering up soiled towels to take downstairs. She paused while they were still mounded on the floor. "What happened?"

"I can't remember, so I don't think it was anything

too traumatic. It was probably something one of my cousins did. All I remember is that Kurt bought me my own bag of Sour Patch Kids, and I wished that he could be my big brother and Rob, my dad." She let out a little sigh. "I think I wished away my big, overbearing Italian family for more years than I should've."

"Well, if it helps, I have two older brothers, and I wished for a sister every birthday until I turned thirteen."

Tess was opening her mouth to say more when Pepper let out a bark-whine that signaled she was ready to deliver again. Tess had exactly enough time to scoop the eighth puppy from alongside her before Pepper unexpectedly stood and began to pace the whelping box.

"Poor girl. She's probably exhausted."

Kurt bolted into a sitting position, his thighs and arms visibly knotting with tension as he cleared his throat.

"She's about to deliver again," Tess said.

As quickly as she stood up, Pepper dropped to the middle of the floor and began to bite at her haunches.

"Something's not right." Kurt swiped the sleep from his eyes and stepped into the whelping box. He sank beside Pepper, running a soothing hand along her side. She whined and reached up to lick his chin.

"I can see something poking out," Tess said, straining for a closer look. "But it doesn't look like the others. There's something long and, oh, it's a tail."

Alarm washed over Kelsey. None of the others had been breech.

Kurt frowned. "They can't always deliver breech puppies on their own. Plus, she's getting tired. Kels, want to keep her calm while I try to get it out?"

Kelsey sank beside Pepper and stroked the top of

her head. Kurt dashed to the bathroom to scrub and wasted only a few seconds finishing getting ready. Tess took the towel from him, gnawing on her lower lip as she watched.

"Are you going to try to turn it around like in the video we watched, or just help it out?"

Kurt gave a stiff, one-shoulder shrug. "I won't know till I get in there. Tess, can you hold a flashlight for me?"

Kelsey forced a few deep, calming breaths and stroked Pepper's head and neck while Kurt worked, occasionally directing Tess to swivel the flashlight in a new direction. "This guy is a giant. So much bigger than the others. And he's coming out backward. No wonder he's stuck."

"Is there room to turn him?"

"No, but I've got him halfway out now."

Pepper whined loudly. Minutes dragged by like hours. Kurt mumbled something about the front legs being more difficult than the back.

If they tried to call a vet now, would he even arrive in time?

"I've got one elbow free. If I can get the other one before the next contraction, I think he could be home free. And I should tell you now, he's incredibly still."

Kelsey fought back tears. Not only might this puppy be stillborn, but Pepper could get hurt in the process of delivering him. "Come on, girl," she whispered over and over. "Push that little guy the hell outta there."

A silence heavier than a thick fog lingered in the room, disturbed only by Pepper's periodic licking of her mouth. Then the exhausted momma gave a grunt and tensed.

"I've got him." Kurt sank back against his heels, a slimy mess in his hands. "Grab a towel."

Tess was already lurching for one. She tossed it over, and Kurt began to wipe the gelatinous sac from the puppy's face. Pepper watched, panting heavily. As soon as the sac was clear, Kelsey suctioned out the puppy's nose and mouth. Unlike the others, there was no twitching or grunting. The puppy was still, lifeless.

Kurt had told her he'd been trained in CPR for dogs in addition to people, but Kelsey was surprised at the confidence with which he went about trying to revive the puppy. Each second that passed was harrowing. The only sounds were Kurt's revival attempts and Pepper, panting as she watched. Kurt went from vigorously rubbing and stimulating circulation to actual CPR. As he switched from blowing air into the puppy's tiny nostrils to chest compressions, Pepper whined. He alternated, back and forth, back and forth, and Kelsey's heart sank.

Then there was the faintest, almost inaudible sneeze, and Kurt began to laugh. He dragged his mouth across his shirtsleeve and then let his head fall back, letting out a giant exhale. "Ladies, he's a she, and she's breathing."

Tess squealed, and Kelsey threw her arms around him. Later, when it was over and everything quieted down, she'd find time to tell Kurt that he was the sexiest and most amazing man she'd ever met. For now, they had a puppy to introduce to its mother.

———⁓⁓⁓———

Shining low in the sky, the October sun gleamed inside the windows, filling the house with cozy warmth. The three of them had finished showering and were on the main floor washing towels, finishing off a second pot of coffee, and grabbing quick, standing breakfasts when Patrick and Megan walked in. Kurt suppressed a smile at the squeals and hugs Kelsey and Megan exchanged. Patrick, who didn't look to be one for physical touch, tucked his hands, palms out, into his back pockets and seemed to lose a beat or two looking at Tess.

Megan glanced Kurt's way as she and Kelsey pulled apart. "Kels said one of the puppies wouldn't have made it if it weren't for you."

"We got lucky with her" was all Kurt said.

"You get naming rights," Patrick added. "We'll hold a contest with the rest of the litter, but you should think of a name for her."

Kurt gave a nod. "I wouldn't mind doing that, but I'll let Kelsey and Tess weigh in."

"I keep a list of the animals we've named since I started. There are eight hundred and forty-seven animals on it, and seventy-six of the names have been used more than once."

When Patrick said things like this, Kurt wondered what sort of stuff he did when he wasn't at work. He also wondered how many of those names Patrick could recite off the top of his head. He suspected quite a few.

The group headed upstairs, and Kurt couldn't help but chuckle over how Kelsey and Tess got just as melty at the whimpers and coos of the pups as they had an hour ago. Patrick took pictures for the shelter's social media accounts, and Megan happy cried as she snuggled the pup with coon-dog ears against the top of her swollen belly.

The big pup, the girl who'd almost been stillborn,

showed no sign of her iffy start. She wriggled about
with more strength than most of them, and Kurt didn't
disagree when Patrick suggested she might be part Saint
Bernard or Bernese mountain dog.

Almost as soon as they were done, Megan headed
back to the shelter, while Patrick stayed behind to work
with Devil. Shortly after he started, the first two volunteers arrived to assist with the morning feeding and
training routine. From the tremendous reactions the puppies had already received on the shelter's social media
accounts, Kurt suspected there wouldn't be a moment of
privacy here today.

Tonight though, come hell or high water, he'd send
everyone away. He had a romantic night to make up to
Kelsey. And after inspecting the room at the inn that
would've been theirs had Pepper not gone into labor,
Kurt knew just what to do.

And it involved a quick trip out this afternoon.

Thankfully, with volunteer help and Tess still here—
she didn't have a car, so Rob was coming back for her
at lunch—they made good time feeding and working the
dogs. Kelsey didn't start yawning until the morning routine was finished. When she started, she couldn't stop.
She looked exhausted. She'd been awake since dawn the
previous morning. Tess, who'd dozed for an hour after
the ninth and last puppy was born, was holding strong.

It took a bit of cajoling, but Kelsey finally curled up
on a couch in the main front room after the morning volunteers headed out. She was asleep in minutes, and Kurt
figured it was as good a time as any to run a few errands.

He nodded to Tess as he grabbed his keys. "Call me
if you need anything. William should be here soon.

He usually comes earlier in the day, but I told him I wouldn't be here this morning. He'll be happy to see you, even if he won't show it."

Tess grinned. "I'll be happy to see him too, and I won't be afraid to let him know it." She stepped out on the porch after Kurt as he headed out. "Since you won't ask, I'm just going to say it. I like her. A lot. I can see her being good for you."

He paused midway down the steps but didn't turn around. "Things slow down around her. Everything gets clearer. Like with the dogs."

Tess crossed over to the railing, locking her arms over her chest as she studied the house across the street. Several painters were there this morning, as well as an electrician's van.

"That pretty much says it all." Her smile faltered enough to let him know there was something she wasn't telling him. Something she was hiding behind that bright-as-the-sun demeanor of hers. He wondered if it was tied to why she'd run off to Europe for a year.

He closed his hand around the metal banister. "Tess, if you ever need to talk…"

She gave a playful wave of her hand, and her smile returned. "If I need to talk, I'll grab Kelsey or someone else with an inherent gift at two-way conversation. Now go, get your butt out of here to do whatever it is you need to do. The day's a-wasting, as they say."

Kurt smiled and tapped the banister with his thumb. As a kid, he'd wished Tess and Rob were family. The older he got, the more he understood it didn't take being a blood relation to make someone that. "Yeah, yeah," he said aloud because the bluff was easier than speaking the truth. "If you're not here when I get back, I'll be seeing you. Rob says you're thinking about sticking around."

She gave a single-shoulder shrug. "Yeah, maybe. I didn't come home with that intention, but you know how it is, family's family."

He headed out, thinking how unexpected it was that everything he could possibly need was all congregating in one city, and most of it was right here, occupying a couple thousand square yards of land. A little over a month ago, as he boarded the first flight home, if anyone had told him that a life he could care deeply about was within easy and short reach, he'd never have believed them.

Chapter 26

IT WAS GETTING HARDER TO PUT ZEUS AND SEVERAL OF THE others into their kennels for the night now that Kelsey knew the dogs so well. The animals wanted companionship as much as they did the playtime, care, and training they were given each day.

Earlier this week, Rob had confirmed that the trial was being expedited, which meant good news for many of these guys. Even when they were deemed ready to enter the shelter's adoption program, the dogs couldn't leave the house until the seven people suspected to be integral in the elaborate fighting ring had been tried in court for the felony crimes of dogfighting and animal cruelty.

Kelsey hoped the evidence would be heard quickly and the case wouldn't drag on. Kurt had confirmed that four of the dogs—Zeus and three others like him who were young enough and lucky enough not to have seen much, if any, time in the ring—could head to the shelter when the go-ahead was given.

As the evening wore on and it was time for the last shift of volunteers to head out, Kelsey's palms began to sweat in anticipation. How would things change now? At Kelsey's initial request, she and Kurt had held off on taking their relationship that final step. She'd wanted time and a special occasion.

Although the special occasion had turned into an even more extraordinary one, it hadn't resulted in any

magical fireworks below the belt. She'd seen the miraculous birth of nine adorable puppies, and Kurt had saved
one puppy's life, so she regretted none of it. But how
would Kurt want to move forward from here?

In case his answer was in line with hers, she quickly
rummaged through her overnight bag for a toothbrush
and deodorant after seeing the volunteers out. Kurt
had been upstairs the last fifteen minutes, and she was
hoping he'd stay up there long enough for her to have a
quick refresher. *Just in case*.

Sorting through the bag, she bumped against something hard and cool. Her fishing float. In all the commotion, she'd forgotten about it. Taking it out along with
her toiletries, she dropped it off on the kitchen windowsill before making a dash for the bathroom. For some
reason, the idea of getting caught with a necessities bag
containing a toothbrush, toothpaste, and deodorant in
her hands felt akin to getting caught shoplifting.

Earlier in the day, she'd showered and changed into
a fresh, cute pair of underwear that wasn't quite as sexy
as last night's. Whatever happened tonight, at least she
wasn't going into it in day-old panties.

A few minutes later, toiletry bag in hand, she headed
out of the bathroom for the front room where she'd left
the rest of her stuff. Dusk was setting in, and a movement in the semidarkened parlor across the hall made
her jump. It was Kurt. He'd been looking out one of the
front windows.

"You scared me. I thought you were upstairs." She
dropped the clutch into her overnight bag and locked her
hands over her hips.

He'd changed while he was up there. He was in a

fresh pair of jeans and a snug-fitting black T-shirt. "I was. Now I'm down here."

Because that's everyday conversation for you.

He closed the distance between them while Kelsey mashed her lips together. There was no reason this had to feel awkward. She'd been alone with him countless times since this rehab started. She'd told him she loved him. He'd admitted to coming here for her—that still rocked her brain whenever she thought about it. And in some phenomenal make-out sessions, they'd done about everything under the sun. Just about.

But not *everything*.

He stopped two feet in front of her. The intensity in his brown eyes made her melt like coconut oil in a warm patch of sunlight.

"Look, if you're thinking of kissing me, you should do it, because I'm really close to sliding into panic mode, and if I do that, I'm going to sweat and—"

Kurt held up a finger, a smile playing on his lips. "Do you remember what you said last night about our first picture together?"

She swallowed and prayed her throat didn't dry up. "Yes."

"This house. I had heard about people feeling like a place was made for them, but never understood it. That wasn't the desert for me, or the jungle, or the post. But this house... When I'm here, I don't feel like a puzzle piece that will never fit in. When I'm with you, that rings even more true."

Kelsey's nervousness thundered away.

"So," he continued, "I'm hoping you'll come upstairs with me. There's something I want to show you."

"Yeah. Sure. Of course."

He took her hand, entwining his fingers with hers.

They passed Frankie's room first. He was sitting by his stair gate and whined softly. Kurt stopped to rub him on top of his head. "Not tonight, boy." Kelsey wondered what that meant, if they had some special evening routine when Kurt was here alone.

Next was Pepper's room. She was in her whelping box, and Mr. Longtail was sprawled atop the empty bed. He'd been eyeing the puppies with disdain half the day. Thankfully, Pepper didn't seem to care. Several of the puppies were nursing, while others were curled into a tangled mess of noses, tails, and legs.

The third room was Kurt's. His door was closed, and he paused outside it.

"To be clear, if you're about to tell me you found another dog who's about to go into all-night labor, I'll probably start crying."

His forehead knotted together ever so slightly. "I'm not, but if you're really that tired, we don't have to open this door. Not tonight. Or we can open it and I can tuck you into bed and I can head to the couch—"

Kelsey giggled and pressed a finger against his lips. "It was a bad joke. I'm sorry. I'm still a tad nervous."

He lifted her finger an inch or two away from his mouth and ran his thumbs over her palm. He pressed his lips against it, causing the hair on the back of her neck to stand on end. Then he slid his mouth down her wrist and along her arm. Just before reaching her elbow, he moved to the hollow of her neck and up her chin. Her legs threatened to buckle underneath her before his lips met hers.

The last of her nervousness melted away. She savored the sensation of his kiss, of his touch, of his body pressing against her.

The temperature of her blood rose from nervous cool to toasty warm.

He swung the door open, and the soft flicker of candlelight caught Kelsey's attention. Kurt's room was aglow with candles. Stunned, she stepped inside. She'd glimpsed this room several times before, and it was always as plain and ordinary as when the house had been donated to the shelter. Tonight, there was a strand of rope lighting along the rim of the headboard and half-a-dozen fluffy pillows and an inviting down comforter covering the bed. And petals.

Kurt Crawford had sprinkled rose petals over the bed. There was a vase of flowers on the nightstand. Beside them, a bottle of champagne was chilling. There were also two delicate glasses and a plate of bakery-fresh chocolate chip cookies.

"It's perfect. When did you have time to do this?"

"When you napped and in bits and pieces throughout the day."

"You didn't have to, but I love it. It's perfect. I'm glad last night didn't happen. I was glad even before I saw this."

"I was hoping you'd say that."

She shook her head, taking it all in. "Everything's so beautiful that I don't want to mess it up."

"Trust me. I'm really looking forward to messing it up."

Kelsey lunged forward, wrapping her arms around him and pressing her face into his chest. "Sometimes I can't believe you're real."

He locked one arm around her waist and lifted her chin with his other hand. His kiss was soft, unhurried. She savored the feel of his lips, strong and soft at the same time, against hers. "I hope you believe me when I say I feel the same way. You're everything I never thought I could have."

She slipped her hands underneath his shirt and ran the tips of her fingers along his torso, appreciating the individual muscles that lined his chest, back, and stomach. With her thumbs, she traced the V defining his lower abdomen until it disappeared into his jeans. As the kiss grew in intensity like a fire with fresh tinder and plenty of air, her blood flowed faster, tingling the tips of her fingers and toes.

The last of her tension melted away. She stepped back and slipped out of her shirt, shoes, and jeans, feeling emboldened and beautiful in the flickering light and by the way he was looking at her.

She loved him in every way a person could love another. A part of it was terrifying, knowing that he could be her everything, but there was a wonderful release in letting go and trusting. Trusting that she was worth his love. Trusting that they had staying power. And surrendering to the beauty that was all of it.

When he closed his arms around her, Kelsey had a sense that she'd been traveling a long time and had finally made it home.

The second time their bodies joined together didn't loosen the words stuck inside Kurt's head any more than the first had. Being inside her while she climaxed was better than any stimulant he could imagine. He'd never tire of being with her physically, any more than he would emotionally. He'd known it before tonight. Known it in the little tastes that had only made him want more.

He loved her. Unequivocally.

More than he'd ever wanted anything, Kurt wanted to spend his life with her. And right now and for as much of the future as he could conceive, he wanted to spend it here in this house. He wanted to fill long-empty rooms with kids, and he wanted a dog for every kid. He wanted to revive the garden and make a workshop in the garage out back that William could putter about in whenever he wanted.

But he didn't know how to tell her any of this. The words were a bridge from that life to this one, and he couldn't assemble it. He was stuck inside himself, loving her and wanting her and not able to say it.

How could he when he'd kept so much from her? The recent stuff to start, but also the stuff that stretched back over years. She'd praised him for his skills at reviving and saving that puppy's life. What he'd wanted to share was that doing so reminded him of losing Zara, of his not keeping her safe, of the helpless way his most favorite dog ever had looked at him as she bled out in front of him.

He couldn't tell Kelsey that, the same way he hadn't told her half of his DNA didn't have to be a forever mystery. Saying those things, building that bridge, was somehow more terrifying than heading out on a trail known to be laden with IEDs. He couldn't control the world. He'd accepted that a long time ago. But he could control himself. He could manage his ADHD with tasks, and he could maintain the same distance from the world his grandfather had long ago mastered.

Letting Kelsey in—or at least acknowledging that he'd done so—was letting in a world of unpredictability. And wanting to be ready for something and diving in were two different things.

So instead of talking, he used his body, his hands, and his mouth to draw one climax for her into a string of them, until she clung to him, sweaty and exhausted, and he found the same release inside her.

Afterward, he collapsed on the bed beside her, savoring his heightened blood flow, his body alive and awake. Their breathing slowed. Kurt heard the October winds rattling the leaves off branches and a soft, gentle sigh from the other side of his doorway. Knowing that sound and who had made it, he couldn't help but chuckle.

He got up and headed for the door. Frankie was curling up on the floor on the other side of it. Kurt shook his head. He'd already raised the stair gate to Frankie's room once. The dog wasn't jumping it during the day, only at night when Kurt wasn't quick enough to offer him use of the floor beside his bed.

Kelsey rose up on her elbow, tucking the covers under her arms. "Did he knock down his stair gate?"

"He jumped it."

Kurt pointed to the rug at the bottom of the bed, but Frankie made for their pile of clothes, claiming them as a cozy spot, and Kurt decided to let it go.

"Are you telling me he sleeps in here? With tougher-than-nails Military Dog Handler Staff Sergeant Kurt Crawford, or however you say it."

"You forgot the ex, and yes, recently anyway."

"That is so freaking sweet. I love your soft side, and that you work so hard not to let it show."

She cuddled next to him as he crawled in beside her again. He pressed his lips over her shoulder and tried to still the jumble of thoughts filling his head, as full of hope as they were doubt.

"Champagne?"

"No." She locked her arms around his torso. "Later, please." Her voice was thick and heavy. He knew how exhausted she had to be. He wasn't far from it himself. "If I doze a few minutes, will you wake me?" she added. "I want to stay awake and savor all this, but now that my heartbeat's slowing down, I don't think I'd have the energy to run from a pack of wildebeests."

"Then it's a good thing wildebeests aren't running free in St. Louis."

She giggled and snuggled deeper against him, laying her head on his chest. Mr. Longtail joined them, seemingly having tired of eyeing the puppies with disdain and determined to fight for his choice of pillow.

"So, this is you every night, snuggling with a cat, and the world's best dog at the foot of your bed." Her words ended in a deep yawn.

He kissed the top of her head, savoring the feel of her long, silky hair against his skin. "I'd like to make one thing clear. I've never snuggled with that cat. We fight determinedly over who gets the best pillow."

"Is that so? Well, I love you anyway."

She was so close to sleep that he wondered if she was even paying attention to whether he would say it back. He opened his mouth, but the words stuck in his throat. Instead, he smoothed his hand along the soft skin of her back until her breathing was deep and even and her body was fully relaxed.

Here it was, the world that he wanted so impossibly close. It would be easy to drift off next to her. Exhaustion beckoned him. He floated between sleep and consciousness, the flickering candles going in and out of focus. Mr. Longtail chose the pillow above Kelsey's head, kneading it along with the top of her hair. Content on his pile of clothes, Frankie was snoring the soft, easy snore that had carried Kurt through the last several nights.

The dreams started even before he was fully asleep. Candlelight burst into flame. The blood of this morning's birth swept into the blood of death. Helplessness and loss encircled him. And somewhere, perhaps close by, perhaps impossibly far away, Nana, draped in a purple-and-gold shawl, reached a weathered hand in his direction, calling him to join her.

He bolted upright, covered in sweat. How much time had passed? Not much, he suspected. Kelsey had turned onto her other side and was sleeping contentedly. Frankie lifted his head off the floor, eyeing Kurt cautiously. Mr. Longtail had obviously been disturbed the most. He'd rolled off the pillow onto the bed where Kurt had just been. With his ears back and low on his head, the cat began grooming himself as if making a statement that the movement had been intentional.

Knowing that getting back to sleep now would be an impossibility, Kurt got out of bed and nudged Frankie off his pants. After dressing, he told Frankie to stay and headed downstairs in the darkened house as quietly as possible, not wanting to rouse the other dogs.

Keeping the light off, he headed into the kitchen, grabbed a glass, and drank two full glasses of water without pausing. He stared out the window into the night. His mind was turning in rapid-spin circles, and his body craved being thrown into movement. Aside from driving, physical labor was the only thing he'd found that could slow the racing in his mind.

From his pants pocket, Kurt felt his phone buzz with a text message. Pulling it out, he looked at the screen. Sara.

Never mind. Good night. We can talk tomorrow.

It was hard to believe it was only ten fifteen. He and Kelsey had gone upstairs about eight, which put him falling asleep at around nine or nine thirty.

Sara had tried calling twice while he'd been asleep or otherwise engaged.

He pressed her number, returning the call as he strolled the length of the kitchen.

"You awake?" he asked when she answered on the second ring.

"Yes, but not for long."

"Everything okay?"

"It's fine. Kelsey told William how you brought a stillborn puppy back to life this morning. He told me about it, which means he was impressed. I thought you might want to know."

"Thanks. The puppy is bigger than the others. A lot bigger. I wouldn't be surprised if she turns out to be part Saint Bernard or Bernese mountain dog. How was your second date? I meant to call. It was a crazy day."

"That's okay. I don't expect this checking-in-with-Mom thing to come as natural as breathing, but we'll get there. And it was great. The art museum was wonderful, and afterward, we walked around Forest Park. It's beautiful there."

"Is there a date number three scheduled?"

"Yes, a dinner one. That's taking a step toward the serious, isn't it? And I didn't sleep with him, if you're wondering."

"Trust me, I wasn't."

Kurt returned to the sink. A glass sphere the size of a softball resting on the windowsill caught his attention. It was cool and smooth against his hand. He'd never seen it before. Though he couldn't imagine why, something about it struck a strong chord in his memory. The bottom had a small lip of extra glass. He flipped on the small light over the sink and blinked as his eyes adjusted. The ball was translucent green and imperfect, obviously handblown.

The hair on his neck and arms stood on end. Memory flooded in. He was a boy curled into bed, and Nana was sitting beside him in her pink nightgown and matching robe, running her fingers through wisps of his hair. There was a book on his lap about a boy and a beach and his grandmother. *Someday we'll go. Just you and I. We'll find a float of our own. And you'll have it to remember your nana.*

"Mom," he said louder than he intended. She was going on about something, and he'd not been paying attention. "What was Nana buried in?"

"Um, her good navy dress. The one she wore to weddings. Why?"

Because in my dreams she's always in purple and gold. But he couldn't say that. "Did she…did she used to wear a shawl when I was a kid?"

"Um, maybe. Probably. I remember I grew up embarrassed about how she was always in a dress like we were living in the fifties. I think she wore shawls to church instead of jackets when it was cool out. She stopped wearing them at some point or another. Her cousin brought her one from Mexico though. She loved it."

"What…" He closed his thumb and forefinger over the bridge of his nose and swallowed. He knew the answer but still needed to ask. "Can you describe it?"

"It's silk, I guess. Probably expensive. I have it, if you want to see it. It's purple with little gold fleurs-de-lis."

Kurt released a shaky breath. "Do you ever dream about her?"

"Sometimes. Not as much recently. At first, almost every night. You probably won't believe me, but the reason I went to get a mammogram was because of a dream I had with her in it."

He closed his eyes and tilted his head up to the ceiling. "You know, I do. I believe you."

He stuck through another few minutes of conversation, then said goodbye, hung up, and headed back upstairs. Frankie was lying at the top of the steps, waiting for him. He clambered into a sleepy stance, then dipped into a stretch as Kurt rounded the top.

He followed Kurt into his room. Kurt slid the closet door open as quietly as possible and pulled out the box he'd tucked into a corner. Frankie sat at attention, watching. Using his phone for a light, Kurt sifted through the contents till he found the book. *Why this? Why a beach over halfway across the continent?*

Knowing there was only one way he'd find the answer, he stood up and moved across the room, blowing out the candles that were still lit. Kelsey's breathing was deep and even, inviting him to crawl in next to her again.

Instead, he grabbed a hoodie and shoes from the closet, and his wallet and phone charger from the nightstand drawer. Everything else he could do without for a few days.

He tapped his hand on his thigh, beckoning Frankie to follow him. He opened the stair gate to Frankie's room and motioned him in. "Back to your room, guy. I'm sure your dreams are a bitch, but it'll be morning before you know it."

Obediently, Frankie crossed the threshold but turned and sat at attention, whining softly as Kurt locked the gate closed, this time a few inches higher. Stocky as he was, Frankie wasn't built for jumping. It was impressive he'd made it as high as he had.

Kurt headed back into the kitchen and sifted through the junk drawer for a pen and a pad of paper. He crossed to the counter next to the sink and stared at the paper in the narrow beam of yellow light that lit the sink area.

There was already so much unsaid. How could he possibly explain? He couldn't. He only hoped she would trust him.

After an eternity of searching for words that were too stubborn to present themselves, he filled the notepad with a few irritatingly insignificant ones.

There's something I have to do. I wouldn't
leave if it wasn't important. I hope to explain
everything in a few days.

He signed it simply "Kurt."

He placed it on the counter where Kelsey would see it first thing and flipped off the light. He headed toward the front of the house but stopped in his tracks twenty feet from the door. Frankie was sitting in front of it. The main floor was filled with cages of dogs, and like the cat, he'd left them all alone.

"Is this your way of telling me you need to crap?" Kurt decided to trust the dog and let him out off leash. He opened the creaky door as quietly as possible and made Frankie wait until he stepped out first. The front yard was empty of possums or raccoons or anything that might be chased away into the night. "Come on, boy," he said, opening the door the rest of the way.

Frankie wasted no time crossing the porch and heading down the stairs. He peed a quick pee on the first bush he passed, then beelined straight to Kurt's Mustang and sank to his haunches, waiting expectantly.

Kurt shook his head, chuckling. Leaving the door ajar, he crossed the lawn halfway and whistled for Frankie to come. Frankie did nothing more than wag his long, thin tail and look at Kurt with his lopsided grin.

Kurt crossed the rest of the way to him and sank into a squat. "Listen, boy, I couldn't take you if I wanted to." He stroked Frankie's smooth shoulder. Frankie cocked his head hopefully. What did dogs know about court cases and house confinement? "How do you even know I'm going? Did I rattle my keys too loudly?"

With a sigh, Kurt stood and opened his door, raising the seat and motioning Frankie into the back. Then he jogged back into the house, grabbed a leash and a couple tennis balls, and added a few more words to the bottom of his note.

By the way, I've got Frankie.

He was locking the door when he changed his mind and returned to the kitchen, picking up the pen and adding one more thing.

And tonight was incredible.

Chapter 27

THE BRIGHT SUN STREAMING INTO THE ROOM WAS disorienting. So was the fur blanket covering the top half of her head. Struggling to shake out of a particularly deep sleep, Kelsey blinked her eyes open. She was on her side, staring at two impressively tall windows overlooking a beautiful oak in full-color foliage.

Her apartment bedroom faced a dark cranny between buildings and never saw direct sun, so even before memory kicked in, she knew she wasn't home. And the hot fur blanket was obviously not a blanket. It was purring.

She slid out from underneath Mr. Longtail as memory returned. She looked around, rubbing her eyes. Kurt was gone. He'd probably gotten up with the sun. Memories of last night flooded her, along with a happy, contented warmth. Like she'd suspected it would be, the two of them being together was beautiful. It was more than beautiful. It was the most incredible thing she'd ever experienced.

The champagne and cookies sat untouched on the nightstand. She was sorry not to have enjoyed them when he'd put in so much effort, but at least the champagne was still corked. They could open it tonight.

She picked up a couple of cookies—her mouth watered at the plentiful chocolate chips encased in perfectly browned dough—thinking they'd make a nice morning pick-me-up for the two of them. At some point, the candles had gone out, but the rope lighting was still on. The closet door was open, and there was a box on the floor she hadn't noticed last night. On top of it was a children's book she'd never seen. It wasn't something she'd have expected to find lying around in Kurt's room. Perhaps the book and box had belonged to Sabrina.

After getting dressed, she paused outside Pepper's room. The proud mamma trotted over to the stair gate, likely needing to pee. "You and me both." Hearing the soft grunts and whines of the puppies, Kelsey clipped Pepper's leash that hung by the door and opened the stair gate to her room. Pepper followed as Kelsey jogged to the whelping box for a peek. The sight of the cozy puppies cuddled together made her insides melt with joy. In a little over twenty-four hours, they already looked bigger and stronger. Of the nine, seven seemed to be all Rottweiler. The other two had marked differences— from their siblings and from each other. She suspected Kurt was right about the puppy who'd given everyone a scare. She was a giant compared to her siblings and had the markings of a Saint Bernard mix.

Cookies in one hand and Pepper's leash in the other, Kelsey headed downstairs. The dogs were awake and ready for the morning routine to begin. Kurt was nowhere in sight. She was dropping the cookies on the counter when she caught sight of his note. Her brow furrowed as she read it.

What did that mean, he hoped to explain in a few days? Certainly it didn't mean he'd be gone that long.

Or did it?

Her chest tightened at the thought.

Seven years of maturity and figuring out who she was seemed to shrink away. She was that girl from sophomore year again, watching Steve grin at her sheepishly. *Sorry, Kels, I just didn't feel it.*

She stumbled out the door onto the back porch, Pepper trailing close behind. Kelsey unhooked the dog after double-checking that no other dogs were out. Pepper trotted down into the open grass to pee, then over to a corner to finish her business.

Kelsey sank into a patio chair and closed her eyes, forcing her breath to be slow and even as she reined in her racing thoughts. She could feel the outline of her phone in her back pocket. She pulled it out and set it on the table. No missed calls, and her battery was almost dead.

She unlocked it and opened her texts, clicking on Kurt's number and typing out a message.

> Saw your note. Things are good here. Take all the time you need. And I agree.

She gave Pepper another few minutes to sniff around, then called her up. She was sliding her phone into her pocket when it vibrated with a new text. Half holding her breath, she looked at the screen.

> Thank you. Will explain soon. Tess will help feed until I get back.

It wasn't much, but it wasn't nothing either.

Her phone vibrated with a warning that she was down to two percent. Then it vibrated again with another text.

I love you, Kelsey.

Tears stung her eyes. She blinked them away and took a single, deep breath. "I think I knew that already, but thank you for saying it, Kurt Crawford."

—◆—

Kurt was hardly even out of the city and over the Missouri River bridge before doubt crept in about the decision to drive over halfway across the country in hopes of a bit of clarity. He silenced it with heartfelt assurance that this was what he needed to do.

He wasn't one to believe in ghosts, but he'd heard enough stories to know not to discount deep, personal connections between people. He'd learned firsthand of military parents and spouses who knew intimate details of their beloved soldiers' deaths before being told. Maybe it was a touch of ESP or something that was yet to be understood. In any case, he was determined not to rethink the decision.

Frankie seemed to enjoy the ride. As soon as the Mustang's wheels hit the highway, he curled up and went to sleep. He wasn't the first dog with a perplexing history. Considering the horrific condition he'd been in, it wouldn't have been surprising if he had little interest in human companionship. The fact that he was so willing to connect was not only touching but a sign that, at some point, he'd been well cared for.

Kurt's short doze alongside Kelsey had provided the fuel needed to drive till dawn. As the sky lightened behind him, he pulled off at a truck stop south of Lincoln, Nebraska. He fueled up and let Frankie drink out of a spigot at the side of the building. Then he led him on a twenty-minute walk down an adjoining two-lane road marked by a narrow strip of woods and fields stretching out on either side. The sun rose over the horizon, and the fields came to life with birdsong in the chilly fall morning. He stopped to watch a hawk on a wire preening its tail while Frankie sniffed and marked new territory.

Determining it wasn't too early, Kurt checked in with Tess to confirm that she would be able to hang out at the Raven estate for the next few days to help with the feeding and keep the training sessions going. Then his phone buzzed with the text from Kelsey. Take all the time you need. Her saying it didn't surprise him. He pulled up her number and was about to hit Dial when he felt his throat locking up. There was so much he wanted to tell her, and it was infuriating that he couldn't. He shot off a text that didn't come close to penetrating the surface. Then, after slipping his phone into his pocket, he pulled it out and added that he loved her, one too-small step in building a bridge between the life he imagined and one he'd grown comfortable with.

When they made it back to the gas station, Kurt drove to the quiet, back corner of the parking lot, cracked the windows, and fell into an easy, dreamless doze. He was thankful he'd taken Thomas's advice to replace the original front seats with models that reclined. The Mustang was doing remarkably well for so much road time, but it hadn't been designed for comfort and cross-country trips. He woke with a kink in his neck that brought to mind some of the soldiering nights he'd spent without a bed and made him wish he'd thought to grab a pillow.

He gave Frankie a pat and headed into the truck stop

for a ready-made breakfast burrito, a gargantuan black coffee, and a small bag of dog chow. When he got back, he led Frankie to a narrow strip of grass in front of the car and slit the bag open lengthwise for a makeshift bowl. Kurt held the leash and leaned against the hood as he ate. Frankie, who was never one to leave a bite of food uneaten, chomped away but kept eyeing Kurt's burrito as if it were the better option.

By the time they were on the interstate again, Kurt felt ready to meet the long miles that lay ahead.

———※———

Kelsey and Tess were upstairs in an empty bedroom working with Louie, a young brown-and-white bull terrier who was one of the dogs who needed considerable retraining, when Kelsey spotted Kurt's grandfather's truck pulling in as usual. Not quite as usual was the sight of Kurt's mom in the passenger seat.

"Kurt's mom and grandfather are here. I wasn't sure if William would come today."

Tess stood up from the floor where she'd been kneeling by Louie and met Kelsey at the window. "I haven't seen his mom in forever. I swear she looked just like that ten years ago," she said, watching Sara climb down from the truck.

Tess hadn't asked a single question this morning when she'd arrived; she'd simply dived into work. As much as it had been a relief not to have to answer questions she didn't have an answer to, Kelsey wondered how much Tess knew. Whenever her mind started to spin like a tumbleweed, she reminded herself of Kurt's last text. He loved her.

Not only had he said it, but he'd shown it last night by decorating the room and with his tender kisses and attentiveness in bed. Kelsey wished he'd been able to share more of what he'd been dealing with these last couple of weeks. She'd caught on enough to know it was something big but was determined to trust that whatever he was doing would help.

"I wonder if they know he's gone." Kelsey readjusted her ponytail.

Tess gave her a sympathetic smile. "I wouldn't be surprised if they didn't. But it doesn't have to be on you to explain. That's the beauty of cell phones, right?"

Kelsey smiled. "True. Did he, uh, tell you where he's going?"

"No, he only asked me to back you up till he got back."

"He didn't tell me either, obviously."

"I wouldn't sweat it, if I were you. I've known Kurt forever. He's a man of actions, not words, but I know he's got it bad for you. Even William refers to you as 'the' girl." She made air quotes at the last part.

"Thanks, that's nice to hear. Everything's still so new, you know? Look, if you're good, I'll get Sara and William settled and be back in a few minutes."

Tess gave her a thumbs-up before dipping into the treat pouch belted around her waist for another bite of turkey and asking Louie to sit at attention.

Kelsey headed downstairs and met Sara and William as they headed in the front door. The house was relatively quiet because the dogs had settled down after their morning meal and exercise time.

William nodded a hello, and Sara pulled Kelsey into an easy hug.

"Kurt stepped out," William confirmed. It wasn't a question. He'd noticed the missing red Mustang out front.

Kelsey nodded, gnawing on her lip. "Yeah. I'm not sure when he'll be back, but make yourself at home…or at rehab, anyway."

"I'm just dropping him off and borrowing the truck for the day, but I wanted to see those little puppies brightening up your shelter's Facebook page. William told me how Kurt brought a stillborn back to life," Sara said.

"It was amazing to watch. I think a full five minutes passed before the puppy started breathing, but you wouldn't know it to look at her. She's the biggest of the bunch and super energetic."

William followed them up for a second look. He'd been here the previous afternoon and had spent a few minutes watching the puppies cuddle, squirm, and nurse, chuckling the whole time. Even someone with an exterior as toughened as his could be melted by fuzzy newborn puppies.

For Sara, who seemed to be the exact opposite of her father in terms of holding back emotion, it took one quick look to be smitten.

"Pepper's a great mom," Kelsey said. "And she doesn't seem bothered with us holding them. We've been staying in here where she can see us though. Let me know which one you want to hold."

Sara chose the pup who seemed to be part coonhound, giggling over his long ears. With his stern look softening, William spent a minute stroking a silky ear before heading back downstairs to work.

"Your father's really transforming this house," Kelsey said after he was gone.

"I think he's finally realized there's life outside the military. I think he'd have been just as happy being a carpenter, and that might have been for the best for all of us. But I guess you can't turn back the clock." She smiled at the pup who was curled against her, belly exposed. He stopped whining quickly and dozed off at her soft touch. "I know we don't each know other that well, but I know how much Kurt thinks of you. Has he been okay? He's been ignoring me lately.

Kelsey sucked in her cheek in debate. He'd clearly had some issues with his mom, but things had seemed better between them lately. Her having breast cancer had to have put things in a different perspective. "He's okay. He's been a little quiet, but okay."

Sara sank onto the bed. "I've been rethinking showing him that letter."

Kelsey tightened her ponytail and looked away.

"He didn't tell you, did he?"

"No. Whatever it is, he didn't." From across the hall, Louie barked twice and Kelsey heard Tess's muffled praise. "But I suspect he's trying to work through it."

"I found his father. For so many years, it didn't seem like a possibility. But then, all of a sudden, it is."

Kelsey's jaw dropped, and she forced it closed. "Do you think he's going to see him?"

Sara blinked. "You mean he's *gone* gone?"

Kelsey shrugged helplessly. "He left last night. He hasn't said where he's going, only that there's something he needed to do. Tess is helping with the dogs until he gets back. She doesn't know anything either, but we both took it that he'd be gone a few days."

"He didn't take the letter, didn't open it even. So

that's not it. Last night he called me late, after ten. I knew something was up; I just didn't know what. He was asking questions about my mom. It's really why I came along today. I wanted to see him." She fell quiet, stroking the puppy, her eyebrows furrowed tightly together. After a minute, she shifted the puppy in her arms and pulled out her phone. "Can you take him?"

Kelsey took the puppy while Sara focused full attention on her phone.

"His phone used to be my mom's. All our phones were tracking enabled at the store when we bought them. I think I know where he's going, but this will tell me for sure." After a bit more searching, Sara closed her eyes. "He's such a Crawford, I swear." She stood up and slipped her phone into her pocket and crossed over to the window. "The little turd is already halfway across Nebraska."

"Nebraska?"

Sara let out a soft sigh. "It's okay. You don't need to worry. None of us need to worry. Even if that crazy car breaks down, he'll be okay. He's a Crawford, and Crawfords endure. But the thing is, I think this is his way of trying to do more than that."

Kelsey felt like the pieces weren't clicking. "Do you know where he's headed?"

"Yeah, I do. The Oregon coast. It seems my son is seeking a bit of closure."

Kelsey blinked, remembering the book she'd spotted by his closet and how her fishing float had been moved off the windowsill and set on the counter.

"Why there?"

"The best I can explain is that he was supposed to go a long time ago, and life got in the way."

Chapter 28

THE THIRTY-TWO-HOUR DRIVE PROVED MORE CATHARTIC than Kurt would've imagined. He settled into a routine, driving as long as he could keep awake and Frankie could stay content, which tended to be eight or so hours. At that point, he found somewhere to park and took a long walk, ate, and slept until something woke him up.

His favorite stop was in Sweetwater County, Wyoming, pretty much smack-dab in the middle of nowhere. At nearly seven thousand feet, the rise in altitude was palpable. The air was thin and crisp, and the temperature was hovering about ten degrees above freezing as the sun set. There wasn't a tree in sight, just rolling hills, tall grasses, and scrubby brush, and a stubby mountain chain in the distance.

A herd of horses grazed near the road. They watched Kurt and Frankie walking by as though they'd never seen anything but cars and trucks.

The way Frankie came to life at seeing them—wagging his tail and barking and dropping into a play bow, enticing the nearest horse to run and buck—made Kurt laugh. After watching the horses a bit, they headed down a dirt road. When they'd made it a safe distance from the herd, Kurt unleashed Frankie and let him run until he was panting heavily and content, his crooked smile wide and drooly.

"Thank God you're getting a second chance, buddy. Kind of makes you want to believe again, doesn't it?"

Kurt blinked away the unexpected tears stinging his eyes. He'd let Frankie in, let them all in, even though he hadn't planned on it. It had started with Kelsey, then the house, then everything else came tumbling along after.

By the time they made it back to the Mustang, it was almost fully dark. The passenger-side door wasn't closed completely, which made Kurt start. He'd gotten Frankie out the driver's-side door. The road was deserted but someone had been here, checking out his car. Nothing seemed harmed, and he'd had the keys and anything of value on him. The glove box was open, and he spotted Nana's rosary inside, lying on top of a few napkins. Lifting it out, he held it in the dim light. The wooden beads were faded and worn from her many prayers. He'd carried the rosary around in his pocket the first few days after getting it but had no recollection of putting it in the glove box. Yet, here it was.

Beside him, Frankie whined as he looked around in the darkness. "Yeah, yeah, I hear you, buddy. We'll head into town before we catch some z's."

Kurt slipped the rosary into his pocket, loaded Frankie up, and continued on until he reached a brightly lit truck stop. He was so fatigued by then that he fell into a doze within seconds of turning off the ignition. He woke a few hours later. Frankie had wedged the front half of his body between the bucket seats and was licking his face.

After grabbing a meal for each of them, refueling, and letting Frankie stretch his legs, Kurt continued west, dipping into Utah, then driving through Idaho. Passing the

Oregon state line renewed his energy, as did the second sunrise of the trip. The green hills of Oregon seemed to stretch on forever. He napped again midway through the day and suspected that tonight, no matter what happened when he reached the beach, he'd need to find a room to stretch out in before heading back tomorrow.

By the time he finally made it to the coast, the sun wasn't far above the horizon, and the western sky visible in gaps in the forest promised a spectacular sunset. He caught glimpses of the ocean as he drove the last few meandering miles to a beach town. A pleasant calm trickled over him, and he couldn't help but feel as if Nana was beside him in the passenger seat.

He should've come home for her funeral. He suspected that's what had been bothering him most of all. He'd extended his service three times. He could've taken leave, but he didn't even try. Instead, he pushed her smiling brown eyes, slim frame, and wrinkled-smooth skin from his mind and immersed himself in duty.

If she'd been here, she would probably have told him there was some pain you couldn't work through. Some pain was so real that there was nothing to do but let it in. Somehow, though, he'd made it through mourning her with his head bent down in duty, first in the service and later at the Sabrina Raven estate.

And even before seeing the beach—the reason he'd driven all this way—he felt deep in his core that somehow, now he was okay. He was ready to let it all go. Ready to move on. Ready to really live. That letter of his mother's could wait. For months, maybe for years. Someday, he'd open it. Or maybe he wouldn't.

Having finally reached the western edge of the

continent, he parked in a public access lot. He stepped out, stretched his stiff back and neck, and sucked in a breath of cool ocean air before raising the seat to let Frankie hop out.

Frankie raised his head as he jumped down, sniffing the sea-salt moisture on the wind. Storm-gnarled evergreens decorated the edges of the parking lot and nearby two-story hotel. Cedar-planked coastal houses dotted the hillside, nestled in a wash of green firs, spruces, hemlocks, and cedars.

Kurt spotted a pedestrian sign for the beach and urged Frankie along. They wound through a dense grove of waxy brush that opened to an expanse of light-gray sand, blue-gray ocean brushed with foamy white caps, rolling dunes, haystack rock formations jutting out of the water, and rocky cliffs surrounded by a forest of emerald green.

A smile tugged at the corners of Kurt's mouth. He chuckled and brushed tears from the corners of his eyes. He'd been a lot of places, but he'd never seen anything so starkly beautiful. He suspected Nana would've agreed with him. He could swear he caught the scent of her lavender lotion in the salty air. His hand slipped into his pocket and closed over the wooden bead rosary.

He led Frankie north on the beach, away from a small group of people wading around a massive rock haystack that rose several stories skyward at the edge of the ocean. A half-dozen beachgoers had dogs with them. Some on leashes, others off. Frankie eyed them warily until they were far enough away, then he turned his attention to the lapping waves.

The sun sank low, sending a yellow, gold, and purple glow across the sky. Kurt unclipped the leash and let Frankie run across the deserted sand. If he could do anything over, it would be to bring Nana here.

A memory rushed in of the day in fifth grade when he beat up Jimmy Varges for spitting on a third grader and got expelled for two days. The worst part was coming home to face the sternness of William Crawford. After a lecture that wounded his pride more than any spanking ever had, Kurt had locked himself in his room.

He let Nana in sometime later. She sank to the bed beside him after having pulled that book out of God knows where. She hadn't read it to him in a couple of years. He was too old to be read to. But he let her read it and still knew every upcoming picture before she turned the page. A boy and his grandma and a cold, windy beach and nobody else in the world.

He held the rosary in an open, calloused palm. A wave crashed over his feet. The water was shockingly cold. A seagull circled curiously before landing a few feet in front of him, eyeing the draping rosary and all but ignoring the dog who was running in and out of the water, barking and kicking up sand.

Kurt walked for a long time, letting the waves numb his feet through his boots, watching the sun disappear below the horizon. Once it was gone, a silver light hung in the air and stars began to dot the darkening sky. The beach was nearly empty aside from a few people huddled around campfires far back from the waves.

When it was so dark he could barely make out the edge of the ocean on the horizon, he pitched the rosary far out into the water.

"I miss you, Nana." Beside him, Frankie looked up and whined as he gave a hopeful wag of his tail. "Yeah, I know, buddy. It's time to go home."

Chapter 29

IDA GREENE PRESSED THE BUTTON TO THE ELEVATOR ON THE entry floor of the Clayton high-rise after checking her paperwork for the correct floor, number seventeen. She gave a silent exclamation over what an intuitive person Sabrina had been, right up through the end. Whatever it was that waited for good souls at the end of this life, Ida was determined her sister was there and smiling over this turn of events.

Inside the crowded elevator, Ida settled in for the ride next to the men and women in tailored suits who were going places without seeming to notice much of anything.

Her sister's law firm, the one that had written her will, was at the northwest edge of the building and had a pleasant view of Forest Park. Megan, the shelter's director, was already there and waiting in a conference room with floor-to-ceiling windows.

Ida was ushered into the room by an assistant but turned down the water she was offered. Megan stood up and wrapped her in a hug.

"Thanks so much for meeting me here and, more importantly, for agreeing to this."

Ida waved her off. "How could I not? It's the best possible outcome I could've imagined for my sister's house, and it's a win for your shelter too. Sabrina's will was so long and tedious that I don't remember the stipulation even being in there. Did you know it all along?"

"Honestly, no, I didn't. It took Kurt calling and asking to have the will reviewed."

"I'm not afraid to say how fond I am of that young man. And of your Kelsey. She was over yesterday. Brought me lunch. She showed me pictures of your special day. It was lovely. And I've been enjoying my wonderful honey pot."

"Thanks, and I'm glad. It's been a bit of a whirlwind, but I'm really happy."

"Well, if I can give you any advice, it would be not to get too busy to stop and smell the roses. Or to bake a pie. That's always been my favorite activity and the one that reminds me of all the good this world provides."

"I appreciate the reminder. Kelsey told me how amazing your pies are."

"Did I hear you right that Kurt's due back tomorrow? If so, I'll bake one in the morning. Stop by and have a slice, if you will."

Megan was accepting the invitation when the door swung open and a woman stepped in. She introduced herself as a legal assistant and said she'd be taking care of the paperwork.

Ida slipped on her glasses and skimmed the passage in the will that gave her permission to oversee the sale of her sister's estate prior to Mr. Longtail's passing, as long as the shelter could provide proof that he would be well accommodated for.

"Well, since Kurt intends to keep him right where he is, I can't see how that mischievous cat could possibly be better accommodated. And my sister's lovely home couldn't have found its way into better hands, of that I'll guarantee."

The assistant smiled. "Great. From what I've been told, the sale won't be final until the dogs have been rehabbed and moved to the shelter so as not to void permits, but a fair price has been agreed upon by both parties. So, if you've no objection, I just need a few signatures and the sale can proceed as directed in Amendment C."

Ida signed in several places and afterward walked out into the main hallway with Megan.

"That baby of yours... Have you found out what it will be?"

Megan's hand closed over her belly. "No, I guess we're dinosaurs that way. Everyone I know has been having gender reveal parties, but we really want the delivery room surprise."

"I, for one, appreciate that. If you ask me, a life well lived has exactly the right number of sincere surprises. It's always good to take it slow and savor them."

———

With Kurt away, Kelsey felt a bit like she was turning into him, flitting from one chore to the next and staying up way past her typical bedtime. She passed her first full night alone in the house with less unease than she might have expected. Tess, who was without a car on her return to St. Louis, had biked in for the day from her grandmother's in the Hill, the Italian-American neighborhood where Tess's family lived. She biked home just before dark, promising to return early the next morning.

After Tess was gone, Kelsey was alone in the quiet house. But rather than making her relive the unease she'd once felt arriving after dark to take care of Mr. Longtail, the house was almost cozy. Certainly, the dogs gave it warmth, but she suspected it was more due to her attitude. The Sabrina Raven estate wasn't the home of a deceased and mysterious donor any longer. It was the former home of a remarkable woman who had cared enough for it and her cat to brainstorm an unusual bequest, and in doing so, had kept the old house from being stripped of its character by indifferent investors hoping to make a few dollars.

Even if Kelsey hadn't been so comfortable staying, leaving the house unattended wasn't an option, not with the protesters still afoot. Locking up the shelter for the night was different. It had a security system and was in a bustling part of Webster Groves. And while the protesters hadn't thrown any bricks lately, when they weren't demonstrating in front of the shelter, they were trying to overturn permits and spamming the social media accounts with hateful comments.

Before going to bed, Kelsey gave serious thought to sleeping on one of the downstairs couches in case the protesters showed up again, but she opted for the comfort of Kurt's room where Mr. Longtail kept her company most of the night.

The next morning, after she and Tess finished the feeding routine, they headed to the side yard with Zeus and Orzo for one of the lighter training sessions of the day. Tess began working on basic training commands with Zeus, while Kelsey added to his challenge by creating constant distractions with Orzo. Once Zeus sat through a series of three basic command routines, he'd be awarded with a morning play session with his buddy.

A young jogger who lived one street over had met

Zeus on a run and was showing serious interest in adopting him when the court determined he and a few of the other easily socialized dogs could leave. Even though she knew she had to let things play out, Kelsey could hardly contain her excitement over the possibility that Zeus could settle so close to the Raven estate. To one day soon be able to see the big, playful dog on a jog with a loving owner would be surreal.

Shortly after Zeus was released from training and the dogs were starting to play, Kelsey noticed Patrick's gray Tacoma coming down the road.

"Patrick's early today," Tess said, surprising Kelsey by how accustomed she'd already become to the routine here. He typically didn't show up until midafternoon to work with Devil.

"Yeah, and who's that behind him?" Kelsey spotted an older-model minivan following just behind. She scrambled over to the rowdy duo of dogs and picked up Zeus's leash in case he developed an interest in checking out the visitor.

Patrick parked and offered a quick nod their way as he headed toward the minivan that had pulled in the circular drive just behind him. Through the lightly tinted glass, Kelsey could make out the profile of a woman whom she guessed to be in her early fifties. Her hair was one length, cropped short, and she was wearing a gray-checkered flannel jacket. When she stepped out to join Patrick, Kelsey noticed she was short and thin, almost frail.

Even though he wasn't talking loudly, Kelsey overheard Patrick saying, "That's his cage there, in the second window on the south side."

Kelsey's heart skipped a beat or two. "Oh my God, Tess, that must be Devil's first owner. She must have called back."

"Wow. I would've guessed she wouldn't come."

Kelsey understood her. Giving away a dog, learning about an ordeal like these guys had been through, and still coming forward took an enormous amount of courage. "Let's get these guys put away. I don't want any reason to get Devil's guard up."

They headed in through the back of the house, kenneled the dogs, and met up with Patrick and the woman on the front porch. He made introductions, then asked if Tina wanted to see the other dogs before reconnecting with Devil.

Tina flinched as the big dog's new name rolled off Patrick's tongue. "I'm not sure I can handle knowing what he's done to deserve that name, but for most of his life he's been Toby. And to be honest, my heart's broken enough without meeting any more of these poor creatures."

Patrick nodded a touch more matter-of-factly than he should've, considering the circumstances. "He doesn't do well with the other dogs. You should stay on the porch, and I'll bring him out."

Tess followed him inside, while Kelsey opted to stay with Tina. "Thank you for coming."

Tina brushed a tear from the corner of her right eye. Up close, it was easy to see she'd shed more than a few this morning. Her eyes were puffy, and her voice was nasal. "I promised myself I wouldn't cry in front of him. He can read me too easily. I had him for four and a half years, and I expected to have him for the duration of his

life, but there were circumstances beyond my control."
She brushed away fresh tears. "Toby was never an easy
dog. I had people tell me they thought he'd be better
behaved with a man as his master. I loved him dearly
though, and it was our life, not theirs."

Kelsey wondered if Patrick had braced her for the
dog that Devil had become in their time away from each
other. A dog who destroyed chew toys within a handful of minutes and was showing no progression with
his zero tolerance for other dogs. He wasn't aggressive
toward people though, or Rob wouldn't have allowed
him to come here.

She was debating whether or not to broach the topic
when Tess pulled the door open wide. "Patrick's walking him out."

Kelsey and Tina backed in front of the rocking chairs
as Patrick appeared in the doorway, holding Devil on a
short leash with two hands.

At first and as was typical, Devil's gaze immediately
locked on the road. Then Tina choked back a sob loud
enough to catch his attention. While his body froze,
Devil's head cocked sideways and he sniffed loudly.

Then, in a burst of commotion so abrupt Kelsey could
hardly register it, Devil dove toward Tina, yanking
Patrick off his feet and half dragging him along behind.
Kelsey braced for the small woman to be knocked down.
But as abruptly as he took off, Devil skidded to a halt
and burrowed his massive, drooly head against her as
he whined. His bushy tail wagged like a set of wipers
on high speed.

Tina sank to her knees and draped her hands around
his furry neck, sobbing. Her words were muffled and

nearly incoherent from her tears, but Kelsey caught the forgiveness being sought in them. The floodgates opened behind her own eyes.

Wanting to give Tina privacy, Kelsey excused herself and headed into the kitchen and toward the mountain of food and water bowls that needed cleaning. The warmth of the water and the silky soap bubbles always helped this chore to be a soothing one.

Tess came in ten minutes behind her. She sank into a chair and collapsed her head and chest on the table. "Wow." For a minute, she didn't add anything else. Then, after a long breath, she sat up and explained that Tina's father, a widower, had been diagnosed with an aggressive form of cancer around the time Tina had been laid off. She moved in with him just over a year ago. His condo had a twenty-five-pound pet limit, and after finding no one willing to care for Toby, Tina had located someone on a big dog forum who lived in Arkansas and was looking to adopt a dog his size. They met up halfway. The man had pictures of his deceased Great Dane, and he'd seemed like a trustworthy, caring person, but giving Toby away had been the hardest thing she'd ever done.

"A few weeks after Devil—I mean, Toby—was adopted, the man dropped out of contact," Tess added. "Tina worried he was blocking her calls, but she'd given Toby away so there was nothing she could do."

"That's terrible."

"Yeah, I know. She says her life has been empty without him. She understands about the trial and how Toby can't be released into her care until he's made a lot more progress, but she's fine with it. She's just across the river in Belleville. She'll come out every day until she can take him home. Patrick's going to time his visits here so they can work with Toby together. I guess he was always a bit stubborn and peculiar, but she knows how to get him to listen to her. Patrick's got her walking him around the yard, and Toby's focused on her every word."

"That's awesome. I was worried he was so damaged we wouldn't be able to get through to him. But that reaction when he saw her…" She teared up again and cleared her throat. "He's just a big, wounded baby. And Patrick was right. He wouldn't bond with anyone else because he was waiting for her. And did she say if her dad—"

Tess shook her head. "She said he passed away a few months ago. She's got his place for sale and is going to look for a house with a big yard for Toby."

Kelsey set the ceramic bowl she was holding on the last empty spot on the dish towel. "Wow. What a journey for both of them! And thank God it's going to have a happy ending. As long as Tina doesn't mind, this is going on the front page of our newsletter. I won't be surprised if Channel 3 wants to air it."

"You know, before I toured your shelter, I'd have thought I couldn't handle shelter work because it'd be too depressing, but I realize now I was only considering half the story."

Kelsey smiled and lifted the stopper, letting the dirty water drain out of the sink. "Trust me when I tell you, I wouldn't be in my seventh year here if the good didn't always have a tendency to outweigh the sad."

Chapter 30

KELSEY SPENT THE DAYS THAT KURT WAS AWAY INUNDATING herself with the dogs and an endless list of chores, and enjoying the company of Ida, Tess, and Patrick whenever there was a bit of downtime. The only part of her normal routine that she missed was swinging by the shelter at night to bring home one of the dogs. That didn't seem like the right thing to do when she was sleeping at Sabrina's. Bringing another dog through the door could add stress and cause undue excitement for the dogs that were here.

She contented herself at night with cuddling the puppies, which seemed to be getting bigger by the hour, and hanging out with Mr. Longtail, who was decidedly more affectionate in Kurt's absence.

By the time Kelsey made it to night four, Thursday night, she tucked herself into bed and pulled out her phone for another quick look at Kurt's most recent text.

I should be home tomorrow midmorning.
Can't wait to see you. It's been too long.

Home. Like *love*, it was a simple, often taken for granted word. She knew he could have meant St. Louis—or even Missouri for that matter, and not specifically this house—but she couldn't help but connect this place with him. She wondered if he had any idea how it fit him so perfectly: beautiful and complex and rugged, and just unpolished enough to have immeasurable character. She also knew he was one of the few people who could love it as much as it was meant to be loved.

She fell asleep listening to the puppies' soft sounds carrying across the top floor of the house and with her hand a barrier between her face and Mr. Longtail's. He wouldn't stop trying to nip her nose as he purred and settled down across two pillows.

Like the other nights she'd spent here, this one passed impossibly fast, and she blinked her eyes open to the first light of dawn. And to the sight of Kurt, asleep but fully clothed, lying atop the covers next to her.

She held her breath and counted out a handful of seconds to be sure it wasn't a dream. It was real. Kurt was back and in bed beside her. A small, brown paper bag was clutched in one hand by his stomach. The other arm was extended, and his hand rested on her hip. Mr. Longtail was at the top of his pillow, curled around Kurt's head.

Four long but busy days disappeared into nothingness. It was if he'd never been away a single minute. His chest rose and fell with ease. The tension that sometimes lined his forehead was gone, and he looked like a cross between an angel and a soldier, impossibly tough and vulnerable at the same time.

She studied him as the sun peeked over the horizon, wanting to commit him to memory, but trusting she didn't have to. He loved her, and he was home.

Then her phone alarm was blaring out Avicii's "Wake Me Up," and Kurt was awake and sitting up. Mr. Longtail rose to his feet, arching his back and stretching. Kelsey clicked off the alarm and sat up next to Kurt.

Frankie, who'd been sleeping on the rug at the bottom of the bed, stood and dipped into a deep stretch.

"Welcome back, traveler. I didn't think you'd be here until lunchtime."

Kurt swiped the sleep from his eyes and grinned. "I ended up driving through last night." He leaned close and pressed his lips against her temple. "Picking between sleeping another few hours in my car and catching a bit next to you was an easy decision." He closed one arm around her and swept her hair back with the other, kissing her neck. "Kels, I owe you an apology. A big one. I'll never leave again without telling you first. Hell, I can't imagine having anywhere else to go."

"I was never mad, just worried."

"I'm sorry," he repeated. "But I was in good hands. I had Frankie."

She laughed. "Yes, you were." She swallowed and thought of telling him that the last time she'd slept with someone, it had led to the end of a several-year friendship, but then decided it was pointless. That was a lifetime ago, and it wasn't with Kurt.

"What happened to make you take off so quickly?" she asked instead. "Was it seeing the fishing float I put on the kitchen windowsill? Your mom figured out where you went. She explained it to me the best she could, about your grandma."

Kurt sat straight and stared at her, blinking. "*You* put that float in the kitchen? I guess there's an answer for everything in time. But why? How?"

She shrugged and smiled. "Because I found it on the beach when I was a kid. I had it on my desk at the shelter forever. The other day, I decided to bring it here."

He dragged a hand through his hair, shaking his head. He was still a solid minute, then he started to laugh. It was a hearty, deep laugh of relief. "Of course. Of course you did. It couldn't have happened any other way."

He stood up and paced the room, the first light of the day glowing in his hair. Frankie watched him pace without missing a beat on the nylon bone he'd begun to chew.

"Did it help?" she asked finally. "Going there?"

"It did," he said, taking a seat at the edge of the bed. "Kels, there are things I haven't told you about my life before, things I may never be able to tell you. Friends, dogs that I didn't or couldn't protect. Choices I made. I'm too much like William for words to ever come easy—"

"It's okay, they don't have to."

He held up a hand. "My grandmother used to say that nothing up to today matters unless you choose for it to matter. Sometimes that makes sense, and sometimes it feels impossible. But a part of me has to believe it, because rather than running, I came here. I saw you six weeks ago on that news story, and I made a choice to stop running, stop evading, and I let you in. I let this house in and these dogs. Hell, when the time comes that he goes up for adoption, I'm going to throw my name into the hat for Frankie, even if it means going down to a one-dog house for a while. As long as you agree."

Kelsey blinked. *As long as I agree to what?*

Kurt lifted the forgotten bag off the bed and got up, walking around until he was directly at her side. He sank into a squat, resting on his heels.

"This isn't a proposal, so you can stop looking like a deer in headlights."

She bit her lip, unable to stop the smile from spreading across her face. "Thank God, because I'd be tempted to kiss you and I definitely have morning breath."

"If it were, this would be a real kneel and I'd have had the sense to let you get dressed first. What am I saying? No, I wouldn't. I love the way you look first thing in the morning in your pajamas with your hair all mussed, and when you're asleep too."

He smiled and passed her the bag. "It isn't much, but it stands for something bigger. At least, I'm really hoping it does."

Kelsey tucked back a strand of hair and sat straighter, folding her legs into a pretzel under the sheets. "Should I open it now?"

He nodded. Frankie had meandered over, and Kurt closed his hand over the top of his head, his nylon bone sticking out of his mouth like a cigar.

It was a plain paper bag stamped with the name of a store in Cannon Beach, Oregon. Kelsey sifted through tissue paper until her fingers closed over a small object. She pulled it out to find that it was a blown-glass Christmas ornament. It was a shiny dog figurine—a tan puppy wearing a Santa hat.

"It's so cute. I love it."

Kurt wrapped a hand over her wrist. "I asked her to keep it a surprise, but I spoke with Megan a few times on my way home. You know that things are moving in court. The first round of dogs, Zeus and a few of the others, might be able to head for the shelter in a month or less. Which means we could have a bit of space on the lower floor by Thanksgiving. Enough at least for a Christmas tree. A giant one. And I'm hoping this is the first of a lot of ornaments, Kels. I love you, and I want to make a home with you. This home, actually. I know you weren't that crazy about it in the beginning, but I'm hoping you've changed your mind."

She tucked a strand of hair behind her ear. "I love this house. It took me awhile to realize it, but I do. I love it. I can't imagine liking a house more than I do this one."

"I was hoping you'd say that because I'd like to buy it. I'd like to live here, with you."

"Kurt, I don't know if that's possible. For now it is, but the shelter will sell it at auction and probably not for years from now, and if you keep fixing it like you've been doing, it'll go for a lot of money. I'm not sure we'd be able to afford it."

He rose and pressed his lips against her forehead, then sat beside her. "What if I told you the attorneys reviewed the will and found a stipulation of sale that works in my—in our—favor?"

"What do you mean? I thought Mr. Longtail would have to be gone—"

"Not if Ida consents to an early sale, which she has."

"How do you know this?"

"Because with a bit of sleep figured in, it's a two-day drive between here and Cannon Beach. I had time to think. Time to make some calls. I wanted to tell you in person. The house is ours, if we want it. I know I do, and I'm hoping you do too."

Kelsey sat speechless, taking it all in. "You want to live with me, here, now."

"Here, yes, and forever. I love you, Kelsey. And I'm not afraid to tell you I want the whole package. I thought you might want to take it slower than a full proposal in less than six weeks, and honestly I wanted to plan it better—"

Kelsey silenced him with a kiss. There was a hint of salt on his lips. She wondered if it was from the ocean or something more recent, like a gas station snack.

She'd gone to the ocean once and found something that she'd been too afraid to admit until now proved she was the luckiest person on earth. She'd just been waiting all this time to let it in.

She ran her hands over the top of his strong shoulders, then his smooth neck, then his silky hair. She had the rest of her life to get used to being with him. As Frankie went back to gnawing on his bone and Mr. Longtail began to knead his front paws into her hip, she knew one thing already. She loved Kurt as much as she'd ever imagined loving anyone.

"Yes," she said. "Yes to everything."

Chapter 31

THE CAMPING CHAIR IDA WAS USING WAS DEEPER THAN SHE would've imagined, and she suspected she'd have to have a hand getting out of it when the evening was over.

With Halloween a week away, the backyard was decorated with happy ghosts, fuzzy spiderwebs, purple-black lights in the bushes, and white rope lighting circling the expansive tree trunks around the yard. Three pumpkins, the last straggling survivors of her sister's old garden, each one more imperfect than the other, lined the steps along the back porch. Pots of steaming chili and an assortment of fixings sat atop the porch table along with hot dogs and s'mores for roasting over the fire. Mr. Longtail was posed once again at the edge of the table, licking his paw indignantly after having been shooed away twice before.

The yard was filled with the rise and fall of laughter from people her sister would have enjoyed meeting. A crackling fire filled the yard with the pleasant smell of woodsmoke, reminding Ida of camping trips in Connecticut when her children were young, and of the circle of life.

Kurt returned from the house and passed Ida the blanket he'd gone inside to find. She thanked him and watched as he settled back down on the bench next to Kelsey on the opposite side of the fire and closed a hand affectionately atop her knee. The young couple exchanged a private smile before returning their attention to the lighthearted ghost story being told by one of the shelter volunteers.

Several kids sat on the ground on blankets in front of the benches and camping chairs, listening attentively. A few of them roasted marshmallows, while others were content to watch the dancing flames.

Having abandoned the table on his own, Mr. Longtail worked his way into the group through an opening in the edge. He walked over to a small girl with bouncy, angelic curls and sniffed noses with her. She giggled and pulled him onto her lap, which he tolerated surprisingly well, even though there was far more of him than her small, pretzeled legs could accommodate.

The girl buried her small hands deep in his long fur and babbled a string of adorations at him. From where Ida sat not far away, she'd almost swear the cat met her gaze. And if she knew anything at all, it was that the sparkle in his eyes was from more than the flickering light of the fire.

Ida Greene's Homemade Apple Pie

Ingredients

Pastry for a 9-inch double crust pie (Ida's crust
recipe is a family secret, so you'll have to find
your own)

½ cup unsalted butter

3 tablespoons all-purpose flour

½ cup white sugar

½ cup packed brown sugar

¼ cup water

1 teaspoon cinnamon

¼ teaspoon nutmeg

8 to 9 seasonal apples (Ida used Pink Lady and
McIntosh), peeled, cored, and sliced

Directions

Prepare and ready pie crust, cutting lattice strips for the
top. Store in fridge until needed.

Preheat oven to 425°F. Melt the butter in a saucepan on
medium heat. Gradually stir in flour to form a paste. Add
white sugar, brown sugar, water, cinnamon, and nutmeg,
and bring to a boil. Reduce temperature and let simmer.

Place the bottom crust in the pie pan. Fill and mound with apple slices. Cover with a latticework crust. Gently and slowly pour the sugar-and-butter liquid over the crust so that it does not run off.

Bake 15 minutes in the preheated oven. Reduce the temperature to 350°F. Continue baking for 30 to 45 minutes, until apples are soft. Cover the top loosely with aluminum foil if pie begins to over-brown.

Enjoy, or share with your neighbor.

Author's Note

While the High Grove Animal Shelter and the Sabrina Raven estate are fictional, St. Louis is full of diverse and charismatic neighborhoods, and some are highlighted in this story. A few of the South City shops and restaurants mentioned, like Gus', a pretzel shop, and Hodak's, one of the most popular fried chicken stops in the city, are real and worth a visit if you find yourself in St. Louis. The underground caves, old breweries, and empty lot believed to be an Underground Railroad site also mentioned are part of the town's rich history. The characters in this book, human and otherwise, are fictional, though Mr. Longtail bears an uncanny resemblance to my family's tetchy Maine coon–tabby mix.

**Read on for a sneak peek at book 3 in
Debbie Burns's Rescue Me series**

MY
FOREVER
HOME

**Coming soon from
Sourcebooks Casablanca**

Chapter 1

AFTER SIXTEEN MONTHS BACKPACKING AND TAKING ON seasonal jobs across Europe, Tess Grasso had racked up a healthy list of once-in-a-lifetime experiences. Especially, she thought, for a twenty-six-year-old who, before then, had never been out of her home state. She'd been back in her hometown of St. Louis for a month, and even though she was no longer seeing famous works of architecture or artwork or meeting people from all corners of the planet every day, the list was still growing.

For instance, before this morning, she'd never traveled alongside a 103-pound Saint Bernard while crammed into the confining back seat of a 1969 Mustang. An oversize, invasive, drooly Saint Bernard.

Not that Tess minded. She'd been a die-hard dog lover ever since she could remember. She wasn't much for classic cars or confining back seats, but snuggling with Fannie, the senior-aged Saint Bernard who belonged to the High Grove Animal Shelter until she was adopted, was almost fun. Tess had yet to renew her driver's license, so it was that or her old Schwinn ten speed.

Today was Halloween, and the last half of Tess's day was jam-packed. It was either miss seeing the High Grove Animal Shelter's Halloween Pet-A-Palooza or catch a ride. She'd been hearing about the event nonstop for the past week and was excited to get to see it firsthand.

Since shortly after returning home, Tess had been volunteering at the shelter's only off-site location, an old mansion where thirty-eight dogs that had been part of an illegal fighting ring were being rehabilitated before they could be adopted out. Even though Tess was trying to get her own career off the ground, she dedicated a part of every day to working with the sweet-natured dogs that were starting to shine after being given a second chance at life.

Earlier this morning, Fannie, who'd been found tied to a post in front of the shelter three months ago, had been brought to the private estate for what was being called phase two of the dogs' resocialization. After several weeks of work, many of the rehab dogs were being rewarded with greater degrees of canine socialization. Those Fannie had been introduced to this morning had previously completed several successful visits with the shelter's laid-back corgi, Orzo, who was also up for adoption.

Due to Fannie's massive size, she was considered a "next-level" dog. Like Orzo, nothing seemed to faze Fannie, and she got along great with other canines. But dogs that had been mistreated the way those at the estate had been were likely to be especially uneasy around dogs Fannie's size, and the rehab team was in the process of rebuilding their trust in other canines.

As suspected, Fannie had done great with the project dogs this morning. And nearly all of those that'd been introduced to her had done fabulous also.

As they neared the shelter, Fannie leaned farther into Tess with every turn. Tess's leg was going a touch numb under the weight of her, so she did her best to wiggle closer to the door. Doing so drew Fannie's attention away from the strip of front windshield visible between the bucket seats to Tess. She gave Tess's long, wavy brown hair a determined sniff and left behind a rather unpleasant string of drool.

Tess lifted the lock of affected hair so the drool wouldn't soak into her jacket. "Any napkins up there by chance, Kelsey?" Tess raised her voice over the load purr of the Mustang's engine.

In the Mustang's front passenger seat was Kelsey, the shelter's lead adoption coordinator. She was co-leading the rehab effort at the private estate, along with Tess's longtime friend Kurt, who was driving. Kurt was an ex-military dog handler and the owner of the Mustang. He was the lead dog trainer at the estate. Tess thought it was just about perfect how Kurt and Kelsey had gotten together while working at the remote estate.

At Tess's request, Kelsey fished through Kurt's glovebox. "Aha!" Craning to reach around the deep bucket seat, Kelsey passed a few napkins Tess's way. "Oh, Tess, there's more space on Fannie's other side than on yours. Can you nudge her over?"

Tess took the napkin and squeezed dry her damp lock of hair. Whenever she worked around dogs, Tess made it a habit of showering at night instead of in the morning. Tonight would prove to be no exception. "I tried, but she only leans harder. It's a good thing I'm a sucker for a cuddly Saint Bernard."

That Fannie had been left the way she had, without so much as a note, was baffling to Tess. Her bad habits were minimal to none. She was potty-trained, dog-friendly, nondestructive, and gentle. And judging by the condition of her coat, her weight, and her trusting temperament, Fannie had been well cared for. If she wasn't already a senior dog, she'd have been adopted several times over. Tess's fingers were crossed that Fannie would go to a great home.

As they neared the shelter, Kurt had to park nearly two blocks away. The street was lined with cars on both sides, and the parking lot had been roped off hours ago for the afternoon activities.

The Halloween Pet-A-Palooza was the shelter's big fall event. Previous adopters were encouraged to return with their pets for a variety of games and a pet costume contest that got more elaborate every year. Pet-A-Palooza was also an adoption event, and Tess had heard that the popular festival often resulted in one of the biggest adoption times of the year: the first typically being the week before Christmas; the other, the week after Parade Day, which was in the spring.

Once they were parked, Tess clambered out of the back seat and out the passenger side door. If the classic Mustang wasn't her friend's pride and joy, Tess would have commented that cars had come a long way in terms of everyday conveniences, such as the ability to get in and out with ease.

Fannie surprised them all with her agile hop over the folded-forward front seat. Free from the confines, Fannie gave a whole-body shake and wagged her bushy tail.

"Oh, hang on," Kelsey said. "Let's get Fannie's costume on here." From a purse big enough to double as an overnight bag, Kelsey pulled out a Saint Bernard–sized whiskey barrel that attached to a thick leather collar.

Fannie didn't mind when Kelsey buckled it around her neck.

"Simple but perfect, don't you think?" Kelsey asked. "It was in our costume collection, so I grabbed it this morning. She's our only Saint Bernard right now, so she had clear dibs."

"Good thinking." Tess rubbed Fannie on the forehead. "I'd say she looks ready to help monks search for stranded travelers along the Great St. Bernard Pass."

Kurt chuckled. "Tess, the dog trivia you've amassed over the years never fails to amaze me."

Tess squinched her nose. "Just remember you want me at your table if the shelter ever hosts a dog-themed trivia night."

Tess could hear the beat of a peppy Halloween song as it pulsed through the beautiful but brisk fall afternoon.

"I'm so glad you guys get to see how cool this is," Kelsey said as they headed toward the shelter. "It's my favorite event of the year. And it's the only time of year I can walk a dog and win a cupcake at the same time."

Kurt shot her a skeptical look. "Are you telling me there's a cakewalk for dogs?"

"Yep. And don't knock it till you see it. It's the Pupcake Walk. Every year, I play with one of the dogs till I win. There are killer cupcakes for adults and specialty pupcakes for the dogs. And the fun doesn't end there. There's a dog-and-owner agility course that's made its fair share of appearances on YouTube, plus several activities just for the dogs, like dog-bobbing for miniature wienies, a sandbox skeleton yard, and the ever-popular game-scented straw maze."

"By 'game,' do you mean like pheasant and duck?" Tess asked.

Kelsey nodded. "It's amazing what you can find at hunting goods stores. And you'll see how crazy the dogs go in the maze. It's not funny how much scent-marking those straw bales get before the day is over."

Tess laughed. "You guys really think of it all."

"It's because we've got a good group, and we've been able to perfect it over the years."

"And you're sure it's okay that I take some of the shelter dogs through the activities?"

"Oh, no question." Kelsey pulled her in for a hug as they neared the shelter, reminding Tess just how much taller her new friend was. Tess had topped out just below a petite-framed five foot four. Kelsey, an earthy blond, was a good six inches taller. "Just because you're helping at an off-site location doesn't mean you aren't a shelter volunteer."

"And in case she didn't tell you, Kelsey's been singing your praises around here," Kurt added. "It's the skilled help you've been giving us every day that is enabling us to train at the pace we've been keeping."

Tess let the compliment roll over her, remembering that the best thing to do with a compliment was to accept it graciously. Whether it was any one person's fault or a random sampling of genetics, she'd reached adulthood feeling a touch inadequate in just about every way except for when it came to her work with dogs.

Thanks to her transformative months in Europe, she'd found a peace and satisfaction with herself she hadn't known she'd been missing. And she'd come home ready to make a success of the healthy-pet canine-consulting business she was hoping to get off the ground. And with it, she hoped to help give financial support to deserving organizations like the shelter.

Tess switched the leash to her other hand as the shelter came into view behind the surrounding trees that were in full fall color. Fannie let out a woof and wagged her tail.

The unassuming redbrick building was decorated with an array of pumpkins, life-size dog and cat scarecrows, straw bales, and spiderwebs. The front parking lot was already a buzz of activity even though the event didn't officially start for another twenty minutes.

In addition to the activity stations, there was a food booth that sold snacks for people and pets, a silent auction, and a booth where one of the shelter volunteers would be drawing caricature sketches.

The shelter was small enough that it only employed a handful of people, and Tess knew each of them. The parking lot was filled with unfamiliar faces that Tess figured was a combination of volunteers, past adopters, and the public.

Many of the leashed dogs in the parking lot were in costume. Tess spotted a black lab who'd had an impressively anatomically correct dog skeleton painted onto his coat, a wiener dog in a banana suit, a three-headed dog whose two papier-mâché heads matched its real one, and a Lhasa apso Ewok. Tess's favorite was a mixed-breed white dog that had been painted so realistically with zebra stripes, she had to do a double take.

With an uncharacteristic burst of energy, Fannie leaped forward, dragging Tess along behind her. It took rebalancing her weight the opposite direction of

Fannie's pull and locking her feet into the ground for Tess to keep Fannie from diving into the throngs.

Kurt chuckled. "Want a hand? I wouldn't be surprised if she outweighs you."

"No thanks. I've got this." Tess pulled a treat from her jeans pocket and asked the excited dog to sit at attention. "I do, however, know which dog I'd like to start with." Fannie gobbled up the treat, leaving a wet spot on Tess's palm. "So, big girl, what do you say we get some of that energy out in the agility course first?"

"I think that's a smart idea," Kelsey agreed. "It's set up around back, along with the game-scented straw maze. That should tucker her out. You too, by the way. That agility course is also a cardio burst for people."

As if in understanding, Fannie tugged Tess onward. "Grab a dog, guys, and we'll see who's buying lunch later," Tess called over her shoulder. "And no, I didn't forget one of you is an ex-marine."

Then she let Fannie lead her away, but not before hearing a duet of chuckles and agreement following her.

The penetrating flash from the photographer's camera made Mason wince. He didn't need to count back days to the accident to know that the effects of the concussion were lingering.

"A few more will do it." The photographer, a middle-aged guy who'd recognized him in the crowd and asked for a few quick shots, was barely audible over the din from the crowd gathered at Ballpark Village for the city's biggest Halloween party.

The woman at Mason's side, the one whose name

he hadn't paid any attention to, moved closer into him, implying a connection they didn't share. This season, Mason's strongest yet, had left it all but impossible for him to go anywhere without being asked to pose for a picture. He'd not minded at first, and he didn't mind it now, but in the days since the accident, he was becoming more conscious of the image each snapshot portrayed.

The woman had approached him after he'd left Thomas for a trip to the bathroom. She'd been coming on to him, holding nothing back, when the photographer spotted him. Mason's left arm was bound in a sling, so she'd drawn in close at his right side. He closed his hand loosely atop her shoulder, keeping his body straight and not leaning in toward her, advice he'd been given by his publicist to help ward off the party-guy image a dozen or so wild nights this last year had created.

She had her hand pressed flat against his stomach, her pinkie resting above the rim of the wool kilt that was currently itching the hell out of him. She was clad in a leopard-spotted faux-fur bikini, long tail, pointy ears, and all, and had the body to pull it off.

Only Mason wasn't interested, however clear her signals were.

It was Halloween night, and he was out here working the crowd and signing autographs and locking his smile in place, for one reason only: to keep a promise to a buddy even though it conflicted with a stronger promise he'd made himself.

The season was over and winter was coming. Mason was craving quiet the way he craved water after a strenuous workout. The insanity that the most successful season of his career had brought would taper down.

It had been a marathon year, and he was ready for the finish line.

The fame he'd acquired still felt oddly surreal, sort of like the Ford Explorer he'd been in had when it had careered across the highway and tumbled into an embankment. Maybe there were some things you were never ready for. Not the things that changed your life in ways you'd never seen coming, and not even the ones your father warned you about.

The photographer snapped another few shots, then Mason stepped back, reclaiming an inadequate bubble of space around him. Leopard Girl's smile faltered. "Oh, come on, I can't let a man who looks this good in a kilt out of my arms without a fight. How about I buy you a drink and we find a spot in the corner to enjoy it?"

Mason read what she was saying with her eyes as clearly as he heard what she was saying with her lips. A year ago, he'd have brought her back to his place and let her rock his world. Hell, who was he kidding? A month or two ago even.

"I appreciate the offer. Maybe another time."

He thanked her again and let the finality seep into his tone. The din of the crowd was starting to hurt his head just like the bright lights were. He'd had enough tonight. The world—lights, sounds, commotion—was still stark, harsh when he overdid it.

Twenty-six nights ago, he'd lain in the ER, disoriented from a concussion and trying to lie still for a CT scan of his left shoulder and collarbone. He'd sworn then and there he was done with the sporadic partying and racy nightlife that had landed him in the back seat of that Explorer.

He scanned the crowds, searching for Thomas. When Mason had left for the bathroom, they'd been talking to a small group of die-hard Red Birds fans. Now, Mason found his buddy and teammate encircled by a small crowd of women who seemed more excited by Thomas's supposedly-worn-by-Arnold-Schwarzenegger Conan the Barbarian costume than his career stats.

Compared to Thomas's dressed-up loincloth, the green-and-black tartan kilt and black silk vest Mason had been cajoled into wearing wasn't so bad. Mason didn't know where his buddy had gotten them, but Thomas had acquired his share of authentic garb. He even had an aboriginal headdress that took up a full shelf in one closet and a top hat supposedly worn by a member of Lincoln's Cabinet.

Mason came up behind Thomas, tapped his shoulder, and offered the very real excuse of a headache as his reason for taking off early. Thomas was disappointed but didn't press.

All it took was heading outside into the night and feeling the cool air wash over him for Mason's release to be palpable. He loved the pulse of the city, loved living in his converted warehouse loft so close to the stadium, but lately, he'd felt an unmistakable stirring in his chest to head home.

When he'd left the serene but stiflingly quiet, rolling farmlands of Balltown, Iowa, for college, he'd never imagined experiencing a longing for the solitude he'd lost. Back then, he'd craved city living, replete with all the culture and chaos nearly as much as he'd wanted to be a pro ball player. He'd been fortunate to have gotten both wishes.

Now, ten years later, he was struck with a wave of nostalgia for the Halloween night he was missing back home. A quieter, simpler Halloween full of people who thought they knew everything there was to know about you, and were largely right.

A glance at the out-of-character Movado watch he'd forgotten to take off showed it was ten thirty. The only Halloween tradition he'd experienced until he was eighteen would be winding down. His extended family and a handful of friends always made for his parents' farm on Halloween night, showing up an hour or so before dark. If the weather was good like it was here, there'd be a roaring bonfire outside and, at the side of the yard nearest the house, there'd be a few folding tables covered with his mom's worn linens. They'd be loaded with all the Halloween regulars, like his aunt's jack-o'-lantern stuffed peppers, his cousin's zombie meat loaf, his mom's pumpkin turkey chili, and his dad's homemade hard cider from apples harvested on their farm.

Dinner would be long finished, and the assortment of homemade pies would be picked over. His uncle Ron would be dozing in his reclining folding chair after having enjoyed one too many hard ciders. His mom and aunts would be wrapping up leftovers while the younger kids and grandkids played the inevitable game of chase after finishing the skeleton hunt his dad set up year after year in the woods beyond the east field.

As Mason walked home, it occurred to him that nothing was keeping him here. He could head home for a few weeks. The season was over. He contemplated the logistics—the physical therapy appointments he'd have to move, the follow-up with his surgeon regarding the shattered collarbone that would hopefully be well-healed before spring training rolled around—as he headed away from the stadium and through empty streets toward his loft.

Three blocks from his building, he caught a glimpse of movement down a narrow side street. Something was down there, just out of reach of the streetlights, watching him in the darkness. He stopped, his muscles tensing automatically as he scanned the cave-like hole created by the century-old brick warehouses on either side.

He was wearing a kilt and hadn't tucked anything aside from a single credit card into the leather sporran around his waist. And even had he not been, Halloween night wasn't the best time to investigate darkened alleys. But Mason had high hopes of what lingered in the darkness, just out of eyesight. He strode into the dark toward it, his night vision kicking in as he left the glow of the streetlights.

The moon wasn't yet out, and the city lights always dimmed the stars. He stopped a hundred feet in, not wanting to scare off the interloper he felt ahead of him in the darkness.

Odds were, it was a homeless person setting up camp for the night. Or tonight, Halloween night, it could also be a couple pranksters having mostly innocent fun.

But it wasn't. Mason finally spotted the four long, white legs and the white fur under the dog's chin. The animal was fifty feet away, facing him. The rest of the dog's body, the parts covered with black fur, was invisible.

Mason sank onto his heels and whistled low and soft. *Maybe tonight's the night.*

The dog made a sound that Mason guessed was half yawn, half whine but didn't move.

"I didn't bring you anything, boy, but if you'd just let go of that stubborn streak and follow me home, I'd cook you up something great."

To Mason's surprise, the dog burst into a trot straight toward him. Mason waited, holding his breath. The animal stopped as abruptly as he started, leaving a mere fifteen feet between them. This close, Mason could make out the white patches just above the dog's eyes in the thick, black fur of his face, giving him an intelligent, inquisitive look.

"It's not the safest of nights to be a stray dog in the city anyway," he added into the silence. "What do you say you hang up your hat and call it a day?"

The dog's tail, black with a white tip, stuck out behind his body, neither relaxed nor stiff. He gave it a single flick in answer, then turned abruptly and trotted down the alley.

Mason stayed in place, watching the spectacular animal retreat until the last visible patch of white, the tip of his tail, disappeared into the night.

"I get it, John Ronald. I get it. You don't answer to anyone. But if you ever change your mind, you're definitely the dog for me."

Chapter 2

BEFORE MOUNTING HER OLD SCHWINN VARSITY ROAD BIKE the following Thursday afternoon, Tess glanced at her watch. She was forty-five minutes behind schedule. She'd been with Kurt and Kelsey at her volunteer job working with the rescued fighting dogs all morning and had lost track of time. The hours she spent at the private estate working with the dynamic group of rehab dogs were often the best hours of Tess's week.

Since she was also determined to get her healthy-pet consulting business off the ground, she'd made a personal commitment to spend the second half of every day focused on it. And while she wouldn't trade the forty-five extra minutes she'd spent with the dogs for being on schedule, Tess needed to getting moving.

She had a meeting with the owner of Pouches and Pooches, a popular and expanding local chain of high-end stores that catered to savvy pet owners with upscale pet products, scarves, and purses. Not only had the owner been open to meeting with Tess, when she'd spoken on the phone with him earlier in the week, but he'd also sounded excited about the services she hoped to offer.

A win today would give Tess a much-needed confidence boost in her business model. From sales calls to drop-in visits at dozens of area stores, she'd not yet had the best of receptions. And Tess's only paying client to date had resulted in a loss.

In hopes of making up for lost time, Tess pedaled hard in between stoplights. One of these days, she needed to force herself to get to the DMV to renew her expired license. She'd not driven since before she left for Europe. Even though biking and taking public transportation were tedious at times, she experienced tiny waves of panic whenever she gave serious consideration to getting behind the wheel of a car. She'd never been in a car accident, and she wasn't entirely sure why the thought of driving had become intimidating, even if she'd never been crazy about it.

She suspected her hesitation had something to do with not fully getting over her dad forcing her to learn to drive using a stick, coupled with the fact that he'd coaxed her into turning down a busy street at rush hour her second time behind the wheel. She still remembered the angry looks on some of the other drivers' faces as she stalled out time and again.

Tess's dad was a good-hearted man but also a very black-and-white one. He was the kind of father who'd scoffed at training wheels and tossed her into the pool before she was a confident swimmer. Maybe this was why Tess had chosen to stay with her grandmother ever since she'd gotten back from Europe a month ago. Tess's parents had worked so much when she was growing up, her grandparents had all but raised her. Tess's other siblings, one brother and one sister, were twelve and thirteen years older and had left home when she was little.

Another reason Tess hadn't moved in with her parents after returning from Europe was that, a year after Tess's high school graduation, they had moved away from the Hill, the Italian American St. Louis neighbor-hood, a tourist attraction and hub for a wealth of inde-pendently owned Italian restaurants packed into a single square mile. The Hill was also where Tess had lived all her life until she'd left for college. Tess's parents now lived, as Nonna put it, a "difficult" twenty-minute drive away in South County.

At her parents' new house, Tess had a bedroom that she'd never spent enough time in for it to feel like hers. Still, it had a newer, more comfortable bed than the worn-out spring mattress at Nonna's, as well as a full-size closet that could be just for her.

But Tess suspected that even if her father had been a more nurturing man than he was, she'd still live with Nonna. If she added up all the weekends and holidays and summers she'd slept over at Nonna's ever since she'd been born, it was no wonder the thousand-square-foot, century-old house felt like the natural place to be. Her grandfather not being around anymore was still taking some getting used to though. He was the real reason she'd come home from Europe as abruptly as she did.

Just a month ago, back in early October, Tess had been finishing transient work with a grape harvest on a small farm in Switzerland. She'd had a considerable stash of Swiss francs saved from a summer spent work-ing in terraced fields overlooking Lake Geneva, the Alps in the distance.

Before she'd gotten the call about Nonno's heart attack, she'd been making plans to backpack into Belgium. A friend, a Spanish girl she'd worked with earlier in the year, promised a few months of work in one of the most picturesque towns in the world—Bruges, Belgium. As one of Europe's best-preserved medieval towns, Bruges received floods of winter tourists and promised backpackers like her an opportunity for temporary work in a new and remarkable corner of the world.

As she cycled into the outskirts of the Hill, Tess remembered back to a few hours before she got the news about her grandfather. Nonno had been in critical condition but was awake and alert. It was time to get home, her dad had said. Using nearly every franc she'd earned over a long, hot summer, Tess packed up her belongings and flew out of Geneva International Airport on the first open flight. He died when she was somewhere over the Atlantic.

Her dad met her at the airport in St. Louis, smelling of cigarette smoke and looking thinner and older than her sixteen months away warranted.

"He was glad you were coming home," her dad had said.

Now that Tess was home to stay, she was determined to make a success of the business she'd dropped out of vet school for two years ago. Tess didn't need to become a skilled surgeon to help animals the way she wanted to help them. Holistic animal therapy was an emerging and exciting field. From therapeutic massage to essential oils to natural foods and products, Tess had become a believer in natural healing for pets. Not finishing vet school didn't make her a failure.

If only her track record for not sticking with things wasn't so long. Or something her big, loud, and vivacious extended family had a knack of reminding her about. Like the fact that she'd quit ballet in preschool or gymnastics in kindergarten. Soccer was a second-grade failure; scouting, a fourth-grade one. She'd dropped out of yearbook in the tenth grade. She ended it with her first serious—too serious—boyfriend during junior year and her second one as a senior. She'd left the Catholic Church in undergrad. Tess was pretty sure grumblings over that one had been heard in Argentina. Most recently, she'd walked out of vet school her second year.

That had been the breaking point. Right after that, she quit the biggest, most important thing of all—her family—and took off for Europe.

Narrowly missing the overturned trash can as she pedaled into Nonna's driveway, Tess reminded herself that what she was doing now was different from all those other things.

She was good with dogs. Dog training was the one thing she'd been introduced to as a kid that had stuck with her. And she'd been more than good at it. Her mentor, Rob, had told her so often enough.

Tess had been ten when she'd been allowed to shadow him for a day—several years younger than Rob was comfortable taking on, but he'd made an exception when he'd heard how dog crazy she was. According to her mom, Tess's first word after *mom* had been *daw* for *dog*, and her first animal sound had been *ruff*.

Over several years of shadowing him whenever she could and trying out what she'd learned on her extended family's pets, Tess had become a skilled trainer. She'd learned how to read most dogs simply by studying them. It was a language that was hard to put into words, but she picked up on their movements, their body stance, the energy in their eyes and in their bodies, the position of their tails and the way they held their heads and ears. It all melded together into a dynamic picture, and she was usually good at communicating back.

The suitcase Tess took along on the business calls she'd been making the last couple of weeks had a binder full of her training success stories: dogs who'd been hard-core counter surfers and dogs who'd all but refused to potty train until Tess had figured out how to reach them. These sort of training behaviors tended to be relatively easy successes for her.

Figuring out why dogs were scratching off the hair behind their ears, why they didn't sleep comfortably through the night, or why they were biting incessantly at their feet were harder questions to answer but didn't always require the costly services associated with vet visits. And deciphering these sorts of problems had become Tess's passion.

Remembering a few of the amazing dogs she'd worked with over the years helped Tess's start-up doubts slip away. She parked her bike and hung up her helmet, ready to head back out soon, catch the bus, and make a success of her biggest business opportunity to date.

―⁓―

Two and a half hours later, Tess stepped out of the old brick warehouse that was a couple of blocks from the Red Birds's stadium in downtown St. Louis and tugged her jacket closed. The thick, dark blanket of clouds overhead was growing more ominous by the minute. She had several blocks to walk to reach the bus stop that served the line with the most direct route back to the Hill.

There was no hurrying either. Not when she was

lugging her loaded-down spinner suitcase. She'd also brought along her old, heavy laptop and was carrying it in her backpack. She was thoroughly exhausted, and with any luck, the rain would hold off until she was on the bus.

To Tess's disappointment, her meeting with the owner of Pouches and Pooches had been nothing less than chaotic and full of interruptions. They met in what was to be the newest location in downtown St. Louis, just blocks from Ballpark Village and in view of St. Louis's best-known landmark, the Arch. What was sure to be a trendy and popular shop in a bustling downtown area was still a chaotic thousand-foot construction zone. The owner's attention had been divided between Tess's presentation and nonstop flooring and wiring questions by the construction crew.

She made it through her still-being-fine-tuned spiel and was attempting to show him some of her products and demonstrate their effectiveness with real-life success stories when he'd held up a hand, stopping her. He was sold. He'd recommend her services to the customers on his mailing list. And he had twelve thousand customers on it.

She'd been ecstatic before finding out that he wanted a 35 percent cut of any business she earned from his referrals. Considering that was Tess's margin, it seemed all but impossible.

Tess was debating how to counter his offer and wishing she had more business savvy when a bigger emergency called him to one of his other stores. He gave her his card and told her to contact him once she'd had time to think about it.

A familiar wave of insecurity rocked her as she headed toward the bus stop. She'd visited almost every independent pet store in St. Louis and several veterinarians too. Why was the concept of truly healthy dogs and cats such a hard sell?

Noticing that the sidewalk ahead was torn up in several places, and that she was about to be forced onto the street, she hoisted her suitcase off the ground. It felt fifty pounds heavier than it had at the beginning of the day. Fat, cold drops began pelting her from the dark gray clouds, which didn't help it feel any lighter.

As the rain dampened her clothes, Tess became uncharacteristically disheartened. When she'd left vet school two years ago, she'd had a vision. Maybe getting her idea off the ground would be easier if she'd taken business classes while getting her undergrad degree. Only, back then, she'd been dead-set on becoming a vet and figured the business end of it would come later.

As Tess neared Market Street and her bus stop, she saw she'd almost reached the end of the sidewalk construction. The muscles in her arm and shoulder were exhausted from carrying her heavy suitcase, and walking on the edge of the city street wasn't the safest of actions. Just as she'd reached the spot where the sidewalk was no longer blocked off, a truck passed by, splashing a wave of cold, filthy water onto her leather boots and leggings. And with the rain picking up, she was starting to full-body shiver. She couldn't reach the shelter of the bus stop quickly enough. Or her grandma's small, cozy home where, after a hot shower, she'd slip into comfy clothes and sip on a mug of hot tea.

Three people were crowded under the bus stop shelter,

two seated and one standing. The standing one, a lanky man in a dark suit, stepped over to make room under the cover. He gave her drenched clothes a sympathetic glance before becoming absorbed in his phone again.

Tess thanked him and attempted to tuck both her body and her suitcase under the thin slip of remaining roof and out of the rain. Her laptop was dry at least. Not only was it in a water-resistant case, but her long-used backpack still had waterproofing sealer on it as well.

The other two people crowded in the small space made no acknowledgment of her arrival. A woman took up most of the space on the bench, or at least her bags did. On the fraction of the bench remaining was an older man with a newspaper open on his lap. Rather than reading it, he was staring across the five-lane street and mumbling in disappointment about the Red Birds, St. Louis's much-loved major league baseball team, and their disappointing end to what had apparently been their best season in nearly a decade. Not that Tess had any idea. To her baseball-crazy family's disapproval, she'd largely stopped following the sport in college, then entirely when she'd left for Europe.

The intensity of the man's stare had Tess following his gaze. On the opposite side of the street was Citygarden, the small but picturesque three-acre fountain and the sculpture park that opened to a view of the old courthouse and the Arch. In the wind and rain, the popular park was all but deserted. The only person visible, not far from the giant sculpture of Pinocchio, was a guy wearing an arm sling, balling up an empty leash and kicking at the grass in frustration.

When there's smoke, Tess thought. She searched for

signs of an escaped dog. She spotted it dashing through the bushes and sculptures at the edge of the park. The dog was small, stocky, and white. From this far away, her best guess was a Westie. She flinched as the yapping animal dashed into the street, causing an approaching sedan to slam its brakes. The dog wheeled to face it, barking as ferociously at the grill as its small stature allowed. After completing a round of rapid-fire barking that stopped traffic in all lanes, it dashed back into the grassy park.

Once again, the dog was watching the guy who was trying to catch it and made sure to keep well clear of him. The man's attempts to make it stay put were only causing it to retreat farther away.

Barely conscious she'd made the decision to do so, Tess hoisted her suitcase and dove back into the cold rain. She had to jog across five lanes and dodge traffic to get to the park. Her suitcase thumped against one calf as she ran, likely creating a few bruises she'd discover later.

Once she closed the distance to a bit less than twenty feet, Tess heard the guy curse as he headed toward the western edge of the park in pursuit of the dog.

"Hey, you!" She was determined to stop him before his frustration drove the dog into the street again. "Stop! Just stop, will you?"

It still wasn't all-out pouring, but the cold drops were soaking her thin jacket. The guy, his left arm immobilized, had thankfully heard her and was turning around to see who'd called out. As soon as he stopped walking, the Westie, thirty feet ahead of him, stopped and cocked its head curiously toward Tess.

"Stop please! Just stop moving! You're too

imposing!" Tess dropped her suitcase and backpack under a bush that had lost most of its leaves but still offered a bit of protection from the rain. She double-checked the small pocket of her jacket to make sure she had a few of the treats she carried with her for emergencies like this one. "You'll never get him back this way."

As she drew closer, Tess noticed that the man was tall. She often thought of people over six feet tall as ones who swam in a different gene pool, and this guy was well over that mark. He also had a defined, athletic build and was broad-enough in the shoulders that some innate, subconscious part connected to her reproductive system responded by emitting a spurt of adrenaline. "Way too imposing," she repeated under her breath as she closed the distance between them.

He was also sans dog, she reminded herself, which was why she'd left the cover of the bus stop.

"Just stay here, okay? If you stop trying to close in on him, I think he'll stop moving away from you. What's his name?"

"Hers," he said, taking in Tess's puddle-splashed boots and clothes. "It's Millie. And please, give it your best shot. She goes berserk off leash. She's my neighbor's, and she doesn't like me on a good day, but even less in the rain. She slipped her collar."

He offered her the leash, but Tess shook her head. A sudden gust of wind blew the chilling drops sideways, causing her to shiver. "Thanks, but she's watching. Do me a favor and act like your attention's not on her for a minute. I'll head down the park next to the street to keep her from heading back out there. Once I'm far enough away from you, I'll see if I can get her to come to me."

"Yeah, sure. And thanks," he called as she hurried toward the edge of the park.

Tess kept watch of the little Westie in her peripheral vision. She headed west along the curb at the edge of the park until she was parallel to the animal. Millie had stopped advancing west and was alternately dashing in crazy circles and stopping to bark in the guy's direction.

Maybe it was because Tess was better with dogs than the imposing guy with the sling was. Maybe it was because frightened and overexcited dogs often found women more approachable than men. Whatever it was, Tess found the little Westie much more accommodating than the guy had.

As Tess moved toward the dog, she kept her gaze averted, approached at a slow, even pace, and offered calm and continuous praise. She stopped walking when she was still a good four or five feet away. She knelt in a squat and offered a treat in her outstretched hand. Millie zoomed over, stopping a foot and a half in front of her. The little dog sniffed the air and wagged her tail, then trotted over easy-peasy. The Westie was quick but gentle at taking the treat. Once Millie had munched it down, Tess dropped another one onto her open palm but didn't extend her hand as far.

As Millie munched the second treat, she let Tess rub a warm, wet ear. When Millie leaned into the scratch, Tess worked her way lower, then locked her hand around Millie's scruff. Once she had it, she nodded to the guy who was watching intently fifty or sixty feet away.

"I'll take that leash now," she called as the soft glow of success filled her. *At least one thing has gone right today.*

A bus had come and gone while she was over here.

Tess suspected it was the line she was supposed to be on and that she'd be waiting another half hour for a new one. It didn't matter though. Catching the cute little Westie and keeping her safe was more important than getting home and warming up.

When the dog showed no resistance or fear, Tess scooped her into her arms and stood.

"Hey, well done!" the guy called as he jogged over, brushing rain from his forehead.

"Thanks. I've had practice." It hit her a second time what a physical anomaly this guy was, too fit and all-American to blend into any crowd. His hair was a wavy light brown and his eyes were a striking blue-green. He had a smile that belonged on a poster, white teeth, and a deep dimple on his right cheek that was visible even with a few weeks of stubble.

"I owe you big time. If anything would've happened to her, I'm pretty sure I'd have been murdered in my sleep—not that I'd have been able to sleep," he said, grinning. "She's a master at slipping her collar. Usually, I'm one step ahead of her, just not today."

Tess laughed as Millie both growled and wagged her tail at the guy. "She seems not quite sure what to think of you."

"You can say that again. My neighbor had knee surgery, and I've been taking her out when I'm home, sometimes three times a day. Just when I think we're good to go, she goes all Mr. Hyde on me."

"Does she bite?"

"No. Just barks and runs about like a Ping-Pong ball."

"It kind of seemed like she was playing. Maybe that's what she needs. A good bout of play at a dog park." Tess nodded toward the leash. "Do you mind snapping that back on while I hold her? I don't want to risk setting her down first. Or can't you in that sling?"

"My hand's fine. It's my shoulder." He stepped in closer than Tess was expecting, and she caught his scent. She didn't know guys' colognes, if it was that and not a shave gel, but his smell reminded her of a walk through the woods with maybe a hint of sandalwood and lemon. Whatever it was, the rain likely accented it. Tess would've liked to bathe in it.

He also had really good hands, she noticed as he clipped Millie's dark-pink collar on. Tess tested the collar with her free hand. It was a bit too loose. She could slip more than the suggested two fingers underneath.

"I can tighten it," he offered, voicing her thoughts.

"That'd be good. They tend to work themselves loose over time from pulling and all."

He stepped in even closer as he whirled Millie's collar around and worked at pulling the extra collar through the tri glide. This close, all that stubble drew her attention like a beacon to his lips and white teeth.

Tess couldn't help but notice that he wasn't wearing a ring.

Odds are a zillion to one that he's got a girlfriend, Grasso. And he's not even your type.

Only, Tess wondered, if you had to remind yourself someone wasn't your type, how could you be sure they weren't?

He's sporty. You like bookish. Besides, getting lost in those arms would be like hugging a tree trunk.

He finished and stepped back, and Tess had to blink herself back to reality. "I'll, uh, put her down now, I guess. You could maybe suggest a martingale collar or a body harness to your friend. Westies are notorious for slipping their collars with those stout necks of theirs."

"I will. Listen, I'd like to thank you, but I'm not sure how. Not only did you catch her, you've gotten soaked in the process."

Tess set Millie on the ground, then stood and shrugged. The little Westie sniffed her wet boots, seeming as calm and content as if she'd never gotten worked up at all. Her tail wagged with the constancy of a reliable clock. "It's all in a day's work, and I was pretty soaked when I got over here." She glanced at the clouds. "I thought it was going to let up, but now it seems like it might get worse. I'd better grab my things and run. Thanks though."

She held out a hand, hoping to look more confident and self-assured than she felt. It didn't help that she was shivering. She didn't need to look in the mirror to know that her lips had become an attractive shade of blue. All the while, Mr. Sporty wasn't in a jacket and the raindrops were beading up and rolling down his water-resistant shirt.

"Oh, come on." He closed his hand around hers but didn't shake it, which caught her off guard. "Are you parked close? Let me walk you to your car. I didn't even get your name."

"I'm, uh, bussing it actually." *Bussing it? Is that even a word?* She needed to pull her hand away, only he wasn't letting go. His skin was warm, and his grip was inviting and strong. Her knees were practically melting into her shins.

She glanced down the sidewalk at the spot where

she'd stashed her suitcase and backpack and blinked unexpectedly. The slightest hint of panic nudged in. She scanned the landscaping for a sign of them, only there wasn't any.

"You're bussing it?" he was saying. "Where are you going? I'll give you a ride."

He must have moved them behind one of the evergreen bushes. Surely that was it. Only he'd been at least ten feet from them and she'd swear he'd never moved until he'd walked in her direction. Only, would she have known if he had? She'd been zeroed in on Millie. Aside from a woman with a poodle at the opposite end, the park was deserted. But had it always been?

"Did you see my stuff?" Panic was flooding in so quickly it was as if a dam had broken. "My suitcase and backpack. Do you know where they went?"

Tess pulled her hand away and hurried down the sidewalk toward the middle of the park where she'd come in. He followed, having no trouble coaxing Millie along. The little dog trotted willingly beside Tess. By the time she reached the bush where she'd set her things, she was in a jog. Her suitcase was filled with her success stories. All of them. And all those dollars' worth of thoughtful purchases. And then there was the laptop in her backpack. The one with all her research. And every single treasured photograph she'd downloaded from her trip to Europe. Dear God, why hadn't she gotten around to backing her stuff up on the Cloud? Her cell phone too. And the cell numbers of dozens of amazing people she'd met while away. All of it. Vanished.

Gone.

A sharp, chilly gust blew so hard she had to adjust her

footing. Rain, in smaller droplets but quadrupled intensity, pummeled sideways into her, stinging her face and neck. Not liking the increased voracity of the afternoon storm, Millie began to whine.

Somehow, impossibly, all of it was gone on a wind she'd never seen coming.

Acknowledgments

Story publication is a process beyond any single person's effort. I'd like to thank the entire, talented team at Sourcebooks Casablanca for bringing *Sit, Stay, Love* into the world. I'm especially thankful for the remarkable insight of my editor, Deb Werksman. Also in my gratitude are Susie Benton for her support and accessibility, Stefani Sloma for being the most enthusiastic and fun publicist possible, and Dawn Adams and the design team for creating covers I want to frame. Thanks to my insightful friend and beta reader Sandy Thal. And then there's Jess Watterson, agent extraordinaire. Jess, all I can say is that I'm grateful to be a member of #TeamWatterson.

I'd also like to thank the many readers who've reached out to me with their real-life shelter pet journeys. The decision to bring some of the more emotionally and physically scarred shelter animals into one's life can require limitless dedication, as well as bring profound joy. I hope this story helps remind readers of the remarkable differences real-life rescuers are making in animals' lives every day.

Lastly, I'd like to acknowledge my family for their patience and support as *Sit, Stay, Love* developed from an idea into a finished manuscript. Like many writers, I squeeze writing time in between a full-time job, my own attention-demanding canines, and the packed schedules of my busy teens. Without the support of my parents and extended family to help catch balls that always seem to be in the air, finishing this manuscript might well have been an impossible task. You have my love and gratitude. Always.

About the Author

Debbie Burns lives in St. Louis with her family, two phenomenal rescue dogs, and a somewhat tetchy Maine coon who everyone loves anyway. Her hobbies include hiking, gardening, and daydreaming, which, of course, always leads to new story ideas.

Debbie's writing commendations include a Starred Review from *Publishers Weekly* and a Top Pick from *RT Book Reviews* for *A New Leash on Love*, as well as first-place awards for short stories, flash fiction, and longer selections.

You can find her on Twitter @_debbieburns, on Facebook at facebook.com/authordebbieburns, and at authordebbieburns.com.

UNTIL THERE WAS US

New York Times and USA Today bestselling
author Samantha Chase continues her
beloved Montgomery series

Megan Montgomery has always been careful...except that
one time she threw caution to the wind and hooked up with
a sexy groomsman at her cousin's wedding. But that was two
years ago. Why can't she stop thinking about Alex Rebat?

Alex has been living the good life. He loves his job, has a
great circle of friends, and doesn't answer to anyone. But
now that Megan's come back to town, Alex hopes he can
convince her to take another chance on him...and on a
future that can only be built together.

"A fun, flirty, sweet story filled with romance."

**—Carly Phillips, *New York Times* bestselling
author for *I'll Be There***

For more Samantha Chase, visit:
sourcebooks.com

LOVE GAME

First in a new contemporary series
from author Maggie Wells

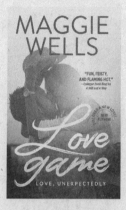

Kate Snyder is at the top of her game. So when the university hires a washed-up coach trying to escape scandal—paying him a lot more than she earns—Kate is more than annoyed.

Danny McMillan gets Kate's frustration, but her pay grade isn't his problem, right? When Kate and Danny finally see eye to eye, sparks turn into something even hotter...and they need to figure out if this is more than just a game.

"Will steal your heart...romance at its finest."

—Harlequin Junkie for *Going Deep*

ONE SUMMER NIGHT

First in the At the Shore series by *New York Times* and *USA Today* bestselling author Caridad Pineiro

Everyone knows about the bad blood between the Pierces and Sinclairs, but Owen has been watching Maggie from afar for years. Whenever he can get down to the shore, he strolls the sand hoping for a chance meeting—and a repeat of the forbidden kiss they shared one fateful summer night.

When Owen hears that Maggie's in trouble, he doesn't hesitate to step in. She has no choice but to accept Owen's help. But what's he going to demand in return?

"One Summer Night is the perfect escape!"

—Raeanne Thayne, *USA Today* bestselling author

For more Caridad Pineiro, visit:
sourcebooks.com